The Redemption
of
Reverend Caine

MountainView Publishing
A division of
Treble Heart Books
1284 Overlook Dr.
Sierra Vista, AZ 85635-5512
http://www.trebleheartbooks.com

ISBN: 978-1-932695-59-5

Thank you for choosing A
MountainView Publishing
ChristianThriller

The Redemption
of
Reverend Caine

Melissa Hart

MountainView Publishing
A divison of
Treble Heart Books

Acknowledgements

I want to thank my family for their endless love and support. Thanks, in particular, to you, Mom, for being my first reader and giving me honest and insightful advice. You improved this book more than you know. Thanks to my perceptive editor, Cindy Davis, and my wonderful publisher, Lee Emory, who was willing to take a chance on me.

Dedication

Foremost, this book is dedicated to my Lord and Savior, Jesus Christ. Without Him, this story would never have been written.

"Beware of false prophets, which come to you in sheep's clothing, but inwardly they are ravening wolves."
—Matthew 7:15

Prologue

Gena Young returned the .38 Rossi handgun to the drawer of her husband's bureau and hurried back to bed. "No more foolish thoughts," she whispered.

Sliding underneath the satin sheets, she gazed above her four-poster bed at the portrait of her husband, Jonathan. Sunlight lay softly over the brass frame and danced in long finger-like strokes across the image of his inverted face. His eyes, an iridescent green in the light, seemed to look down upon her. Knowing eyes. Had they seen her at his bureau just the night before last stroking the muzzle of his gun, thinking those horrible thoughts?

"Dear God, forgive me."

She sat up and leaned backward against the headboard. Wind whistled against the glass panes of the balcony doors. All week, the weather forecasters had been calling for thunderstorms in Redemption, North Dakota, but so far Gena hadn't seen one drop of the baptismal rain for which she longed.

She turned her head and glanced at Jonathan's face as he slept beside her. "But you've come back to me, haven't you, Johnny? And you're never going to leave me again."

Past the faint lines that had formed along his forehead and sunk deeper with time, past the ruffled gray hair at his temples and the dark circles under his eyes, was the man he had been before he had started working with the reverend. The man he had been before Jolie had vanished.

Gena was certain he was still every bit of that man she had painted in the portrait hanging over her bed. And if he had stopped working for the reverend like he promised he had—if this had been the last evangelistic mission trip he would take with Reverend Caine—she knew the painting would stop haunting her. She knew it like the difference between right and wrong. Peace would settle into and soften those faint lines on both their faces. It would wrap itself around both their hearts. And they would start attending a new church, a church where God sat in the pews and behind the pulpit.

Watching the one she loved second only to God, Gena's chest tightened. Jonathan snored softly with his pillow crumpled in the crook between his chin and his chest. A slight frown bowed the corners of his mouth.

She shivered as a chill snaked through her. *The honorable Reverend Caine.* Her eyes glazed over, and the room seemed foggy. An image settled into her mind—the image that had been haunting her dreams. At first, a shadow appeared, but then, a light so bright it could only have been fire. From a mountaintop overlooking the small town of Redemption, she met Reverend Caine's paralyzing gaze as his body writhed in flames. The skin of his charred face dripped like candle wax into the white collar of his shirt. His cerulean eyes washed over her, soaking her body with their icy stare. But his coldness did nothing to extinguish the flames around him. His eyes glinted to the side, widening. His mouth opened in a scream. He craned his arm at her and mouthed her name, but the flames closed around him, silencing his screams in a vacuum of fire.

She shook her head, hoping to banish the image from her mind. *Oh, Lord, what's wrong with me? Why do I have such horrible thoughts?* She glanced at Jonathan's bureau where she had returned the gun. Its dark walnut stain seemed a shade darker than usual. Its meticulously carved claw feet seemed a size larger. The contours of its edges seemed a degree sharper.

"No more foolish thoughts."

Rolling over, she lay down and nestled against him. She kissed his shoulder and trailed kisses down his back. "I love you more than anything, honey. Now remember your promise."

Sunlight flickered over the church pamphlet still resting on her nightstand. The reverend's wife had brought it over the previous afternoon, four short hours before Jonathan had returned home and nearly collapsed into Gena's trembling arms. Long fingers of sunlight seemed to be moving it now. Gena blinked hard, and the fingers withdrew. "Honor the reverend, indeed."

She sat up and rolled her shoulders as she stretched her arms behind her. Sunlight glinted into her eyes through a gap between the lace curtains of the balcony doors, and she raised a hand to block the glare. Across the street, the slender spear-shaped church steeple Reverend Caine had used to replace the supposedly damaged cross steeple gleamed. "Oh, Reverend Lamont, I miss you. Why did you have to die and let this man take your place?"

She swung her legs over the side of the bed and felt a crick in her hip. Rain was coming. And not the kind of rain she wanted.

Her bare feet glistened with sweat even while she shivered. She reached for her silk camisole and edged toward the balcony doors. The lace curtains easily parted. She glanced at Jonathan's face. It amazed her how peacefully he always seemed to sleep with his eyelids so heavy against the world.

The curtains fluttered when she opened the doors and stepped onto the balcony. The leaves of the trees were just beginning to turn. The elm trees lining the streets of the old town swayed in the breeze to phantom love songs. All was nearly right with the world now that Jonathan was home.

The delicious scent of lavender and honeysuckle filled her with memories. She leaned her head back and closed her eyes. *There is just one more thing, Lord. Just one more missing piece to this old broken heart.*

The scent carried memories of her daughter's youth, memories so strong she thought she could almost reach out and touch the lovely oval face. Could almost hear the soft timbre in the tiny voice. And could almost see the tilt of Jolie's head and the child-like glimmer in those inquisitive eyes— eyes the child had carried into her adult years—had even carried away with her into her marriage to that tyrant. *Oh, Jolie, surely you will return to me one day too. I'm so sorry, dove. Surely you won't let Richard keep you away from me and your father forever.*

Gena blinked back tears and opened her eyes. Was their daughter even still alive? Was she happy with her husband, Richard? Did she ever have her baby? It had been a little over a year since Jolie left home. Maybe Richard was preventing her from visiting, from calling, from even writing. And maybe she was dead. Maybe the monster had killed her and dumped her body somewhere. Gena shook her head, trying to free her mind from the grip of deadly thoughts, and forced her eyes away from Jonathan's bureau. She had hired so many private investigators to track down her daughter, and all of them had failed. If Jolie was still alive, she might never be found.

Gena looked out at the mountains in the distance bordering the valley town and thought of all the old family photos in a chest downstairs. She'd have to go through them again tomorrow. This time with Jonathan now that he would no longer escape the pain by occupying his every thought with work.

An ache seemed to swell from deep inside her heart. Soon oranges and yellows would dominate the mountainsides, and she would paint Redemption with the precision she had painted the masterpiece hanging over her bed. The lush colors would become a tapestry of ominous faces in her portrait, appearing like the proverbial man in the moon. And she would see her daughter's face among them somehow, calling to her from far away, promising like the ghosts in Gena's mind always promised, that Jolie would return soon.

"Redemption. My precious little Redemption." The words tasted bitter upon her lips. She glimpsed something out of the corner of her eye.

She veered backward with her heart banging, and drew the door shut. She nudged the curtain and peered through the glass. Reverend Caine darted across the street. In his right fist he clutched a red Church pamphlet with bright gold lettering. She knew what he wanted. It was the same thing he always wanted. She looked back at her clock radio. Eight a.m., one hour before Church services. *Not today, Lord. Please, not today.*

What does everyone see in you, Reverend Caine? She peered into the sky as though she were trying to decipher a message from the scattered clouds. *Lord, is there something wrong with me? They've all but forgotten about Reverend Lamont and his teachings.*

The sun loomed behind the church steeple, projecting sunlight that capered along his back, warping the shadow in front of him. *Maybe you're something other than a man, maybe something unnatural or*—she lowered her head—*maybe something supernatural?*

Even from her elevation, she could see the grooves in his cheeks and the sunken flesh around his fierce eyes. She wondered what kind of life he had led before he and his young wife, Amanda, had moved to Redemption.

She reached for her robe, then snatched up the church pamphlet on her nightstand and slammed it into the wastebasket by her drawing table. Rapping sounds faint like a woodpecker hammering the bark of a poplar then a sound like a karate chop splitting several rafters of the house seemed to reverberate through the walls of the ground floor and refract into the floor beneath her feet. Gena clapped her hands over her ears. Her knees buckled. She braced herself against the wall and forced herself upward.

Sucking in her breath, she glanced over her shoulder at Jonathan. He snored softer than before. Somehow, he had slept through the explosion. "No one is going to bother you today, dove. Not even him."

Her knees wobbled on her way out of the bedroom, and she found it impossible to run.

They buckled, and she almost slipped on the staircase. Up went one hand in front of her against the recess of her robe. The other hand clamped to the railing. Looking down, the floor tiles seemed to swim in circles like sharks. *Come on now, Gena. He's only a man. No matter what he thinks.* She knew she was holding her breath, but she couldn't force herself to breathe until she reached the foyer.

Rain speckled her forehead and the bridge of her nose when she swung open the front door, but no one stood on her porch. The iron gate at the end of her driveway clanged back and forth into the fence, hinges squealing.

She slammed the door and hurried into the kitchen. With her back to the entryway, she thought she heard someone breathing behind her. She twirled around. "Jonathan?"

No one stood there.

She shifted her gaze to the counter. Her black and white tabby was slinking toward her, meowing. "Get down." She swatted at the frizzled tail. The cat dove off the counter and sprinted from the kitchen. "Going to give me a heart attack."

After being reprimanded, it usually darted upstairs. But from the sound of its nails scraping the marble foyer tiles, it seemed to have made a sharp right and skirted into the living room.

Sweat dripped from her shoulder blade to the small of her back. Her forearms prickled with goose bumps. She switched on the ceiling fan and went to the radio on the corner section of the counter flanked by the gas stove and the refrigerator. She cranked up the volume. Her body went limp in the arms of the music. Now she could concentrate on making the celebratory breakfast she had planned for Jonathan's return home.

When she had two plates of eggs and toast and two glasses of juice on the tray in front of her, she switched off the radio. Another sound erupted from upstairs. In the bedroom? She had definitely heard something drop. Hadn't she?

Carrying the tray into the foyer, she held it close to her, intending to use it as a weapon or a shield. But no intruder came running down the stairs or loomed in the shadows. Only the cockeyed tabby stared at her from the corner of the foyer, looking skittish.

Her laughter, sharp and unnatural, seemed to echo across

the house as though none of the furniture existed to buffer the sound. *Don't lose it now, girl. He's home. He's finally home. Don't lose it now.* She laughed again before going upstairs. The shrill sound seemed more frightening than the ghosts still haunting her mind. *No more foolish thoughts.*

Rounding the corner into the bedroom, she realized Jonathan was no longer snoring, and she wondered if something had woken him.

Sunlight streamed through the balcony doors and pierced the surrounding darkness as she set the tray on her nightstand. Hadn't she closed the curtains before going downstairs?

She raised her gaze to Jonathan's face and nearly toppled backward. Sunlight beamed into his open vacant-looking eyes. She smacked her mouth with her hand, hardly noticing the sting. The sun seemed to sear his pupils, shrinking them to the size of pinpricks.

She rushed to the balcony doors and drew the curtains shut, praying he would wake up when she touched him. She crawled across the bed and leaned over him. A lock of her hair feathered his cheek. "I love you, Johnny. Do you love me?"

Silence.

She slid her lips over his mouth and kissed him. His lips seemed cold. Too cold. Her eyes locked on his dead stare, and her heart banged in her chest. She leaped off the bed. The balls of her feet thudded against the floor, sending tremors she barely noticed up her legs.

"Jonathan? Honey? Wake up." She clutched his arms and shook him. "Jonathan! Jonathan, wake up!"

She lowered her ear to his chest and listened, but heard nothing except the droplets of rain splattering the balcony doors like liquid fingertips drumming the glass.

"No!" Tears blurred her vision. She raised her hands

above her head, holding her palms open to the ceiling. "Not now. Not after all I've suffered. Dear God, if you'll only let me have him, you can have everything else." She jerked her head back and forth until her vision blurred. "No! No! No!"

Spinning on her heels, she darted toward the bureau. She flung open the top drawer and tore through its contents. Jonathan's undershirts and socks flew about the room like flight-resistant birds. *It's like someone just up and took it while I was downstairs.* Surveying the room, she spotted no traces that anyone else had been there and quickly dismissed the thought.

She continued to tear through the bureau. A pair of scissors she often used to cut the tags off new clothing rocketed into the glass pane of one balcony door, shattering it. "Where is it? Where is it?" A large pullover sweater flew into the lamp on her nightstand, knocking the lamp onto the breakfast tray. Eggs and juice splattered the bed sheets.

She slammed her fists on the bureau. There would be no celebrating today.

Her legs bowed underneath her, and she dropped to her knees, screaming into her hands and pounding her fists into her legs. Her tabby leaped into her lap, and she flung it across the room. It skidded on its heels and hissed at her. Fresh tears stung her eyes while she stared through her watery gaze at Jonathan's body. "Jonathan. Wake up, dove. The love of your life wants you to wake up now. Wake up and tell me you love me."

Nothing answered her but the howling sounds of wind outside.

She thought again of the rapping at the front door. Realized it hadn't been very explosive after all. Realized it in a way like déjà vu is realized. That it had only been firm knocking from the reverend before he had given up and left, not fisted pounding from mischievous boys. Her mind had been so used to silence from Jonathan's absence all these months that she could easily misperceive almost any sound. Or maybe it hadn't even been knocking. Maybe it had only been the wind or her imagination. Maybe Reverend Caine hadn't even been coming to see her.

The cat. Hadn't she thought someone was behind her in the kitchen? Someone tall and male when it had only been her tabby. Surely she had imagined the male presence.

She shook her head again. The thoughts left her mind, and she ran to the balcony doors. Shards of glass from the shattered pane sliced into her bare feet. She recoiled, reaching down to pry them out. Then Jonathan's ghostly gaze flashed in her mind, and she raised up and marched forward, no longer feeling the pain.

She flung the doors open and stepped onto the balcony. Rain rolled from the sky and pressed down on her with the weight of nearly a year of mourning. Her body seemed to stride toward the balustrade, propelled by its own force.

With her fingers tightening around the slick iron rail, she heard a voice amidst the cacophony of the storm and peered downward. A face blurred by the torrent seemed to be beckoning her back inside the house.

She shook her head, raising her arms and her eyes to the swirling gray sky then leaned forward and fell over the balustrade.

Chapter One

Seven Years Later

Raising her head, Jolie Needham pressed upward until she stood without cleaving to the bank. Three miles outside Redemption, North Dakota, she could no longer stifle what was rising inside of her. What was rising even now, but hadn't yet emerged before her, unlike the tantrums of her stomach.

She stumbled backward, brushed the yellow grains off her sundress, and cocked her ear toward the sound of whistling air. Something snapped under her shoe. She flinched and lunged forward onto the bank, instantly realizing she had only broken a twig. When she twisted to verify what she had crushed, a choked scream died in her throat. A few more steps would've sent her sailing over a cliff into the gaping valley below.

Blood rushed to her face and hands, stinging her. Sandy grains filtered through her fingers while she clutched the bank, desperate for something solid to anchor her. She moaned into the muffling mound and tried not to think she was sliding backward off the cliff into the swirling rush of whistling air.

Scooting further away from the edge, she concentrated on her heartbeat until it slowed. She wiped the sand from her face and spat out what had gotten into her mouth. Just ahead, past a gravel bed, her husband, Richard, sat in the driver's seat of their Mercedes with the windows powered up, eyeing her while he drummed his fingers on the steering wheel. His head bounced between her and his Seiko like a plastic bird oscillating in and out of a Cuckoo clock.

Something stirred inside her she thought she had buried under impenetrable stone.

She looked down at her feet clad in the pink cream flats Richard had bought her. A stronger force overtook the others wrestling inside her. She stared at her ridiculously perfect little shoes. At the lacy hem of her perfect little dress now encrusted with sand.

It was undeniable.

She slammed her fist into the bank and worked her knuckles through the sand. "No more tears." *And no more foolish thoughts*. But were those promises she could keep? They certainly hadn't been ones she had kept before. Even for her daughter's sake.

"Emma, honey," she whispered. Thoughts of her eight-year-old daughter drew her to her feet.

Richard was facing the backseat of the car, hammering his fist into his seat to punctuate his words. His large clumsy lips moved, but his words were indecipherable.

Emma stared back at him, clinging to the puppet Jolie had given her for their trip. Emma's face tensed. The skin between her brows puckered and her lips became a thin firm line. *My brave little soldier*. Jolie felt herself smiling, her smile straining against the dimensions of her mouth.

Richard suddenly spun toward her. She veered around, pressing her shoulders into an elm tree. Her heart hammered over painful gasps for breath. *Oh, God, don't let him have seen me smiling like that. He'll think I was laughing at him, and he'll punch me in the stomach again. I'll have to see this new baby or whatever's moving around inside me in the toilet tomorrow.*

Jolie closed her eyes and concentrated on the tides rising again inside her. But it wasn't Richard or a new baby who caused them. She realized that now, staring over the edge of the cliff.

The sprawling sky darkened. "Why, God? Why am I so afraid of returning home?" *Sure, eight years is a long time, but...Dad, I'm so sorry. I should have come back sooner.* "Can you ever forgive me?" Jolie sniffled and closed her eyes, damming back tears. She hung her head. *Yeah well, I guess I'll never know the answer to that one.*

Her father's death seven years ago had been a shock she had yet to overcome. A heart attack...wasn't that what the woman had said over the phone? A heart attack...and in his mid-forties? "Dear God, make me strong for Emma's sake. I'm so tired of letting everyone down. What good am I if I can't be brave for my little girl through all this?"

A cool breeze dried the sweat on her forehead while she eased toward the edge of the cliff and peered into the valley. Window light illuminated the encroaching darkness.

Redemption.

She lifted her gaze to the bordering hills and mountains enclosing the valley town. From this elevation, Redemption looked like a foreign land. Slithering tendrils of fog coiled around the borders and crept over the buildings like giant spiders' legs softly blurring each window's light. The embryonic mass wound its way around everything, between everything, enveloping the little town until it was reduced to a dark formless abortion.

Mom, which house is yours? Jolie wondered. *Will we be living anywhere even close to you?* Jolie hadn't seen the house Richard had purchased, and she hadn't wanted to see it either. It would be just another extravagant purchase, complete with several extra rooms she would have to dust but never enjoy using.

Will you even recognize me, Mom? Jolie raised her hand to her temple and depressed the pulsing vein.

Why had she married Richard and moved away from Redemption only to return now? What would her mother think of her? She hadn't even attended her father's funeral. And Richard had prevented her from even writing to her mother. Jolie bowed her head, recalling her last words to her father: "Don't cry, Dad. Richard is a good man. He'll take care of me, and I'll be back soon. I'm still your daughter, you know?" How many times had those words woken her from a nightmare?

Something swirled around inside her again, but didn't pin her to the bank and put her at the mercy of her stomach.

"Jolie, get back in the car." Richard had powered his window down, and he was shaking his fist outside the car like a madman pounding some invisible bird out of the sky. "I swear you...you test me like no...don't make me leave you out here."

Jolie gulped. Emma was sitting up, twisted around and straining against her seatbelt. Emma's panic-laced voice filtered outside. "Dad? Where's Mom?"

"I'm still waiting for your mother to get in the blasted car."

Emma's jaw dropped, and she whirled toward him.

Jolie wanted to scoop up her little girl, but the feeling of nausea overpowered her again. She slumped against the bank, trying not to collapse. Her quaking limbs were impossible to control. Tremors wracked her spine then shot into her back and shoulders and into the nape of her neck, inciting a fit of wheezing and coughing. *That's it. All his hatefulness is finally killing me.*

With one hand on the bank so she could clamp her other hand over her hacking mouth, she prayed Emma wouldn't meet her eyes.

"Where is she?" Emma bounced around on the backseat. "Where's Mom?"

A breeze stirred the leaves of the elm beside Jolie, and she realized her tremors were fading. She took a deep breath. The sweat cooled on her chest and brow. "Thank You, God. It's going to be all right now...for awhile, isn't it?"

"She's outside. Over there."

Jolie jolted upright and frantically wiped her cheeks and forehead. She smoothed the sticky strands of hair off her face and stared at the Mercedes.

Richard swiveled around and wagged his index finger at Emma. "Leave your seatbelt alone."

The child's eyes locked on Jolie before Emma thrust her head into her seat. By her trembling shoulders, Jolie knew her daughter had started crying.

Richard's voice seemed to echo a little. "I don't want to spend the night out here with the wolves. Don't you feel better yet? There isn't exactly enough light on these mountain roads to see through *total* darkness."

Jolie didn't know if she could trust her legs, but she had to test them for Emma's sake. *Okay, God, let's go. On three, okay? One. Two.* Jolie released the bank and headed for the car.

"You don't want me driving us over a cliff because you were too sick to stay in the car, now do you?"

"Wolves?" Emma curled into a ball.

Richard leaned forward and plopped his fists on the dashboard.

Jolie shivered and wrapped her arms around herself. A sliver of silver-tinged moon hung overhead. "Lord lead me through this. I can't do any of this without You." She ran her hand over her hip pocket and found her little Psalms book.

"Ready to go, Emma, sweetheart?" She lifted the hem of her dress off her ankles and skipped over the jagged stones glistening like teeth in the moonlight beside the front passenger door.

"What's that?" Richard's nostrils flared. He clenched his jaw. His forehead shimmered with perspiration as he craned over the center console. Jolie's door rocketed open, but she caught it before it smacked her knees. A blast of air-conditioned air chilled her.

"We won't be getting there tonight if you don't hurry up."

She clambered into the car. "I'm ready." She latched her seatbelt and looked at Emma. A dimple bloomed in the child's left cheek. One dark red curl bounced forward when she leaned toward her mother.

"What happened to you out there?" Richard started the car. "I felt like I was talking to myself."

"I just needed to catch my breath."

"Dad does drive kind of fast, doesn't he, Mom?"

Jolie reached around the driver side headrest and slid the back of her hand over Emma's icy cheek.

"Are you cold, sweetheart?"

Richard frowned, slamming the heel of his shoe on the accelerator, jerking the car backward. Jolie faced forward, grabbing the dashboard. He braked hard and switched gears.

She sneaked a glance at Emma in the side-view mirror. The child's granite expression had returned, but it was a much harder expression than Jolie had realized from outside.

Richard stamped the accelerator again, and the car thrust forward. The tires spun gravel as he forced the car back onto the winding mountain road. And Jolie's stomach started churning again.

Chapter Two

"Turn off that faucet! You know how much I hate when you waste water."

Realizing she had been lost in thought, Jolie lunged for the hot water knob. Her soapy fingers slipped, and her hand collided with the sink sprayer. She bit down on her lower lip to stifle a shriek and gripped her wrist. The offended tendons pulsed.

She pulled a china plate out of the sudsy water that filled one side of the double sink and wiped it with the dishcloth she held in her wriggling left hand. "What is wrong with me, Lord? Why can't I feel bad about this morning?"

Jolie gripped the plate to her chest and dropped the dishcloth into the water as she drifted off in thought again. She had woken from a nightmare with a sudden urge to use the bathroom. But she had been unable to pee. When something hot and wet had slid out of her, she had known without looking into the toilet that she had lost the child that had been growing in her womb. But she had gotten up and

looked anyway. Its remains had rested bloody and tangled in
its watery grave. Jolie had flushed the toilet without calling
for Richard, but Richard had been standing in the doorway
with his arms folded and his red hair plastered to one side of
his balding head, looking down on her with enormous eyes.
His face had been nearly as red as his hair. Then he had started
yelling, and Jolie had been nearly certain he would never stop.
And the whole time he had yelled, she had kept thinking, I
have Emma. Emma is all I need.

She looked out her kitchen window at the movers who
had arrived just as Richard was on the threshold, wavering
between anger and acceptance. Richard had badgered her with
questions. Was the child a boy or a girl? How long had she
known she was pregnant? Why didn't she tell him she needed
to see a doctor? But in the end, the arrival of his collectibles
and the realization that he could make another child, a stronger
child—maybe even a son—with her pacified him.

The men smoked their cigarettes and laughed as they
lounged behind one of the moving vans, oblivious to how
they had impacted her morning. A smile split her face, and
she nearly laughed in relief.

She realized she still held the china plate Richard's
mother had given them and was about to continue with the
dishes when a Crown Victoria pulled up alongside the curb.
For some reason, Jolie imagined the woman inside was her
mother, the confidant and assertive woman Jolie had
remembered from her childhood. Yes, her mother had finally
come to rescue her poor spineless daughter after having heard
about Jolie's return.

Absentmindedly placing the plate next to a stack of
freshly washed ones, Jolie stared at the tiny woman emerging
from the car. This was definitely not her mother. The woman
couldn't have been over five foot two. Dressed in an outdated

blue blazer that hung tent-like over a streaming white dress, the woman seemed lost inside her clothes. A white scarf covered most of her bright yellow hair and obscured nearly half of her face.

One bony leg more like a tree branch than a healthy limb poked the underside of the dress as the woman stepped onto the curb.

Jolie gasped, feeling foolish, and silently scolded herself.

The woman stopped at the end of the driveway and lowered her chin. Her dress billowed behind her in the breeze. For a moment, the wind seemed intent on carrying away the tiny body. Her lips began moving as in a prayer. When she raised her head and strode forward, her round eyes burned with determination, and Jolie flinched, ramming her hip into the counter.

The movers looked up from their conversation. One man tossed his cigarette on the ground and stood from the back of one of the vans before calling out to the woman. Her eyes grew wide, and she moved faster. A couple of the men laughed. The woman started to raise her hands to her face, maybe in an attempt to somehow hide. Then she snatched her wrists to her sides and bounded onto the porch.

Jolie went to the octagonal lookout window in the corner of the kitchen that faced the stoop. The woman removed her scarf and raised her fist to the door. Mounds of short blond ringlets tumbled down to her chin, giving her stern emaciated face a girlish quality.

Richard jerked open the door before the woman could knock. "Come in. Come in." His voice echoed from the barren foyer.

The woman stumbled backward, losing her footing, and grabbed for the bush beside the kitchen window, turning her face toward the pane. Jolie gasped and backed away, but not before the image of flesh sunken over bone imprinted itself in her mind.

The woman disappeared into the house. "Hello, sir. My name is Amanda Caine." Amanda's birdlike voice filled the foyer. Chills wracked Jolie's spine. "I'm here on behalf of the local church to welcome you to Redemption."

Richard coughed hard and thumped his chest. "Please come in. I'm Richard Needham."

Jolie pictured him sweeping out the length of the entryway with his arm like he had been accustomed to doing for his clients in Chicago. His portly frame moving aside to accommodate the invitation.

Amanda's heels clicked across the marble. "Pleased to meet you, sir."

Jolie fled back to the sink. No more plates left to rinse. She griped the sides of the basin and tried to will her shoulders to stop shaking. She stared into the murky water, wondering if Amanda had seen her at the window. *God, what's going on? What am I so afraid of?*

The aroma of freshly cooked eggs and bacon wafted through the house. A breeze from outside seemed to have stirred those ghosts back to life. Jolie had been too sick that morning to eat anything. Now her insides growled. But was it for food or was it in dread of whatever Amanda had come to discuss with them? And how could Jolie know the strange woman had come to discuss anything? Jolie had just lost a child without shedding a single tear. Surely, she was headed for a nervous breakdown. That was what was happening to her.

Jolie wiped her forehead with the back of her hand. It came away damp. She ran it across her apron and edged toward the doorway. She lifted a hand towel off the back of one of the breakfast table chairs and dabbed her forehead.

Past the doorjamb, Amanda spun, her white dress ballooning around her, like a princess in a fairy tale. "My, what a beautiful home you have."

Richard didn't need anymore incentive to lecture her about the many fine antiques he had collected over the years. Jolie cringed, recalling how he had spent the larger part of the morning meticulously unpacking and aligning them after their fight.

She rubbed the back of her neck with the towel. He was telling Amanda about the origins of the lamps and the quality craftsmanship of their ornate stained glass lampshades—the fine Egyptian or Swedish or something upholstery of his leather sofa and recliner—and the many intricate details of the sculptures from famous dead Indonesian artists and African priests and... "Oh God, stop him," she whispered before realizing Amanda might hear her.

Richard explained the craftsmanship of a few more items in the living room, most still in boxes. He riffled through them, dislodging several sheets of protective plastic. Then stepped on a sheet of bubble wrap and grunted when it popped. Just like her hopes and dreams, she thought. At that moment, she finally admitted she hated him. But no reproach followed her confession. *God, what is wrong with me?*

Jolie sucked in her breath and started into the living room.

"My you have a lot of things. But there aren't many feminine touches here, not that you're done unpacking yet of course. But does your wife decorate mostly upstairs?"

Jolie froze. Richard let his reading glasses fall to the tip of his nose while he examined Amanda. After so many years of marriage, Jolie could read his silences as well as his words, and she prayed he wouldn't say what he was thinking. Amanda took a step back from him, maintaining a friendly gaze. He finally smiled then tucked his glasses into the pocket of his suede jacket.

Jolie fled back to the kitchen, remembering a task that could stall her entrance into the living room, and pulled out the stepping stool between the refrigerator and the counter. The rubber feet skidded over the tiles. She mounted the stool and lifted the stack of plates to the cabinet above the refrigerator, ignoring the lingering pain in her sides from the miscarriage. Listening for movement behind her, she slid the plates onto the bottom shelf and closed the cabinet doors.

Jolie became aware of how she was gritting her teeth and forced her jaw to relax, remembering how often Richard teased her about the habit.

"Would you like to meet my wife? I think she's in the kitchen."

The frantic clicking of Amanda's pumps made Jolie cringe. Then the sound of Richard's heavy Clydesdale-like gait made her knees quake.

Desperate for something to do with her trembling hands, she seized the plate she had set aside while watching Amanda climb from the car. She mounted the stool with the delicate china clenched in her hand.

"Hello, Mrs. Needham."

The stool tipped, and Jolie hopped to the floor. The plate slipped out of her hand.

"Mom's china!" The gaudy plate—only one of the detestable items his mother had given them on their wedding day—sailed past Richard's grasping hands and smashed into the floor. He knelt before the pieces sprawled underneath the table. "Jolie, this is Amanda Caine," he grumbled.

"Are you all right, my dear? I'm sorry. I didn't mean to startle you." Amanda came toward her with both skeletal arms extended. "I'm the reverend's wife."

Jolie shivered and wondered if anyone noticed. "I never knew Reverend Lamont remarried."

Jolie shook Amanda's hand instead of hugging her even though it was evident Amanda had intended to be hugged. But the thought of how it would feel to embrace a walking corpse was too much to bear.

Richard bumped his head on the underside of the table and muffled a curse word.

"No, no." Amanda waved her hand, letting it crest onto Jolie's shoulder. Jolie flinched under the bony digits. A grandmother's touch. Not the touch of a woman barely in her forties. "I'm sorry to have to tell you this, dear, but Reverend Lamont passed away a few years ago. He had a heart attack. Died in his sleep. My husband took over the church for him. I'm so sorry. Were you two close? I know a lot of people admired him. My husband surely most of all."

Jolie blinked hard and swallowed the lump rising in her throat, knowing she wouldn't be able to do that later when the shock dissipated. "He was the kindest man I've ever known."

Richard grunted. "Reverend Caine took over for the great Reverend Lamont?" Seeing the smile on Richard's lips was like tasting poison. Jolie turned away before the whole knot of emotions inside her could unravel.

"Yes, Sir. And oh, my dear, Jolie, I know you'll approve of him just as much as you did of dear Reverend Lamont. Probably more." Amanda's eyes were suddenly bright and piercing, the eyes of a feral cat about to pounce on its prey. The skin around them crinkled as she smiled.

Jolie felt the blood draining from her face.

Richard prodded her ankle with the dustpan he had lifted from the cardboard box beside the refrigerator. She winced, bending over to take it from him. He swept the china into it with a hand broom while she held it at a fifteen-degree angle with the granite tiles, exactly the way he would have instructed her to hold it.

"Oh, Jolie. You're so fortunate to have such a patient husband. A lot of the women I counsel at Church and in my home Bible study have to bear such coarse short-tempered men." A ghost of an emotion loomed behind Amanda's dull blue orbs. For a moment, Jolie wondered about the new reverend. Did he realize how sickly his wife looked?

Richard snatched the handle of the dustpan and stood to empty the mess into the trash. "We saw the church when I was driving in. It was modernized. I hardly recognized it."

Amanda's soft blond curls bounced at her chin as she stepped backward and folded her arms. Gazing into Amanda's face, Jolie suddenly suspected the reverend's wife had more secrets than she had.

Amanda patted her hip pocket then reached inside and pulled out two bright red pamphlets with highly stylized gold lettering. She handed one to each of them. "I know they're rather thick, but my husband strives to impress everyone with his church. Just like he does with his very profitable business."

Richard dropped the dustpan, pulled his reading glasses back out of his pocket, and affixed them on the bridge of his nose. Jolie didn't like the look that had crossed his face at the mention of Reverend Caine's business. He stared down at the front of the pamphlet. "The Church of His Redemption, huh?" He smirked at Amanda then opened the pamphlet and narrowed his eyes on Jolie. Jolie opened her pamphlet, but she had to squint to read it through the glare of sunlight reflecting off the gold lettering on the waxy surface.

"You remind me a lot of my husband," Amanda said.

Jolie's heart clenched. She peered at Richard from behind her pamphlet, hoping he wouldn't say anything sarcastic.

"How so?" He was staring at Amanda, but saying nothing with his eyes.

"I don't know how to describe it, but please take it as a compliment."

Richard beamed, and Jolie fought the urge to sigh. "I'm in good company then? With a man of God no less?"

He lowered his head. His lips moved in a whispery cadence while his wide, intense eyes streamed back and forth, his gaze sweeping across the open pamphlet. Jolie shivered, recalling how she had woken just a few mornings ago while they were still living in Chicago and found him doing the same thing with a fax she had heard coming in before he had gotten on the phone with his accountant. The next morning, he was looking for a house in Redemption.

"You can read all about our church in there. I brought them in case I couldn't convince you and your husband to attend tomorrow morning's service on my own."

Amanda leaned toward Jolie. "Are you at all religious, dear?" Amanda's eyes looked serpent-like now.

Jolie started to say something, but Richard interrupted her. "We're religious, but not as much as we'd like to be."

That was a lie. Jolie wanted to stomp her foot and demand he admit it. He had never supported her interest in studying the Bible or any other book for that matter. It had probably been the mention of the reverend's business that had sparked Richard's sudden interest in feigning religiosity.

"Well then, I definitely hope to see you there." She winked at Jolie as though they were sharing a confidence. "My husband has planned a special sermon for tomorrow, and I can't wait to introduce you around." Amanda glanced out the window. When she looked back at Jolie, her face was nearly as pale as her dress.

Jolie laid her pamphlet on the counter and took Amanda's elbow before Amanda careened into the breakfast table. Richard dove to pull out a chair.

Amanda waved away the offer to be seated and steadied herself against the table. She took Jolie's outstretched hand

and patted it. "I'm fine, dear. I shouldn't keep doing this. I told myself I wouldn't let her keep getting to me. I just get a little upset when I think about all the trouble one of your neighbors is always causing. I hope she doesn't cause you any trouble." Blood slowly returned to her cheeks. "When she lived in the Colonial a few houses down from us, I could keep a better eye on her. The fall she took off her balcony shocked everyone. Some say she slipped. Some say she meant to kill herself to end the misery in her life after her daughter left her and her husband died."

Amanda waved her hand over her watery eyes. "Well, it was just a good thing she only broke her leg. The reverend moved her here because he was worried about what taking care of her was doing to me, but now I worry about what taking care of her soul is doing to him. Maybe if Gena would just come to church, she wouldn't be so depressed anymore. God is the greatest physician you know."

Amanda pointed out the window at the Cape Cod across the street with powder pink vinyl siding.

"Gena?" Richard asked.

"Yes. Gena Young."

Jolie sank to her knees.

Amanda dove for Jolie's arm. "My God, what's wrong, dear? Has she been bothering you already?"

Amanda pulled out the chair she had been offered. Jolie slumped onto it, clutching her chest and leaning over the table. She heard the cap pop off the Valium bottle Richard had put behind the toaster for her, and she tried to raise her heavy head. Her mind seemed to have suddenly filled with water. She felt like she were drowning. Richard grabbed her hand and shoved one of the pills into it then plunked down a bottle of water in front of her.

Jolie forced down a sip from the bottle, but dropped the

pill into her dress pocket. Richard frowned, but he wouldn't make a scene in front of the reverend's wife. Jolie clenched her hands until the tingling in her arms dissipated. Then she looked up and met Amanda's wrenched face. "Gena Young is my mother."

"Your what?" Amanda grabbed her chest.

"My..." Jolie clutched the edge of the table. "Mom." Her voice startled her. It sounded vulnerable like a child's voice. Then she looked at the doorway and saw who had spoken over her.

Emma stood there cradling herself in the red footed pajamas Jolie had dressed her in last night. Her face was flushed. The combination made her look like she were on fire. "Mom," Emma repeated, scampering into the kitchen.

She halted beside one of the breakfast table chairs and peered through the back rails at Amanda. White tear marks trailed down Emma's chin and neck. Jolie stood up and spread her arms, instantly forgetting her problems.

"Don't lift her if you still feel nauseous," Richard warned. "She's not as light as she used to be."

"Mom, I got scared." Emma pressed the heels of her hands into her eye sockets then bolted into her mother's arms.

"Scared of what, Emma?" Jolie lifted her daughter, ignoring the pain in her sides that had been lingering from that morning's ordeal.

Emma pressed her face against Jolie's ear and spoke loud enough for everyone in the room to hear her. "I dreamed there was a monster in the house."

"A monster?" Jolie glanced at Richard.

He rolled his eyes and turned away from her. Jolie knew he gave the wall a reprimanding scowl.

"Awe, what a precious face." Amanda raised her hand to touch Emma's cheek. The child cried out and buried her face in Jolie's hair. Amanda flinched, stepping back. "You know monsters don't exist, now don't you, Emma, honey?" Amanda's birdlike voice had gone an impossible octave higher.

Richard cleared his throat. "Emma, that's not very nice."

Jolie bounced Emma higher in her arms and carried the child to the counter. Emma kicked the pamphlet. The pages fluttered up when the spine smacked the floor. Her sobs were quickly chased by great heaving gulps of air.

"Emma, shh," Jolie whispered into her ear. "I love you so much."

Amanda picked up the pamphlet and laid it back on the counter out of Emma's reach. "That's all right, Mr. Needham." There was a sour note in Amanda's tone, and Jolie suddenly realized Amanda was capable of shouting in anger. "She's just scared. She had a bad dream, and I'm a stranger."

"She's probably just hungry," Jolie offered. "She gets upset sometimes when she naps past snack time."

"But it wasn't the kind you can see." Emma glared at Amanda. "Not the kind of monster you can see."

Amanda glanced at her wristwatch. "My look at the time. I'm sorry, but I've got to be going. The reverend will be expecting lunch soon. It was nice meeting all of you. I hope to see you in Church tomorrow."

"Let me see you to the door." Richard jumped to his feet. He had been leaning against one of the stools behind the breakfast bar, probably lost in thought about the reverend's business ventures.

Jolie spotted the tension in his shoulders when Amanda stepped past him. He glared at the top of Emma's head before disappearing into the foyer.

* * *

Jolie stood at the kitchen table dabbing milk from Emma's chin when she looked up and found Richard's gaze upon her from the doorway. She shuddered, wondering how long he had been watching her.

"You baby her, you know. That's why she's still afraid of monsters. You need to let her grow up." He stepped closer.

"I don't think it's such a good idea to attend that church. Did you see that woman? She's anorexic."

"Why do you say that?" Two converging veins bulged on his forehead.

Emma stopped nibbling her cheese sandwich and looked at her father. Her feet stopped dangling from her chair.

"We're going to that church. And furthermore, we're going to become members." He started out of the room. "Oh..." He pulled something out of the back pocket of his pants and tossed it on the table, "you might want to brush up on this after all."

"I don't want to go." Jolie realized she was whining and inwardly scolded herself. She knew how much Richard hated weakness. She thought she could feel the insufferable heat of his body now as though his presence consumed the room. She imagined the heat it would have in their bed tonight when he would lie on top of her and try to make another baby her body would reject.

She shifted her gaze to the floor and couldn't help cowering like a frightened child as she reached for her little Psalms book. "I'll have Emma ready early."

He turned and left the room.

Chapter Three

Relieved to be in a pair of jeans and a T-shirt, Reverend Timothy Caine stepped in front of his dearest friend.

The stout man shut the limousine door behind him and slapped him on the back. "Dontcha take too long in there now, Rev." The man winked his one good eye and patted the front pocket of the blue blazer of his chauffeur uniform. His slur was getting better since he had started speech therapy. Timothy hoped the man would one day be able to regain the feeling he had lost in his face from the accident. "And don't forget to call me if she gives you any trouble. I'll pick right up."

"I know you will, Edmond. You'd save my life all over again if I needed you to."

Edmond smiled. One side of his face raised in a grin while the other side lay flat. Timothy chuckled, but inside his heart felt heavy with guilt. How long would he carry this burden?

He waved over his shoulder then edged up the

cobblestone driveway. Clusters of white carnations grew along both sides like planted wedding bouquets in front of the Krenshaws' two-story Victorian.

His thoughts turned to Gena Young. In his mind, her china doll face was framed by ringlets of glorious black hair through a sheer white wedding veil. God's masterpiece. Her eyes so powerfully blue he shivered thinking of them. Thank God she had survived the fall from her balcony. If she'd have died, he would've regretted what he had done to her husband, what Edmond had helped him do.

He felt his smile slip from his lips. "Jonathan," he spat out.

But just as easily as ever, his thoughts returned to Gena. "Those eyes," he grumbled, unable to stop picturing her. They were in everything. The sky. The ocean. The flowers. His dreams. Even other women's faces. Even Barbara's face when he wasn't careful. But lately, those eyes had changed their expression. They seemed to accuse him of something. What did Gena suspect? Did it have something to do with Jonathan's death? He couldn't help smiling. *Jonathan's death. Even you refer to it that way, you sorry excuse for a man.*

He hung his head. No, he couldn't bear to think about what that emotion had made him do so long ago. Not today, his first day away from the business and the church in three weeks.

Gena had never said anything about it. Never made any accusations clear. Maybe it was only his guilty conscience forming accusations now.

He dragged his feet toward the carnations. Their aroma was as fresh as the skin of the woman inside the house. Barbara Krenshaw. But Barbara would never fill the void in his heart, the place he reserved only for Gena.

The void only I can fill.

He shrugged off the soft voice pressing against his

conscience and looked down at a meadowlark fluttering past. It fanned its tail for lift and landed on one of the fence posts enclosing Barbara's vegetable garden. It opened its beak and sang. Either to stake its territory or to attract a mate, it didn't matter. Either way Timothy thought of Gena. How he sang for her in his own way, to mark her as his own, with every sermon he created that she never came to hear.

He thought of how she flitted through her house when she was suffering one of her spells, trilling and cackling, beckoning him to her with her song of helplessness. Then, more than ever, she seemed ethereal. A beautiful, untouchable, oblivious little nymph cresting over the horizon of his heart and disappearing into the sun of another man's memory. He cursed Jonathan to Hell.

His dead father's voice snaked through his mind. Isn't that where you're going, old boy?

Leave me alone! Timothy's heart cried out. *Both of you.*
Is she more important to you than your Lord?

The soft voice froze him. He felt a twinge of shame.

No. Of course not. It's just that with all I do for You, I'd think You could just give me this one thing.

Give her up, Timothy. I am your God. You will have no other gods before me. Give her up. She's not yours anyway. And tell her the truth. Tell everyone the truth. Everyone. Reveal yourself to them so I can repair what you've broken.

The limousine's engine revved, one of the alert signals Timothy had worked out with his business partners, and Timothy turned as though he had been snagged by a fishing hook. Edmond glanced at him, and he followed the man's eyes.

An unfamiliar olive green Mercedes rolled past the limousine and stopped in front of a neighbor's yard. Strangers in Redemption were never a good sign. A heavy-set man with unruly red curls and an obnoxiously freckled face sat perched behind the steering wheel. A young girl bounced up and down on the backseat playing with some kind of stuffed animal. But the young woman in the passenger seat refused to look at him. The back of her head was all he could see. Her long dark glistening hair. Like Gena.

He was about to wave at the driver when she faced him. Their eyes met, and he couldn't help but return her indecipherable smile. Gena, his mind whispered. But he had no way to explain it. If anything, those had been Jonathan's eyes. But surely she was no ghost from the past come to haunt him for his past indiscretions. He shook his head. *No Timothy, don't start that again. No one can undo what has been done.*

The driver scowled at the limousine and leaned over the steering wheel before zooming down the street. Definitely not a good sign. The passengers could be spies from his last business conference for all Timothy knew.

He nodded at Edmond, and the man pulled out a cell phone and started dialing. Timothy relaxed. His friend would be calling Peter. By the end of the day, Peter would know more about those strangers than they knew about themselves.

He glimpsed a woman on the porch next door and froze. The woman's arms were crossed over her flat chest. She was drumming her fingers on her biceps. When he locked stares with her, her mouth bowed at one corner in a frown. She flung her hands over her narrow hips.

Easy there, don't draw your weapons. He wanted to laugh. At least she didn't have binoculars dangling from her neck this time.

He waved at her, and she scowled, jutting her chin at his limousine, engine still idling curbside.

But he wasn't worried. Handling jealous women was his specialty. "Such a blessed day, isn't it? Hope to see you at morning services tomorrow."

She refolded her arms. "Maybe Mrs. Krenshaw will give me a ride if she's not too tired. Seems she's had a busy day today." She spun and disappeared past her slamming screen door.

Busy day, he wondered?

Timothy continued down the driveway and sprang over the final step onto Barbara's porch. The door instantly opened.

Wound into a tight orange pantsuit, Barbara hid nothing of her womanly assets. Her over-bleached hair stood almost by itself in medium-length spikes, a new style she was trying out that he hoped would be short-lived. Her small brown eyes twinkled. Her collagen-inflated lips drew back in a sinewy smile. "I'm just fine and so happy to see you too. I've been excited about your return all day. Did everything go the way you and Peter expected?"

He nodded, sensing something queer in her tone besides sarcasm.

"I'm afraid we have a little problem." She wagged her finger at him. "Gena's inside all zombie-like on my couch. You should know she assaulted my dog again. The poor animal is traumatized. She can't keep thinking he's her dead husband come back from the grave. When I opened the door to rescue my poor baby, she ranted that I was trying to steal Jonathan. She chased the dog inside then suddenly gave up and plopped down on my couch. She's been almost catatonic since. I suppose she's been waiting for either you or her dead husband to show up. Anything you think you might be able to do about this before I lose my mind? I almost called the police this time."

"You think she's waiting for me?"

Barbara looked wounded.

He leaned toward her, intending to kiss her cheek, and she veered backward over the threshold, wagging her finger, letting the corners of her mouth draw back to expose the creases around her mouth, something she did when she thought she was being mocked.

"Come in and ask her yourself."

Blood throbbed in his ears as he followed Barbara's swaying orange backside into the living room. He shrunk from the blurry face he glimpsed amidst the glare of the living room track lights. The last time he'd seen Gena she had been angry with him about confiscating her photo albums. Why couldn't he just call it all off? Why couldn't he just tell her he was sorry and let her go? But he already knew the answer to that. She held him captive just as tightly as he held her.

"Gena say hi to the reverend." Barbara clapped her hands together. "Come on now, Gena. Be a good girl." Barbara rolled her eyes at Timothy. "You know I'm getting pretty sick of this. This is the third time this month. She surprised me with a bucket of ice water—I didn't tell you that part. Can't that nurse of hers keep an eye on her? I had to change clothes." Barbara glared at him, but he looked past her at Gena. "But then again, this outfit is much nicer than the one I had on."

Still covert in the light, Gena stood from the sofa and stepped toward him. Her head bobbed.

He nodded at her, but she backed away from him. *God please don't let me startle her.* Any sudden movement could send her into a limb-flailing tirade that would send Barbara straight to the phone for the police. Sure Peter would intercept the call at the department, but Barbara didn't need to know the extent of Peter's power.

"Those medications are taking a toll on her, you know. They're making her old before her time."

Timothy edged closer to Gena. He concentrated on her tiny waist and the jutting bones of her ribcage evident under the knitted sweater he had bought for her. It wasn't a girdle that made her look so fragile. She was losing weight again, and he was the only one to blame. He'd have to have her medicine adjusted again.

"Why won't you dim the lights, Barbara? After all, we're not in an operating room."

He sat down on the stool at the wet bar while Barbara adjusted the light. Only with great effort could he resist embracing Gena. He glanced down at the counter and noticed the pile of bills awaiting Barbara's husband, Aiden. *How does it feel to be on your own, Aiden, old boy? Should've stayed in the business with me and Peter. But oh, no, you had to get out like Jonathan. Course we both know what happened to him.*

Barbara tilted her head. "Aiden was never one to take much responsibility for his actions or to remain true to his commitments." Barbara dropped her hand onto his shoulder. "But I've always been more than true enough for the both of us."

Cupping the base of her square jaw, Barbara slid her other hand down her side and rested it on her ample hip.

Gena skirted around them. Timothy glimpsed her movement, but dared not look directly at her. His heart raced ahead of his brain. The urge to reach out and grab her was almost unbearable.

Gena stood close to him now. Her knees nearly touched his as he resisted taking her hands. She was summoning his eyes toward her with her blind trust. He'd already determined he wouldn't look into her face for long, but when his gaze met hers, he was sure his eyes would never be able to completely look away again. This new soft nonjudgmental expression would haunt him for the remainder of his life, maybe longer. Maybe the medicine was working after all. *Oh, Gena, my love, my one and only. Why can't I have you now that Jonathan's gone?*

He couldn't help but stare at the subtle line of her delicate nose, the pert bow of her pink mouth, the long black lashes that framed her piercing eyes. *Oh, Gena, could it be possible that you're even more beautiful than the day I first met you?*

Gena covered her mouth.

Was she trying to communicate with him? No. But then again, she always seemed to have special powers of communication, special gifts. Like her ability to paint portraits of people, penetrating their physical facades down to the depths of their souls—their purest motivations—which was one of the reasons he had never asked her to paint his portrait. His sins wore many masks, but Gena's paintings would reveal all of them.

No. Gena wasn't that perceptive. Was she?

Despite the daggers he knew Barbara's eyes were throwing at the back of his head, he continued to concentrate on Gena. Her lips parted. Was she going to speak to him today? *Oh God, if you love me, let her speak to me.*

"I'm pleased to meet you, sir," she said in her tiny distant voice. He felt himself frown and tried in vain to raise the corners of his mouth. She didn't recognize him today. She didn't even think he was Jonathan today. But she said it so sweetly part of him was glad she thought she was meeting him for the first time.

Then came Gena's slender hand toward him. He didn't move. "You're supposed to shake it, sir," she explained.

He eased his hand into hers. His body tingled. He wished hers did too, but he knew it didn't.

Offering his hand to Barbara, she swatted it away. He looked up at her. "You silly man, we've been introduced." She laughed with effort and snapped her head toward Gena. "You're very lucky, Gena Young," Barbara said, "that your reverend is such a patient man. You should try harder to remember who he is."

Maybe if Gena hadn't stolen his heart, he could've given it to Barbara or to his wife. Part of him hated how he had used them while he waited for Gena to open her heart to him. "Amanda will be expecting me soon. I should probably be leaving. Edmond and I will escort Gena home as usual. And again, I'm very sorry about all this, but I'm immensely grateful for your unending patience."

Barbara slid her arm around his back. He barely noticed the pressure until it had coiled around him like a reptilian handshake.

"Couldn't you stay and visit a little longer?" Gena asked. There was a new brightness to her eyes. A coherent brightness perhaps?

Patience, old boy. "I suppose I could stay, my little dove." The liquid texture of his voice surprised him.

"Don't you dare call me that," Gena snapped. "Only Johnny can call me that."

Timothy felt like he had been punched in the gut.

Barbara gasped, but it had been to conceal a smile. "I would think you could show a little more gratitude toward your reverend, Gena. He has been more patient with you than you realize."

Gena locked stares with Barbara, but said nothing more.

"You know where Aiden's office cot is, right?" Barbara placed her hands on her hips. "I do remember your nurse calling and saying you skipped out on your afternoon nap an hour ago. If you don't mind, I'd like to spend some time with Reverend Caine, I have a personal matter to discuss with him, so why don't you go lie down like a good girl."

Gena left the room, glancing over her shoulder at them as Barbara pulled him to the sofa. He hadn't time to react. He was still reeling from Gena's reprimand.

A door slammed shut down the hallway as Barbara sat

down next to him and began to force part of him to forget, at least temporarily, the power Gena held over his soul.

Chapter Four

Timothy slammed his office door and balled up the letter he had found in an old trunk in the attic. His father's old trunk. He shook his fist. The letter had been hidden underneath a pile of old sermon notes. An old snippet of dialogue for tonight's sermon had been what he wanted, not this ghost from the past.

Staring down at the wad of yellowed paper, his thoughts were interrupted by Amanda's shrill voice. She was whistling again from their master bedroom. "God give me strength," he muttered through clenched teeth. "Can you hear yourself in there? It sounds like a squealing pig is going in for the slaughter." A single tear escaped down his cheek, but he knew it wasn't because of Amanda's voice.

He stormed down the hallway and stopped at their bedroom door, knowing he wasn't angry with Amanda as much as he was angry with himself. He fought the urge to scream at the sight of her wounded expression. Maybe if she wasn't so good all the time, so merciful with everyone else but him, maybe then he could stop hurting her. Maybe if she didn't always have to take his dead father's side when he confided in her about his past. Maybe.

"What are you thinking about?"

"Mind your own business," he snapped.

She fled into their master bathroom.

He sighed. The news Peter had brought him yesterday evening after he had left Barbara's house with Gena had been difficult enough. Now faced with the fresh assault of discovering some new trace of his father in his home, exhaustion crept into his bones. Timothy recalled the words in the letter. "A preacher will never make enough money to support his family. Better to be a businessman like your old man, Son. Besides, God can't make any man rich."

Timothy opened his fist and examined the wadded letter his father had written him after Timothy had been accepted into Bible college. He had it memorized. He slammed it into the trashcan by the door and stomped toward the bathroom. "Amanda. We'll be late." He punched the door, hating the sound it made under his merciless fist. Deep down he was no ogre. Though only Gena knew that.

"I'll be right out. For goodness sake, Tim. Why are you always so short with me? Are you depressed again?" He waited, not knowing what to say first as he listened to her fiddling with things in the linen closet.

"I'm not depressed." He laid his palm flat against the door. "I'm sorry. I didn't mean to be so rough, but I'm not depressed. Only sinners get depressed."

"Aren't we all sinners?"

Don't let her get the upper hand on you, Tim, old boy, he heard his father's voice echo in his mind. *If you start letting her do that, who knows what she'll start holding over you.*

"But I know you, Tim," Amanda continued, *"I know when you're depressed."*

"You don't know anything."

"All right. All right. Whatever you say. I'll be out in a minute."

Timothy kicked the baseboard and cursed under his breath. Why did Amanda always try to counsel him? She wasn't a pastor. She hadn't even read the Bible one full time through. Why did so many people in his life think they knew what was best for him when he should be the one telling everyone else what to do? Even his dead father still had a say in his life. It wasn't fair.

Timothy stared at the baseboard when he suddenly began to chuckle.

What had he found the courage to say to his father in the nursing home? *Oh, yeah...* Timothy looked up and watched himself smile in Amanda's vanity mirror. *Well, Dad, looks like I'm making more money as a simple preacher than you ever made as a CEO. How does it feel to know you were wrong about God?* But that hadn't felt right. The words had left him empty because the cancer had drained his father of all pride and most of his coherency, and because the things Timothy had done to the minds of his parishioners and wounded souls all over the world left a deep sore in his heart that might never heal. But then that was before he had found Gena. One look at her face from that pew the first time he had visited Reverend Lamont's church, and he had realized she would be the one to fill that void in his heart, to heal him. She would provide the soft womanly understanding he needed. After all, she had the same strength of faith in God he had. They were kindred spirits. They were meant for each other and no one else. Why she couldn't see it was a mystery.

Oh, Timothy, how deceived you are, my son, the soft voice whispered. *Don't tell me you believe these lies.* Timothy blinked hard to clear his eyes. He had been hearing the voice for a full year now. He supposed it was his conscience, or maybe it was God. He couldn't think straight when he was emotional. He had to get control, or he'd be useless at Church tonight.

"Jolie seemed like such a sweet young lady." He flinched and felt the tension return to his face. The pressure behind his eyes made him wish he could skip the prayer meeting that would follow tonight's sermon.

The bathroom door creaked open and Amanda emerged wearing a loose robe that had clung to her two weeks ago. "And she's a mother like me. I have this feeling we're going to become very good friends." She giggled while dabbing perfume behind her ears. "You know, she wasn't even mad at me when I told her about Gena being her neighbor. Sure, she got a little upset but..." She lowered the glass vessel to her vanity and looked in the mirror.

"What?" Timothy stared at her as she swerved past him, avoiding the look in his eyes. "You warned them about Gena?"

"You didn't want me to? You told me to smooth her behavior over with people so they'd understand when you visited her all the time."

"Yeah, but none of them happened to be Gena's daughter."

"You knew?" She spun to face him. "You knew and you didn't tell me before I went over there and made a fool of myself? The poor girl almost fainted when I told her."

Trying to steady his nerves, Timothy chewed his bottom lip. He couldn't let all his hard work with Gena be obliterated by her prodigal daughter's return to Redemption. "I didn't know then, Amanda. I found out later when Peter showed me the names on the buyer's contract. But you should still have been more careful, considering they were strangers."

Don't show weakness, Tim.

Timothy shuddered at his father's familiar refrain.

"In fact, I believe, Amanda, that I specifically told you not to bring her up to anyone unless they brought her up first." Timothy slapped his hip and rolled his eyes. *"Jolie Needham of all people. Gena's long lost precious daughter. What's next? A reunion with Jonathan? I don't know how this one could've slipped past Peter's radar. I'm going to need someone else to pick up some of the slack. I think I'm finally over-extending him."*

"Did Peter find out anything about Jolie's husband, Richard? He seems a little strange. You should've seen all those antiques and collectibles he was showing me. I think he's more fond of them than his own family."

"Don't worry about him. I'm way ahead of you. I know the type."

"I bet you do."

He ignored the comment. "Peter says Richard is a businessman. Running away from a business scandal in Chicago. The man knows how to cover a paper trail—much harder to cover than a computer trail—I'll give him that. If I can get Richard interested in taking over Aiden's old role in the business and get the pompous fool under my thumb, I can control his wife. I'll dangle a little money in front of his nose, and the rest will be history."

"Timothy, you won't hurt Jolie, will you?"

He folded his arms.

"Jolie has such a reserved demeanor just like me. I bet we'll get along great. I'll be able to keep her in line. You won't have to hurt her."

"And don't forget she has a husband—*golly gee*—just like you too." He rolled his eyes at her again.

She went to her closet and opened the louvered doors.

He gritted his teeth. "I just hope little Jolie Needham

doesn't try to become the devoted daughter she hasn't been for eight years when she sees how much Gena has changed."

"So, you are going to let them meet?" Amanda selected a dress from her closet. She turned as though she had felt his gaze on her back.

"Honey, why don't you wear one of your other dresses. You don't exactly have a body like our dear Gena."

"What do you mean? You said this was your favorite dress on me."

"Exactly, Amanda. Was." Timothy hated the words that came out of his mouth. Hated that he had to say them to distance himself from her. Hated that it would only make her anorexia worse. "And is there any way you could wear a little more make-up? There's got to be something in that box of yours to cover up those horrible blotches."

"Why do you always compare me to Gena?" she whined, running back to her vanity mirror. "You promised you'd stop doing that."

"Don't talk down to me. Remember your place."

She tucked her chin toward her chest like she usually did when he hurt her in new ways.

It was only when she cowered that he knew he still had the same control over her as he had over his congregation. Why did it always take a clerical collar around his neck or a show of aggression to get the respect he deserved? Why couldn't he be the soft-spoken man he ached to be around them?

Because no one ever took a soft-spoken man seriously, his father's words echoed in his head.

Only Gena had ever allowed him to show his true self without challenging him. Only Gena deserved his kindness.

He blinked away tears. His father had been the first person to misunderstand him, to hurt him so deeply he had no choice but to wound others before they could hurt him.

Timothy hadn't just been a starry-eyed boy who wanted to grow up to become a famous preacher and change the world with his gift. He was the man who had accomplished all that boy's dreams and had potential for so much more because of his unique gift from God. Gena saw it. Gena knew. But getting Gena to admit it when she wasn't strung out on drugs—getting Gena to admit his faith was just as strong as hers, as Jonathan's—well, that was his only unfulfilled dream.

He glared at Amanda while she scurried past him toward her closet for another dress. "Besides, you're the one who keeps feeling threatened when I even mention her. Obviously, you're the one who's at fault. Can't you at least try to be more of a Christian?"

"You know, Tim, it isn't about being more like a Christian. It's about being more like Christ."

Amanda slipped into a dark blue dress. He averted his eyes from her mass of jutting bones. She sat down at her vanity and leaned forward. She ran her fingers across her face, evidently searching the mirror for the illusive marks. He felt a sick grin stretch across his face when she seemed to spot something she hadn't been expecting.

"What a fine woman Gena is." He edged toward Amanda. "Will she be attending Church today?" He fought the urge to rest a gentle hand on her shoulder and apologize. But that would be backing down. That would be weakness. He couldn't start letting her be the strong one, so she'd have to be the first one to apologize.

"She still refuses to come," Amanda whispered, squinting into the mirror. She slid the lighted magnifying mirror toward her and squinted harder into it. "Milly said Gena was going through the house again, looking for traces of Jonathan. She had to give her a mild sedative."

Timothy rolled his eyes. "She'll accept that nice new

home I gave her, but she won't come out to my church. Mind boggling. I swear women reason in an alternate plane of reality."

"You're not doing anything you shouldn't be with her, are you, Timothy?" Amanda stared at him the way she rarely did, and he suddenly felt exposed. "Or to her? You remember you said yourself people were getting the wrong impression about Barbara?"

"Of course I remember, but I'd be blind not to notice what a beautiful woman Gena is." He backed to the foot of the bed behind her. "Would you have me close my eyes to the beauty of God's creation and stumble around blind?"

"These blotches, I only see a few little freckles, but I think they might've always been there. What blotches were you talking about?" She stood up and brought her face close to the mirror.

"You don't see them?" He pointed to the base of her chin then to the center of her forehead. "There. And there." He waited while her facial expression changed. She seemed to be trying to decide whether to believe him. "Your pores are so large I can practically fit the tips of my fingers inside them. I don't suppose you can see those either?"

She pressed her nose against the mirror then moved her face back to inspect her pale, but otherwise, flawless complexion. She crinkled her brow at him. "Do you think a little more make-up would help?"

"I've got ten years on you, and I look ten years better than you. Nothing's going to help that." He went to the doorway. "By the way?" He grabbed the doorframe, and turned his back to her. "Did you get Richard and Jolie to agree to attend Church today?"

He heard faint sobbing behind him and blinked hard. "Amanda?"

"Yes. Yes, I did."

"Good," he whispered, swallowing hard. "At least you can do some things right. Don't worry with the extra make-up. They've all grown accustomed to the way you look anyway."

That familiar far away look greeted him when he faced her. That ghostly I'm-looking- through-you-not-at-you look. He narrowed his eyes at her, hoping she would toughen up. Maybe then he could respect her.

"I try to please you, Timothy. I try so hard."

He grunted and folded his arms. "She hasn't seen her mother in eight years, and she moved in right across the street from her. I just can't believe Peter didn't pick up on that before you went over there and embarrassed me." Timothy slapped his hip, narrowing his eyes on the wall behind Amanda. "Well, I know what to do with her if she starts to get in my way." His chest tightened. "But then...who knows? Maybe I can use this to my advantage. A distraught mother and daughter reuniting after all these years and falling into each other's arms? Might even knock some sense back into Gena. Might rouse her back to sanity. Might open her heart up to Church. Course..." He stared at the floor. "There's a chance it might send her farther away from me too, from God that is. If that happens, I'll know who to blame."

"Why'd you bother giving her old photo albums back? Jonathan's not in them since you doctored them. Neither are pictures of Jolie." She rolled her eyes at him when he didn't answer.

"Don't you dare." He shook his finger at her.

"I know. You said you had your reasons. But I'm your wife, Tim. I see more than you give me credit for."

He drummed his fingers on the doorjamb. "I don't know what you mean." His ragged nails clicked into the wood, spurring new thoughts, new plans for his business and of course what those plans would mean concerning Gena. If he could just prove to her that he was accomplishing more for God than her dear Reverend Lamont ever dreamed of accomplishing. Course, he also had something to prove to himself and to his dead father.

You'll never impress a dead man who's probably spending his days and nights in the place you're headed. And a mad woman certainly won't save your soul.

Timothy shook his head at the biting voice of his conscience.

"You won't hurt Jolie if she upsets Gena?"

"That's none of your concern. I told you, what I do is between me and God. Besides, it's not like I can move Gena in here with us again. Not after what you did to start all those rumors that have finally dissipated."

"I can't help but hold my breath whenever you tell me not to worry."

"Gena is special, Amanda. I care deeply about her soul." He met her eyes. "Don't look at me that way. You read too much into things. That's a product of your sin, not some imagined sin you keep accusing me of committing."

"It's just that I don't always think the way you lord over her is right even if you say she needs all that help. Maybe if you just lighten her medication a little. Or get your brother to prescribe something else. Just try something different. Maybe all she really needs is time to mourn."

"What are you doing, Amanda? Are you doubting God?"

"No, I didn't mean it that way."

"Then what did you mean? Are you doubting me?" He balled his hands into fists and spun away from her.

"I'm just saying I don't think those drugs are helping her like they should."

He spun toward her and flexed his hands. "If I don't have your complete support, Amanda, you're not giving me what I deserve as your husband."

"But she doesn't want to come to our church. She still believes in God. Who are we to judge her because she doesn't care for the way you preach?"

He wanted to tear down the walls with his bare hands and beat Amanda over the head with the joists. "It would be like you to feel closer to the sinner than the saint."

She cocked an eyebrow at him. "Who is the saint, Timothy?"

"She tried to commit suicide. If I take her pills away and she doesn't have God to lean on, she'll try to kill herself again. Do you want that on your conscience?"

"No. But I don't think she'd do that. Things pass. Emotions settle. We learn to cope if people let us."

"You don't think she'd try to kill herself again, huh? She's already tried it once. Should I let her soul be on your conscience if I take her off the drugs and she does kill herself?"

"I…I don't…" Her forehead wrinkled.

He rolled his eyes. "Well, you don't have to frazzle your brain thinking about her anymore. I think it's obvious to you now how foolish you've been. You have to weigh everything, Amanda. You can't just do things based on your feelings."

He stormed out of the room and down the hall into the foyer. "We're going to be late if you don't come now." He looked back for her.

She hesitated at the mirror in the hall, holding up the sides of her dress, before running after him. "Is that why you spend so much time away from home, because of the way I look?"

"It doesn't help."

He touched her face, letting the tips of his fingers glide over her cheek.

She seemed surprised.

With his thumb, he strategically wiped a tear that had escaped her eye, being careful not to smear her blush or eyeliner. He withdrew his hand, straightened his collar, and looked away from the disappointment shadowing her face.

What, Amanda, you thought I could start loving you now? A bedraggled old lovesick fool like me? "I'm sorry. You know I've got a lot on my shoulders. I don't mean to be so hard on you, but you give me no other choice. Sometimes I think you don't have any faith in me at all. How do you think that makes a man feel, when his wife doesn't respect him? All that I've given you...you don't want for anything. You'd think that you could just give me this one little thing."

Tears flecked the corners of her eyes. "I'm sorry too. I'm sorry I ever married you."

"I'm opening the door now, Amanda. Remember yourself in front of the children."

The door opened and a familiar numbness fell drunk on his heart. He again became Reverend Timothy Caine.

She seemed oblivious to the tightness of his embrace as they stepped outside and approached their limousine. Edmond held the door open for her. She wrenched her hand out of Timothy's grip before he could think to release it and climbed into the limousine.

"I guess it doesn't matter what you wear." Timothy took his seat across from her. "You'll never change."

Their two daughters looked out the windows of the limousine.

Amanda's face tensed. He knew she'd be spending most of tomorrow on the treadmill again, and he wished he could somehow undo all the horrible things he had done to her.

"Couldn't you have worn your black dress?"

"I will next time," she hissed.

Timothy stared at his daughters. They were studying him again, probably evaluating him like Amanda often did. Neither of them meant much to him anyway. It only mattered what they said about him to other people and how much they devoted themselves to him at Church. Now a son, a son from a woman like Gena would mean something.

Timothy nodded at the reflection of Edmond's eyes in the rear-view mirror, and his friend started the engine.

Amanda clasped her hands together and seemed to at least pretend to enjoy the landscaping. It rolled by like memories on an old film reel. In a few minutes, the reel would run out and stop on the last slide, a pink Cape Cod with—and these had been the most important features, he thought—fixed-pane upstairs windows and no balcony.

When the limousine reached its destination, he stepped out before Edmond could get out to open the door for him. Timothy reached back into the limousine and grabbed Amanda's knee, compelling her eyes to his. "You just make sure you don't say anything else to the Needhams that could embarrass me," he whispered.

She nodded, and he slammed the door.

Edmond powered down Amanda's window as Timothy leaned toward the tinted pane. "I'll be along shortly. Just make sure you do me proud today, Mandy." He knew the soft way he had used her nickname would please her somehow.

Amanda opened her mouth when he raised his hand. Edmond nodded from the driver seat and powered up the window. The car pulled away from the curb. Amanda twisted against her seatbelt and stared at him through the rear window. From her expression, he knew she still loved him. God help her, she still loved him. Timothy turned from the fading vehicle, trying to banish the look on Amanda's face from his mind.

Chapter Five

The sky darkened like God had pulled a large blanket back up over the world at the sound of some heavenly snooze alarm. A storm was threatening to break, one that might eventually cast its full fury on Redemption and test the faith of all its inhabitants.

Jolie shielded her eyes, swallowed against the lump rising in her throat, and rubbed her sore shoulder. *After Church. After Church I'll get away and go see Mom. Richard can beat me black and blue if he wants to when I get back, but I'm going.*

On the announcement board beside the church, in bold blocky letters, was printed: Welcome to The Church of His Redemption. Underneath, in smaller letters, was written: what we try to hide from people is always seen by God.

Storm windows had replaced the large stained-glass windows she had cherished from her childhood. The replacement of the steeple was a mystery. Where a shiny golden cross had once been was now a vertical spear that conveyed no comprehensible message. Two plastic benches sat cattycorner to each other beside the wide mouth of the concrete steps leading into the church. More sturdy wooden benches had once occupied their place. Jolie could just see the whisper of her father's form sitting in one of them now, and she fought to gain control of her emotions. How could she enter this church after all these years? What memories would haunt her inside?

Precisely sheared hedgerows enclosed the sides of the churchyard, even leading back to the graveyard where her father was supposed to have been buried. Jolie's chest filled with acid as she tried to breath. Visiting her father's grave after having missed the funeral and the last years of his life seemed wrong to her. She was unworthy of his forgiveness, and of her mother's. Even if Richard insisted on taking her back there, she would refuse to go.

Jolie blinked and shook her head, and the distant sound of a lawn mower registered in her memory. For a moment, she saw Reverend Lamont waving to her from his riding tractor as he mowed the grass of a much simpler landscape. Somehow she couldn't picture Reverend Caine with his flashy church pamphlets more like vacation brochures doing anything so submissive. She blinked and the memory was gone.

The hem of her skirt fluttered, tickling her ankles. A breeze kissed with juniper and pine made her shut her eyes before she looked down at the smooth pavement beneath her taupe flats. She imagined the sound of her mother's shoes clicking across the old cobblestone walkway on their way across the street to Church.

Even now, she could look up and see her parents' old Colonial between the parted trees in the distance, the infamous balcony in plain sight. Odd that her mother no longer lived there.

Her father's laughter drifted into her mind, and she almost felt the playful yank on her ponytail he would often give her when he walked close behind her while she walked arm in arm with her mother on their way to Church. He'd tickle the back of her neck with it, and she would giggle. Then he would turn to her mother, and their eyes would be filled with a love Jolie had prayed for in a husband ever since.

She sighed. Would home ever be the same for her now that so many things had changed?

She lifted her index finger to her temple and depressed the pulsing vein. It was still early, but it seemed very late in the day.

Richard arched his back, pushed out his large round belly, and moaned. His sideways glance made her spine stiffen. "You really should make Emma sit in the back seat no matter how much she whines. She's too old to ride without a seat belt."

"She looks like a statue, Mom." Jolie looked down at her daughter, and followed the little extended arm that pointed up the Church steps. Amanda stood at the top, shaking hands with a steady stream of parishioners. Her dress hung on her like a fitted shower curtain and flapped in the wind behind her rigid body.

"I have a stomach ache, Dad. I want to go home."

Emma clung to Jolie's leg, gripped her belly, and pursed her lips. Jolie leaned down and kissed Emma's forehead, noticing the light moisture there. "Sweetheart, it's not going to work this time." Then the same queasiness settled into her stomach.

Richard's eyes bulged. "You're going in there." He grabbed Emma's shoulder and trudged across the pavement. The breeze ballooned, puffing Jolie's skirt. With her hands clamped down over her sides, she followed them. Wind whipped through her hair and seemed to muffle his voice.

"Don't either of you embarrass me," she thought he said.

Richard urged Emma up the concrete steps despite her pleas that sand had gotten into her eyes.

"Honey, it'll be all right."

Emma stumbled and almost fell on the top step, looking back at her mother. Jolie's heart caught in her throat as she lunged for her daughter's elbow and lifted her over the last step.

Amanda knelt in front of Emma. "No more monsters, I hope."

Jolie found herself frowning at her daughter's down-turned head.

Two men held the mahogany doors open. "Thank you, Peter," Amanda said to the taller, thinner man on the right. A port wine birthmark covered the left half of his face. He winked at Jolie before she passed him, and she couldn't help but stare at his otherwise handsome face.

"You look a lot like your mother," he whispered.

Goosebumps seemed to spread from Emma's arm to hers. She forced her gaze away from him.

Instead of the floor plan Jolie recalled from Reverend Lamont's pastorate, the sanctuary split into a lower area and a raised stage. A lectern stood beside the stage, and a pulpit stood in the center. Newly stained wooden pews aligned each side of the lower part of the sanctuary and glistened in the light streaming through skylights that had been installed in the old vaulted ceiling. Chairs for the choir sat directly behind the stage facing the pews instead of off to the right side. Nothing was the same as she had remembered it. Even the walls seemed to have been moved.

People walked up and down the aisles. Some emerged from heavy pink curtains draped over thick brass rods on the left and right sides of the rooms. A woman shoved aside a curtain, dabbing at her eyes with a handkerchief. An older woman stood from a nearby pew and draped an arm over the younger one's shoulder as they sobbed in each other's arms.

A tall lean man with medium-length caramel-brown hair stepped out next with a red book underneath one arm. His head was down. The strong line of his jaw was all that was evident of his face. She could just make out the gleaming inscription, Holy Bible, on the book. It made her think of the church pamphlets Amanda had brought over. The man's black suit tapered perfectly to two polished black shoes. He seemed at immense ease with the two women he now held by the shoulders. He looked up, and Jolie almost bit her tongue at the sight of the white collar around the man's neck. He locked stares with her, and she felt a twinge of embarrassment. His hot blue glare seemed to penetrate to the secret depths of her heart.

Reverend Caine?

He shifted his eyes as though he had seen something distasteful and went up the aisle to the stage. He caught Peter's arm, and the man cocked his head at her. His face grew red, and his birthmark seemed to pulse with a life all its own.

The knots tightened in her stomach. *Surely they're not talking about me.* When the reverend turned to look at her, she imagined his eyes might have turned her face into stone had she not believed in Christ.

The reverend patted Peter on the shoulder before climbing the stage. Sliding his hands down the sides of the pulpit, he raised his head to survey the pews. Now his gaze was upon the crowd. His glistening hair fell backward, catching the light and exposing his sharp nose. Shadows settled into the deep groves of skin along his tan cheeks, directing a path to his white collar as though to make a moral point.

Jolie tugged on her skirt, but it was already down to her ankles. She barely noticed when Emma clung to her hand.

The man smoothed his hair behind his ears and took a deep breath, his chest rising like he was a play-actor who needed his actions seen from the back of an auditorium. The pulpit lacked a microphone, and she doubted her voice could ever be loud enough to carry very far without one.

"My husband is a fascinating man. Isn't he?"

Jolie flinched, bringing her hand to her chest.

"How beautiful your hair is." Pain of some nature Jolie could almost feel resonated in Amanda's hollow-looking gaze, and Jolie suddenly wished she had hugged Amanda when the woman had come to the house. "I used to wish for hair that long and such a deep shade of brown, like mocha, almost black like your mother's. The reverend would have loved it too, but this style is so much more practical for me." Amanda's fingers fussed with the tips of her hair. "What a fortunate man you are to have such a breathtaking wife, Richard. Was she into modeling where you used to live?"

Richard raised his hand and coughed into his palm. The hint of a smile faded from his lips. "No, she doesn't work." He puffed up his chest. "She doesn't need to with what I make. Her job is at home with our little girl, Emma."

"That *isn't* work?" Amanda looked away before Richard could reply. Jolie wondered if she'd pay for Amanda's comment later.

"Amanda, dear." A woman with spikes of white-blond hair and a dark mask of foundation and smoky eye shadow slid her arm around Amanda's waist and hugged her. "It's wonderful to see you on this fine day. How lovely you look, dear."

Amanda fidgeted like a child who had just soiled her Sunday clothes. Barbara seemed to take the hint and released her.

"Barbara, this is Richard and Jolie Needham and their daughter, Emma. Barbara is a deacon of our church."

A tall man with wavy dark brown hair stepped around Barbara and offered Richard his hand. Richard looked up at him and must've noticed the extra foot of height separating them. Jolie fought the urge to chuckle. "I'm Aiden Krenshaw, Barbara's other half." His voice was warm and rhythmic. It soothed Jolie's frazzled nerves, and she absently wondered where she had heard it before.

"But not necessarily my better half," Barbara added.

"Now, Barbara."

Richard elbowed Jolie, and she raised her head, realizing she had been avoiding eye contact with the Krenshaws. Aiden held out one well-tanned hand to her. The cinnamon-colored skin flowed upward along tight muscles on his forearm.

She wiped her palm on her skirt and quickly took his hand. She dropped her gaze when they touched, and she pulled her hand free. His skin had been too warm, too soft. His grip too gentle, too unlike Richard's. His hazel eyes too kind and expressive when he smiled and dimples formed underneath cheekbones that popped to life. His mouth too...she shut off her thoughts.

"Aren't you adorable." Barbara narrowed her eyes on Jolie.

Jolie froze, suddenly recognizing the voice of the woman who had phoned her about her father's death.

Barbara smacked her lips. Jolie felt a chill looking head on at those little animal teeth that amply filled the space between Barbara's thick red lips.

"Nice to meet you, dear. You must have dinner with us so I can catch you up on all the town gossip. And don't worry..." Barbara tapped Amanda's shoulder with one long reflective fingernail, "I don't mean gossip, really."

"We'd love to come over," Richard said. "How about sometime this week?"

"This Wednesday at four would be great for us." Barbara focused on Jolie's face. "Hey, don't I know you? Your name sounds so familiar." Barbara gasped, covering her mouth. "My goodness." Her eyes widened. "You're Gena's daughter. You probably don't remember speaking to me, but I was the one who phoned you when your father passed six—no...what was it?" Barbara drummed her fingers on her chin and sucked on her bulbous bottom lip.

"Seven years ago," Jolie whispered.

The look and feel of Barbara's spidery blue-veined hand on Jolie's arm was almost too much to bear. The long fingernails nudged her skin. Now she thought she knew why Amanda had seemed so nervous about Barbara's hug. "Redemption lost a great man, my dear. I'm sorry you couldn't be here for the funeral. I bet your mother will be overjoyed to see you, considering how she's faring nowadays. Tell me, dear, have you had a chance to visit your father's grave yet?" When Barbara withdrew her hand, Jolie almost gasped. "Well, I'm sure you'll get around to it." Barbara glanced at Amanda.

Emma yanked Jolie's skirt. "I don't like it here, Mom. This is a spooky place. Can I go home?"

Barbara leaned toward Emma. "Oh, child, don't be silly."

Emma smashed into Jolie's hip.

"This is a holy place, child. Nothing can hurt you here unless you have a guilty conscience."

Jolie patted Emma's clammy arm. She choked on her words, "This is Reverend Lamont's old church, honey. Remember me telling you about him?"

Emma nodded, snuffling. "I remember, but Reverend Lamont's dead."

Barbara grimaced or tried to grimace. Some of the

muscles around her eyes didn't contract, but the lines around her mouth furrowed. "Oh, Jolie. A child who's fearful of Church. Don't you ever take her?" Barbara faced Richard.

He shrugged at her and shook his head. "I've tried to get her to see how important it is. Maybe now she'll understand. From what I'm hearing, Reverend Caine will have an effect on her heart."

"That's..." Jolie croaked. She stopped herself. The Krenshaws stared at her. The look in Richard's eyes had been all the warning she needed.

"You all right, Jolie?" Aiden put a warm hand on her shoulder.

She nearly burst out in tears.

"She's fine." Richard slapped Jolie on the back. "She's just fine."

"Would you want us to bring anything for dinner?" Jolie asked, her voice monotone.

"No, that's not necessary, dear. Just bring yourselves." Barbara's gaze swept downward to Jolie's feet. Her smile slipped from her face then returned in what was more like a smirk.

"Let me give you my card." Richard slid a magnetic business card out of his vest pocket and handed it to Aiden. "You can give us a call if plans change."

Aiden looked surprised to find the card already in his hand. He glanced at it then slid it into his jacket pocket and withdrew his own card. Richard snatched it away. Aiden covered his mouth with his hand to hide what Jolie suspected was a smile.

Richard slid his arm around Jolie's waist, and she reflexively looked at the floor.

"She's more reserved than I remember," Aiden said.

Jolie raised her head and stared into Aiden's eyes, trying to remember him.

"You know my wife?"

"Sure." He laughed. "But from the look on her face, I can tell she hasn't a clue who I am."

"Who are you?" Jolie whispered.

Richard nudged her in the rib. She hoped no one noticed when she flinched.

"When Jolie was a little girl, I used to deliver the Young's groceries. She always had her nose in a book when I came over. She probably didn't even know I was there. Man that was a long time ago. Congratulations, Richard, on getting her nose out of those books and her eyes onto you."

Jolie fought the urge to punch him in the chest. She knew better of course. She knew he was only trying to be nice, but his comment still stung. Her head filled with lava, and she couldn't look anyone in the eyes. She vaguely recalled a delivery man, and she certainly didn't recall one so annoyingly handsome. Finally, it was Emma's little face that provided her escape from their stares.

Barbara took Aiden's arm and led him away into the crowd, and Amanda finally spoke up. Jolie was relieved to see Richard's attention shift back to the reverend's wife. "We're very blessed with a large membership. Everyone in Redemption attends our Church at least once a month."

A long-fingered hand tapered across Jolie's shoulder, and she winced, momentarily thinking either Barbara had returned or a serpent had slithered over her. She spun and met the reverend's eyes. "Amanda is almost right." His voice was deep like a cavern. "Your mother is the only person in town who doesn't attend my church. This greatly concerns me." A wry grin crept across his wide thin lips. He locked arms with Amanda as Jolie reached for Emma's hand, but found Richard's instead. "She rarely speaks of you anymore, but then she was hurt by your departure. Barbara Krenshaw, a deacon of my fine church, found your name and unlisted number on a scrap of paper buried in your mother's dresser. That's how we knew to call you. I always wondered why you didn't attend the funeral. Why was that, Jolie?"

Jolie opened her mouth to speak, to tell him that Richard had prevented her from traveling, but nothing came out.

"She has been pining away for your father for seven years now, believing he has yet to return from that last business trip we went on together." Remnants of that wry grin surfaced on the reverend's lips. "I think she pines for you in a different way."

Jolie wavered forward and leaned into Emma, hoping the reverend's relentless gaze would shift to someone else's face.

"Lately she thinks the Krenshaws' dog is your dead father." Blue flames seemed to flicker in his eyes. "She's always out on the Krenshaws' lawn petitioning for release of Jonathan. Or she's out there talking to the dog while the little guy's peeing on the lawn—all the while thinking he's Jonathan. Or she's chasing him up and down the street. The dog loves it too, which makes the neighbors laugh harder. But it breaks my heart." His face grew stern. "You live right across the street from her, you know? I hope you don't plan on a bittersweet reunion with her. I honestly don't think she'd remember you...under the circumstances."

Jolie covered her mouth, feeling something rising in her throat, and bowed forward again.

"It's no laughing matter. I assure you," Timothy added.

Jolie shook her head. "I'm not laughing." Her words seemed heavy on her tongue.

Timothy faced Richard. "How'd you feel about doing a little work for me? I have a little business you might be interested in, and I hear you're quite the investment whiz."

Jolie stared into Amanda's eyes. Amanda said nothing. Her face was a blank sheet of paper.

"How did you know about the line of business I'm in?"

"You should come over some time and we could talk about it. I know all about all the lines of business you're in. I'm sure you'd make much more money working with me than what you've made before, that is if you're the kind of man I think you are. I'm looking for someone to replace Aiden Krenshaw and become a third partner in my business."

"You are a reverend and a businessman?" Richard clapped Timothy on the shoulder. "How does that work out?"

"It works out fine. My business has grown so much this past year. I must confess, your reputation in Chicago has preceded you to Redemption. It's, if I may be honest, one of the main reasons I asked Amanda to visit you so soon after your arrival."

"I might take you up on that offer." Richard patted his vest pocket. "Maybe just for curiosity's sake. Let me give you my card." Richard withdrew another magnetized business card.

Jolie sighed at the gleam in her husband's eyes. She prayed they wouldn't have to move again. She wanted to resolve things with her mother now more than ever. *Mom will recognize me. She couldn't be as crazy as he says.*

Timothy took the hands of two teenage girls who came up behind him. His and Amanda's daughters, Jolie assumed, looking at their faces.

"Nice meeting you." Timothy tipped an imaginary hat at Richard and winked at Jolie before letting the girls lead him away.

"What kind of business is your husband in exactly?" Richard asked.

"He ministers to people all over the country. All the

donations he collects go to charities, but he is paid for his services. We've been blessed with prosperity."

"So he's an evangelist?" Richard asked.

"Sort of...He's also an adviser trying to unite different religious organizations seeking to have a greater impact on the world around them."

"How long has he had the business?" Richard asked.

"Well, for years, but it really started gaining momentum eight years ago when we moved here and he started working with Jonathan Young and Aiden Krenshaw." Amanda glanced at Jolie. "Your father did a lot of good for a lot of hurting people before he left."

"Before he left?"

Richard grumbled. "She meant before he left the business or the earth, before he died Jol. Really." He rolled his eyes. "She was trying to be polite."

Amanda's eyelids flickered. She scratched the back of her head. "Yes, thank you, Richard."

"What killed my father?" Jolie eased around Richard, knowing but not caring how much she would pay for it later. Peripherally, she glimpsed Richard's scowl and his folded arms and locked jaw, but she continued to study Amanda's face for an answer.

"A heart attack. Don't you remember, Jol?" Richard demanded. "The stress from the business was probably what did it. I've heard about this kind of thing. It happens a lot in the line of work I'm in."

"Oh yes. Richard," Amanda added, "you're absolutely right. In fact, the night before Jonathan died, on the plane home with Timothy, Jonathan was having what we later realized were palpitations. Timothy blamed himself for Jonathan's death for a long time after that."

"And the following morning when my mother found him dead in their bed?"

"For a long time after Gena's accident, Timothy spent most of his spare time trying to console her, but she just seemed impossible to reason with until he finally had medication prescribed for her."

"What's her obsession with Barbara Krenshaw all about?" Richard asked.

"I don't think Gena knows what she's doing. The only thing I can think is it's because Barbara has helped Timothy out so much with her that she has developed some strange infatuation with Barbara."

Jolie kept staring into Amanda's face, searching for a glimmer of truth. "You don't think she knows what she's doing? I thought you just said the medication made her more reasonable."

"Sure…on and off it does."

Richard slid his arm around Jolie's waist. She flinched. "Come on, detective, I have a few more business cards to pass out, and I want to introduce my fashion model wife around before services start." Richard winked at Amanda.

Amanda nodded. A strained smile perched on her lips. She batted at the wisps of blond hair around her eyes. Jolie had seen that look before. It was one she often gave Richard when she was hiding something from him.

"Mom?" Emma whined.

Jolie squeezed Emma's hand then straightened her posture in the pew, but she didn't turn her head.

Video recorders rested on triangular slats around the stage.

"Mom?" Emma whined again.

Jolie slanted her gaze at Emma then back at Richard. He seemed entranced by Reverend Caine's performance.

Sermon, Jolie corrected herself. She looked up. Reverend Caine seemed to be staring at her. His voice grew louder, his mannerisms more agitated, as if he were solely speaking to her. She was afraid to look away.

She had expected his words to inspire her mind, not just stir her emotions. The word pictures he created sounded beautiful, poetic, full of emotion. His lyrical voice and the pacing of his movements might've entranced her if she hadn't spoken to him before the sermon.

"Prosperity!" He slapped the sides of the pulpit. "We can all have it if we just care a little bit more about giving to God's kingdom. Remember, what we give to God, He returns tenfold."

Jolie bit down on her lip, trying to restrain her temper as the collection plates were passed around the room and quickly filled to overflowing.

He spoke about a woman's wifely duties, but didn't mention the husband's responsibilities. He emphasized the importance of tithing, but didn't mention the proper heart of the giver. He mentioned God's grace, but didn't speak of the Savior who had made redemption possible. Jolie wanted to stand up and shout into the video recorders that the reverend was lying if he didn't tell the whole truth, but she felt paralyzed between the man sitting beside her and the man preaching in the pulpit.

Many of the people sitting in the pews cringed and buried their faces in their hands as though convicted of secret sins. *Mom. You're not here. According to the reverend, you're never here. Maybe deep down you're saner than the rest of us.*

"*Mom, I see a bad man,*" Emma whined. "*He's a monster.*"

Jolie glanced at her daughter then followed Emma's gaze to the stage. Jolie shook her head at Emma, but Emma persisted, raising her arm to point. Jolie tapped Emma's elbow and the child lowered her arm, but her gaze remained locked on the stage, on the reverend.

"Don't stare," Jolie whispered.

Reverend Caine's hair now clung damply against the sides of his face. He was leaning forward with closed eyes, asking his congregation to join him in a prayer for Gena's soul. Richard jabbed his elbow into her ribcage, and she lowered her head, but she didn't shut her eyes. When she was certain he wasn't watching her, she raised her head.

Two women in the first pew, as though on cue, cried out and fainted.

"Amen." The reverend raised his head.

Richard's eyes burst open, and he clapped along with the crowd.

Two men who had been standing beside the stage, looking more like bodyguards than deacons, offered the women ice water from glass pitchers that had been perspiring on a table beside the stage.

Jolie wanted to grab her daughter's hand and walk straight out the church doors, but didn't for fear Timothy would interrupt his sermon to ask the congregation to join him in a prayer for her soul.

Emma nudged her arm. "Mom? What are you so afraid of? Do you see the monster too?"

Reverend Caine continued pacing the stage. He stopped and clutched the sides of his pulpit then surveyed the crowd. If Jolie had to pick one doorway she had opened for the devil in her life, she'd have to pick her emotions, mainly fear. Emma was right. Jolie was afraid of something—of so many things. And the thing she feared here went deeper than the man in the pulpit and the man beside her.

Fear had veiled her eyes to scripture, to truth, to the

repeated promises of God that He would never forsake her. For the first time, she admitted to herself that she had remained in her abusive marriage out of fear of what life would be like if she left, not out of obedience to God. She had stayed away from her parents for eight years out of fear, not out of respect for Richard's headship in their marriage. And fear had kept her and her daughter in danger. Emma in danger? Yes. She had hurt Emma by staying with Richard, and staying not because she thought Emma should have a father.

What she needed was faith in God that He would provide a way of escape for them if she would only take the first step toward Him.

She looked up at Reverend Caine again. The deep grooves in his face looked slick with sweat. Suddenly, she felt uncertain. *God, how can I know what I'm thinking is right? Here in this of all places?*

God usually didn't answer her prayers right away, but this time He did.

"Mom?" Emma's voice sounded like it rose from a fog. And maybe it had. The spiritual fog surrounding her in this church, seeking to consume her and strangle her heart and mind with the reverend's dead words.

Jolie turned from the stage. Emma met her with a smile.

"But Mom, there's a good man here too."

Chapter Six

Emma's impish cackles filtered down from upstairs, filling Jolie's ears. "There's a good man here too," Jolie whispered, holding her hand over her heart. *Lord, how could I have forgotten that You're always with me everywhere I go?*

Richard sat behind his computer in the study to her right working on some paperwork the reverend had given him after Church. She hadn't liked the look exchanged between the two men. But what could she do to stop what had already started when she wasn't even allowed to know what it was?

Richard's fingers thundered over the keyboard. His typing broken only by flourishes of epithets that brought Jolie's mind back to the urgency of her task.

She stood in the foyer, staring at the front door. She grasped the knob and swallowed hard. The hinges creaked when she pulled the door open. The pounding at Richard's keyboard stopped dead. Her body tightened in rebellion. She listened. Waiting. Hoping. She rubbed her left eye, thinking a blood vessel was about to burst there.

Emma squealed with pleasure from upstairs, nearly masking the sound of Richard's heavy footfalls.

"Jolie?"

Her heart and mind raced.

"Jolie?" Richard's voice registered only vaguely from behind as she marched out the door.

She could tell by the sound of his frantic steps, lighter than usual, that he was trotting after her down the driveway. His cell phone rang. For once he ignored it. "Where are you going?"

"I'm going to see my mother. I'll be back in a little while." She faced him for emphasis. "You should answer that. It could be the reverend."

"Why don't you let me come with you?" He was running now, reaching into his jacket for the phone. His stubby little legs had hardly more flexibility than pogo sticks. Jolie couldn't remember the last time he had even briskly walked. Then another thing occurred to her. Why was Richard being so... so what? So polite?

"I need to do this by myself." She searched his eyes for a hint of his familiar irritation.

"No, maybe I should come with you. Tim said your mother's changed."

Tim? He was on a first-name basis with the reverend now?

"You might not be able to handle things alone."

The phone rang again. Stopping to shield it from the sun's glare, he shook his head at the display screen. "It's not important. Let it go to voicemail." Something beamed in his eyes she wasn't used to seeing. Apprehension? Yes, she was certain of it. And she was certain of something else. Reverend Caine, having anticipated her reunion with her mother, had given her husband instructions not to interfere.

Jolie pointed past him at Emma who stood cradling her puppet on their front stoop. She raised one raggedy arm of the toy and used it to wave to her mother. Jolie waved back.

"I won't be long." She waited, searching his eyes again.

He bit his lip then spun on his heel, heading back to the house. His short legs pumped like they wanted to break into another run, but couldn't quite muster the strength. What kind of power did the reverend have over her husband that no one else had ever been able to harness?

"Don't say I didn't warn you," was all he offered.

Jolie sprinted across the street. She rang her mother's doorbell and knocked, hoping the combination would deliver a faster response.

The front door swung open. A red-faced woman with ash blond hair dangling loose from a bobby-pinned bun slapped her hands to her hips and glared at Jolie. The sides of the woman's white nurse's uniform were torn and stained in a menagerie of faded and fresh colors. Jolie smiled, hoping to soften the woman's expression. The woman frowned, and Jolie noticed the streak of smeared lipstick running from lip to cheek.

Jolie stammered, "I'm…I'm sorry to bother you, but I was…I am looking for my mother, Gena Young. My name is Jolie Needham. I'm her daughter. Is she here?"

The nurse rolled her eyes. "Well, do come in. I've been expecting you."

Jolie darted into the foyer. It reeked of lemon oil and ammonia. She nearly gagged. Photo albums with torn pages sprawled across the carpet. Crumbled photographs lined the floor. A vase had shattered at the bottom of the stairs. Violets lay in a bed of glass splinters. Something reflected light into Jolie's eyes. The crumbled red waxy paper with the intricate gold lettering was easy to recognize. The pamphlet seemed to be missing its white interior pages like someone had ripped them out.

"Well, close the door," the woman said through gritted teeth. Jolie shut the door a little too hard, and the nurse flinched. "The reverend warned me you might decide to visit. Of course the little dear is in. But I'm afraid I only vaguely remember her talking about any daughter. Just hold on. I'll get her."

She went up the stairs and stopped at the top, clutching the banister. She pointed toward the cluttered living room. "Well, do please go in and have a seat, Your Majesty." The nurse sighed. "I'm sorry. She's just more than I can handle sometimes. You picked a great day to return. I'll tell you that." She threw up her hands. "I'll see if I can tear her away from her pictures. It's photo album day, you know. Course, most everyday is photo album day."

Jolie took a seat on the living room couch and folded her hands in her lap.

Someone upstairs shrieked. A door slammed. Muffled voices filtered downstairs. Jolie dug her nails into the fabric of the armrest and stared into the foyer. "Dear God," she whispered. Another shriek, sharper, as though someone were enduring the horrors of a medieval torture chamber.

"Mom," Jolie whispered.

"What are you doing!" The nurse shouted from upstairs. Something rocketed into a wall. Maybe a door that had been flung open. Two pairs of footfalls thundered down a corridor. Jolie stared at the ceiling. A pair of footsteps shuffled across it. Then someone seemed to be running down the staircase.

Jolie leaped from her seat and tensed, facing the archway leading back into the foyer.

A tall woman with long dark scraggily hair slammed her feet together at the living room threshold, body frozen like in a snapshot. Her large manic-looking eyes watered. The part in her hair zig-zagged down the center. "Jolie?" she whispered hoarsely. "My girl, is that you?" The woman's tears seemed to be washing away mental cobwebs.

"Mom?"

Jolie backed up as two arms clamped around her middle.

"My sweet girl. At last I've found you." The woman smelled of sweat and sorrow. "Dove, you've flown back to me. Now part of me will have some peace."

"Mom?" Jolie's tears flowed as easily as blood from a sliced artery. "Mom, it's really you?"

The nurse appeared in the entryway, bent over, gasping and panting, hands clasped against her bowed knees. More loose hair dangled in front of her face. Some strands were flecked with white. "I'm shocked she remembered you, given the circumstances." She raised up, wiping her face with the backs of her hands. She shook her finger at Gena. "You behave, Miss Young, while your daughter is here. I don't suspect she'd like to know what kind of trouble you've been getting yourself into lately." The woman lowered her voice, evidently for effect. "We don't want her leaving again, do we?" The nurse started out of the room, then peered back over her shoulder. "How long has it been since you've seen your mother, anyway? I've been her nurse for three years, and I've never seen or heard of you."

Gena brushed back Jolie's hair and whispered, "Look up, dove. What have I always told you? Don't be so afraid of what other people think."

"You two standing there like that, side by side. You look like time projection photographs. Mrs. Needham, do you like what you'll probably look like in twenty years?" The nurse ambled out of the living room and disappeared into the foyer without waiting for an answer.

"Have a seat," Gena whispered and lowered herself to the loveseat. Jolie joined her, unable to tear her gaze away from Gena's face. Her mother was the ghost of the woman Jolie remembered. So much had changed in those eight terrible years of Jolie's absence. Her mother was still a beautiful woman. No one could deny that, but there were faint creases sprawling all over her face like cracks in a fine sculpture damaged by time, particularly between her eyebrows and down-turned at the corners of her mouth. There were no smile lines though. Jolie couldn't help but grow weak with the knowledge that her mother had done considerably more frowning than smiling during Jolie's absence.

Tears sprang to her eyes. "Oh, Mom..." She leaned against her mother's shoulder and wrapped her arms around her mother's neck.

Gena patted Jolie's arms. "It's all right, dear. Timothy has taken good care of me while you've been away."

"You're on a first name basis with Reverend Caine?" Just like Richard is, Jolie thought.

Her mother didn't seem to hear the question.

Jolie looked up and narrowed her eyes on the prescription bottles lined up on the mantle like miniature soldiers. Wouldn't Reverend Caine have wanted them concealed before her arrival? Surely, he must have known what she would think.

"Don't let them upset you." Gena nodded at the bottles. "They're mostly empty. Milly keeps them out to remind me of what a mess I am. It helps motivate me to get off them one day, seeing them out in the open like this. She never has to worry about me taking them on my own. I would never try to kill myself again."

Jolie winced. Again? So her mother hadn't accidentally fallen from her balcony. She had tried to jump to her death. "How many different pills do you take? What kinds are they?"

Jolie moved to get up and check the bottles, but Gena pulled her back down.

"Mom?"

"I missed you so much, dove. I'm glad you moved back to Redemption. The reverend told me you might be coming to see me."

"Is that why you were looking through your photo albums today?"

Gena nodded. "I get weepy when I look at them. I know I should stop, but I have trouble remembering things, important things, without them."

"Mom, I'm so sorry." Jolie bowed forward.

Gena took Jolie's hand and cradled it between hers. "Course I can never find pictures of you or your father anymore. I think I lost them, but there were so many of you and him. I don't know. If I just wasn't so disorganized."

Jolie shook her head. "I don't understand. Where did they go?"

"I missed you so much, dove."

"I should've come right away. I should've at least called when we got here, before we got here...way before we got here. Please forgive me, Mom, I couldn't bear it if you hated me. My life has been so confusing these past years with Richard. Please say you don't hate me."

"Shh. I don't hate you. I love you. And you're here now. We can start over like we were never apart. I've been praying. Now dry those tears." Gena stretched past Jolie and yanked a tissue from the box on the end table.

Jolie took it and blew her nose.

"Now, that's better. Let's not talk about any such silliness any longer. Tell me, how's Richard?"

Jolie leaned her head onto her mother's shoulder and let the tears come. Tears for her mother. Tears for her father. Tears for Emma. Tears for her broken marriage.

And tears for herself. "Mom, I'm so sorry. I thought you'd be so upset with me that you wouldn't want to see me. Every year that passed, I thought, this will be the year I call her. This will be the year I leave Richard and come home with Emma if she'll have me."

Jolie trembled under the weight of her tears, but her mother's body was a rock upon which she could cling. Except that rock was more like a sandy bank, and Jolie could already feel herself slipping, falling backward over the cliff.

Gena placed her finger under Jolie's chin. "How's my grandchild?" Gena glanced at Jolie's belly. "Was it a little boy or a little girl? I never did find out."

Jolie fought the urge to lose her mother's face in a mask of tears. "You knew?"

Gena nodded. "I should've told you it would be okay. That we'd work it out somehow. That you didn't have to leave with him. But I was too proud. I lost you because of it."

"Did Dad know?"

"I don't think so. Not at first. It was harder on him, but he felt the way I did. We just wanted you safe."

"It was a little girl. We named her Emma. I just lost a child," Jolie blurted, "because Richard has been hitting me in the stomach. Oh, Mom, you and Dad were right. I should never have married him, but I didn't think you would forgive me for getting pregnant with Emma. I wanted to hurry up and get married to him so you would never know. I never suspected he would keep me from seeing you all these years."

"I hired so many private investigators to find you. Even Timothy tried to help, but he couldn't."

"But Barbara Krenshaw said she found my number on a slip of paper in your dresser. Are you sure one of those investigators didn't find me after all?"

Gena shook her head, looking agitated. "I don't know."

Jolie heard a noise and looked up. "I said would you like some tea?" The nurse stood by the sofa, grinning over her serving tray. She slid the tray onto the coffee table in front of them, nudging magazines to the floor.

Jolie looked down and saw her reflection in the tray's shiny surface. Her image grossly distorted.

"Funny how things are never quite what they seem," the nurse said.

Two tea cups, an ornate glass sugar bowl, and a fluted vessel of milk obscured one side of the distorted reflection.

"How do you like your tea, Mrs. Needham?" The nurse lifted the sugar bowl. "One lump? Two?"

"Leave us, Mildred," Gena commanded in a voice that made Jolie wonder if the real Gena Young was just buried underneath all those medications. "We can serve ourselves."

Mildred started to open her mouth then snapped it shut, set the sugar bowl down, and tramped out of the room. Jolie heard a door slam in the distance and felt the corner of her mouth lift in a smile.

"Emma is the light of my life."

Gena nodded her head and raised the cup of tea that was closest to her. She took a long gulp then returned it to the tray.

"Without Emma, I probably never would've stayed with Richard. He's so different from the man I married. I can't explain it, and I'm ashamed to admit it, but I was glad when I lost this last child. I knew I couldn't handle raising another one with him."

"He's not different, honey. You are. And I understand how you feel."

"He's always making me nervous. Sometimes I can't even wash a dish without him giving it a full inspection and accusing me of using too much soap, as if with what he makes we need to save every cent. Once, just for spite, and I know it was wrong, I didn't use any soap and when he accused me of using too much, I shouted, 'I didn't use any!' Guess what became of that?"

Gena nodded her head again and pulled Jolie closer.

"You forgive me, Mom."

"Of course I forgive you. Do you forgive me, dove?"

Jolie rested her head against her mother's shoulder. "But you didn't do anything wrong."

"Even if that were true, I didn't do much right."

"Of course I forgive you," Jolie whispered.

"So, what did he do about the dish?"

"I don't remember exactly. I know he made Emma cry and then blamed it on me. He's forever doing things like that."

Gena shook her head and furrowed her brows then glanced at her empty cup of tea. She rubbed her forehead and sighed. "We've both suffered so much for so long, but now those long years are finally over and we can be together again. I don't think I'll need my medicine anymore." Her voice sounded strained. "And I only know they were years going by because I know what year it was when the circuits started shorting out in this old loose wired brain of mine."

Jolie's eyes watered. She thought again about her number supposedly written on a single slip of paper hidden in her mother's dresser, the one Reverend Caine had mentioned. "Oh, Mom. How can you forgive me for not being there for Dad's funeral?"

"Did you visit his grave yet?"

Jolie bowed her head. "I can't. I don't think I can face him."

"I keep meaning to go out there myself, but somehow I never make it. It's so weird knowing he's gone. The autopsy said he died of a heart attack, but I wonder if God didn't take him from me to test me."

"To test you?"

"To see if I loved him more than I loved God." Gena's eyes glazed over. Then the fog shifted like clouds parting to reveal the sun. "I should've never asked God to return Jonathan to me. You can't bargain with God. I think it was the way I found him in bed with his eyes open, almost like he was still alive, just pretending to be sleeping that made me try to strike that bargain. Then I got scared. I panicked and tried to join him in Heaven by jumping. I'm being punished now, aren't I?"

Jolie touched her mother's elbow. "I'm so sorry I didn't come to the funeral. You're not being punished. God forgave you if you asked Him to."

"It's all right that you weren't there. I made it through. The reverend and his wife helped me." Gena clapped her hand to her mouth. "Oh, I'm sorry. But I guess if you've been to Church, you already know about Reverend Lamont."

"Yes, Mom. Mrs. Caine told me."

"Not that I didn't love him, but Timothy and Amanda have been a constant blessing in my life since both Jonathan's and Reverend Lamont's unfortunate passings. And his precious daughters...what a blessing they've been as well. Have you met them, dove?"

Jolie shrugged. "I think I've seen them. We weren't introduced."

Gena smiled. An indecipherable smile. "One looks like a mirror-image of Amanda. Don't remark to the reverend on that point. As for the other one, make sure you mention how much she resembles me, won't you?" Gena laughed. "No, don't do that either."

"Mom...has the reverend ever done anything to you that you didn't want him to?"

"Good. Then you know how kind he is."

"Mom? Did you hear me?"

The fog settled over her mother's eyes again and seemed to thicken.

"I must confess though that I didn't originally approve of him or his leadership in the church when he took over for Reverend Lamont. The church just seemed strange to me after Reverend Lamont's funeral, almost like God had left it. I never wanted to step foot in there again. I went once to one of Timothy's sermons. But afterwards, I felt numb, dried up. It was like the anointing on the church died along with Reverend Lamont. Maybe that's why I don't go there now. Timothy doesn't understand me, but I don't understand myself, so..."

Jolie spotted what had evaded her upon entering the room. Her mother's artwork was strewn across the room amidst the clutter of magazines, books, papers, and various misplaced items from around the house. Some of the larger full-sized portraits sat half-finished on easels. Most of the creations lacked clarity and a focal point, but they still had her mother's uniquely perceptive touch. Watercolor drawings and pencil sketches lay on top of the TV hutch and along the floor. A drawing had even been constructed from the layer of dust clouding the TV screen. Faces Jolie didn't recognize stared back at her.

One portrait hung above the mantle. It was of a woman and a child with their backs facing the viewer. They were walking along a beach in an evening storm. The child was dressed in a simple navy sailor dress with white trim and white pantyhose, her feet disappearing into the sand. The woman wore a long red sequined dress with a sloping v-shape down the back. Her silhouette was a shockingly seductive image. Her hair was piled high on her head. A lightning flash in the painting made the hair color indistinguishable behind a glow of silver. Yet the strange light illuminated the side of the child's face. Jolie faintly distinguished worry between the raised brows. A title ran along the bottom.

The Unforgiven.

A flicker of white caught Jolie's attention. She leaned closer and saw that what drifted onto the sand behind the woman was a wedding veil.

"Mom, when did you paint that? Is that us? Where's Dad in it? What's that veil about?"

Her mother didn't answer.

Jolie let her gaze return to the pill bottles that lined the mantle and fought the urge to get up and knock them all off with one sweep of her arm. "How ill are you, Mom?" Jolie whispered. "Or should I ask, how ill do they keep saying you are?"

Gena stared at the painting as though seeing it for the first time. "I've never been able to let go of your father, or you. I don't know what comes over me sometimes. I just start thinking these wild thoughts then, next thing I know, I'm face down in someone's rose garden or passed out in their gutter and Tim is coming to get me. I can't help myself, and sometimes I think he's Jonathan. Just for a moment, but then I kind of wake up again and realize Jonathan's dead." Gena lowered her head into her hands and sobbed.

Jolie hugged her mother and rocked her back and forth, wanting to hold onto her forever. Bones that had once felt so sturdy and reassuring now felt frail and breakable. "Mom, I'm here, and I'm never leaving you again. You just need to mourn. No one has let you mourn, have they? They just keep feeding you pills because they're afraid of what you'll do without them. Who is prescribing them for you?"

Gena stiffened then pulled away. Her face was suddenly different. Infinitely different. Her eyes, wide staring orbs. Her lips pasty trembling folds working at an imaginary sentence.

"Let go of me. I don't want you, sir. You aren't my husband. Get out of my house! Get out!"

Jolie lurched back and scrambled off the sofa.

Gena yelled past her, and she spun around, but no one stood behind her.

"Who are you talking to? It's only me, Mom."

Jolie heard heels clunking through the foyer. The nurse sprinted into the room, wielding a syringe. "I knew this was going to happen. I'm sorry you have to see this, Mrs. Needham."

Gena fled to the far corner of the room, sobbing. Jolie watched with her hands clamped over her mouth. Mildred lunged at Gena and slammed into the wall as she bolted past. Gena skirted around the coffee table and knocked Jolie aside on her flight into the foyer. Jolie ran after her, but Mildred shoved Jolie away and darted up the stairs after Gena.

"I'm sorry things have to be this way for you. For her."

"Mom!" Jolie tried to shove past Mildred, but the woman grabbed Jolie's shoulder and spun her around. Fireworks shot through her upper back. Pawing at the banister for support, she fumbled her way down the stairs.

"I'm so sorry, but your mother is dangerous when she gets like this. I was hoping your visit would be good for her." Mildred started up the stairs again. "I hope you enjoyed what little time you got to spend together. I hope you resolved some things, but the plain truth of the matter is that your mother needs professional care twenty-four hours a day."

"I can take care of her. I'm her daughter."

"Please, Mrs. Needham." The nurse held up the syringe as though to make a point. "You don't have what it takes to care for someone who's delusional. Be grateful. At least you know she loves you. At least you know all things past have been forgiven."

Jolie averted her eyes. "Does she really forgive me? Does she even know who I am? One moment she seemed like she did, but the next I was a stranger and she was afraid of me. Afraid of her own daughter. What kind of pills is she on? What's in that needle?" Jolie hesitated. "What did you put in her tea?"

Gena howled from upstairs as though in pain. The nurse ignored her and narrowed her eyes on Jolie. "She knew who you were, honey. Please understand that. Those precious moments she spent with you just now were as real as the conversation we're having, but they don't last long."

"How real is that?"

Mildred smirked. "Listen to me. You can't give her the attention she needs. I'm sorry. You can come over to see her whenever you like. Be assured the door will always be open to you, just as if you lived here with us. But please, please leave the responsibility in my hands. We don't want another suicide attempt. I've handled her for three years, and I'm not at my wit's end just yet. If I need you, I'll call you, and you can come right over. Now, please, go home and see about your daughter's needs. The reverend says Emma is a very lonely little girl. Go be with her. She must be missing you."

Jolie opened her mouth to speak. Mildred raised the syringe even higher. Jolie's lips lay mute.

"You have been gone a long time. Be careful what accusations you form about me and the reverend's care of your mother. Sometimes what's good for people may be the hardest thing for them to accept."

"Who's my mother's doctor? I want to at least speak with the man." Jolie's chest burned, but thankfully nothing rumbled inside her.

"Careful, Jolie. You're treading on dangerous ground. You'll have to talk to Reverend Caine about that. I'm not at liberty to say. He's her legal guardian. Trust me. You don't want to see how bad your mother was before the medication. How lonely she is without your father." Mildred took a step down the stairs toward her. "You didn't even call." If the woman's lips could have spewed poison, Jolie thought she had heard it in the texture of those words.

"You don't understand. It wasn't all my fault. Richard..." Jolie blinked hard to clear her eyes. Maybe her mother was better off here. Mildred was harsh, but maybe that was the only type of person who could control her mother. Jolie looked up the stairs and called out, hoping Gena would hear her and know who she was. Her chest burned so badly she thought the words might not come out. But they did. "I'm leaving now, Mom. I love you. I'll see you again soon. Rest now. Please rest. And let Milly take care of you." Jolie waited for her mother's response, but heard nothing.

Mildred lowered the syringe and came down the stairs. She placed a hand on Jolie's back and ushered her out the door. "You're doing the right thing, honey."

Jolie peeked back inside the house as Mildred shut the door. Secrets filled those rooms like air.

Chapter Seven

Cherry and locust trees hedged the borders of the Krenshaw estate. Strobes of light swept the length of the unfenced front yard, undoubtedly searching for trespassers like Gena Young.

Jolie raised the zipper on her windbreaker and looked at Richard. She didn't like the gleam in his eyes. She couldn't help but wonder what the reverend had told him about Aiden Krenshaw. A breeze ruffled a cluster of yellow rose bushes and shook loose a swarm of velvet petals. Richard raised his hand to the onslaught while Jolie peered through the swirling mass trying to find her way.

"My dear child, don't you know I'm with you?"

Jolie flinched. "Richard, did you hear that?"

"Hear what, you moron? Just hurry up."

He yanked her hand, and she realized the voice had been in her mind. Hadn't it? He jerked her around an oversized orange clay pot. She stumbled to catch up and nearly tripped on a large crack running down the center of the door stoop.

Richard caught her arm and grumbled something before

pressing the door buzzer. The front door creaked open. A tall broad-shouldered form stood cast in silhouette under the foyer light. The form drew closer, and Jolie recognized Aiden. His dismantling smile made her greeting catch in her throat. She swallowed and stepped forward trying to assert herself, but Aiden's liquid gaze wouldn't release its hold on her. He smiled wider, and a few handsome wrinkles sprawled at the corners of his hazel eyes. Her chest fluttered. Earlier that evening, she had decided she wouldn't let the Krenshaws inside her heart, but now she wasn't so sure she could keep this man out. But that was ridiculous, wasn't it? A man who had once delivered groceries to her parents couldn't possibly know her as well as his eyes said he did.

Dear God, that's how Richard used to look at me, like I was the only person in the world. Don't let me fall for this man, Lord. Please. I'm just desperate for someone to talk to, for someone to understand me, that's all. Please keep reminding me of this.

My dear child, don't you know I'm with you?

She smiled, and Aiden seemed to think it was directed toward him. It didn't seem possible, but his smile grew wider.

"Welcome, Jolie. It's so nice to see you again so soon." He reached for her hand. Desire she thought had died on her wedding night awakened in her when Aiden's warm and gentle fingers made contact with hers.

"Please do come in." Aiden nodded at Richard. "Nice to see you too." He chuckled.

Such a charming sound, Jolie thought. She could spend the rest of her life listening to it. But no, that wasn't right. She mustn't think like that.

"Barbara is just finishing up in the kitchen. It won't be long before dinner is ready."

Richard tugged Jolie into the foyer. She spotted two red

splotches on the black and white marble floor and swerved to avoid them. She looked up and locked gazes with Aiden again.

His eyes sparkled with mischief. "They're not real. It's just a pattern in the marble. The designer called it moonlit arcade. Doesn't make much sense to me. It reminds me more of a bloodstained chessboard. But you know how these interior designer types are always saying stuff that's over your head." Aiden held out his hands. "Here. Let me take your things."

She flinched, finding Richard's hands busy sliding her jacket from her shoulders. "What's the matter with you, Jol? Why are you so jumpy?"

Suddenly, her face seemed to be on fire. Her cheeks burned like they were turning a bright shade of red. Aiden took their jackets and her purse and hung them in the closet. Thankfully, he didn't seem to notice her unease.

"This way, now. Barbara is so excited to see you."

The marble tiles flowed into a stream of oak hardwood as Jolie and Richard followed Aiden down a short flight of stairs into the sunken living room. It was at least twice the size of her and Richard's living room, a disparity Richard would surely notice. She looked up at the four spinning ceiling fans. The bulb housings glittered with soft amber light. Richard's fingers tightened on the small of her back. She lowered her eyes and tried not to think about how long it would be before she could go home and start planning her next attempt to visit her mother.

Aiden led them through two elegant stained glass french doors into a large carpeted dining room that looked more like a basement without any windows. Her stomach muscles tightened, but it wasn't just the recognition of the aroma of wild game that was starting to make her ill.

Two partially illuminated hallways flanked a swinging

door and a look-out cove to a gaping stainless steel kitchen. Not even a reckless fuzz ball polluted the sea of perfect Persian whiteness beneath her black flats.

"Thanks for inviting us over." Richard slapped Aiden on the back. "It smells great in here."

Aiden gave him a tight-lipped grimace.

"If you don't mind me asking, how do you afford this place? I guess you made a small fortune working with Reverend Caine? Too bad you don't work for him anymore."

Aiden glanced at Jolie. "I made very good money working with Timothy, but it wasn't really my money to make."

Something clattered in the kitchen, and a muffled curse word rose from behind the row of hanging pots and pans.

"What do you mean?" Richard asked.

"I think you'll find out soon enough. So, where did you meet Jolie?"

Richard smirked. "Oh, yeah, that's right. You used to have a thing for her." He strolled to the figurine cabinet in the corner of the room and tapped his stubby finger on the glass pane, undoubtedly leaving his greasy fingerprint behind. "I'm just kidding. Lovely collection. What are they?"

"Doulton," Barbara called from the kitchen. "Glad you two could come. I'll be right in. Just finishing up. Where's Emma?"

"With a sitter," Richard said. "The reverend recommended a girl. I've got quite an assortment of prized collectibles at my place too. Jolie isn't my only prized possession. You two should come over some time and see them."

Aiden faced Jolie. "So where did you meet your doting husband?"

Richard screwed up one eyebrow at Aiden.

"We met in Church to answer your question," Richard

snapped. "I was in town on business. I was there to speak
with Reverend Lamont after services about the way he was
filing his taxes and some of the things he was and wasn't
claiming on his returns. Turned out he wasn't up to anything.
And that was fine with me. I couldn't wait to get out of there.
He was too intense. His eyes carried a weight when he looked
at you. Jolie goes on and on about him, has ever since we
met. Thinks he's a saint, I mean was a saint." He slanted a
look at Jolie, and she put her hand to her mouth. "He was the
most stodgy old man I've ever met, but he knew his Bible,
could beat you over the head with it anytime."

"Reverend Lamont was the most honorable man I've ever
known," Jolie whispered. "He didn't beat anyone over the
head with anything. It must've been your own conscience
weighing on you."

She thought she heard the static electricity spring from
the carpet under Richard's Oxford's as he whirled toward her
and came across the room. When he placed a hand on her
shoulder, she didn't feel the shock she had been expecting,
but flinched anyway. She wondered if she was the only one
who noticed the catch in his voice before he spoke again.
"So, where did you meet Barbara?"

"We worked in the same law firm for two years before
we met. She was shy back then, believe it or not. The years
have a funny way of trimming that stuff off of you."

"Hmm." Richard nodded then arched his back, placing
his hand on the small of his back, and yawned. "Last year I
cleared two hundred grand. Reverend Caine promises I could
make more than that. You have any idea if he's for real? After
all, you used to work with him."

Aiden stared at him. "You could probably make as much
as you want, but everything has a price."

Dishware clattered in the kitchen, and a utensil jangled

onto the floor. "You make him sound nefarious, dear. Richard wouldn't want to be involved in anything illicit. Now stop joking with them."

"You all right in there, Barbara?" Richard asked.

"Fine." A pot banged. "Sorry. Just fine."

Aiden leaned close to Richard's ear. "Your life will never be the same if you team up with him. I promise you that. You have your wife and daughter to consider. I'm just looking out for someone I hope I can call a friend."

Somehow, the offense slipped away from Richard's face, and the knot in Jolie's stomach finally loosened.

"Well, I thank you." Richard placed a hand on the back of a dining chair. "But I don't think it will be a problem. Jolie is used to my erratic schedule." He scratched his head. "Hey, I don't see any lawyer for hire signs up in your windows. No seriously, I bet it's hard getting that kind of work in such a small town. You must miss working for Reverend Caine. What happened? You two get to a crossroads and call it quits like Jonathan did?"

Barbara laughed from the kitchen. "Aiden is retired, Richard."

"What? Lost your license?" Richard slapped Aiden on the back again. "Just kidding. But it must be hard to afford your standard of living now, huh? There's no shame in it. Maybe I could help you."

Aiden shook his head, but he didn't shift his gaze from Richard's face. "I own several houses all over the world free and clear, but Redemption is the place you live when you want to leave the rest of the world behind. The reverend would agree with me there." Aiden's eyebrows arched. "And I bet you would too."

"Nah. Not me. But you're running from something?"

Aiden laughed and shook his head again. He stared across

the room at nothing in particular. A rueful look loomed behind his hypnotizing eyes. "No. I've finally stopped running."

"All that money make you as happy as it does me?" Richard leaned against the chair with both hands. "Make Barbara as happy as it does Jolie?"

Aiden's back tensed. He looked down at the table then up at Jolie. "Money makes you happy?"

"Jolie would still be floundering around here, probably still living at home, doing nothing with her life—maybe taking part in her mother's pathetic artwork—but never really doing much if she hadn't met me. I'm the best thing that ever happened to her. She'll tell you that if you ask her."

Aiden folded his arms. "I thought she couldn't speak for herself."

Richard's jaw dropped, but he quickly collected himself and laughed off the remark. "She's just quiet, that's all, at least in front of people she hardly knows. You should hear her at home. Sometimes I can't get her to shut up."

Aiden glanced at her. What was it in his eyes that made her want to cry?

Silence filled the room, and Jolie's stomach threatened to roll over. She stepped forward and grabbed the edge of the table, certain she would vomit or faint or maybe both until Aiden spoke again. Something strange in the tone of his voice soothed her.

"Everything you can buy." Aiden peered into Richard's squinty eyes. "I had it. I had a good house. I wanted two houses. I had a good job. I wanted a better one. Got married. Wished I was single."

Jolie glanced through the kitchen alcove. At the sink, Barbara sipped from a wineglass and patted her forehead with a dishcloth.

"I wanted more money, so I started working with Timothy.

The more I made, the more I wanted. I was too busy trying to impress everyone, to make them all so envious of what I had, that I forgot how impossible I was making it for them to stand me. None of us are indispensable. I realize that now." He looked at Jolie. Something in his expression made her feel naked. "I wondered what I would look like to a stranger when I was old and a young person had replaced me at work. Would I be sitting all alone, maybe having outlived everyone I ever cared about or maybe having driven them all away? I wondered what I would regret more, not having made more money or not having more time with the people I pretended to care so much about while I was making my fortune?"

Richard grunted. "I never plan on retiring completely. I don't believe what you said about no one being indispensable. I'm the kind of man who will always be needed. And Jolie and Emma mean the world to me. They know they come first, that's why I work so hard."

Jolie felt her face warm and turned away to wipe her forehead on her sleeve, not caring what it looked like or how much she would be punished for it later.

"It will be a pleasant change to sample someone else's cooking." The bite in Richard's voice nipped at her heart. It always amazed her how little she pleased him, despite how hard she tried.

She turned back around when the kitchen door revolved open. Barbara bustled into the dining room with a steaming bowl of creamed asparagus and set the dish on the table. The look of frenzy about her made Jolie wonder how much wine Barbara had been drinking that evening. "Glad you two could make it." She flung up her hand, rattling the chandelier. She wavered backward on unsteady legs, and her eyes went wide. The swinging chandelier cast a shimmering outline over her as she braced herself against the back of one of the dining chairs and regained her balance.

Jolie held her breath as she watched Richard, waiting for his expression to change, waiting for him to laugh. When he stepped toward Barbara and offered her his hand, Jolie allowed herself to breathe again.

Aiden came up beside her. The heat of him pressed against her shoulder. "Are you all right?" His breath was warm against her neck, but she was certain he hadn't meant to stand so close.

She admonished herself for the tears pricking her eyes. *No, Jol, don't cry because of him.* But it wasn't only because of him, was it? The ghost of a woman who used to be her mother haunted her dreams and her consciousness now. *Mom, I'm going to help you. I'll be back, and I'll let that nurse have it. Maybe I'll even give Reverend Caine a piece of my mind. Maybe I'll give everyone a piece of my mind.*

She looked across the room, trying to avoid Aiden's powerful gaze.

A squeak escaped her throat when she saw the portrait hanging over the fireplace mantel.

Aiden stepped closer and placed his hands on her shoulders. Richard and Barbara didn't notice. They were lost in their own conversation. Aiden whispered into her ear, "You bear an eerie resemblance to him in the eyes. And you are pretty much a dead ringer for your mother everywhere else."

"How did you get that?" she snapped, unable to soften the edge in her voice, and shoved past him.

Her father's bright green eyes stared down at her. Sadness seemed to loom over his features. Jolie wondered if her mother had meant to paint that emotion or if Jolie was imagining it. "Dad," she whispered so no one else would hear, "I love you. I'm so sorry. Forgive me. I'm here now." A shadow indicating movement eclipsed one side of his chiseled face, and Jolie wondered if she had imagined her father turning to face her. The veil of sadness had lifted, and the hint of a smile seemed to surface on his pale lips. Thank you, she mouthed, and backed away from the portrait.

Aiden cleared his throat. "The reverend said she used to cry when she looked at it, so Barbara offered to take it for safekeeping. Personally, I think that's why she comes over here so often looking for him."

Richard paused in his conversation with Barbara, and silence filled the room. He came over to Jolie and slid an arm behind her, digging his short nails into her back as he pulled her to their seats at the table. Jolie forced herself to breathe.

"Your father was a good man," Aiden said. "I worked with him for nearly three months before he passed away. You have his gentle way." Jolie couldn't be certain, but she suspected Richard had taken offense to the harmless comment.

A buzzer went off in the kitchen. The corners of Barbara's mouth drew back. The woman seemed to be holding back a smile. "Let me just get one last entree and we can all sit down and eat before this delicious meal gets cold. Our other guest will just have to eat hers a little on the tepid side."

Aiden lowered his eyes. "You really shouldn't have invited her, Barbara."

"Invited who?" Richard smacked his lips and unfolded his cloth napkin across his lap.

Jolie glanced once more at the painting. She couldn't see it well from this angle. But her father's smile was gone, and she was certain a frown had taken its place.

"Now don't tell." Barbara wagged her finger, letting her eyes get wide. "It's a surprise."

* * *

Staring down at her plate, Barbara folded her hands and began praying. Jolie stared in disbelief as Richard joined in by bowing his head and closing his eyes. Aiden stared at his plate, but kept his eyes open. His forehead tightened in a knot of concentration until Barbara finished. The Krenshaws had accomplished in one short visit what Jolie hadn't been able to do after eight years of marriage, or had it been the reverend's work? And more importantly, did it mean to Richard what it meant to her?

"I hope Gena won't mind that we didn't wait for her before saying grace," Barbara said.

Jolie dropped her fork.

Barbara flipped out her napkin then tucked one corner under her collar so the rest of it spread across her ample chest. "So, how do you like my surprise?"

Aiden grumbled.

Barbara's nose wrinkled when Jolie stood.

The light from the chandelier cast an eerie glow on the silver trays, china bowls, glazes, and sauces. Even Barbara's face was a target for the mean games of light and shadow.

"What's wrong?" Richard slid his hand up her forearm.

"I think I need to use your restroom."

"Barbara, how ever did you learn to cook like this?" Richard still held Jolie's arm in an attempt to change her mind, but it wasn't going to work. "Maybe you could teach my wife to prepare a meal like this."

Barbara blushed. "I'm sure Jolie cooks very well, but if you like I can show *you* some cookbooks after dinner that I live by."

"That sounds great." Jolie tried to tug free, but he wouldn't let go. "She can follow a recipe. After all, she's a quick study. Always has been."

"Quicker than you?" Aiden's voice rolled low and deep like an ocean wave in a dream. Jolie concentrated on the spinning table then closed her eyes and clung to Richard's arm, leaning over his shoulder for support.

"For crying out loud you two!" Aiden leaped to his feet and rushed around the table. His hands locked around her waist, and he pulled her away from them. She leaned against him. "I'm showing her the bathroom. We'll be back." Richard opened his mouth to protest then clamped it shut when Jolie grabbed her mouth.

Aiden led her down the hallway. "You're all cold and hot at the same time." She leaned her head into his chest, indulging in the scent of him. *Why couldn't Richard ever hold her this way, with such unbelievable kindness? Or was this kindness? She couldn't quite remember what it felt like.*

His breath felt cool against her throbbing ear as they reached the door at the end of the hallway. "It's going to be ok. You just need to get away from all that for a little bit."

"My mother…If she sees that portrait."

"I'm so sorry about Barbara, but the next time you visit us will be different. I promise."

She tried to smile. *The next time I visit?*

He stopped at the door, looking uncertain. She pulled away and stepped into the bathroom. "Will you be all right by yourself? Should I wait by the door?"

"I'll be fine." She gazed into his soft eyes. They were more golden brown than green in the hallway light. "I'll be just fine. Thank you, Aiden."

He smiled when she said his name then turned and edged back down the hallway, glancing over his shoulder at her.

She shut the bathroom door, flipped on the light, and careened toward the toilet. Thank God, she thought as her knees smacked the marble. *Thank God the lid was up.*

* * *

When Jolie returned to the table, she found her plate filled. No way would she eat everything, considering the pains exploding in her like fireworks. She sat down, hoping she wouldn't bolt right up again. She stared at the slices of dark meat and the congealing red sauce that reeked of roasted chestnuts. She coughed, and Richard patted her back. His hand felt harder than usual, like he had been making a fist. Or maybe she was only noticing the contrast between his touch and Aiden's.

Jolie raised a forkful of meat to her lips. The scents of rosemary, anise seeds, and juniper berries assaulted her nose, and she fought not to drop her fork again. Spasms coursed up and down her throat as she slipped the morsel into her mouth. For a moment, her stomach wrenched, and she thought she was going to throw up, but then her stomach relaxed and the meat slid all the way down her throat. It held the subtle taste of perfume even though Jolie knew that was probably ridiculous. Or maybe she just didn't have the delicate palate to enjoy Barbara's sophisticated cuisine.

The doorbell suddenly rang, and Jolie let her fork go. It clattered across the side of her plate and fell to the floor, leaving a small brown stain on the carpet. Richard grunted as he reached for it. He lifted it, but said nothing about the mark. Jolie opened her mouth to speak when Richard ground his nails into her thigh. She snapped her mouth shut, finding Aiden's gaze upon her.

Barbara leaped from her chair and dabbed her chin with her napkin before tossing it onto her chair. She spoke with her mouth full, swallowing hard between words. "That must be your mother. Be back in just a sec."

Jolie grabbed Richard's hand and turned her pleading

eyes toward him as Barbara disappeared through the dining room doors. His nails finally relented, and she couldn't help but gasp. She took several deep breaths, keeping her face away from Aiden and concentrated on the sound of Barbara's high heels clattering across the living room hardwood and up the stairs into the marble foyer.

Jolie waited through her swirling vision, hoping she wouldn't faint. When the dining room doors burst open and Gena strolled in, evidently laughing at something Barbara had said, a great peace filled Jolie's heart. "Mom."

Gena met her daughter's eyes. For a moment, Jolie wondered if her mother would recognize her.

When Gena cocked her head and smiled, holding her arms out, Jolie stood up and went to her. Gena wrapped her in a tight hug. The fruity scent of shampoo filled Jolie's nostrils. Her mother no longer smelled like sorrow. She even wore a little lipstick and eye shadow, and her part went straight down the center of her hair.

Memories of life before Richard and Reverend Caine filled Jolie's mind. She glimpsed her father's face as he bent over his sawhorse and called to her to help him inspect the dollhouse he had just finished for *some special little girl's birthday*. She saw her mother as the young woman she had assumed she would be returning to see after eight years. Her mother with her long dark hair glistening in the moonlight during a stroll along the beach to gather seashells and inhale the salty ocean air.

Tears of joy pushed against her eyes.

Gena released her, holding her at arm's length to look at her. "I'm glad we can be together again, dove."

Gena frowned as she faced Richard.

He held out his hand for Jolie to return to him. "Nice to see you again, Mrs. Young." He kept his eyes on Gena until they took their seats.

Jolie raised another forkful of the greasy meat to her lips, entranced by her mother's face.

Richard jabbed her in the thigh with the prongs of his fork until she looked at him. "You want to stop staring already?"

A diamond bracelet glittered from Gena's wrist and clanked against the butter dish when she reached for the cranberry sauce. "Who gave you that, Mom?"

Gena smiled like a child with a secret. "The reverend. On his last visit." Gena filled the rest of her plate.

"I just finished setting out the meal before you arrived," Barbara interrupted. "Hope it's still warm."

Gena took a small bite of meat and chewed under Barbara's inspection. Jolie wondered if she had imagined the subtle friction between the women.

"How do you like it? It's a delicacy you know. Only the most refined taste buds can appreciate this sort of game."

"It's quite good."

Barbara stared at her. "So Gena, what's it like getting cleaned up and going out for a change?"

Gena started to choke and thumped the center of her chest with her fist until she cleared her throat. She reached for the pitcher of water. Aiden intercepted it and poured her a glass.

"Mother Young?"

Gena snapped her head toward Richard.

He dug his short nails into Jolie's thigh. Jolie leaned forward in her chair and gritted her teeth. She pictured the red half-moons those stubby nails were leaving in her skin, but said nothing.

"Mother Young, you look nice tonight. Did your nurse help you get ready? The reverend tells me you've been having a hard go at it with all the stress from losing your husband and all. If I would've known how bad off you were, I would've insisted on Jolie coming to visit you sooner."

Red-hot rage erupted like a volcano inside Jolie.

Gena craned her brows and looked otherwise unfazed by Richard's remarks. "I'm not an invalid. Not only can I dress myself, but I can even bathe myself too. But as far as stress goes, it's a wonder to me that you could possibly have enough of a heart to know what stress over the loss of your family feels like. So, maybe I'm the one who should be pitying you."

Jolie wanted to whoop and pump her fist in the air, but Richard still had her pinned with his nails. Nails that were now peeling off her skin. She jerked her leg away from his grip.

Gena winked at her, and Jolie's face cooled a little.

"My daughter and I have been away from each other for far too long, and I'm so looking forward to getting to know her again."

"Oh...um..." Barbara frowned. "Does the reverend think so many visits right now would be wise? You do remember your spells?"

Jolie glared at Barbara, but Barbara wouldn't back down. "I mean, he is your legal guardian and your reverend. He would know what's best for you."

Gena dabbed her lips with the cloth napkin beside her plate. "I know what's best for me."

"Yes, dear, of course you think that now. But tomorrow you could wake up crazy again." Barbara glared at the bracelet on Gena's wrist and raised a tiny piece of meat to her lips. She narrowed her eyes at Aiden who sat gaping at her.

"Crazy?" Gena smiled like she hoped there wasn't anything caught between her exposed teeth.

Jolie would've interrupted the conversation if Richard hadn't turned to pinching her thigh.

Barbara's nose twitched. "Yes, well...I'm just being

honest. I care more about your welfare than I do about hurting your feelings."

Aiden slapped his palm on the table. "You and Jolie should visit each other as often as you can. I know that would be the best thing for both of you now that Jolie's back. Too much time has been spent being unhappy. Contrary to popular opinion, the reverend doesn't always know what's best for everyone else."

"Nonsense!" Barbara rapped the underside of the table with her fist.

Jolie flinched, and Richard's hand slipped off her. She rubbed her thigh and found a slight dampness there. Blood of course. She knew it without looking.

"Jolie doesn't know it yet, but she won't want to be burdened with an invalid. She has a little girl to raise."

"Jolie loves me. And I'm no invalid. I'm perfectly fine. I'm perfectly sane. If Mildred didn't keep feeding me pills all the time, I could gather my wits about me."

"I'd never think Mom was a burden. No matter what you say, you withered old Barbie Doll!"

Richard pinched hard enough to leave a bruise, but she recoiled and smacked his shoulder. He clapped his hand to his arm and glared at her, eyes bulging.

"And you can't keep me away from her either, so stop pinching me underneath the table." Jolie ran to her mother's side. Gena stood and buried herself in Jolie's embrace. Gena noticed the blood and glared at Richard as though he were the devil.

Barbara cleared her throat for effect. "Funny how some kids are. Don't call. Don't write. Don't think about you for years. Then just come waltzing back into your life. Wonder what Jolie wants."

Gena's eyelids fluttered like she was going to cry.

"Barbara how can you be so cruel?" Jolie whispered.

"It's a shame," Barbara said, "that such an ordinarily nice young woman would have had to grow up in a house with such a loony mother. Course, you weren't always loony, were you, dear? But then it's so hard to remember how sane you supposedly used to be before Jonathan's accident. Such a strong woman, everyone says. Such a strong woman of faith. Stronger than most. Imagine that. Seems like such a long time ago to you, I'm sure."

Aiden fisted his hands. "Barbara, don't you think that's enough?"

Barbara gave him a look Jolie couldn't decipher. "I'm just trying to get things out in the open so people can start healing. I'm sorry if the truth is so offensive."

"I'm very smart," Gena whispered. "I know when someone is trying to make a fool out of me."

"Yes. I must say, a woman who looks like you with brains as well is rare. Oh, Gena, your dress. Did the reverend buy it for you too? Looks like his taste, but then I should know. All the gifts he has given me over the years...I'm sorry I didn't notice how lovely it was until now. It's so..." Barbara shook her head, "So flashy. Where did you ever get the nerve to wear such a daring frock to my house? I'd never be able to pull off something like that, not that they sell those kinds of dresses in the stores I shop in. Somehow people would think I looked cheap in something like that, maybe even foolish, but on you, it fits."

"I really can't believe you, Mrs. Krenshaw." Jolie finally drew Barbara's gaze.

An inexplicable look of torment twisted Barbara's features. "You won't believe me now, but later you'll see. I'm only looking out for you."

"Jolie, sit down," Richard mumbled.

Gena looked like she was going to scream and knock over the table or at the very least, throw her plate at Barbara or Richard. "I'm not a fool. I know when I'm being mocked."

"What ever do you mean, Gena? Please calm down. You're making a scene."

"Why did you invite me here tonight? You wanted to demean me in front of my daughter, try to make me look like a crazy old fool? I would never be so cruel. I treat others with respect."

"Is that what you were showing me when you flirted with Timothy in my own home, that day you came over here like a zombie and plopped right down on my couch? Ah...sometimes I think you just pretend to be out of it." Barbara shook her head, tears brimming in her eyes. "You knew he would come for you. Half the time I think you really are crazy, and half the time I think you're perfectly sane and trying to drive me crazy."

"What are you talking about? What day did I come over?"

Barbara thumped the table. Gravy sloshed in the gravy boat, but somehow, it didn't spill onto the lace tablecloth. "You just continue to prove my point. Are you that in and out of it that you really don't remember dousing me with ice water?"

Jolie couldn't believe what she was hearing. She had no idea what her mother had been doing all those years Jolie lived in Chicago.

"Is that what you think I did? Is that what's bothering you? Your precious reverend's behavior toward me? Now I get it. I don't want Reverend Caine. I only want my Johnny." Gena started to cry. "All I've ever wanted was him." She turned and stared at the portrait hanging over the fireplace. "I don't know why Timothy won't let me keep it. I painted it. It used to bring me such comfort. It still would if I had it."

Barbara's cheeks puffed then she burst with laughter. "Would it make you angry if I told you how much comfort it brings me now, or if I told you I had slept with Jonathan on one of those long business trips?"

"You miserable old woman." Gena shook her head.

Jolie felt her jaw drop.

"That must be why you come over here so often looking for him. In your deluded mind, where the past and the present are all screwed up, you think he's here with me."

"That's enough!" Aiden rose from the table. "You're making a fool of yourself. Everyone knows how faithful the Youngs were to each other. They had a love like no one else. A love like I wish I had with you."

Barbara waved her hand at Aiden and rolled her eyes. "You're so melodramatic. Just be still, and let the truth be said."

Gena glared at Barbara. "I may be delusional sometimes. I may be a nuisance to you." Barbara leaned back in her chair. "But I'm not a jealous, insecure, judgmental barracuda of a woman who enjoys demeaning other people so she can feel better about her own pitiful life." Gena's voice softened. "At least I don't hide from real life."

"Don't hide from real life?" Barbara slapped the table. "That's crazy. You hide from everything. You hide from the truth behind all those medications. Jonathan's dead, Gena. I saw his dead body just like you did. His wide open eyes locked in that eternal dead stare before he was hauled off to the morgue."

Jolie's knees bowed. She thought she was going to faint, but found when she clung to her mother that the tiny woman was strong enough to support both of them.

"I knew I shouldn't have come here tonight. But I'm glad I got to see my daughter."

"You didn't exactly get here without help. Edmond drove you. Can't even drive yourself anymore. I've got to get the reverend's chauffeur to do it. Locked in that house all day with that half-psychotic nurse of yours. It's a wonder you have any life left in you."

Gena slumped to her seat, clinging to Jolie's arm.

Barbara stared at Jolie. "I had hoped inviting you here tonight would be good for you. But she ruined that, just like everything else." Barbara slapped the table. This time gravy splashed the tablecloth, and Barbara cursed, craning over the table to dab the spot with her napkin. The small spot grew larger as she rubbed. She cursed again and threw the napkin down. "So seriously, what are you going to do for her now that you've returned to Redemption after all these years? Are you going to be able to take care of her when she goes into another one of her delusional episodes and starts picking up any sharp thing she can get her hands on and running at you with paranoia dripping from her bleary psychotic eyes. You can take my word as gospel. When she gets like that again, she won't know who you are even when the blade pierces your well-intentioned heart."

Jolie stood paralyzed by Barbara's words. Was the woman telling the truth? Was her mother dangerous? Was that the point Barbara had been hoping to make with this dinner arrangment? Did Gena need all those drugs? There seemed to be so many. Too many. Surely they would interfere with one another after awhile. Maybe that was part of the problem. Maybe she needed medication, but she was over-medicated.

"Jolie is a good daughter. And she's going to surprise us all one day soon."

"Why is that?" Barbara smiled at Gena's down-turned head.

Gena raised her face. "Because she has so much of her

father in her." Gena bolted for the dining room door. With one hand against it, she turned and smiled at Jolie then faced Barbara. "And one more thing."

Barbara adjusted the neckline of her dress. "What's that?"

"The duck...it was rather tough. Tell your cook, the one who sneaks in and out like it's a crime that you can't cook, that she needs to start paying a little more attention to what she's doing." Gena slammed the door as she left.

Barbara grunted and mumbled something.

Richard scratched his head. "Well, I certainly didn't expect that."

Jolie wondered what kind of man could tolerate a wife like Barbara. Then she looked at Richard and wondered the same thing about her ability to tolerate him.

Aiden cleared his throat, but when he spoke, gravel still filled his voice. "I hope you'll accept my apology for my wife. I hope you won't judge her too harshly. She has a very unique way of trying to help people. And sometimes, she gets exactly what she deserves."

Jolie offered him a weak smile. Maybe only she knew it, but this had been a good night somehow, and she had a feeling things were only going to get better. Her mother loved her. That was clear. And she needed help. No matter what happened, Jolie would never abandon her mother again.

Chapter Eight

Goosebumps prickled Jolie's skin as she jolted upright in bed.

Wrapping her arms around herself, she shivered and lay back down, pulling the bedcovers over her chest. They came freely, without the weight that usually held them.

Rolling over, she found the right side of the bed empty and cool, not warm. She sat up, examining the shadowy outline of the room, blinking hard to clear her vision.

"Richard?" Her voice seemed to echo as though she had spoken in a dream. "Richard, are you there?"

No answer. Was he playing some kind of game?

She swung her legs over the side of the bed and slid her feet into her slippers. "Richard?" *Probably downstairs in your study working on something for the reverend.*

Just before she reached the doorway, the cordless on Richard's nightstand rang. She spun toward the noise. Her slippers scuffed the hardwood, sounding unnaturally loud, as she went to the phone.

She stared down at the caller ID. *Blocked call.*

The handset felt cold in her hand, and she shrugged away the ridiculous thought that she was still dreaming. "Hello?"

A muffled voice sobbed from the other end of the line. "Hello?"

Sniffling.

"Mom?"

"No, Jolie. It's me, Barbara. Are you busy? I guess you probably were busy sleeping. I just wanted to call and apologize for dinner. I couldn't wait any longer. I was eaten up with guilt all night long. I don't think I got one bit of rest." Jolie opened her mouth to speak, but snapped it shut and listened when Barbara started to cry. "You probably want to get some things done while he's away. Maybe I should call back later."

"While who's away?"

Silence.

Jolie thought she could hear Barbara starting and stopping to speak several times. Words finally came through the line. "You didn't know?"

Jolie clutched the handset with both hands.

"Richard left on a business trip with the reverend and one of the other deacons of the church. He probably got an early start."

"Peter?" Jolie stared at Richard's side of the bed.

"Yes. You met Peter? He has that large birthmark on his face. Course I hardly see it anymore. Such a delightful man. Very smart too. Has a degree for every day of the week." Barbara laughed. "Well, not that many, but he's the guy to ask if you need an answer to a tough question."

"I bet." Jolie eyed the doorway, thinking Emma was standing there, but she wasn't. "When will they be back?"

"Don't know, dear. Aiden never used to say when he would return."

"Why not?"

"It's what's best." Jolie heard a smile in Barbara's voice.

"Is Richard punishing me for what happened at your house yesterday?"

"Don't be silly, Jolie." Another smile entered Barbara's voice.

Jolie lowered one hand and spoke very deliberately, "If you have any information that might make me feel a little better about this, Barbara, please tell me right now."

"I'm sorry, dear. I'm probably just being a worrywart. I do that sometimes. But I was afraid you'd still be angry with me for trying to help you, I meant well, Lord knows I meant well."

"Never mind that Barbara. Consider it all in the past. Just please, tell me, is Richard in any trouble?"

"Trouble?" Barbara laughed. "Well goodness no. He's with Reverend Caine. Preaching to the masses. What could be wrong with that? You know, Jolie," Barbara hesitated, "you might want to consider trying to see things through the reverend's eyes now that you're in his town. He is a very wise man. Just as wise if not more wise than your dear Reverend Lamont."

One look back at the empty bed then at the empty spot on the floor where Richard routinely left his socks and underwear before his morning shower made Jolie's back stiffen. "Seems to me you couldn't be more devoted to the reverend if you were his wife."

Barbara responded without a hitch. "I am most devoted to God. Reverend Caine just happens to be God's chosen vessel. I am sorry to have bothered you so early. And I'm very sorry if I upset you again. I figured Richard left you a note. Aiden used to do that." Barbara laughed. "Oh, but then you probably haven't even gotten out of bed yet, so you wouldn't have seen one."

"Barbara, you know how crazy this sounds?"

"I feel much better now." Barbara yawned. "I think I'm going to catch some sleep. Please feel free to come over later if you have any trouble with Emma. Richard did leave the car for you, right? Well, either way, give me a call. Aiden or I can pick you up and bring you over."

Jolie nodded then realized she hadn't spoken. "Sure, Barbara. You go ahead." She turned off the handset and lowered it to the charger. The handset clattered into place.

Jolie glimpsed something white on the floor.

She went to her dresser and bent down. She lifted a slip of paper. Richard's dark handwriting bled through it. She turned it over. Her stomach churned at the sight of the scrawled writing.

Jolie,

I've decided to help Timothy out with some business out of town, kind of on a trial basis. I'll be back soon. Don't worry. Tell Emma I love her, and try not to burden your mother too much with unnecessary visits. You know how ill she is.

Richard

A strange emotion gripped her. One she didn't quite understand. She smoothed the note, paying special attention to the corners, and folded it in half. Thinking of Emma, she tucked it into her jewelry box and stormed downstairs to confirm Richard had already left.

She got her answer when she saw he had taken the car.

With a steamy mug of coffee in one hand, Jolie watched the sun set from the bow window in her kitchen, thinking how this first day without Richard in nearly eight years had been the worst and the best day of her marriage. The smell of roasted hazelnut wafted in from the kitchen and she tightened her grip on Richard's letter. She had made Emma a cup of hot cocoa not long before bedtime, secretly hoping the caffeine would keep the dear child awake for an extra hour of shared bliss. It was amazing how peaceful the house was without Richard. Even Emma seemed calmer without her father around monitoring them and yelling at them.

Jolie had even found time to visit her father's grave with Emma. They had placed daffodils on the headstone and stood hugging in front of the grave. "What does humble mean?" Emma had asked, pointing at the inscription carved into the stone. "It means you know that anything good that comes from you was given to you by God, so you never think you're better than someone else." Emma's brow had furrowed at that answer, but then it had relaxed, and a look of understanding had crept into the little freckled face. "Was Grandpa humble like it says?" Emma had asked, pointing at the headstone. Jolie had nodded with tears filling her eyes, unable to speak.

Now the tears came again as she remembered the afternoon and how it had felt, knowing she could never make ammends with her father. But her tears were bittersweet because the gravestone had said it right: Here lies Jonathan Young, a humble man of incredible mercy.

Blotting her eyes with a tissue, Jolie shifted her thoughts.

She could visit the Krenshaws if she could bear it. Barbara had begged her to visit. What had Barbara said when she called back at two after Jolie and Emma had returned from the graveyard? "You'll need all the support you can get here. Don't want to end up like your mother, wandering around your big house seeing ghosts in every shadow. You don't keep a gun, do you, Jol?" Now what had prompted that question?

According to Barbara, Gena had been lonely for some

time before the attempted suicide. Lonely for half a year without her daughter to console her. There had been no one to confide in except the reverend. Supposedly, it was only when Reverend Caine had started visiting Gena that she had stopped acting suicidal. Then he had gotten someone to prescribe medication for her. But surely all those pills were hurting more than they were helping.

Gena wasn't crazy. Jolie had seen evidence of that. Hadn't she? Barbara was trying to deceive her. What had Amanda said? Gena hadn't been allowed to mourn. Yes. Gena had been put on medication when all she needed to do was mourn. But the suicide attempt had occurred before the medication was prescribed. Surely mourning wasn't the answer either. But what was?

Gena had never seemed crazy when Jolie was younger. Her mother had an artist's moody temperament, sure. She was a walking stereotype in that regard, but she wasn't mentally ill. *I don't know why I have my reservations about a reverend, but I do. Lord. What is wrong with me?*

Jolie sighed, cupping the mug in both hands. The warmth was good. She shut both eyes and thanked God for Emma and for the time God had allowed them to spend together today.

Then she thought about Aiden. Why had he quit working for the reverend when Barbara was obsessed with the man? Why hadn't he given a straight answer to any of Richard's questions at dinner when Barbara seemed to have an answer for everything? What was Aiden hiding?

What was Amanda hiding?

Jolie looked up. A pew Bible rested on the shelf over the table. Richard must've brought it home with him. Maybe the reverend had given it to him to study. Jolie reached up and pulled down the book. She took another sip of her coffee and opened the Bible to the table of contents. She scanned the list. Genesis. Exodus. Leviticus. And all the other books of the Old Testament. Jolie paged back to the table of contents. Where were the books of the New Testament? Flipping through the pages again, she realized the New Testament was missing. She closed the book and stared down at the cover. It didn't say it was just the Old Testament. Where was the story of Jesus' life?

She stood, staring down at the book. It had the same thickness as the pew Bibles she had used in Chicago when Richard allowed his family to attend Church there. It had the same thickness as the pew Bibles Reverend Lamont had used. The text was twice the size though.

Of course, she thought, none of his sermons were about Jesus. At least not any she had heard. For all she knew, his god was just a generic supernatural entity.

In her bedroom, she retrieved her Bible from the bottom drawer of her nightstand. She had kept it hidden in various places throughout the house since Richard had discovered it during the first year of their marriage. Lately, he seemed only to complain when she wasn't reading it.

She carried it downstairs and sat at the table.

Would the Old Testament verses be equivocal?

She opened the pew Bible to Genesis and compared the verses at random places. They were different versions, but similar enough to please her. Then Exodus. Same thing. She closed it and placed it back on the shelf then opened her Bible to Matthew. She had always gotten so much strength and gratitude from reading the Psalms, but Matthew always challenged her heart.

Paging through, the highlighted verses soothed her, and she thanked God for the peace settling over her heart.

Emma called from upstairs. "Mom, can I sleep in your bed tonight?"

Jolie smiled to herself, feeling the first euphoric waves of the evening. About to close the Bible and join her daughter upstairs, her eyes locked on a verse she had never underlined or marked in any fashion.

Matthew 7:15. "Beware of false prophets, which come to you in sheep's clothing, but inwardly they are ravening wolves."

"Dear God," she whispered. "Are you talking to me?"

She was never one to run to the Bible impatiently trying to force an answer from God by opening it to a random section and plunking down her finger. But here it was just the same. An answer of sorts.

The print appeared foggy past her glazed eyes. An image settled into her mind. She saw herself standing at the top of the mountain she had stood upon just before her return to Redemption, overlooking the town. Looking down, she didn't see the houses. Reverend Caine rose up from the dark mass. He was yelling at her. Screaming at her. The deep grooves in his face grew deeper with every word. Behind him, a fire consumed the dark valley. Jolie saw herself staring into his paralyzing eyes as the flames closed around him, swallowing him up and silencing his screams.

Pushing the Bible away, tears formed in her eyes, and she stood up. "Dear God, what do you want me to do? Surely someone like me can't stop him...or is it that you actually want me to help him? What can I do? I need help myself."

Child, won't you trust me?

Four weeks after the departure of her husband, Jolie sat in the swivel chair behind his hulking mahogany desk, listening to the rain keeping time with the Royal Philharmonic

Orchestra playing on the CD in Richard's computer, trying to lull the beast of a migraine in her head to sleep.

No thunderstorms tonight. Weather man was wrong again. But she suspected a nasty storm might be brewing anyway.

Jolie had been sitting in Richard's study staring at his monitor for nearly an hour daydreaming about Aiden and worrying about her poor mother. She wasn't angry with Barbara anymore. The phone calls over the last four weeks had changed that. If anything, she was starting to pity the woman. Deeper than the sarcasm and the condescending tone in the woman's voice, an inexplicable sadness drove all Barbara's actions. Sometimes her eyes held the look of a dog wanting to come in out of the rain.

Jolie sighed and leaned back. The smell of the leather upholstery comforted her. It was the first smell she remembered from the beginning of her marriage when the money Richard had been making had seemed like a blessing. It was an expensive smell. Something she had enjoyed before everything in her life had become too expensive. She gazed down at her body. She wondered how much weight she had lost while Richard had been gone and hoped she wasn't starting to look as frail as her mother. She hadn't been able to eat or sleep very much in the last month, maybe in part because of the residual sadness of losing the child. Recently, she had allowed herself to wonder about the sex of the child, what he or she would've looked like. Which parent the child would've favored more. But she had kept a smile on her face for Emma's sake. Ultimately the only ones that mattered were the ones who were still alive. She had to remember them. They still needed her.

She rubbed her temples and then her eyelids. The bags under her eyes would soon be too prominent to hide with makeup. But for once, Emma hadn't had the perception of an old sage or an emotional Geiger counter, or if she had, she wasn't letting on.

Jolie sighed. She was getting nowhere with Aiden when she visited Barbara, but she still kept trying. It was clear he kept secrets about the reverend. It was clear he had been wanting to tell her something about her mother. Who was he protecting? And the strangest thing of all since Richard and the reverend had been gone. Supposedly, her mother had been admitted to Covington Hospital, evidently for another attempted suicide. No amount of pleading with Mildred had convinced the nurse to allow Jolie to visit her mother.

When Jolie stormed across the street and banged on the front door and then the windows, demanding to see her mother after seeing Edmond drive her mother home, she realized something very important. She would never be allowed to see her mother again unless she started playing by the reverend's rules. Standing outside one of the living room windows, getting ready to bang against the pane again, she had realized it. In a way like a woman realizes having fallen in love with a man. All at once and with such clarity it can't be denied. Just like knowing she had fallen in love with Aiden.

The next step was unknown. Nightly prayers that God would reveal His plan started coming harder. So far, she had felt like a gnat buzzing in the eye of a giant.

Beware of false prophets.

Who could she trust? She needed help to divulge the reverend's secrets. But so far, no one wanted to speak up.

She had imagined that if Richard ever gave her breathing room, she would inhale the whole world and forget all about him. But as the weeks passed, she felt she were slowly suffocating on that world.

The sound of a vehicle turning into the driveway made

her break eye contact with the dancing robot screen saver and shut down the computer. Upstairs, Emma's footsteps scrambled across the floor.

Jolie jolted out of the chair as Emma's tiny feet thudded down the stairs. "Dad's home! Dad's home!"

Jolie rushed into the foyer as Emma heaved open the front door and flew into her father's outstretched arms. Richard kissed their daughter on the crown of her head before setting her down. Jolie winced. He had never kissed their daughter with any tenderness before. What had caused this sudden change?

He lifted his bags off the stoop and brought them into the house. From the side compartment of his suitcase, he removed a gift-wrapped package, pink and white striped with an oversized yellow bow.

"What is it? Is it my birthday already?"

"No, my little oyster poop."

"Dad!" Emma giggled. "Don't call me that."

"All right then, my little pearl. It's a gift for being such a good girl while Daddy was away."

"What's the occasion?" Jolie folded her arms over her chest.

Instead of looking at her, he handed the gift to Emma. Her eyes sparkled as she tore through the paper and found a doll inside. "Yippee!" Emma hugged the doll first, then her father, and trotted into the living room.

Richard finally acknowledged Jolie. From the pocket of her sweater, she pulled out the note he had left her four weeks ago. "I see you've decided to come home. I trust you're going to stay awhile before you leave again?"

She followed him into the study. He threw his briefcase onto his desk and plopped into his swivel chair, evidently wondering what kind of new boldness a mere four weeks had produced in his wife. Jolie chose the seat on the opposite side of the desk and sat down with her arms still folded. He yanked off his tie and draped it over the monitor, eyeing her every move.

"Why didn't you wake me instead of leaving me this ridiculous note?"

He bolted from his chair and skirted around the desk to shut the double doors of his study. He wiped his forehead with the back of his hand then returned to his seat and slammed his fist down on the briefcase, spilling papers and a ceramic pencil holder on the desk. Freshly sharpened pencils rolled free. He raised an eyebrow. "You've been in my office?"

He flicked one of the pencils teetering on the edge of the desk, and she winced when it shot past her.

"Yeah, so?"

He ground his teeth and clenched his eyes. A thick vein bulged on his forehead. His nostrils flared. He rubbed his temples. "I don't want you in here anymore."

"Fine. I won't come in."

He took a key from his pocket and unlocked the briefcase. Then unsnapped the clasps. The lid popped open. A vinyl portfolio lay inside. Before Jolie could get a good look at it, he snatched it up and slammed the lid shut.

He leaned back in his chair and licked his index finger and thumb before paging through the document. Facial contortions masked whatever he was thinking. Finally, he pulled one sheet free and slammed the folder on the briefcase.

"Well?"

He looked at her. "What?"

"What is that?"

He shook his head. "Not important."

"Why didn't you wake me and tell me you were leaving?"

He put down the paper then stood, pressing his palms

against the top of the desk, and craned toward her. "I don't have to tell you anything."

She wanted to scream. It took all her resolve to control herself. She was suddenly glad she hadn't been pregnant again. Such stress could only hurt another child. Then she wasn't so glad. Pangs of regret over losing something so fragile and full of hope because of this monster seized her, and she nearly grabbed one of the sharpened pencils and plunged it into one of his flattened hands.

He stared at her, and she realized she had been partly smiling and partly scowling at him like a mad fool.

He sniffed before straightening his spine. He collected the paper and put it back inside the folder. She stared at him, amazed at how much she could hate him, the father of her child, the man who was in part responsible for one of the greatest joys in her life.

She stood up and went to the recliner behind her and guided herself to the seat. Holding the sides of her head in her hands, she waited for her eyes to stop throbbing, and when they did, she allowed herself to look up.

Richard was staring at her, holding the folder at his side. His forehead was furrowed in the center where a massive wrinkle was threatening to take permanent residence. "I decided to sign it, Jol. Timothy's contract for making me a partner in the business. This is the copy." He shoved the document into a desk drawer and locked it.

Two snaps and the briefcase locked too. "You know, I might have to start reminding you of who's the head of this household. I left you the note, didn't I? I didn't have to do that."

"What if I wouldn't have found it? I would've thought something horrible had happened to you, and you didn't call once while you were away. Why didn't you at least call to make sure Emma was okay? And where did you go?"

"Timothy said it was best I didn't disturb my train of thought, and I knew Emma would be safe with you. Didn't Barbara call and make sure you were okay? We had a lot to go over on the plane ride, and I needed to give work my full attention. I'm tired now." He raised his eyebrows. "I'm going to bed. I don't look forward to discussing this any further when I wake up."

"What kind of business is this that you're expected to leave suddenly in the middle of the night without any notice and fly to God knows where? What were you doing while you were away?"

"My work doesn't concern you."

"What do you mean? Of course it concerns me. I'm your wife, aren't I?"

"All you need to know is that I'm going to be making more money than I ever could've dreamed of making in the stock market in Chicago."

"I don't want you to go away with him anymore."

A slight smile parted his lips. "I'm glad you missed me." He seemed to study her face, waiting for a certain reaction. "Why your father ever thought so highly of you, I'll never understand. You'll have to stop making demands. You're overreacting. Tim warned me you might be upset. Your mother didn't understand when your father traveled either. Maybe this is really all your mother's fault. I saw how different you treated me in front of her. She might be filling your head with bad ideas."

"Mom needs me. She has nothing to do with how I feel about you? I want to know what kind of a business you're in?"

"We are taking God's message all over the world. Timothy has a vision for me. He sees greatness in me. You've always been insistent on making me more religious. Why are you getting so upset now when I'm trying to do something you've always wanted?"

Jolie shook her head. "It's not about being religious. There's something wrong with this business of his when you can't even feel comfortable telling your wife the details— the very basic details—like where you're going and when you'll be back."

"You don't get it." Richard inched toward her, and she felt a familiar stab of unease. "His business has grown so big since he took it over from your father. Jonathan's narrow expectations pale in comparison to what Timothy's promised to show me, to what he has *already* shown me. Aiden was a fool for giving this all up. Barbara must be kicking him."

"This doesn't make any sense!"

"Will you lower your voice? I'm trying to tell you something important and you keep interrupting!"

"Why didn't you discuss this with me first?"

"What would you have to say that would matter?" He had just been teasing her, making her think she could get away with her new assertiveness. His face revealed the truth now.

Jolie backed up.

"I mean, what do you know about making business decisions? You're a housewife." He dragged his finger across the top of his desk. "And not a very good one at that. Those cookbooks Barbara loaned you are just sitting in the living room collecting dust like this."

"But you told me you didn't want me in here."

He snarled at her. "And yet you continue to come in." He stepped closer and draped his arm over her shoulder. She hated how she trembled under him. "Just trust me, this is going to work out ten times better than anything I've ever done before, and I won't be going on that many trips. I wouldn't dare leave you alone for too long, wouldn't want you to end up like your mother." He chuckled. "That trip you made over to her house while I was gone." He wagged his finger at her and clucked his tongue. "Shame, shame, Jolie. I guess I'm going to have to start being more firm with you. No more visits with your mother until I say differently, not so much for your sake, but more for Emma's." He dug his nails into her arm. "Do you understand me?"

She nodded, gulping down the bile rising in her throat. He shoved her away. She caught the edge of a bookcase and bit back the pain in her thigh from where an ornate bookend stabbed her.

"I know you thought a lot of Reverend Lamont, but Reverend Caine is the kind of man I'd prefer you believing in. Trust me. Have you ever met a more righteous man?"

Self-righteous, she thought, but said nothing.

Richard seemed to study her face again. He seemed to be delighting in its many subtle changes. Then he lifted his briefcase and went into the foyer to collect his suitcase.

She watched him head up the stairs. She didn't follow. She had learned everything she needed to know from the note by the foot of her dresser.

Chapter Nine

The sounds of clattering and shuffling drew Jolie toward the kitchen. Richard had let her sleep in without prodding her for breakfast, and now she feared he was in the kitchen throwing a tantrum to prove a point. Emma had been the one to finally rouse her from her dreams. Well, her nightmares.

She tripped on something and fell into the revolving door, batting it open. It thumped against the wall. She bent to remove one of the Velcro arms of Emma's puppet from her fuzzy pink slipper. Ever since Richard had given Emma the doll, the puppet had been forgotten. Jolie had felt a twinge of remorse, but hadn't mentioned anything. Even Richard's smug implications hadn't prompted any discussion.

Jolie looked up. Aiden's alarmed expression froze her. He held one hand on the refrigerator door. The other was in his thick tousled hair. A hint of a smile dimpled one of his cheeks. So *he* had been the one making all that noise.

She gripped the long arm of Emma's puppet to her chest and let the stuffed body dangle against her pajama-clad leg.

Unicorn pajama-clad leg. *Yikes!* She twirled away from him, feeling her face warm, and cast the puppet onto the ledge of the bow window. Streaks of morning light painted the floor in bursts of yellow and orange. Hopefully the soft light masked some of her disheveled appearance.

"The men wanted a beer." Aiden's voice felt like satin sheets against her ears, ears that had grown too accustomed to Richard's grating voice. "Tim says we'll think better with some refreshment." She took a deep breath, trying to calm her racing heart, and faced him. What was he doing here? He motioned at the crowded shelves of the refrigerator, turning his back to her. She reached up and raked her fingers through her hair, hoping to smooth some of the wild strands. He met her eyes again and offered a grin that would make a celebrity jealous. "But I can't find any."

"You can't find any what?" Jolie searched her mind for any clues about what Aiden had been talking about, but found none.

"Beer. I don't see anymore of it. Do you keep extra someplace else? Maybe in the pantry behind you?" He took a step toward her, and she backed up before she could think how it would look. Her hip crashed into the newly installed wet bar, and a single tear escaped her eye.

His face erupted in concern. "What's wrong?"

"I'm fine." Instinct made her body react. She leaped toward the refrigerator and bent to survey the shelves. "I thought there were two left." Before she could nudge the milk aside, she caught the scent of him. Fading tendrils of cologne mingled with the unmistakable scent of clothing that had been slept in. She felt a twinge of emotion she barely recognized. How long had it been since she had let herself register anything tender toward a man? She shook the mental images of Aiden away and concentrated on her task. She wished he would give her more room. Did he know how close he was standing to her? *Dear God, don't let him hear my heart banging.*

"I thought there were two left," she repeated and reached as far past the milk as she could. Her fingers grazed a cold bottle. "Got one." Something tickled her neck, and she stood up, suddenly worried were Richard was.

Aiden averted his gaze, but not before she glimpsed the goofy-sad expression on his face. She wondered if she had only imagined him touching her.

"Barbara isn't so lovely in the morning."

The warmth of his body heat made her back up. "Where's Richard? Do you know?"

His forehead wrinkled, and he stepped back from her. She resisted the urge to sigh in relief.

"He's in the basement with Timothy. I'm teaching him what he'll need to know to replace me. It won't be long before you'll have so much money you won't be able to think straight."

"I don't care for any of the money Richard has made cheating his clients over the years. I hate the things he's done since I married him. I have these nightmares sometimes about all the terrible things he's yet to do. And I know this new business arrangement with the reverend is just going to turn out bad." Jolie laid her hand over her mouth, surprised how much she had just revealed. Things she was barely able to admit to herself.

He was silent while she reached back into the refrigerator and fished out the two bottles of cold beer from behind the milk. He swept her hair back over her shoulder, and her spine stiffened at the sensation. She stepped past him, clutching the bottles like they were the stress balls Richard often brought home from business conferences.

"It's beautiful, but it's so long I guess it makes it hard to see when you lean over."

She plunked the bottles onto the table and cleared her throat. "Guess I might have to go out for more. Two won't be enough." She went to the pantry for her purse. "I was hoping to stay home though. Last night was so exhausting. I talked to Mom on the phone because that nurse of hers wouldn't let me see her. She never lets me see her anymore. You know, I think she was listening in, making certain Mom didn't tell me anything she wasn't supposed to." Jolie's hand froze on the pantry door. What was wrong with her? Did she have to tell this man everything that was on her mind?

"I'm so sorry. I wish I could help you."

Jolie squeezed her pajama shirt like it was a rag she wanted to wring out. "You know things," she whispered. "You know things about my mother and the business my husband is getting involved in that I don't know. Dangerous things." He said nothing. Nothing in his expression changed. "Don't you, Aiden Krenshaw?"

He grunted and glanced at the basement door. "You don't know what you're asking." Sounds filtered up from below. Reverend Caine's heavy voice. Richard's high-pitched snorting laughter. Jolie realized Richard had let her oversleep so she wouldn't try to interfere with whatever was happening downstairs.

Aiden still wouldn't look her in the eyes. She edged toward him. "Tell me something. Anything."

He kept his gaze on his feet while she drew closer, feeling a sudden and inexplicable boldness. His dark hair dangled over his eyes. "Please, Aiden. I'm not Barbara."

He looked up. His eyes danced with desire she couldn't explain. There was a heat in them that nearly burned her. "Are you always so eager for the truth?"

"The truth is all that matters."

He nodded at the bottles sitting behind her. "And are you always so eager to please your husband? You seem to jump at his every command. I know he hurts you in ways you think you can't tell anyone. You could tell me."

"What do you mean? I never really give anything to anyone but Emma. She's my life, has been since I got pregnant with her and married Richard." *Lord, help me, what am I saying to this man?*

He craned his eyebrows. "Emma's the reason you married Richard?"

She shrugged. "You don't think so highly of me anymore, do you?"

"He's running from something, isn't he? That's why he's let you come back here. He needs a place to hide, to blend in. And he knows coming back here won't look like running. It'll look like coming home. Isn't that right?"

She cocked her head. "Why'd Barbara call me and tell me about my father's death? And where'd she really get my number?"

One side of his mouth lifted in a smile. He glanced back at the basement door.

"Come on Aiden, you first, then I'll tell you about Richard. Why didn't she call me when my mother started having trouble? And if Reverend Caine was thinking about becoming my mother's legal guardian, why didn't someone give me the option? I'm her daughter."

"Because Timothy drew up papers and…"

"And?"

"Your mother signed herself over to him…Barbara got your number from one of the private investigators your mother hired to find you. She never knew. Timothy wanted you to know about your father's death so you would return to Redemption and he could have Peter deal with you so to speak, but Richard told Barbara he wouldn't let you return and that he certainly wouldn't allow you to take in Gena. That worked out better for Timothy. No one had to get any blood on his hands."

Jolie clapped her hand over her mouth. "Are you saying Timothy was at one time thinking about having me killed to make my mother his?"

He glanced at the basement door again and nodded.

She nearly crumpled to the floor. Aiden grabbed for her arms, but she pulled away and forced herself to her feet.

"You said you wanted the truth."

She shook her head, trying to deny what he was saying.

"You had been gone half a year when the verdict finally came in. Amanda's dutiful care of Gena since their arrival in Redemption immensely helped his case. Your poor mother. She never even had a chance with all the people working against her on Tim's behalf. It appeared all perfectly legal, but it was all perfectly wrong."

"Has Mom mentioned me much since I've been gone?"

"More often than you can imagine." He eyed the door again.

"Did you hear what she did while Timothy and Richard were away? Tried to kill herself again. Just this time she didn't have a balcony to jump off of." Her laughter was harsh, awkward, but she didn't care. "When I asked her about the attempt yesterday, she didn't know what I was talking about."

Aiden touched her wrists, and she felt a chill. "Maybe she didn't remember it because it didn't happen."

Her heart wanted to explode. Her body felt flushed. Her skin tingled. She covered her face with her hands. "I'm sorry." She pulled away, wiping at her eyes.

"Jolie." He hesitated. "There's so much you don't know about Timothy and my wife."

"Then tell me," she whispered, glancing past him to

confirm what wasn't there.

"Listen to me. Mildred is a horrible woman. She's closer to the reverend than you think. Don't trust her, and don't trust my wife. Don't trust anyone. If you want to know if something's true, run it by me first. Your mother has improved since you returned to Redemption. I know because I saw her lucid at dinner. I haven't seen her that way in seven years, but if the reverend has anything to do about it, I doubt any of us will ever see her lucid again. I've had to see her often over the time you were gone. She factored heavily into my so-called business dealings with Tim. Most of those business trips your father took with him were designed to weaken your parents' relationship. You can't even begin to imagine how obsessed he is with her." He shook his head.

Jolie stared into his eyes. They seemed to have taken on a soft blue tint in the changing light. She wished she were married to him instead of Richard. *God help me. What am I thinking?*

"You're a good person, Jol. I know how much you love your mother. I know you've been away only because he kept you away."

She spoke before she could stop herself. "Help me find a way to get Mom out of that house so I can leave Redemption with her and Emma."

He shifted his eyes.

"I think you know something you're not telling me that could help me free her from his custody or you wouldn't bother telling me all this."

He shook his head. "You don't know what you're asking. You don't know the fight you're in for if you try, and I'm not talking about the courts. You said you got to call her. I don't know why he's still allowing Richard to allow you to call her, but it could stop. You'll have to be prepared for that if it happens. Just like how the visits have stopped. We all play by Tim's rules one way or another here. Even me."

"I can't believe you're telling me this. She's my mother."

He shook his head and paced, again eyeing the basement door. "No. Jolie. I can't help you. I won't help you—for your sake as well as Emma's."

A cool breeze rattled the screen door. She shivered and draped her arms across her belly, fastening her hands to the sides of her waist. She watched Aiden's shadow draw back from the floor. Outside, two locust trees swayed in the distance, their leafy fingers almost touching.

"You want to know the real reason why I agreed to come over here and help Timothy instruct Richard?"

She said nothing.

"You're so much like Gena used to be. It's no wonder Timothy longs for her the way he does."

She shook her head, trying to deny what he was saying.

"Your face lights up like a Christmas tree when you get embarrassed. Did you know that?"

She let her gaze fall to the puppet sitting on the bow window. Its cold button eyes caught some of the changing light and gleamed as though possessed. She picked it up, partly to avoid its phantom glare and partly to avoid Aiden's stare. "Richard brought me back here because the investment company he used to work for went under. He was stealing money from them. Richard said we would stay here while the storm blew over, but I don't think it's even begun yet." She tried to raise her face, but found she couldn't. "I keep thinking I could easily get custody of Emma now that I have something to barter with, but…"

"I'm glad Richard hardly notices you except when he wants something."

"That's not a very nice thing to say," she whispered,

turning away from him. She felt the air change. Something in the temperature or the humidity.

"And I'm glad he trusts me with you. I'm glad Barbara does too." His voice was closer, but she didn't dare turn around to look at him. "I had a crush on you since the first day I saw you sitting on your parents' porch. You were sketching something. A tree I think. Your face was all screwed up in concentration. You didn't even notice that your hair was flapping behind you, getting caught in one of the windmill birdhouses your father used to make for his shop in town."

"Richard won't trust you with me after I tell him what you've said."

Even closer. Almost a whisper on the back of her neck. "But you won't tell."

Large warm hands slid over her shoulders, and she wanted to melt into his embrace, but she fought the urge and kept her back to him. He spun her around and pulled her closer. She dropped the puppet. Its hard plastic nose slapped the linoleum. She quivered under the weight of his stare. She put her trembling hands against his chest to push him away and nearly fainted as his muscles flexed beneath her palms. *Say no, Jolie. Open your mouth and tell him to stop.*

"Why won't I tell Richard?" She pressed harder against him. Her legs seemed to be wet noodles now. *Just open your mouth and say no real firm like they taught you in self-defense class when Richard still approved of your independence.*

"Because he'd blame you before he got around to dealing with me. He'd say," his voice deepened, "look at how you flaunt yourself in front of him in your pajamas no less. No wonder he looks at you that way. I know Richard's type, Jolie." His hot breath tickled her cheek when he tilted his head and brought his lips near her ear to whisper. "We could be happy together. I could be the man you wished you'd married, and you could be the girl I fell in love with all those years ago, the girl you still are."

She leaped sideways away from him, shoving as hard as she could, but she didn't have to shove hard. He easily let her slip out of his embrace. Was he just toying with her emotions like Richard often did? *Surely, he wasn't cruel like Richard.*

She faced the basement door. Timothy was leaning against the doorjamb, almost looming over them from the doorway. Yet nothing in his eyes indicated he'd seen Aiden holding her. Nor had he seemed to notice the emotions that must have been evident on her face.

"Did you forget what I sent you up for, old man?" His ragged nails drummed the wood trim, and he smiled.

"They're right here, Reverend Caine." Jolie lifted the bottles.

Timothy held out his hands, and she brought the beer to him. He took them with one hand.

"I'm going back down." He lifted one eyebrow. "Are you coming, Aiden?"

Timothy started downstairs then turned around as though something had bitten him. He stared at Jolie. She backed up and gripped the counter behind her.

He glanced at the clock on the microwave above her head. "Noon already? Where's Emma?"

"Still sleeping."

"You're sure?"

"Of course."

"I'm not trying to pry. I'm just curious how carefully you monitor her. My girls. I always know where they are and what they're doing, but then, I have a few people to help me keep track of them. If you'd be more understanding about these business trips, Richard could provide you with help for Emma. I heard about the little tantrum you threw when he got home. Really, Jolie, you have to set a good example for her if you want her to grow up to honor her future husband like a good Christian wife should." He thumped the jamb with his fist. "You should never be too careful with your girl. She's a fox that one. So pretty and so smart. Maybe too smart. Maybe too pretty."

Jolie's knees locked. Her jaw became stone. She saw what Timothy was trying to do, what he had been so successful doing to her before. She had Aiden to thank for that revelation.

Timothy looked back at Aiden again. "Let me know when it's five o'clock, old man. I'm riding down today to pick up Gena from the women's center."

Jolie stepped forward. "My mother went out?"

"She wanted to talk to Amanda at Church. Go to the women's group and get some counseling for the things you've had a hand in stirring up in her. I trust you heard about the second suicide attempt?" He turned to go back down the stairs then faced her again. "You know, I allowed that phone call yesterday. Richard didn't want it, but I allowed it as her legal guardian. You have me to thank for it. You should remember that the next time you complain about these business trips or try to force your way past Mildred."

Jolie dry swallowed. "Thank you, Reverend Caine." She realized she was gritting her teeth and forced her jaw to relax. "I was hoping you might allow me to see her tomorrow if she's feeling up to it. Maybe I could go with her to the next church group. Maybe I could learn something too."

"You?"

Jolie winced. Tears sprang to her eyes.

"I didn't think the all-knowing Jolie Krenshaw needed counseling."

Jolie cocked her head. Aiden was staring at him with his mouth slack.

"What did you call me?"

Timothy shook his head. "What do you mean? I called you by your name, Jolie. Jolie Needham."

"That's not what you said."

He winked at Aiden before heading down the basement stairs then shouted something to Richard. The door slammed shut behind him. "Hurry back, Aiden." Timothy's voice filtered up from the basement. "We still have a lot of work to do."

"In a minute."

"I'm sure Jolie will be happy to fix you anything you want if you're hungry," Richard called up the stairs. "Course it won't taste like Barbara's cooking. Probably won't even taste much like food." Richard's ridiculous hyena-like laughter assaulted her ears.

Jolie stooped to retrieve the puppet. She hugged it, refusing to cry.

"I'm sorry," Aiden whispered. "I'm just as trapped as you are. I can't protect you or your mother."

Tears streamed down her cheeks. She raised one Velcro arm of the puppet and used it to wipe her face.

Timothy knew he had surprised Gena. He was sitting in the back of the limousine holding his reading glasses on top of a pile of business papers when she climbed in and sat down across from him. He capped a felt tip pen and stared at her, but she avoided his gaze. The contract he had drawn up for Aiden could wait. "Who was that sitting on the bench with you?"

She remained silent.

Timothy remembered meeting the man at church. A trial lawyer or something like that. Not a good idea to have one of those nosing around Redemption unless Timothy could get the man on his side. "What were you two discussing?"

"Nothing much. Just bragging about my daughter mostly. He seemed nice enough…I thought Milly was going to pick me up."

"You're not disappointed, are you?"

She shrugged.

"I wanted to pick up my little dove. You still are my little dove, aren't you Gena?"

She stared at him.

Timothy glared out the window at the back of the man's balding head as the poor fool sat on the bench outside the church scratching his neck, oblivious to what grave sin he had just committed. Timothy's chest clamped down over his heart. "Has this man ever talked to you before?"

"No. I never saw him until today. He asked me how I enjoyed the women's meeting. He was in the men's group. It was okay, but Amanda and Barbara really didn't say much I haven't heard from them before. I had more fun talking to that man."

Take a breath, old boy. "I don't want you talking to him anymore, dove. Is that okay? I have a bad feeling about him. Do you still trust me?"

She nodded, but her frown unnerved him. At least she had let him call her by the precious nickname she had shared with Jonathan. It was a good sign, a sign she was starting to see him in the role of her future husband, her one true husband, a man who would never abandon her to go off on business trips. A man who would share all his secrets with her, well, all but one.

She leaned back against the leather upholstery and sighed, then gazed out the window. Was she looking at the man, maybe imagining Jonathan's head on his shoulders? Timothy threw up his hand, and the limousine peeled forward.

He was going to say something, then stopped himself. He could hardly stand when he made her angry with him. He wanted her to remain as sweet as she was on the days they looked through her photo albums together and he almost convinced her he was her husband. He loved when she smiled at the pictures of them together. Those were always good days, but Gena wasn't always up to them. It took too delicate of a balance of medications to keep her there.

"I'm sorry, Gena. I just want to protect you. I know what men like him are like. I do love you so much. You must forgive me."

"I forgive you if you forgive me." She met his gaze.

His heart raced ahead of his thoughts.

She smiled at him. "I don't always understand what's good for me. I wish all people cared as much about me as you do."

No, you don't, he thought. No you certainly don't. He wanted to hug her, but decided against it. He couldn't rush his new plan if he wanted it to work. Soon Gena would be losing Jolie forever. Richard would make sure of it. Then Gena would fall helplessly into Timothy's consoling arms, having lost the last person who mattered to her, and needing someone to show her how to live again.

Jolie stared into her vanity mirror at the image of her pacing husband.

He moved with an unparalleled stride, almost effortlessly cruising through her life, crushing every dream she had ever had the courage to dream. The venom she suspected of coursing through his veins seemed to aspire to blood as human as her own, but Richard was no human. He was a monster.

Maybe he would just turn off the lights and roll over. Go right to sleep. Maybe tonight she could fall asleep too.

If she had known him as a child, seen him through a mother's eyes, then maybe the mere sight of him now would not inflame her, maybe her pity would not abandon her, maybe every child after Emma who grew in her womb would not abort itself under the weight of his relentless cruelty.

"Blasted trial lawyer," Richard muttered. He whipped the bed sheet back and plopped down on the mattress. The bedsprings protested with a loud squeak. Then he rose and repeated the display. "Can you believe our luck? Poor Timothy. On top of everything else, he has to deal with this now."

Her hairbrush startled her when she lowered her hands to her lap. She had forgotten she still held it. She laid it back on the dresser and tried to understand what was so threatening about Rakes. He had seemed very pleasant and soft-spoken in Church. The graying hair at his temples and the gentle way he laughed at Barbara's lame jokes had made him seem precious and kind, certainly not a threat to Richard or Timothy.

"Jolie, are you listening to me?" Richard had moved to the doorway of their bedroom.

She hadn't even noticed. She nodded, raising her gaze from her lap. She squeezed her hands into loose fists. In her vanity mirror, her eyes seemed hollow and dark like those of a decaying corpse. *What ghost is this?*

"Sorry, Richard. What were you saying?" Her voice was flat. She wondered if he even noticed. If he even cared that she was shutting down emotionally in preparation for whatever he was going to do to her tonight. She rose from the table and climbed into bed, pulling the blanket up over her legs.

"Timothy has this strange feeling about the man. Has he said anything strange to you about Gena? I know he spoke to you after services last week."

He touched her shoulder. She tried not to recoil, feeling the warmth from his hand so soon after he had seemed so cold to her. She looked into his eyes, but couldn't, as hard as she tried, find any reproach in them. Her eyes watered.

"Why are you shaking? Is it really that cold in here?" He got up to turn the thermostat up and then climbed back into bed. "So, have you noticed anything strange about our new resident?"

His hand lingered on her pillow, and it wasn't balled into a fist. Just for a moment, she thought about stroking it, about forgiving him for everything he had ever done to hurt her and Emma.

"I might have to put an end to this for Tim." Richard spoke like he wasn't sure his words were true and like nothing in the world would be able to stop him from making them true. "Not that I plan on having any trouble with him. Now Aiden, he was a little trouble to the reverend once, but he's Barbara's husband, so Tim can't do much, won't do much, hasn't yet at least. And now that you're behaving, the reverend can concentrate more on his sermons. But this man…"

Jolie cringed. Had Richard just revealed something important to her? Something she hadn't even asked for? "What kinds of things does Reverend Caine ask you to do for him?"

Richard glared at her. She had gone too far. That fast he became the old Richard. "You would start putting your pretty little nose in places it doesn't belong."

"I…I didn't mean it like that." But it was too late. He had taken it the only way he was going to take it.

"If this guy causes any legal trouble for the reverend, he won't have to bother thinking about moving. I'll buy him a nice home in the ground next to your father. In fact, I'll take care of anyone who interferes with Timothy's plans for my future."

Jolie thought she knew this man so well. What had Timothy done to him in so short a span of time? Would Richard take care of her if she interferred with his future?

Richard looked down at his folded hands then up again like he had become someone else. He reached to turn off the lamp. "When did Emma finally fall asleep?"

"About an hour ago."

"Still having those nightmares about the monster with the melting skin?"

Jolie gulped. "Yes, I'm afraid so."

Richard shook the bed until he got comfortable. "I've been thinking maybe I've been a little too hard on her lately. I might let her stay home from Church next week. We'll use that sitter again."

Jolie didn't dare ask if she could stay home with Emma. She knew the answer before opening her mouth. She knew it like she knew her own name.

"Goodnight, Jol. I hope you sleep well. You deserve it. Rest in peace."

His words echoed in her spinning mind when her head hit her pillow. *God help me. I still don't know what You want me to do.*

Chapter Ten

Timothy raised his hands from his sides and slammed his fists down on top of the pulpit. Silence filled the pews.

Jolie was glad Richard had decided Emma could stay home with a sitter. At least the woman wasn't permanent—at least for now. But would Emma be any safer from the reverend's mind control games at home with a stranger.

Timothy glared out over the sea of bodies. His voice rolled over them like a hypnotic current as they sat like zombies before him. "You can all have what I have if you'll just give what God calls you to give. The only way He's going to be able to reward you for your faith is if you exercise it by giving into His ministry. This ministry!"

Richard squeezed Jolie's hand, but he remained entranced by Timothy's words, and he didn't look at her. She turned her head, searching for familiar faces and spotted Aiden. He sat beside Barbara with his arms folded over his chest and a scowl across his face. Something in the expression lines of his face confirmed he was trapped like he said he was. He didn't approve of the reverend, yet Aiden somehow sat in the pew watching the man preach. What held him to that spot next to Barbara? Was he playing by Tim's rules like he had said?

Barbara's eyes grew round and moist. Her face was one large knot of enthusiasm and praise.

In a way, Jolie wished her mother would attend Church. At least that way they might be together. But she felt like Aiden looked, and she knew her mother would be trapped here too.

The reverend's voice built to a crescendo. "In a few moments, the collection plates will be passed around, and I want you all to give whatever God has placed on your hearts."

Missiles swam through Jolie's lungs, defying all the physical laws of her body, as she tried to breathe. She had only the veneer of her calculated smile to deflect the emotional tides. Tides that seemed attuned to her beating heart and her groaning mind.

The congregation nodded as one creature. Except for her and Aiden and one other man. Norman Rakes. The man Richard had been complaining about last night. Rakes leaned back in his seat. His face was stone. He turned his head and spotted Jolie. Blood rushed to her face, making her chest feel like it was going to explode. He mouthed something at her, but she couldn't read his lips.

The reverend was still prancing across the stage. She placed a cool hand across her hot forehead and shut her eyes. Some of the parishioners sat with their heads bowed as though they were praying. Others suddenly lay down, making phantom snow angels on the floor as tears ran down their temples.

Timothy's voice boomed from the front of the Church, and Jolie's eyes sprang open. She thought the sound had shaken the pew beneath her. "What is it God wants to give you?"

People stared in what seemed like awe just like Barbara had. Many nodded at every verse he emphasized from scripture only to use it in a context that brought guilt and confusion to their faces. They clung to his sermon like his words were life preservers for their drowning souls.

There was something bigger than Jolie in Redemption. Of course she knew that, but knowing it and experiencing it like a slap across the face were different. She reached up to her forehead again and felt its dissipating warmth. Yes, she thought, and this bigger thing is bigger than all my petty fears and insecurities, bigger than my unresolved guilt over being away from my parents and not attending my father's funeral.

The fog of depression was lifting off her mind. Pain registered in the many confused faces surrounding her. She had looked like them not very long ago. Still looked like them at times. Sure she didn't have all the answers, but there was always an answer when she opened her mind to it, always the same answer.

Trust God. You can't trust yourself.

And maybe she didn't have to have all the answers before taking a leap of faith. Maybe that was the point. But what leap of faith would she take?

She had to find a way to get her mother out of that house and out of the reverend's custody. Maybe she could talk to Norman Rakes about her mother's situation when Richard wasn't watching. Rakes was a lawyer. If Aiden wouldn't help her, maybe this man would at least give her some impartial legal advice. Then she could call the police and tell them a little about what the reverend seemed to be doing to her mother. Maybe she could take Gena and Emma and leave Redemption before anyone had a chance to stop her.

She closed her eyes and prayed for them and for Aiden, Barbara, Amanda, and the woman she'd seen crying during her first visit to the reverend's church. She prayed for so many of these people, and for herself—that they would be able to see the reverend's sermons for what they were and look to God for His answers.

There is a good man here, Jolie reminded herself, and smiled despite the grave faces surrounding her. *And His name is Jesus.* She held a hand over her heart.

Then she looked at Rakes. The man nodded his head in a covert greeting. Relief edged its way up her body, and she thanked God for what she thought was His answer. She would talk to him after Church while Richard was preoccupied with handing out his business cards and making more new friends.

But when she turned back around, Richard was staring at her.

Ten minutes after Timothy stepped from the stage and disappeared into a huddle of animated women, soft music played from the speakers at the corners of the room, teasing the parishioners into a frenzy of laughter and conversation. Mr. Rakes had disappeared into the crowd. Some parishioners began dancing, jumping up and down in the aisles, waving their hands over their heads. If it wasn't the Holy Spirit that had overtaken them, Jolie could only guess what had.

She leaned forward then sank back into the pew, watching them while Richard still sat beside her with his hands folded in his lap. She scanned the crowd of heads that eventually blurred like she were looking directly into the sun. Heat poured off her, and she knew she might faint. She smoothed back her hair. It was slick with sweat. Richard patted her on the thigh.

Instantly, she stood up and reached for Emma's hand. But Emma wasn't there. She was home with the sitter.

"Wasn't Timothy's sermon moving, Jol?"

"I think my mother's right in not coming here."

He leaned close to her ear. "You better just watch it, for Emma's sake. Remember that. I can get her a nanny who will give her the same level of dedication that Mildred gives Gena."

She shrunk from the heat of his gaze.

Timothy emerged from the blurry maze of people and strolled down the aisle holding the hand of a young woman. Barely in her twenties, the woman's makeup made her look at least five years older. Her short skirt and low-cut sheer blouse seemed to attract numerous male stares.

Barbara whistled them over to her small cluster of friends.

The group fell silent at his approach. *What are they expecting? Him to impart some divine message through this stranger?*

He placed his hand on Barbara's back, still holding the hand of the young woman, and gazed upward. The skylights ushered in amber light. He stood bathed in a golden glow that softened the harsh lines of his face and made him look almost handsome. He shook his head, and the hair tucked behind his ears came free and spilled over the front of his shoulders.

Someone tapped Jolie on the shoulder, and she realized Richard had left her. She bit her lower lip and flinched at the pain as she spun toward Amanda. Jolie swallowed the faint taste of blood.

"Another substitute for the woman he really wants," Amanda whispered.

"What?"

Amanda's mouth twisted. A small vein bulged at her temple. "Barbara couldn't possibly be happy."

Timothy's group of admirers nodded their heads while he spoke. "Barbara is the most generous member of my congregation. She's given countless hours to our church, weekends and weekdays alike. She's spent many a holiday handing out food to the poor and many hours counseling the fallen."

"Praise be," a voice said.

"Thank God for her," another said.

"And this lady right here..." He raised the young woman's hand. "Thanks to Barbara's assistance, is one of my most accomplished young converts. This young lady standing before you, who used to be lost on our very streets, has opened her heart to my church. Now she has overcome a life of death. Glory be."

People outside the group raised their voices. An assortment of heads bowed, bodies swayed, and arms waved in the air to the rhythm of the psychedelic music. "Praise be." They kept saying. "Praise be." The music grew louder.

"What kind of singing is that?" Jolie expected to see a crazed piano woman playing from somewhere in the room, a bottle of bourbon mounted to the top of her piano like a hood ornament.

"Mood music." Amanda's smile seemed barely tolerated by the lips upon which it sat. "It adds to his performance."

"Now she's a true woman of righteousness." Barbara threw up her hands and leaned in to hug the young woman whose hand was still wedged in Timothy's grip.

"Yes, that's right." Timothy raised the young woman's hand. "My newest convert! Glory be!"

"Amen," a few people added.

Barbara gazed into Timothy's eyes the way Aiden had gazed into Jolie's, and Jolie bit her tongue, certain of Barbara's feelings for the reverend. "Aiden and I would be honored if you, Amanda, and our new friend would have dinner with us tonight."

"Barbara, aren't you the selfless giver the Bible praises." Timothy raised his free hand and closed his eyes for a moment, shaking his head to the music as though overcome by the Holy Spirit. He looked like a colt about to whinny with his shoulder-length hair splashing his cheeks.

Jolie wanted to rush up on the stage and scream at them to stop this blasphemous performance. How could this so-called church not burn to the ground under God's fiery gaze?

"We will be honored to join you and Mr. Krenshaw tonight." The young woman offered Barbara a coy smile and squeezed Timothy's arm.

Barbara's eyes flickered with contempt.

"Richard." Timothy looked past his growing huddle of listeners and raised his free hand.

Jolie turned her head. Richard was talking to Rakes. *God no. Please don't let it be true.*

Richard patted him on the back and hurried down the aisle. Jolie swallowed hard.

"So?" Timothy laced his arm over Richard's shoulder and glanced at Jolie.

She took a step back. She hadn't realized Timothy had noticed her.

"You got a taste of what it's like to work with me? Timothy shifted his gaze to the young woman still standing beside him. Richard followed Timothy's gaze.

"Sure did. God has really blessed your business, reverend. It's an honor to work for you."

"To work alongside me. You're my partner now, Richard." He glanced at Jolie again, and she turned away.

She opened her mouth to speak, but Amanda had left. With her mouth still open, Jolie raised her hand and touched the tip of her tongue, confirming the soreness there. *What about God, reverend? What about the power of Jesus in the woman's heart? What about this young woman being His convert, not yours?* Jolie glanced down at the diamond wristwatch Richard had insisted she wear to Church. Noon already? How much longer would she have to endure this charade before she could be with Emma again?

Timothy hadn't expected the papers to take so long to sign. But then Aiden wasn't making an effort to speed things up. Timothy let his mind drift off for at least the third time since returning home from Church. He could hardly believe it was already mid-afternoon. He had missed his luncheon with his beloved Gena and had sent Edmond in his place.

"So, I'm out and Richard's in?"

Timothy eyed his former friend. "You know I don't have to let you out so easily."

Timothy leaned against the living room archway when the doorbell rang. "Will you get that?" he called into the hallway.

The butler scurried out of the den. "Sorry, sir. I..."

Timothy waved his hand, and the man fell silent on his way to the front door.

Aiden looked up from the papers on the coffee table and dropped his pen as Edmond's voice rang through the house. "She sure was feisty today."

Edmond appeared in the archway.

"But she's not disappointed with me, is she?" Timothy clutched his dearest friend's shoulder and looked the man in the eyes.

"Nah. She's jus missin her daughter. You know what I think don't chu, Tim?"

Timothy lolled his head. Aiden was staring at him, that

condescending look on his face. He wanted to punch the arrogant pig in the mouth. What made Aiden think his feelings for Jolie were so pure?

"You can't lettum see each other again. Jolie upset Gena bad after dat reunion. What a mess. She was tryin to stop takin her meds today, actin like she didn't need em or *you* anymore. You shouldn't even allow dose phone calls."

Timothy faced Aiden. "And that little episode at your house, what on Earth happened there? How did such a simple thing go so wrong. Gena was a mess when she came home. Your wife choreographed that little play, didn't she? You two are both lucky I'm such a patient and forgiving man."

Aiden said nothing, not that Timothy expected Aiden to defend Barbara.

Timothy caught Aiden by the arm. The man stared him down, his glare dark and contagious. The burdens behind those eyes were too great for most men. But then Timothy and his little circle of brothers were not most men.

"Don't think I don't see right through you, Tim."

"Sure. You think you know me, but you don't even know yourself. The sins you accuse me of committing are hidden in your own hypocritical heart. And so what if you have a problem with what Peter and me are doing. So what if you don't like the way I feel about Gena. So what? I've been misjudged by greater men than you. And when I stand before God on the day of judgment, my sins will be covered. Will yours, Aiden? I know how you feel about Jolie. I know the kind of man you used to be. I know the man you still are. How does that little dagger of irony feel twisting into your own back?"

Aiden turned and reached down for the papers. "You're wrong about me. I've changed." Aiden thrust the papers at Timothy and slid the pen back into the pocket of Timothy's dress shirt. "Here. They're finished. And I expect to be out of the business. I expect it to be legal now."

"You're the lawyer, old man." Timothy took the papers and slapped Aiden on the back. "I'll be sure to have my secretary take care of them."

Timothy paged through the document. Because of some shred of incriminating evidence Aiden had locked away in some corner of the world even Peter couldn't pinpoint, Aiden would be free of the business and all the ties that close friendship had afforded him. But if Timothy was ever prosecuted, Aiden would be a scapegoat just like Jonathan had been. Aiden would only remain free and clear as long as Timothy remained that way.

"I just hope Jolie doesn't learn anything she shouldn't. You're pretty safe, but she's not."

Aiden stepped around Timothy. "You leave her alone."

"Or what?" Timothy raised one hand in a mock sign of defeat.

Aiden rolled his eyes.

Timothy laughed and smacked Aiden on the shoulder. "Why are you so adorable? I swear. Now I know why Barbara has you twisted around her pinky, Marcy."

Aiden sighed. "I'm leaving now, Tim. Our work is done. I don't have to deal with you anymore."

"Oh, but you shouldn't overestimate that dirt you think you've got on me, little girl."

"Don't you underestimate it."

"She's your Achilles heel. That Jolie. So you see, I still have you right where I want you."

"Don't play games, reverend. I can throw the threats right back at you. I know Gena wouldn't want you even if Jonathan had never existed, and you know if I really wanted to I could sacrifice myself to make sure you never saw her again. They don't let criminals retain custody of people, you know."

Timothy shook his fist. Aiden seized the hand and forced it down. "You remember my threat too if you decide you want to try to mess with Jolie." Timothy's eyes widened. "I'm not as much of a pushover as Jonathan was."

The young woman Timothy had introduced to his church family that morning sauntered out of his bedroom, a wineglass in one hand. A distorted version of Gena's face stared back at him over that torn low-cut blouse. Just a girl, not much older older than his eldest daughter, but old enough to play his games.

"What's the matter with him?" She patted her chest and belched. "The devils you gave me earlier just won't stay down."

Aiden glared at her, and Timothy fought the urge to laugh.

"Honey, don't worry about him. You're more my type than his anyway. Go back in the bedroom and wait for me, okay?" She grinned at him before slinking back down the hall. "And don't make too much noise, dear, I'm expecting my wife home shortly."

The bed rails squeaked in the distance. The girl had probably collapsed.

Timothy faced Aiden. Almost anyone else would've been startled seeing the prostitute in his house. But Aiden had once been his closest friend, and they had shared more secrets than he could remember. The loss hit him hard in the chest, and he found it difficult to breathe. He suddenly wanted to be alone with Gena.

"How can you justify yourself to God, reverend?"

Timothy glanced at his wristwatch. Maybe he could squeeze in one quick visit to Gena's before meeting up with Richard to discuss their next trip. "You just remember what I said." He waved over his shoulder at Aiden as he headed down the hall, his throat burning with unexpected emotion. "Now get out. I've got some personal business to attend to."

The front door slammed, and his mind filled with thoughts of Gena.

Chapter Eleven

Jolie carried two full mugs of coffee into the living room. Richard loomed in front of the bow window. She strained to see past him, but the tensing muscles of his back obscured her view. *What was wrong now?*

Richard sighed, jerking away from the window. "Guess what else I have to put up with for the reverend?"

Raising a mug to her lips, she tried to feel something for him that would quench her blooming desires for Aiden, but there was nothing redeeming to feel for a man who hated everything about you except your pretty face.

"She's out in the street again talking to your dead father."

"What?" Jolie choked and dropped her mug. Even as the steamy liquid splashed her shoes and nylons, she couldn't get her mind to understand what her heart had instantly realized. "Mom's out in the street?"

"Yes, stupid. Didn't you hear the loon this morning?" Richard glared down at the stain seeping into the tapestry footstool where the mug had rebounded. "She woke me up serenading him. Tim promised he'd take care of it, but he hasn't gotten here yet. Maybe he should raise the dosage on her meds."

He boxed his fists at the ceiling then paced in front of the window with his arms folded against his chest.

With one hand, she caught Richard off guard, and shoved him away from the window. He frowned at her, but she didn't care what he'd do about it. Her mother, clad only in a slip, stood barefoot in the street. Random strands of her long dark hair lay loose all the way to her waist, having escaped the cockeyed bun on her head. Her hair streamed around her while she twirled with her arms raised to the sky. "Jonathan!"

Jolie burst back from the window, feeling breathless. "My God, help me bring her in."

"No can do." Richard made a sign of the cross and rolled his eyes. "The reverend's coming over for her. He said not to let you near her. She's having another one of her spells, and she shouldn't be touched. No telling what she might do if she's antagonized."

Jolie sprang toward the window again, but Richard caught her. "I'm not going to antagonize her, Richard. Let me go. She's my mother." Her hands slipped past the sill and she grabbed air, straining for the window. Her feet slid backward over the Oriental rug as Richard dragged her. "Mom!"

Gena turned and cocked her head.

Richard flung Jolie onto the couch where she bounced once before scrambling for the front door. Unable to keep her balance, she skittered into the china cabinet and sunk to the floor, cradling her ribcage. It seemed to be exploding with pain.

"Don't defy your husband." Jolie was only thankful Emma was at school, unable to hear the cold and calculated tone in Richard's voice.

A screech followed the sound of squealing tires. Jolie burst upward despite the dizziness that overcame her and flew past Richard before he could grab her.

"Dear, God," she prayed and threw herself into the door. She fumbled with the doorknob, imagining Richard's breath against her neck, then flung the door open. "Mom!"

Gena flailed her arms and skittered past a van into their front yard. At least she isn't hobbling, Jolie thought. *That's a good sign, right? She wasn't hit?*

Richard growled and yanked Jolie back into the house before slamming the door. She stumbled and toppled onto the stairs. "Almost got your wish, didn't you?"

"I don't want her to kill herself. Let her in."

Gena rammed the door, pummeling it with her fists.

"That psycho?" He flicked a certain finger he was fond of using at the door. "No way."

"Jolie!" Gena clawed at the door. "Let me in!"

Jolie tried to get up, but Richard stomped his foot on the floor and raised a finger to his lips to silence her. She settled back down. The ache for her mother expanded in her chest. Jolie slapped her hands against her face and raked her fingers down her cheeks, not caring if she drew blood with her fingernails. "What the neighbors must be saying, Richard. What would the reverend say about them?"

Richard hesitated, staring at the door. "Nice try, Jol."

"The town nut's on your lawn, Richard, carrying on one of her delusional conversations with her dead husband, your deceased father-in-law, her true love, la de DA." She stomped her foot. The lamp on the mail table vibrated.

Richard smiled down at her and shook his head.

"Mom. Calm down. Help's on the way."

Gena's clawing intensified. "Not Timothy! I don't want any needles!"

Jolie buried her face in her sleeve. "Richard," she whined, "you're my husband. Can't you think about what's best for me just this once?"

The clawing suddenly stopped. Something smacked the door, and Jolie knew Gena had thrown herself against it.

"What you want and what you need are on opposite poles."

Jolie screamed into the sleeve of her dress. Then with all the composure she could manage, she said, "Wouldn't the reverend be interested to know what you call his precious Gena when he's away?"

His face didn't change. His eyes remained two dimly lit bulbs.

She screamed again.

"Are you going to start flipping out now too? What about Emma? Do I need to hire that fulltime nanny the reverend has been talking about?"

"Emma will never see me like this. When she gets home from school, I'll be ready for her." She bit out, "Just like always."

Richard held his hands over his heart and pushed out his bottom lip. "I'm touched. Really, Jol. You are so much the parental role model for me."

"You pathetic excuse for a man."

That time his expression did change, and he spun toward the door and came down hard with his fist. "If you don't want to see the reverend, then get your sorry hide back across the street!"

Gena kicked the door as though in response, and Jolie felt herself smile.

"Crazy kook," Richard grumbled.

Tires squealed outside followed by a slamming door. A strong knock at the front door came moments later. Too steady to have come from Gena's hand.

Richard yanked open the door. Timothy held Gena against him. She was wearing his trench coat now, buttoned halfway up the front over her slip. Heat poured from Timothy's eyes.

"Thanks for the call, Richard. I've got her now."

Timothy guided Gena to the chair in the foyer and knelt before her while the Needhams were in the kitchen making the tea he had requested for Gena. After trying so hard to reach her daughter, he couldn't immediately take her back home. It would cause at least a month's setback.

How could she look so breathtaking with her hair all messed up and her eyes so puffy? Thankfully, he had gotten his coat around her in the yard before he lost it right there.

"I never meant for this to happen, dove." He held Gena's face in his hands, but she wouldn't meet his gaze. He ached to test her love by confessing. Would she forgive him? Would she, dare he hope, thank him. "It was me at your door that morning so many years ago. Not the wind."

Nothing. Not a flicker of understanding.

"Oh, dove, I was going to honor his wish to be let out of the business, but when you didn't answer the door right away, I knew what you two had spent the better part of the night doing, and I decided against my better judgement. I watched you answer that door then shut it. You were so beautiful. You left the door unlocked like it was a sign from God that it was time for me to do what I had planned. Edmond and I slipped in so easily. Then I knew I was right about it being the right thing to do. But I never meant for things to turn out like this. Jonathan was special to you. I know now I took away a part of you that day."

She averted her eyes, but he turned her face back to him.

Had he said too much too soon? She continued to let him hold her. Was she debating whether to forgive him?

"It wasn't your fault," he continued. "You weren't really delusional when Jonathan was away. Amanda was feeding you prescriptions even back before the accident. She put them in your tea when she came to visit." Her face felt soft in his hands. "I'm so sorry, but I was worried about what his absence during all those trips was doing to you. I thought you needed them, and yet I made him continue to work with me." He searched her face for a reaction.

Fire lit her eyes, and she jerked away from him.

"My Johnny's alive. He's just on a long trip. He'll be back soon. I know it."

He gripped her shoulders. "I wish you'd let me take you home with me. Amanda could keep an eye on you whenever I'm gone. Just like the old days. You could come to Church with us. Jonathan would want that."

She violently shook her head.

"Why must you insist on living without me, dove? Don't you know I'd be a better husband to you than Jonathan ever dreamed. One day, you'll see, it's better he's gone."

She stared at him. "Jonathan? Is that you?"

An odd sense of hope filled his chest. He smiled and hated himself for it. "Yes, Gena, my little dove, so sweet, so pure, fly away with me. I've missed you, but I'm home now."

She hugged him, lingering in the embrace. He closed his eyes, feeling her relax in his arms. "I'm never leaving again." *Why, Lord, can't I just be Jonathan?*

"Good, Jonathan, good." She kissed his neck, and his body trembled with desire.

Don't do it, Timothy. It's not right. The voice he had once so closely heeded was now only a whisper in his mind. "Gena, you're so beautiful."

"Oh, Jonathan."

He glanced over his shoulder to confirm the Needhams were still in the kitchen. The faint sounds of arguing trickled down the hall.

Gena's expression had changed when he looked back into her widened eyes. She shoved away from him and rose from the chair. "No, you're not Johnny. You're someone else. I don't know you."

Timothy shook his head as tears filled his eyes. He stood up, frantically wiping at his cheeks and whispered. "No, it's me, dove?" Timothy patted his chest. He splayed his arms. "Me. Jonathan. I've come back for you. I know I've been gone a long time, but I'm back now. Don't you recognize me?"

Gena's gaze shifted. He turned to see Jolie holding a ceramic mug in her hand. Her face was a white sheet of uncertainty. He hadn't heard her leave the kitchen.

"What's going on? Mom?"

"Get this man away from me. He thinks I'm his wife."

Jolie swung the mug at him. Hot liquid slashed his face.

His father's voice raged in his head. Are you going to take that?

"Jonathan!" Gena bolted for the front door. "Where did you go! Don't leave me!"

Timothy caught her around her fragile waist and held tight. She felt like a tiny bird fluttering to get free, but she had no place to go.

"I'll kill you!" Jolie swung at him. He grabbed her wrist and threw his hip into her, knocking her off her feet. He flung Gena around and pushed her up against the wall. He pulled a syringe out of his back pocket and thumbed off the cap. "I was hoping it wouldn't come to this, but your mother is severely ill." Jolie's fingernails felt like claws around his ankle. He plunged the syringe into Gena's hip. She squealed overtop Jolie's cries. He kicked Jolie's hand free. How he hated himself. But no amount of hatred could change what had to be done.

He tossed aside the syringe. Jolie's nails dug into his calves. He kicked at her again, and she recoiled, grabbing her chest. He held Gena against him until she stopped struggling. *Dear God, why can't I stop? Why can't I just be happy with my wife?*

You mean happy with me? the faint voice asked.

Richard waddled into the room. "What's going on?" He pulled Jolie to her feet. He grabbed her wrists when she tried to strike him and twirled her around when she started kicking him. "What's gotten into you? You're acting like your mother."

Timothy glared at him.

"Sorry," Richard whispered.

By the gleam in Jolie's eyes, she was about to bite down on Richard's arm. Before Timothy could decide if he wanted to warn the man, Richard slapped her hard across the head. "Stop it."

Brave young woman, Timothy thought. *So brave yet so defenseless.*

The tremor in Timothy's voice shocked him. "Jolie, I'm sorry, but you don't know what I've had to deal with while you were gone."

Jolie met his eyes, and his heart almost stopped. She was looking directly past his defenses into his heart the way Gena often did when Gena was coherent and the way Amanda sometimes did. Jolie had heard what he had said to Gena, and he could never take it back. But how much had she heard?

Something would need to be done about Jolie. Barbara wasn't getting through to her the way he had planned. At the very least, he would have to have another talk with Richard.

* * *

Timothy strolled into Gena's art room and dropped the duffel bag he had found stuffed into the closet at the top of the stairs. It made a heavy thunk, but she didn't look up from her art table. On an easel beside him stood one of the paintings she had yet to finish. It was of a young woman stooping to kiss a child. That made the second maternal painting he had seen since Jolie's return to Redemption. Gena's obsession for Jonathan seemed to have been replaced by her growing obsession for Jolie.

Oh, how he wanted to be the one to give her another child, to blot out the memory of her daughter, if only she would love him and let him into her heart.

"What were you going to do with this?" He pointed at the bag. "Jolie doesn't want you moving in with her. She said she has enough on her hands to worry about without you adding to the mix."

She said nothing, keeping her back toward him. She was punching a lump of modeling clay. The force of her thrusts were muted by the dense mass. She clutched the corner of her art table and ground her nails into the clay. Slowly, her fingers sank in up to the knuckles. "You won't even let me have my drawing pencils anymore because you're afraid I'll injure myself." She turned and threw the clay at him. He ducked out of the way. She was too coherent today. Too close to unlocking the truth about Jonathan if the conversation went that way. Lowering her medicine had been a terrible mistake. "If I don't have my pencils, I'll go mad. I'm not a sculptor!"

She would see one day how much she needed him, but until then, he couldn't risk loosening his grip on her. That was what his father had done to his mother, and that was how the man had lost her.

Timothy glanced at the duffel bag. "Jolie didn't call you for eight years. Do you really think she'd want to take care of you now? And you can't go around harassing her and your son-in-law and expect to get off your medication either."

Gena looked so wounded, he wanted to hold her, but he knew she would fight him.

"This room is so modest," he said sitting on the cot beside her, scooting aside an easel to accommodate his feet. Lightly, he slid his fingers up her arm. "Maybe I could do something about that, and maybe I could ask the doctor about letting you have your drawing pencils back. It wasn't my decision to confiscate them."

She said nothing. She just looked at him then swatted at a bottle of pills on her desk. It bounced twice then rattled across the floor.

"I heard Jolie was here once. Did it help seeing her?"

Gena's eyes watered. "I...I don't quite remember. I miss her. Please let me see her again. Tell Richard to let me in."

He leaned toward her. "Honey, what makes you think anyone is stopping her from visiting you? She lives just right across the street."

She looked down.

He leaned back. "I'm sorry about all the medication, but it's for your own good." He reached behind the cot and lifted a gift-wrapped box to his lap.

"What's that?" Gena's eyes lit up. That fast she had drifted back into that mental fog where she saw him through different eyes. Enough residual medicine still drifted through her system after all.

He tensed at her advance and sat back, holding the gift out to her. "It's for you."

Smiling, she took it.

Her hand grazed his, and he swallowed hard. "I wanted to apologize for what happened at Barbara's house. I know

I've told you Barbara is someone you have to take with a grain of salt."

Gena's blue eyes glistened in the light of her art table lamp. Her hair took on a subtle red hue. "Actually, Barbara is someone I think should be taken with two fistfuls of scotch."

He laughed, surprised how good Gena could make him feel, even now, so many years after he had first fallen in love with her. He reached out to smooth back her oily hair. She'd need a shower soon and a hearty meal. He hoped the nurse wasn't too rough with her when he wasn't around to oversee things.

She covered her mouth. "Please don't tell anyone I said that about Barbara."

He crossed his heart with his finger. "I wouldn't dare."

Looking satisfied, she set the package on the art table and unraveled the ribbon. Timothy watched her gentle fingertips fiddle with the wrapping paper then tear into the box. He couldn't help smiling.

The box toppled to the floor as she pulled the long white wedding gown free. Holding it against her while gazing down at the streams of lace, she twirled around. Tiny flecks of diamond handsewn into the fabric sparkled. "It's the most beautiful thing I've ever seen."

His body tightened. He felt winded as though he had just run a mile without stopping. "You are the most beautiful think I've ever seen."

She placed it on the cot beside him and stepped back to admire it further.

"Timothy, why are you spoiling her?"

Timothy flinched, twisting toward the doorway. Barbara stood there with her hand on her ample hip. She looked Gena up and down then waddled toward him in her short yellow Spandex dress.

"I'm not spoiling her. She deserves even more than I can give her."

"I've got to try this on." Gena sprinted across the hall into the bathroom.

"You haven't given me anything lately."

He glared at her. "That's because you have so many nice things already."

"And Gena doesn't?"

He started out of the room.

She pinched his elbow. "It's a shame. I don't think she is ever going to realize who you are. Not really."

He slipped past her down the hall. Why couldn't she just leave him alone? Sure, he needed her there to keep the neighbors from talking when he visited Gena too much, but still. Why couldn't she just once stay downstairs and wait for him?

Her heels clicked behind him down the stairs into the family room they used as a makeshift office. She shoved aside a sack of folders she had been working on and sat down on the couch next to him. "I try to please you, Timothy. I always smooth out all the wrinkles when you're gone. Even Peter wouldn't be much use to you without my legal guidance."

He let that comment slide. It wasn't true.

"And you do please me."

She stood up, bending over him. Hands on her hips.

"But you could learn to respect the relationship we have for what it is." He reached for the remote and turned on the small TV mounted in the corner of the room.

He could still see her out of the corner of his eye. She was looking around at all his paperwork. At the legal pads with scribbled notes. At the desk with its drawers hanging open, spilling with crumpled papers and battered reference books. And the typed pages of a manuscript in progress. She sniffed and lifted his red leather Bible from the minature bookshelf beside her. "Funny how you keep this in such good condition compared to all your other books." She opened it and fanned through the pages. "Not even dog-eared I see. Nothing highlighted either."

He snatched it from her. Anyone else would've been punished for the implication Barbara was making.

"Why don't you buy your wife some nice things? I bet the little woman would appreciate some attention now and then."

Timothy punched the seat cushion. One of the sewn buttons tapped his knuckle, and he shrieked in pain. Barbara caught his hand and kissed it. He stared at her, waiting for her to release him. She was tenacious. He had to give her that. Had to admire it in a way like he hoped Gena admired his tenacity.

Barbara dropped his hand and bolted toward the door. He had never seen her move so fast in her high heels. He expected her to lose her balance and spill over. "Better yet, why don't you tell Amanda you're giving up Gena to show her that you are a changed man." She held the door open.

Heat flooded his cheeks. "There's only one woman for me, Barbara, and you swore to me that you accepted that. Why don't you go home and tell Aiden you love him?"

She stepped back, but kept her chin elevated and snatched her coat from the nearby chair. She slipped it on. It concealed her tight outfit. The neighbors wouldn't look twice at her when she left.

"Gena is the only one who appreciates and understands me."

Barbara mumbled, "Yeah, when she's heavily medicated." She raised her voice. "You know, Tim, just because your parents didn't believe in God and didn't understand your desire to go into ministry, doesn't mean that converting Gena or making her your wife will give you any closure about the fate of their souls."

He leaned forward and threw his face into his hands. "Why do you keep testing me?

"All right." Her voice had softened. "How about a truce?"

He looked up and sighed.

She stood with her hands on her hips, a hint of worry shadowed her face. "I'm sorry."

He reached up and took her by the hands when she came toward him. "Are you feeling a little neglected? You need a little attention?"

Barbara blushed, gazing into his eyes. "That's all I ever wanted."

He shook his head. "That's all I have to give you." He pulled her down next to him and draped his arm over her shoulders. Noticing movement by the stairs, he snatched back his arm. Gena wore the elegant white satin gown he had bought her, looking even more angelic than she had looked holding it against her upstairs.

Barbara snorted. She stood up and cleared her throat. When Timothy didn't look at her, she stomped past Gena toward the door.

"Don't trot, dear. Your feet will develop hooves." Timothy knew he was trying to distance himself from her like he did with Amanda by reeling her heart in then casting it back out, but he hardly cared. What Barbara had said about his parents had been close to the truth. He couldn't risk letting her know how close she had come. Only Gena, if she wanted it, could have that intimate connection to him.

Gena covered her mouth.

"Go ahead and laugh. You're nothing more than a child with all those pills in your head. I refuse to hate you."

"Ignore her, Gena. She's always so dramatic."

Barbara's hand froze on the doorknob. Looking over her shoulder, she met his glare. A faint frown bowed her mouth. Her teeth drew back in that familiar expression. She gingerly gripped the knob and slammed the door shut behind her.

Timothy winced, feeling soft fingers slide over the tensed fist he had laid atop the armrest. He looked down and saw Gena's tiny hand.

Stifled sobs choked her voice. "Why does she hate me?"

Before he could change his mind, he reached up and pulled her down to the couch, wrapping her in his arms, amazed she was letting him hold her. She wept against his shoulder. The ruffles of the wedding gown pressed against his lap, creating a barrier between her flesh and his. He closed his eyes, breathing in the earthy scent of her, savoring this unplanned, but perfect moment. *Oh, God, how could You forbid me someone so pure and beautiful, someone so befitting for a reverend's wife? Surely You want me to be happy.*

Chapter Twelve

Emma whined from the kitchen doorway.

Jolie hung up the phone and bent to scoop her daughter into her arms. She hadn't expected Gena to pick up, but she had needed to try again anyway.

Emma returned the bear hug Jolie gave her then clambered across the kitchen and sat down at the table. "What's wrong, Mom? You can tell me."

"Nothing's wrong, sweetheart. I was just thinking, that's all."

"Silly Mom. You're not supposed to think that hard."

Jolie peeled Emma a banana and chopped it into tiny chunks overtop of a saucer. *Thank you God for this precious gift You've given me amidst all the suffering in my marriage.*

Jolie sat the saucer in front of Emma, kissed the child's cheek, then went into the living room to stoke the fire. Jolie spread her fingers in front of the embers that had swallowed the letter from the Seattle doctor. The contents from the syringe Timothy had abandoned on the end table had been Chlorpromazine or by its trade name, Thorazine, a major tranquilizer often used to treat psychotic episodes in schizophrenics, but not usually available in such high concentrations. And certainly not used just for the hopelessly heartsick.

Jolie looked up at the clock. It had been two hours since she had called the local police to report the drug. Peter had answered the phone. She hadn't recognized his voice at first, but when she had, she quickly changed her story. According to Richard, no one had worked more intimately with Reverend Caine than Peter. Except for maybe Aiden. And if Peter came looking for the letter she had sort of mentioned, he would not find it. Then maybe her altered story would stick.

No one had called back. No one had come out to the house to check on her. Richard hadn't come home and punished her. She wasn't sure if Reverend Caine had sunk his teeth into Norman Rakes' mind yet, but she was going to hold out until she could talk to the man. If he didn't have any suggestions, she was going to contact the FBI or the CIA.

Closing her eyes and trying to settle her rambling thoughts, she inhaled the smoky sweetness of the cherry logs and contemplated how frozen the turkey still was in the bottom of her refrigerator.

The buzz of the doorbell jolted her eyes open. She folded her arms across her chest and waited. A chill had settled in the air and into her bones, but it had sulked inside—not past weather-stripping or mere flesh—but through the seams of her carefully stitched persona. Now, as at other times, she felt no more real than a sewn doll with its pincushion face.

The doorbell buzzed again. Longer. Jolie scuffed the heel of her dress shoe against the blue brick of the hearth and tried to ignore it. It might be Peter. Maybe Richard or Reverend Caine. And maybe whomever it was would give up and go away. A ridiculous thought of course.

A round of knocking, then pounding, followed a long steady buzz of the doorbell.

She bolted across the living room into the foyer, her heart thumping.

She was relieved to see Amanda fidgeting on the doorstep. In a long black dress, Amanda looked like a widow in mourning. Jolie wondered if between them, they owned a single pair of jeans.

"Sorry to bother you, but I was hoping you had a moment to talk."

Jolie nodded. Richard was due home soon, but he wouldn't have any gripes about Amanda visiting. She could stall Amanda in the family room and at least get the turkey in the oven while Amanda waited, then she could invite her to stay for dinner.

Yanking down the sides of the black dress, Amanda looked like what Jolie would be in ten years if something didn't change, and it was a sharper image than any mirror could provide. Jolie led Amanda into the family room where Amanda chose a seat on the ottoman and raised her trembling hands to the fire.

Jolie opened her mouth to tell her that she would be just a minute in the kitchen when Amanda's eyes filled with tears. Jolie slumped into the rocking chair. Amanda seemed to stare at the powdered ash clustered in front of the shriveled crackling logs.

Emma scampered past them. "Were are you going?" Jolie asked.

The child spun to face her and lowered her eyes when she spotted Amanda. "Up to play."

"All right, but make sure you don't play too loudly."

Emma nodded and raced up the stairs.

"I have a miracle waiting for me," Amanda whispered.

"What did you say?" The rocker creaked under Jolie's shifting weight.

The prominent bones of Amanda's face seemed to glow with firelight. Shadows filled the harsh hollows of her sunken flesh. "It's a line from a song or a poem I heard a long time ago at about the time I met my husband. I have a miracle waiting for me. It's far outside the gates where I want to be. Where nothing that I know is unkind. And all that I need is mine."

Jolie didn't know what to say. Funny. Amanda had come here to talk, determined not to be turned away. *And somehow I have rendered her heart mute. No, that's not right. She's ready to tell me something.*

"Has Richard ever cheated on you?"

Jolie clenched her tingling fingers, making two fists before drawing them into her lap. "No. That's one injustice I don't think I've ever suffered from him."

"Well, Timothy cheats on me on every so-called business trip. All the time really."

Jolie felt her mouth spring open before she could raise her hand to cover it.

Amanda seemed to stare into the distance. The look of fiery determination Jolie had noticed when Amanda had first come down her walkway flashed in Amanda's eyes.

Jolie's mind swirled with probabilities. Hard facts about Timothy's actions formed one theory while intuition catapulted her into another. Further analysis made her mind swell with new questions and uncertainties. She circled through theories like Timothy's sermons circled around scriptural points, and she realized if you say everything, you say nothing, so she chose one question she wanted to ask more than anything else. "Does Reverend Caine cheat on you with my mother?"

A storm of tears Amanda must've long ago dammed back finally broke in her eyes and spilled from her cheeks, dampening her blouse, but she made no sound. Her silent quivering was the worst thing Jolie had ever seen.

"How can he pretend to be a man of God when he doesn't live like one?"

Amanda leaned over in a fit of laughter then slapped a hand to her mouth. Tears filled her eyes, and her laughter became strained. She bowed forward then raised back up. Hysteria lit her eyes. Firelight danced across her forehead, nose, and cheekbones, and Jolie winced before she realized she had only imagined sparks striking Amanda's face.

The house slowly drained of the laughter and seemed unnaturally quiet. Even Emma was silent upstairs.

A hard couple of blinks allowed Jolie to focus her mind and break the silence. "When you came to our house to invite us to Church, Emma had just had a nightmare. And when Richard and I first came to The Church of His Redemption, Emma got a bad stomachache. I know this sounds crazy, but I think God uses her to speak to me." Jolie stared into Amanda's unblinking eyes. "How can you invite people to a church whose reverend is…"

No tears marched forward to the frontlines of Amanda's eyes. They seemed to have retreated into her heart where they would recover for a future battle. "Tomorrow I'll wake up and my life will have all been a dream. You know, it doesn't all happen at once. Most things are slow. Most things don't just suddenly become clear to us. We find ourselves caught in the spider's web only after we see the spider. And when you marry young or naïve or both in my case, you have a kind of inherent blindness to certain very important things."

"And my mother? I suppose Timothy doesn't want us together because of what seeing me is doing to her mind?"

The wink Amanda gave her said everything she needed to know.

Tears started to swell in Jolie's eyes, but she made no attempt to conceal them. "So, what are we going to do about it?"

Amanda shook her head. "All I wanted was to tell you. I knew you were a kindred spirit from the first time we met. I knew you wouldn't judge me for my confession. I've sinned too, Jolie, by staying with him and being a part of his madness by covering for him." Amanda pounded her fists into her thighs. "I wish I could do something more, but I'm weak. I'm just a shell of a woman. I can throw around words with the best of them, but deep down in my bones, there is no fight. I've been married to him for twenty-three years now—since I was nineteen. I'm spent. I don't even know who I am outside of Amanda Caine, wife of Timothy Caine."

Jolie waited until Amanda met her eyes. "You know my mother doesn't want him, don't you?"

Amanda nodded. "The only man she wants is your dear father. I wish I could tell you something else, but I don't think it would unburden anyone but myself, and it would probably turn out bad, worse if I did, because of the hell gates it would unleash in the fight for Timothy's soul. You see, Jolie, I am a reverend's wife, but I pray daily for the redemption of my husband's soul."

"Tell me what you're afraid to say, Amanda. Tell me how my father really died."

Amanda shook her head and rose from the couch. "I've got to be going now. The reverend doesn't know I'm here. He thinks I'm at Church leading the women's group, but Barbara is covering for me."

"Amanda..." Jolie stood.

Amanda raised her hand. "I know the way out, thank you, sweetheart." She headed for the door. Jolie didn't try to stop her. Amanda would probably never divulge her secret, but with the right coaxing, Aiden might help her now that she had a better idea of what she was up against. And there was always hope that Mr. Rakes would have some invaluable legal advice for her if she could just get past Richard's radar and get the man alone again.

Jolie leaned back in the rocker. Emma's footsteps shuffled overhead. She smiled up at the ceiling. *Thank You, God, for Emma. Please keep her safe through all this and help me make contact with Mr. Rakes.*

Jolie looked up at the clock in the foyer and scurried into the kitchen five minutes after Amanda had left. Passing the granite island, she switched on the TV encased in the wall above. She cut a sharp left to the oversized refrigerator and pulled out the large circular plate that held the turkey. She poked the bird and decided it was thawed enough. She set the oven to preheat, plopped the turkey into a roasting pan, and buttered it in a frenzy.

She was again Jolie Needham, the obedient wife of Richard Needham. She shut the oven door and lifted the TV remote. She flipped around the channels past soap operas and infomercials and settled on a documentary she knew Richard would watch. She returned to the island and pulled out a cutting board from a lower cabinet. She was chopping vegetables, smiling at the memory of her conversation with Amanda, and dreaming up her next attempt to uncover the reverend's secrets when an emergency local news bulletin appeared on the screen.

"Dear Jesus," she whispered, coming down hard with the knife. She winced, thinking she had sliced her finger. But when she looked down, there was no blood. A jab to raise the remote's volume control convinced her she hadn't imagined the words, *local murder*.

"The body of a recent occupant of Redemption, North Dakota," the journalist continued, "a man who has been identified as Mr. Norman Rakes, a retired trial lawyer from Minnesota, was found in a wooded area today, just three miles from his apartment building. Authorities are not yet certain if the man was assaulted. From the claw marks surrounding what appeared to be a grave, it seems a wild animal may have uncovered the body. A resident near the local park, who declined to be named, discovered the apparent grave on his way home from work earlier today."

Jolie's head throbbed so loudly she could no longer hear the report. She switched off the TV and ran down the hall into the bathroom for some Tylenol.

Standing in front of the medicine cabinet, she refused to look at herself in the mirror. She'd have to touch up her makeup before Richard got home and at least run a brush through her hair, but first she had to get rid of the train wreck in her head. The lid to the Tylenol bottle popped off in her jittery hands, and when she reached for it, she dropped the bottle. Capsules sprawled across the counter. She managed to save exactly two from hitting the floor. She cupped the precious items into her mouth and swallowed with a handful of tap water.

She set the empty bottle on the toilet tank and lowered herself to the floor, nearly forced there by gravity and a sudden inability to maintain her balance. Capsules pressed underneath her, but she hardly noticed the pain. When she reached behind the toilet for a cluster of them, her vision grayed out. The white capsules evaporated into the white ceramic tiles. *Don't pass out, Jolie. Richard doesn't like a mess.* Slowly, her vision returned, and she struggled to stand on wobbly knees. Without falling, she somehow managed to brush off the capsules embedded in her shins. "Come on now, Jolie. The broom is right there in the hallway closet. Come on, girl."

She made it to the doorway then did the very thing she feared most. She fainted.

"What in the name of all that is holy are you doing, Jolie?" Richard crouched over his wife. "You're lucky Emma was upstairs playing and didn't see you. What would she have thought?"

Jolie peered up at him, raising her throbbing arm to shield her eyes from the hallway light. She tried to sit up. Lightning erupted in her lower back. Richard's eyes narrowed on her. Her thoughts refused to assemble. A thin line of teeth showed through his parted lips, making him look like a dog about to growl.

She blurted, "The TV."

"What?" He grabbed her by the hands and hoisted her to her feet.

She leaned against the wall until her vision clarified. At least she didn't have a migraine anymore. Until he belted her across the face. Her nose and part of her right cheek felt like it had been stung by the world's meanest wasp.

Winding his fingers around the base of her neck and squeezing like she were a giant tube of toothpaste, he drove her to her knees. They thudded against the tile.

"Dad! What are you doing to Mom?" Emma's voice rang out behind them.

Jolie felt paralyzed by her daughter's sobs.

Richard spun and belted Emma across the mouth. Jolie clutched her chest. "Richard!"

"Go up and play, you little..."

"Just go, Emma." Jolie tried to keep her voice light and sweet. "Mommy will be right up."

Emma scampered away.

Richard stomped into the living room and flicked on the TV. "What channel were you watching?"

She massaged her sore throat while her mind raced. Then she calmly stood and hobbled into the living room.

He was staring at the screen, watching the news report she had seen earlier replayed. Then he clicked off the TV with the remote. "Looks like it's only playing on local channels." He gritted his teeth. Worry creased his brow. His cell phone rang at his hip, and he jumped. He unclipped it and looked down at the caller id. "It's Peter. I've got to take this."

Jolie turned and walked down the hall and into their bedroom. The muffled sound of his voice drifted off. She looked around. There wouldn't be much to pack.

Ten minutes later, he strolled into the bedroom with a bottle of Jack Daniel's in one hand and leaned on the dresser beside her. "What are you doing now?"

Jolie kept shoving the pile of clothes she had placed on the bed into the suitcase, eyeing the bottle. Since he had started working with Timothy, his choice of alcohol had gotten much stronger. Had he been drinking when he had botched the disposal of Norman Rakes' body? "I'm doing what I should've done the first day I met you. I'm getting as far away from you as is humanly possible."

"God forbids such language. And you're not going anywhere. You're my wife. Who's making you talk to me like this? Your mother? She's finally turning you against me."

"In case you didn't notice, I haven't even been allowed to talk to my mother. And you don't own me."

"I knew it!" He slammed the bottle down on the dresser, and she flinched. Liquid spilled into the open drawer onto her underclothes.

"I never gave you a reason to leave. I never beat you."

"You never beat me? You beat me everyday. You beat me down with your silence *and* with your words *and* with your fists."

Richard thumped the dresser, but she didn't flinch. She had anticipated the reaction. The veins on his forehead bulged. The divot that had only been a faint expression line between his eyebrows before they had moved to Redemption had become a gully splitting his forehead in half. For a moment, she imagined his brain might come popping out, and she fought the mad laughter prickling her insides. "What is with you lately? Why are you always challenging me? You're the reason I hit Emma." He faced the window that overlooked Gena's house and flexed his hands. His arms dropped to his sides, and he let out a heavy sigh. "What am I going to do with you?"

"Did you kill that man on the news? That Rakes guy? Did you screw up his burial? Is the reverend angry with you?"

Something flickered in the corner of his eyes.

"What was that? A yes or a no?"

He whipped toward the doorway.

"How did Timothy get you to do it?"

He thumped the doorframe. "Who would take you if I kicked you out, Jol? If I decided you're finally more trouble than you're worth?"

"Maybe I'd be happier without a man trying to control me all the time."

"Don't be foolish. You can't make it through life without

a man. You're not the type. You'd have ended up like your mother if I hadn't married you when I did. You were just itching to get out of that house."

"I haven't had you since we were married and I've done just fine."

He laughed.

A paralyzing darkness consumed his features as he slowly raised his gaze to her face, but the darkness did not originate from any argument between them. It lay deeper near the heart of the monster she called husband with her lips and Satan with every step she tried to take away from those hateful eyes.

She looked away from him, afraid that his darkness would snuff out what precious light still flickered inside her. *Oh, how patient God is with me.* She sucked in a deep breath, remembering what Amanda had told her about weakness. She didn't want to wake up one day and realize she was no more than a shell of a woman. "Got to control everything, don't you? Well, not me. Not anymore." She closed the suitcase and lifted it off the bed.

He stared at her, standing midway between her and the door. "Will Emma suffer for your sins, Jol?"

"You wouldn't," she croaked.

The answer in his eyes made her drop the suitcase.

"Now, don't be foolish. Get this nonsense out of your head. I'm hungry, and I've been more than kind about dinner being late."

The aroma of nearly burned turkey wafted into the bedroom.

He brushed past her. She gasped and backed around the side of the bed.

He reached down and wrenched the suitcase off the floor then flung it into the wall behind them, sending the contents flying about the room like heavy flight-resistant birds. "Now look at all *this* mess." His stomach gurgled, and he sighed. "You can clean it up after dinner."

Chapter Thirteen

Laying his red leather Bible beside him on the church steps, Timothy looked up at Aiden. "I saw that little display in Richard's kitchen between you and Jolie Needham. I'd be very careful if I were you."

Aiden wavered on his way down the steps, dangling the keys to his Ranger. He squinted into the sun, shielding his eyes as he looked back over his shoulder and smiled. "And I've seen how you treat Gena Young. So what?"

Timothy folded his arms across his chest and leaned back against the concrete riser, smiling. "You tell me once and for all if I need to watch my back with you."

"I'm no threat to you. Remember our agreement? You leave me alone, and I'll leave you alone."

"I'd be very careful, Aiden. Jolie is married to the man I expect will help me take my forum to the ends of the earth, and I don't want him being distracted by any marital foolishness at the hands of one of my former associates."

"Don't try to buffalo me. I know why you're so interested

in that pompous idiot. We all saw the same news report. You're just trying to get him on your side so you can control Jolie. Peter had to scramble at the station to cover that big boo-boo for you."

"Don't forget who you're talking to, Aiden."

"I don't do business with you anymore," Aiden snapped. "I'm not yours to control."

"Ah, but agreements are only good if both parties keep their promises."

"What's that supposed to mean?"

Timothy pivoted on his hip and squinted at Aiden, knowing his eyes twinkled like those of an ornery child.

"I have proof of more than you think I do, Tim. I could hurt you more with those records than you can imagine."

"Big words for such a little girl. If I find out you're feeding Jolie any privileged information, it'll be her neck, not yours. Then we'll see how much you really know."

"I'm not feeding her anything." Aiden turned and looked up the steps to the church door. "So, where's Amanda? I didn't see her here today, and she's always there sitting frozen like the good little zombie wife beside you."

"Deathly ill. Today was the worst I've seen her in awhile. She'll be fine once she gets a little rest. She hasn't been eating right. Poor dear."

Aiden snorted and continued down the stairs. Timothy grabbed Aiden's calf, and Aiden flailed his arms to keep his balance. He plopped onto the riser beside Timothy.

"I'm warning you, Aiden, stay away from Jolie."

Aiden ground his teeth at him. "You think your so-called love for Gena would still exist if she gave in and started attending your church, if she believed in your convoluted sermons like Amanda somehow still does. It makes you crazy to think there's a woman in this world who doesn't adore you, who doesn't think you're God's voice. You would hurt Gena like you hurt Amanda if she gave you half a chance."

"I love Amanda, Aiden. I would never try to hurt her. Do you love Barbara?"

"Of course he loves his wife."

Timothy flinched and looked up the steps. Holding open one of the double doors, Jolie scowled down at him. How long had she been standing there? A breeze stirred her long dark hair. It fanned out behind her face, and she casually pushed a few strands away from her eyes. No, he decided, she hadn't heard Aiden's accusation.

Emma sprinted out the doors and down the steps.

"Come back here. You're going to get your dress dirty." Jolie eased her way between them, gliding down the steps. Timothy swallowed hard. *Beautiful like her mother.* He couldn't blame Aiden for falling in love with Jolie, but he could stop him, he hoped. That phone call Peter had intercepted at the station had meant something. But what?

Emma squealed at the edge of the sidewalk and lay down, thrashing from side to side. "I want to go home! I want to go home!"

Emma looked more like Richard than Jolie. Unruly red curls framed the puckered red face. The crinkled snotty nose in the center was Jolie's though, and the inquisitive accusatory green eyes...well, they belonged to Jolie and Jonathan. Timothy bit down on his lip, trying not to frown.

Timothy raised his chin for emphasis. "Why's she acting like that? How old is she now?"

Jolie took her by the hand and wrestled her to a sitting position then leaned over and scooped her up. The child clamped her legs around her mother's waist and pitched her arms around Jolie's neck. Jolie bounced Emma higher to get a better hold and smacked off bits of dirt that still clung to

Emma's ruffled skirt then struggled to set Emma down.

"She's upset." Jolie wiped the child's brow. "Something Amanda said to me."

Timothy glanced at Aiden. The man hid his smile behind his upraised hand, but he could not hide the crinkling at the corners of his eyes. Emma smiled back at him. Flickering sunlight made imps dance in her eyes. Jonathan's eyes.

Timothy shuddered. *So you've got something to say, do you, little imp?*

She turned to face him with a boldness in her expression he hadn't expected. Her voice was like a tiny dagger plunged into his side. "What did you do to my grandpa?"

Timothy blinked hard and clutched his Bible against his thigh. "What's that child talking about?"

Jolie's eyes narrowed. "Nothing really. Amanda just mentioned something about my parents I wasn't aware of. Emma took it the wrong way."

"And what might that have been?" He hoped no one noticed the beads of sweat rolling down his temples.

"It was just something about my father's funeral. Amanda mentioned it was closed casket." Jolie glanced down at her daughter and slowly let go of the child's shoulders. Emma remained put, but stared as though entranced by the church doors. "Mom might not have taken the news too well that Dad wanted to be buried up north with the rest of his family. It was just too soon to know after her attempted suicide, so no one broke the news to her that he had willed to be buried there instead of in the plot behind the church which I've come to learn is empty." Jolie shook her head. "You know, Reverend Caine. I never realized how unstable my mother was all those years. I honestly didn't know how much I could've helped her."

He fought a smile. Was Jolie petitioning for permission

to see her mother? If so, it was a good ploy. Just not good enough. "I honestly believe you couldn't have helped your mother back then, even though I know you would've wanted to, just like I know you can't give her the help she needs now. You know how..." He paused, eyeing Aiden. Of course, Aiden wasn't buying the routine, "...well, you know how very unstable your mother became shortly after your reunion."

Aiden laid his hand over his heart. "Well, I for one wondered why the funeral was closed casket."

Timothy turned away, leaning over the concrete wall of the stairwell, hoping he wouldn't be sick.

He flinched when Aiden grabbed his shoulder. "So, that wasn't Jonathan I saw being buried in the graveyard behind the church?"

Timothy snapped his head around so only Aiden could see his sneer. The church doors opened. An elderly couple emerged and headed down the steps, glancing in Timothy's direction as he smiled and leaned back, patting his chest. The woman's gaze lingered too long, but he pretended not to notice. He watched the door a moment longer until he was certain no one else would emerge.

Staring down at the Bible in his right hand, he blinked, damming back tears he never meant for anyone but God to see. From where are these emotions coming? he wondered.

Jolie tugged on Emma's arm. "Let's go back in now." But the child wouldn't budge. Emma scuffed the pavement with her patent leather shoe.

"All right. You can stay in the car, but I can't stay with you. I've got to go back in to be with Daddy."

"No." Emma lunged forward and yanked Jolie's arm, ignoring Timothy's blazing glare. "You have to stay with me, Mom. It's not safe in there."

"Emma!" Timothy slapped the Bible against his thigh. "Good little children listen to their parents."

When Emma glanced at the Bible then looked him in the eyes, Timothy's lungs almost clamped shut, and he could barely breathe. *What are you thinking, girl?*

"She knows that, Reverend Caine," Jolie snapped. "Thank you for the reminder, but I can handle this."

"I'm sure you can." Timothy's eyes felt like they were pulsing with laughter. Heavy rolling laughter thundered from his throat. Laughter he usually reserved for Amanda. "Oh, Jolie Krenshaw, I'm sure you can handle just about anything you set your mind to."

Jolie spun on her heel, whirling Emma into her hip. She stared, but said nothing. Then she glanced at Aiden. Then around the parking lot. The elderly couple who had come out of the church hesitated before shutting the doors of their car, but that was all. No one else had overhead them. She returned her gaze to Timothy.

Emma gripped her mother's legs.

"Reverend?" Aiden whispered. But Timothy didn't shift his gaze.

Jolie broke eye contact first, turning around and taking Emma's hand and heading across the parking lot.

Aiden tapped him on the shoulder. "What are you thinking now, reverend?"

Timothy craned his eyebrows then stood and headed down the steps. He looked back over his shoulder from the sidewalk. "Oh, ye of little faith, Aiden. Oh, ye of so very little self-control." Timothy laughed, but it was a strange laugh that frightened himself even more than he had meant for it to frighten Aiden.

Jolie unlatched the screen door, and Aiden rushed into her kitchen. He stood before her, trembling, at first, unable or maybe just unwilling to speak while she backed away and lifted a pan of sautéed mushrooms from the stove. Then the words came gushing out. "Jolie, I love you. I want to take you and Emma away from here. We'll leave Redemption and go wherever you choose. I don't care as long as you'll tell me right now that you'll come with me."

Jolie dropped the pan of mushrooms back onto the burner and stared at the disheveled man trembling in her kitchen. Sweat trickled down his temples along the strong line of his jaw. His fists shook at his sides. His lips were a quivering line mouthing unspoken words she longed to hear.

"Aiden?" She glanced behind herself at the swinging door leading into the living room and listened. The volume on the cartoon program Emma had been watching didn't change.

"Aiden," Jolie whispered, "What do you think you're doing?"

"Where's Richard?"

"Upstairs napping."

He smiled and stepped toward her. He took her hand and buried it between both of his.

Words, reason, whizzed through her head in a jumble. If she had uttered them, they would not have made sense to anyone else, maybe not even to herself. The rush of protests slowed to a trickle. Then stopped altogether. She could only gaze hopelessly into his watery eyes. "Do you know what you're asking?"

"Have you ever been so completely alone, without the one person in your life you know could fill that void in your heart? Then found that that person was standing right in front of you."

She shook her head. "You can't think like that."

He stepped closer, but she pushed him back.

"Aiden, slow down. I can't help you unless you slow down." He refused to sit and tried to pull her closer, his smile widening and shrinking then widening again. "What fills that void in your heart, Jolie? Does God?"

He settled his gaze on the floor. I'm sorry. I shouldn't have said that. But you don't understand. Barbara's dead— dead inside—I accepted that a long time ago. A part of me is even..." he hesitated and raised his head, "it's even glad to be rid of her."

"Aiden? Barbara's not dead. She's full of life."

"She's dead in here." He pointed to his chest. "And here." He pointed lower.

Jolie leaped back from him and reached for the door he had entered. She struggled to sound calm. "Aiden. You need to go home. If you leave now, we can forget this ever happened."

She turned and found his hand in mid-flight to her. He lowered it when he met her hard gaze. "This is about you. I love you, Jolie Needham. God help me I love someone who doesn't even like me."

Holding open the screen door, she said nothing. *Dear Jesus, help me. It would be so easy to love this man.*

"Please, Jolie," he whispered, scuffing his shoes as he approached the door. "How can you stay with a man like Richard and run away from a man like me?"

Still, she said nothing.

He reached for her, but she shook her head. "I won't ever let myself love you," she lied. "And I can't leave Redemption without my mother. Every day, I'm afraid I'll wake up to find she's disappeared off the face of the earth because I've gotten too close to the reverend's secrets."

He stood outside the screen door, peering in at her while she locked it. "Jolie, I can't change how I feel about you."

She glared at him, letting her eyes get wide. "Try, Aiden. Try because I won't be in another relationship God doesn't want me in. I just won't."

He raised his hand to the screen. She met it with hers and smiled like she often smiled at Emma when the child was being difficult. "Now go home, Aiden," she said, using the voice she reserved for Emma, "and pray God will strengthen your love for Barbara and fade your desire for me."

He swallowed hard as she latched the screen door. Then he backed away. "You're an amazing woman, Jolie Needham. An amazing woman."

A sour stench mingled with the scent of lilac bushes. Jolie looked out at the trashcans along the wooden privacy fence. Richard hadn't taken them to the curb last night. Flies buzzed over the loose lids.

"I don't know if God will answer that kind of prayer, but I'll pray it. There's something about you that makes me want to be a better man." He winked at her and started jogging backward. A smile spread across his lips.

She turned around and trudged back to the stove. The mushrooms were smoking. She turned off the burner and raised the pan to scrape most of the contents into the sink. She salvaged what she could on a plate. She glared at the screen door, at the latch that separated her from Aiden's arms, then rebuked herself for giving his proposition half a thought. "Marriage is sacred," she whispered.

"What'd you say?" Richard yawned behind her.

She spun around and swung mushrooms at his feet. He backed up, wiping at his puffy eyes. "Watch it!"

He eased past her and went to the breakfast table, ignoring the mess on the floor, and pulled out a chair. "Emma eating?"

"No. Just us." The dead tone in her voice made her wonder if she were as dead as Aiden claimed Barbara was. Tightness settled into her lower back while she carried the plate to the table. She set it down between the bowl of macaroni salad and the plate of glazed chicken before taking her seat.

"Good. I'd like a little peace while I eat my lunch. Got a meeting with Tim over at the church. He decided his office would be a better place to discuss his plans for me. Our basement seems to have ears." He glanced at her before pulling the bowl of macaroni salad toward him. "You're not a chef like Barbara, but you make a mean pasta salad, Jol."

She stared at the mess on the floor while he finished loading his plate. He stabbed his fork into a hunk of chicken and raised his eyebrows at her. "What are you looking at?"

"Nothing," she whispered, struggling to catch her breath. She lowered her head and flipped a napkin across her lap.

"Good. Then let's keep it that way." He tilted his head to take a bite of his chicken while looking at her. She knew what he was examining, the bruise fading on her collarbone she covered with the neckline of her dress.

Aiden's words echoed in her mind. How can you stay with a man like that and run away from a man like me?

Amanda lay the stack of ironed dress shirts on the king-sized bed and began refolding the pile of undershirts.

Timothy watched her from the doorway with a smile he could barely control. She failed to notice the lump lying motionless underneath the covers. "Amanda?"

She raised her head. Her eyes grew wide. Had she seen his little surprise?

"What kinds of things have you been telling Jolie Needham? She called down to the police station on me. Peter couldn't tell me what she wanted. I thought maybe you might know."

She reached down and raised the laundry basket at her feet. "Don't you come near me with that look in your eyes."

No, he decided, she hadn't seen it.

"What are you going to do, Amanda? Slug me with that."

She tightened her grip. Her eyelids flickered. "Maybe. Or maybe I'm going to hit her!" Amanda spun on her heel and flung the basket at the wall, missing the girl slinking out of the bed. Amanda wrenched the covers off the bed, spilling the dress shirts onto the floor.

"Timothy, you selfish fool." Tears choked her voice. The bedspread sailed down over her head. She clawed at the offending material and pulled it free from her static-infested curls. "I don't know what you want from him, but if you think he really wants you, you're as stupid as you are a whore."

"Amanda, honey, please calm down. I had a craving."

"A craving? She's not junk food. She's not edible."

"Yes I am." The girl sprang across the bed to avoid the swat of Amanda's hand.

Timothy felt a twinge of shame for the joke, but shoved it aside.

Oh, Timothy, how far you've turned away from me, the soft voice said. *But there's still a chance to turn back.*

But it was a joke, his mind protested. *Meant to teach her a lesson. She has no respect for me. I was just trying to teach her a lesson.*

And what kind of lesson have you learned?

"No," Timothy whispered, grabbing the sides of his head then resting a hand over his aching heart. "I can't. Don't ask me to."

"Timothy?" It was Amanda's voice now. He looked up and saw her crinkled forehead. "Are you all right?"

He glanced at the girl bouncing back and forth between the bed and the door, the same girl from Church. His latest convert. How could Amanda still care if he was all right? Oh, how he hated himself. Then again, what could Amanda have been so upset about? The girl was fully clothed. It was obviously a joke. "Go on." He waved his hand in the girl's direction. She ran from the room. Her footsteps clattered down the hall.

"I'm sorry, honey," he whispered, realizing this had been too cruel of a joke, even for him. "I don't know what I was thinking."

Her face tensed. "You never think about anyone but yourself. What would have happened if our daughters would've seen that girl in here?" She raised her fists and batted his chest, but her tiny protests were like flies buzzing around a bull's face. He grabbed her wrists.

She froze. "Oh, I know. They never would've gotten the chance to see her if you didn't want them to. One of your men would've made certain of it." Tears finally fell to her cheeks. Still she refused to blink.

He reached for her waist, and she pulled away from him. Anger boiled inside him, bubbling up to the surface. How dare she not forgive him when he humbled himself to her? How could she step all over his pride?

"Come back here!" He trailed her down the hallway to the guest bathroom where she slammed the door in his face. He jerked away just in time to avoid a broken nose. "It was a joke, Amanda. You should realize that. How does it feel to be made a fool of?"

"What's that supposed to mean?"

"What exactly have you been blabbing around Redemption about Jonathan Young to people like Jolie Needham, for instance?"

"Is that what this is all about? Your insane infatuation with Gena? I don't believe it. You're still afraid he's going to come back one day and rescue her, aren't you?"

"I'm upset, Amanda, and getting madder by the minute. I'm wondering what else you've been telling Jolie."

"I didn't tell anyone else anything. Jolie caught me in a fib, that's all. A couple of fibs really. She is smart. Wouldn't it be strange if sweet little Jolie was the one to finally reveal you to the rest of Redemption? And to the world."

Her laughter sounded mad and her body pulsated against the door.

"What fib, Amanda?"

"The first time she came to Church, she caught me in a slip of the tongue about her father. Smart. So smart. And that girl of hers-"

"Amanda." He rapped against the door and twisted the handle. "Open up."

"Forget it. Not with that look in your eyes."

He ran his hand through his hair and stared at the wooden impasse between them. "Well? What was all this talk about the funeral being closed casket? Why did Jolie need to know that?"

She cleared her throat. "I swear to you no one knows your dirty little secret. I covered all my bases. Jolie is satisfied with what I told her. She's not up to anything. I promise you. And neither am I."

"You better be telling me the truth." Timothy felt the threads of reason loosening inside him, unraveling. "I might need to do something drastic if things don't start running much smoother around here."

"Don't, Tim. Don't you dare try to do to her what you almost did to Jonathan."

"Who else has Jolie been talking to?"

Silence.

"Amanda." He calmed himself and faced the door. "Either you tell me or I'll have Peter find out."

"The Krenshaws. That's it. Far as I know. I doubt they've said much to her. I know Barbara is loyal. And Aiden...well, you know he wouldn't risk violating your agreement."

"Aiden?" Timothy gritted his teeth. "I'll just have to see about that." He rapped on the bathroom door. She gasped and seemed to pull away.

He smiled, knowing exactly what had to be done. He returned to the bedroom and squinted into Amanda's vanity mirror. He smoothed his hand through his disheveled locks, bringing a distinctly human look to his eyes. From down the hall, a lock disengaged with a click. He listened with amusement to Amanda's scuffling footsteps.

After awhile, she appeared in the doorway. "Why do you always have to make me cry before you'll believe I'm sorry?"

He stared at her. "What are you talking about?"

"My heart can't take much more of this. You don't love me. You couldn't love me." She threw her face into her hands. "Don't you remember how it used to be? There was no one in the world who could separate us."

He couldn't help wondering what kind of scars he was leaving on her heart with his obsession with Gena. *God, help me. I just want this one thing. This one person, and that's it. Just give me Gena, and you can have everything else.*

But I want you Timothy, the soft voice said more firmly than it had ever said anything else.

Timothy swatted his eyes with his sleeve. "No one will ever separate us, Amanda. That's a promise you can take to your grave."

"What am I really here for? Why do you keep me in your life?"

"You're the mother of my children."

"And what am I to you? I'd be very careful, Timothy Winston Caine, of the things you do in God's name."

"Blasphemer!" He raised his hand to slap her, and a tremor coursed down his arm. He recoiled. How could he even think of hitting her when she had never done anything to deserve his wrath?

"Maybe you never did love me. Maybe you never will, even if I spend my life trying to please you."

"But you'll stay with me for the sake of the children, and for the sake of the church. You know you will. You'll stay for my sake too." He wanted to say he loved her. He wanted to tell her he didn't mean to hurt her, that he was powerless to stop himself, but he knew it would be a lie. He could stop himself, but he wanted Gena more than he wanted to be fair.

She didn't answer, and he let her walk away. Maybe, he figured, he owed her that much.

Chapter Fourteen

Aiden raised a hand to his red-rimmed eyes and squinted into the porch light while Jolie cowered on his door stoop. "What time is it?" He glanced at his wrist, but he wasn't wearing a watch. He hadn't shaved in days, and his dark hair curled haphazardly behind his ears. His dark silk pajamas reflected gray-green in the light over his tanned legs.

Jolie swallowed, more to clear her mind than her throat, and glanced back at the taxi in the driveway, wondering if she had made a mistake in coming here.

A warm hand touched her arm, and she jerked her head. Aiden held her, looking more alert now.

"He's getting ready to leave again," she blurted, "Richard. I think Timothy's got something bad planned for him. I found a plane ticket for Sacramento in his desk drawer with a note to remember to take his gun. I didn't know Richard had a gun. I searched the whole house over twice for one. I was just looking for some tape to seal a letter to my mother. I know." She waved her free hand, more as a nervous reflex than anything else. "I know I shouldn't bother trying…And then Richard ran out of the house just an hour ago after an emergency phone call from Peter. He took Emma with him. Said he didn't want me running off with her while he was gone. He didn't take the ticket yet, but…"

He squeezed her arm. "Come in. You'll catch cold standing out there ranting like that."

She tightened her shawl around her shoulders as his large hand settled onto the small of her back. "You think Emma is safe? I ran after the car, yelling for him to stop."

He drew her into the foyer. "She'll be fine. She's his only tie to you. He wouldn't ruin that." The door whispered closed behind them. In the living room weakly lit by the lawn and garden lights shining through the window, she worried she had woken Barbara. "I was afraid you'd never speak to me again."

"Nonsense," he whispered. She took a seat on the end of the couch, hoping he'd sit in the recliner opposite her. He glanced at the cushion beside her then looked like he thought better of sitting there, and slumped into the recliner. "So, what's this all about now?" he whispered.

Tears stung her eyes. *Dear God, please help me.*

When he leaned toward her, his expression seemed edged with irritation. "You know, you remind me of your mother's ghost. Your hair is almost black like hers. Your feet are barely audible on the floor when you walk. But you're stronger than your mother, aren't you? Why is that? Is it God?"

Jolie opened her mouth to speak, but nothing came out.

Aiden hung his head. "Poor Gena. Trapped in that horrible house with that horrible woman the reverend thinks takes good care of her. You won't buckle under the reverend's heavy hand, will you?"

Jolie shook her head. "No," she whispered, "God help

me I won't. But do you think Richard's supposed to kill someone for Timothy on this trip?"

"I always took a gun too. It's just for Timothy's protection. Richard will be helping guard him. I never used mine. Richard won't be expected to actually use it either."

Jolie let her shoulders relax a little. "What if Emma finds it?"

"She won't if you couldn't."

"But what if—"

Aiden touched her shoulder. "You're going to have to pray about that. Warn Emma about it. That's the best you can do. I'm so sorry you have to go through this."

Jolie let out a long sigh.

"You asked me once to help you get your mother out of there, and I told you no. You want to know why?"

Jolie nodded and ran her hand up her arm, feeling a sudden chill.

Aiden took a deep breath and gazed across the living room. A light came on at the top of the stairs.

"Everything all right down there?" Barbara's razor-sharp voice filled the room.

"Yes, fine. Just fine. Go back to bed. I'll be up soon."

She huffed. "Fine."

A door slammed in the upstairs hallway.

Aiden touched Jolie's chin. He began whispering again. "You're not going to like what I tell you."

She tried to smile, but her lips curled back, revealing her gums. She raised a hand to her face then snatched it back to her lap.

"Timothy's infatuation with Gena extends back almost eight years. It wasn't long after you left town that he moved here and started eyeing Reverend Lamont's place in the pulpit." Aiden put his elbow on one knee and lowered his head into his hand. "Oh, God, Jol, don't hate me, please."

"I won't hate you." Jolie touched his forearm. He looked up, his glazed eyes brimming with hope and desperation.

"You have to believe me when I tell you I never knew how power hungry the reverend was. I didn't have a strong relationship with God back then so my eyes were clouded like Richard's are now." He gazed across the room. "Even now my faith isn't as strong as it needs to be."

"Please..." Jolie took his hand. "You can tell me anything. I won't be mad at the man you used to be."

He sighed and ran a hand through his dark curls. Pain flashed across his face like lightening. "I remember the moment like it happened yesterday. The moment that changed my life forever. I was sitting beside the Caines, listening to one of Reverend Lamont's sermons. It was one about how regardless of the level of suffering we experience on Earth, our pain is just a whisper of what Christ suffered on the cross.

"Timothy had been trying to get me interested in his business ideas. I had been over to his place for lunch a few times. He had a lot of connections, people he had me meet in secret. But he needed some key people to help him make things work in Redemption. He was bored with the sermon, but he was there to keep up appearances as a reverend himself. And your parents were in mourning over your absence. I was a little in mourning myself. You never knew how much I thought about you after you left—or while you were here."

Jolie shivered and glanced toward the stairs, thinking she had heard Barbara. But no one was there. She faced Aiden again.

The same worry creased his face. He started to stand as he peered through the darkness. The soft sound of snoring filtered downstairs, and his shoulders visibly relaxed. He slumped back into the recliner with a long sigh.

"Well," Aiden continued, "Timothy spotted your mother, and something changed in him. He started coming to more and more of Reverend Lamont's sermons to sneak glances at her, watching her smile in adoration at your father and lean against him for support before looking up at Reverend Lamont as though lost in deep contemplation over the man's words. Finally anger filled Timothy. It was all over his face. Jealousy greener than your pretty eyes. I believe it was then that he decided to take Reverend Lamont's place and your father's place, and it was then that I started working for him. Jonathan's interest in missionary work gave Timothy all the opportunity he needed to start becoming a part of Gena's life through working with your father. And it gave me a chance to practice my legal skills in ways that stretched the imagination, so to speak."

"So, how did Reverend Lamont die?"

Aiden shook his head. "I can speculate all I want, but there's no proof."

"You think Timothy killed him?"

"Maybe had him killed. Maybe, but I don't know."

"And my father? Do you think Timothy killed my dad?"

Aiden blinked several times. "I do, but I have no proof. Barbara knows something though. I know she does. But she refuses to tell me. She was there that day when the ambulance took your father away." Aiden looked down at his hands.

"Who prescribes all those pills for my mother. What's his name?"

Aiden shrugged. "I've tried to find out. But no one knows."

"Where does he live?"

"No one knows."

"Why my mother? What is it about her that makes Timothy want her badly enough to destroy her and everyone else around her?"

He wouldn't meet her eyes until she touched his hand. Then he looked at her the way he had when she and Richard had come over for dinner. Those first butterflies swam through her all over again. "Your mother's faith intimidates him. It took me years to put my finger on it. He's partly jealous of her, jealous that she still loves Jesus after all the suffering she has endured, is still enduring. He'll never admit it, but it's the reason he never teaches directly from the New Testament about the story of Jesus' life. Timothy is in awe of her, because deep down, he doesn't love God enough to give Gena up, but Gena loves God enough to give up everything else. Over the years, his obsession has slowly shifted away from God and onto Gena. He almost sees winning her love as his redemption."

"You make it sound like I should be pitying him."

"If you can't love your enemies, what good's love, right? Believe it or not, he suffers even more than he makes your mother suffer because he carries his wounds in his soul."

"You talk about him like you know him better than he knows himself."

Aiden rose and turned his back to her. His shoulders bristled.

"Aiden, what's wrong?"

"Maybe we should talk about Richard now."

She reached for his arm and tugged until he sat beside her on the couch.

His stare darkened. His nostrils flared.

She scooted back from him.

He raised his hands. "I know, Jol. I won't touch you. We're just going to talk. We're going to be friends, as good of friends as you will let us be. So, tell me about the plane ticket."

The soft lights of a passing car streamed in from the window behind the couch, illuminating the corner of a pillow sham. The edge of an end table. One side of Aiden's fierce jaw. She wondered if he could see her as well as she could see him in that instant, if he could see the tears glistening along her cheeks. "I misjudged you. I was looking for an excuse to compare you to Richard. But your faith is stronger than you realize…than I realized. God has helped you forgive Reverend Caine, but I still…"

He leaned back. "Don't be sorry. I wouldn't say I forgive the man. I just understand him. Maybe because deep down in my heart of hearts I am still like him."

She touched his hand. His stare intensified. Then he snapped his head away. "You see?" He let out a clipped laugh. "Right there. I can't apologize enough for that. It's as strong as what Timothy feels for your mother, but I can't seem to change it. And I wonder if Timothy can change how he feels. I can't shut off my feelings for you. I pray for them to stop, but maybe Timothy prays for the same thing."

"Maybe I shouldn't be here, but I have no one else to turn to. Amanda isn't any help. All the people at Church raise their eyebrows at me if I even so much as question any aspect of Timothy's sermons or his business affairs anymore. And Barbara is Timothy's head cheerleader. Now Richard keeps performing these disappearing acts. I just…"

"Richard isn't acting any differently than I used to act. I'd leave in the middle of the night for those long so-called mission trips or business trips. Only difference is, Barbara always knew about them. I didn't need to hide anything from her. She was in on it before I even knew there was an it. I started getting suspicious of Timothy's business practices, of how Barbara always seemed to be making excuses for him, covering for him. I knew I stretched some boundaries, but I had no idea how many Barbara was stretching behind my back."

He glanced in the direction of the stairs and blinked. He seemed to be studying the darkness. "It was like he was a drug for her. Whenever he was around, she was a different woman. She was intoxicated with him."

"Please tell me more about the trips. What did you do when you went away?"

He cleared his throat. "We traveled to different locations all over the world. We were never in the same place twice. Timothy always had a different name, but the routine was the same. We went into large Churches, schools and hospitals and any other place where he could draw a large crowd, but without publicity. Always without publicity. Course we'd have our own cameras. Just to make the people feel Timothy was bigger than their petty problems. Any place that had been hit with some kind of disaster. The people would come out, usually in droves and always with needs they hoped would be met by *giving to the ministry what God laid on their hearts* as Timothy always calls it. We'd hand out religious pamphlets and other items, do a little miraculous healing, preferably on someone disabled who was hit hardest by the disaster, and then he'd deliver a sermon that would shake loose any residual money from their pockets. He'd have them throwing it into the collection plates like it was a terrible disease of which only he could free them. As though not giving more was the reason they had suffered the disaster in the first place.

"But I promise you your father never knew what was happening. He never found out about the offshore accounts or the phony charities through which Timothy funneled the money. Mostly I believe your father only traveled with us to keep his mind off having lost you and to do something for God. It was his way of coping, of forgetting about his problems and focusing on other people.

"Barbara did all the paperwork after a certain point. I

learned to stop asking so many questions. She kept asking me how I could question the integrity of a reverend. That one always got me, at least up until things started getting too big for her to hide by standing in front of each problem. I started doing a little research behind her back. When Timothy found out, he tried to blackmail me like he tried to blackmail your father when Jonathan told him he thought God was calling him back home to be with his wife. But he didn't intimidate me. I stole some incriminating paperwork. I have it hidden away in case he ever decides to come after me."

She gazed into his eyes, eyes so unlike Richard's, and wondered how she could have ever disliked this precious man. "What is it? Give it to me. We can use it to get him to let my mother go."

He shook his head. He seemed to hesitate. His eyes shifted back and forth until he finally looked at her again. Was he hiding something? His forehead seemed to glisten with a light sheen of sweat. "It's not enough evidence to convict him of anything. It's only enough to keep him off my back. Besides, only the hand of God could make him give up your mother. And threatening him with legal action could only make him take her and run. And you'd never find her, just like she couldn't find you all those years she thought she had those investigators trying to track you down."

"Why doesn't he just take her and run now? What's there in Redemption for him?"

"You mean besides a good place to hide and a whole town that would swear to his good character?" He smiled. "He's a rat. He won't run unless you chase him. And he'll bite you if you corner him."

She glanced toward the stairs. Still no sign of Barbara.

Aiden touched her elbow, and she leaned into him, wanting to let the tears drown her. He wrapped his arms around her, arms she'd never have to fear.

Dear God, why is life so cruel? She forced herself to sit up and push away from him. He didn't move.

"Jol?"

She started to laugh, but nothing was funny anymore. Maybe it never would be again. She cupped his jaw. He closed his eyes and pressed his mouth against her hand. His lips brushed her palm. His hair tickled her wrist, and she fought the urge to draw him closer.

"I should go." She stood.

His face grew stern. "Watch out."

"What?" She looked behind herself.

"So that you don't corner him. He'll hurt you. I mean it." He pointed, and she wondered if he had meant to indicate the bruise on her collarbone. "Worse than Richard can."

"You knew?" She sat back down.

He nodded, putting his hands on his knees. "Richard will protect Reverend Caine's reputation with his life. Timothy will have it no other way if he's feeling confident enough in Richard to take him to Sacramento. He has a lot of connections there. He's grooming Richard for something. Best thing to do is keep quiet like me, and..." Aiden grasped her shoulders. She felt paralyzed by his gaze. "There's nothing you can do to help your mother, but you could think about Emma. Is she safe with Richard? My offer still stands."

Jolie pictured the rest of her life. The next countless nights she would spend in bed beside Richard, listening to him snore, being comforted by the sound because it would mean he was sleeping and not getting ready to roll over and climb on top of her. The days she'd spend taking care of Emma while she glanced over her shoulder, hoping Richard wasn't glaring at her from the doorway. The afternoons when Emma would come home from school, and Jolie would have to hurry and get herself cleaned up so Emma wouldn't see what Richard had done.

Aiden bit his lip. He grimaced and slid the back of his hand across his mouth.

"I just want to get my mother out of that house." She leaned toward him. "If you could help me get her out of there, I'd leave Redemption with you."

"And if your husband pressed child abuse charges?"

"But you said I should think of Emma's safety. Why would you offer to…? Why would he do that? How could he do that?" Jolie suddenly understood what Aiden was trying to show her. They could leave Redemption together. They were free, but Emma and Gena were not. He was offering her the only freedom he could. "Reverend Caine would help Richard get sole custody of Emma, wouldn't he?"

"And don't forget that he's your mother's legal guardian. If we did somehow manage to escape Redemption with your mother, the police would hunt you down and bring her back."

"But if I just had some evidence against him, to prove someone is helping him poison my mother with all those drugs. Or if I had some paperwork to discredit his business so he'd go to prison." Aiden flinched. "I already know he's giving my mother Thorazine which is way too strong for what is supposedly wrong with her. But that isn't enough. Not hardly."

Aiden wouldn't look her in the eyes. She hated the dawning realization that she had been trapped since the day she had left home with Richard.

"What's wrong, Jolie?" It was Aiden's soft voice again. "Jolie? You look like you've seen a ghost." His hand pressed her shoulder. She felt dizzy, but too angry to faint.

"If I just had some incriminating evidence against him that he killed my father or Reverend Lamont or had them killed. If I could just prove Richard killed that Rakes guy. If I just…"

"But you don't, and you never will. They all clean up after each other. Peter, Timothy, Barbara, and now Richard. Even Edmond, not that I think he's just the reverend's hired help. And others too. In other places across the country. They exchange favors."

Jolie's eyes watered. "So there's no hope? No hope at all?"

Aiden sighed. "Before I met you, I thought about killing myself."

Jolie said nothing, replaying the words in her mind, trying to determine if she had heard them correctly.

"You want to know why?"

She stared blankly at him, unable to move.

"I was making more money than ever before. I had a bunch of people I called friends." He blinked away tears. "But, I was very unhappy with myself. When I told Barbara I was getting out of the business, she grew bitter toward me. She started telling everyone I had retired. The money either helped drive the wedge between us, or it helped reveal the wedge already there. I started to stay out late at night to avoid the tense moments at home. One night, I came home early with the thought of rekindling our sex life and found her in bed with another man. That night, in the bathroom, I had a gun to my head. I was going to pull the trigger when I...I had this feeling, almost like a vision, that if I killed myself, I'd miss out on meeting someone who might fill that hole in my heart."

Jolie raised her hand as he leaned toward her. The look of rejection that crossed his face made her wish she had thrown her arms around him instead. But she kept her hand raised, knowing she couldn't let him think they had any chance of being together. "Only Jesus can fill that void, Aiden. Not me. Not anyone else. Not even your wife is supposed to be able to fill it. No one is responsible for keeping you happy. Nobody can carry that burden for another person."

He turned away, and her heart ached for him.

"I'm sorry. I didn't mean to sound uncaring. I do care about you…so much more than I know I should."

He faced her. Heat rushed to her face, and she tried to distract him from what she knew he wanted to say. "What ever happened to the man you found Barbara with?"

"The affair ended as far as I know. We never talk about him. It's almost like it never happened."

"Have you forgiven her?"

He ignored her question. "I still wonder if I ever really wanted to be married to her. I've gotten so good at pretending not to be sad, but I've grown very tired of pretending. Seeing you again was like being reminded that I'm still alive. You dredged up feelings I thought I had buried. I keep trying to understand why you married that man. But then I have to ask myself why I married Barbara."

"He raped me," she blurted.

"What?"

"That's why I married him. I was too embarrassed. I thought it was my fault."

"Oh, honey." He slid his arms around her, and she went weak in his embrace, unable or maybe just unwilling to keep him at a distance any longer.

"When I'm fortunate, I feel numb. I don't think I knew what I wanted when I met him. It's strange, Aiden, it took the words of my little girl to make me understand what people really need. The day after Richard left that first time, we were having lunch next to a little dress shop in town. She had this great big smile on her face, ketchup at the corners of her mouth. We were celebrating being alive. Just being alive. I asked what she'd do if her father or me weren't around one day and she had to live with someone else. She got real serious, and I almost regretted asking the question, but then she answered with a little bit of a smile still on her face. 'I'd miss you, Mom,' she said, 'but I'd be all right because I will always have Jesus.' Can you believe that?"

His eyes grew round. His smile playful. "Why is it so easy to talk to you, Jolie Krenshaw?"

She leaped to her feet and backed up.

"Where are you going?"

He followed her through the darkness. She nearly tripped on the stairs leading back into the foyer.

"I'm sorry. I just keep wondering what it would be like to have someone like you as my wife. I've wondered that since I first saw your sweet face. There's an unshakable kindness in your eyes even when you're trying to push me away. I wonder what it would be like to be your husband."

The rush of movement toward her made her eke out a tiny scream. His arms entwined her waist.

"What makes Jolie Needham angry?" He pulled her toward him. "Does this make you angry?"

She tried to pull away. "Stop it," she hissed, trying to keep her voice down. "You're scaring me."

He kissed her hard on the mouth. She wrestled her lips away and twisted around. Puffs of his warm breath lapped at the back of her neck and threatened to drive her body into convulsions. But she struggled harder, remembering Barbara upstairs, and burst free from his embrace, her body tingling so badly she could hardly stand.

"Could money turn you into a hypocritical snob, Jolie?"

Feeling her way backward up the steps, she kept her gaze trained on him the best she could in the dark foyer. Surely, she knew he would never intentionally hurt her. Surely, she knew he was only hurting himself. She heard a sound like someone plopping onto the couch in the living room and knew it was Aiden.

"Please forgive me," he moaned as she headed out the door.

She stopped in the middle of the street, having charged past the taxi. The driver looked up with raised eyebrows. She stood there, knowing she should get into the cab, but unable to shake the mental image of Aiden inside the house. His eyes clenched shut as he tried to quiet his racing thoughts and desires. And when she saw him reaching out for her in the darkness, she hated that he had to reach out and find himself alone.

Chapter Fifteen

Standing in the shower with her back to the mirror and her head craning toward her reflection, Jolie gazed at two black fist-shaped bruises on her lower back, one on each side of her spine. One for each of Richard's fists. Punishment for her refusal to reveal her whereabouts when she had arrived home in the cab. And punishment for her impetuous plan to rescue her mother shortly after her return.

She had only packed one suitcase, mostly with Emma's things, but she hadn't gotten past the new alarm system the reverend had convinced Richard to have installed. She was a goner before she even got across the street, armed with that ridiculous crowbar from the garage she was going to use to break down Gena's front door if Mildred didn't cooperate. That stupid crowbar she should have used on Richard before he attacked her in the street. Before he had swatted Emma across the face for interfering. He hadn't threatened her with the gun, so maybe he wasn't keeping it at home.

Already the skin around Jolie's bruises had erupted in a

sunburst of yellowish green. Near the center of the bruise on her left side was the tiny divot made by his wedding ring. That side had stung the worst. Fire had ripped through her lower back, and her kidneys had pulsed with a deep and intimate soreness. Pressing her hands against the shower wall, she leaned forward into the cascading water. Hot streams soothed her aching muscles. Her entire back had become one elongated knot of agony while she had slept with a pillow wedged under her. *But how could Richard blame her for trying to rescue Gena from that house? The reverend was drugging her mother with high dosages of Thorazine. It was Timothy's fault Gena seemed psychotic.* "Dear Lord, how am I ever going to get out of here?"

Just run to me. Trust me, my child.

Harsh laughter erupted from the den.

She dropped her arms and stared down at her feet. She had thought they'd be all she needed to escape Richard. Why weren't they enough? And if Emma was so precious to her, why hadn't Jolie protected her daughter? Why hadn't that smack that had left Emma's lip a little puffy given Jolie the gumption to run? Why did she let Richard drag her back into the house and wrench the car keys out of her hand and fling her against the wall? Next time it would be harder to escape. Surely she knew that. If there would be a next time, and if she really did want to escape. But of course she wanted to escape. Why did she keep risking her daughter's welfare by remaining here? Was it that the unknown seemed even more frightening than her life with Richard? Could it be that fear superceded her love for her daughter and her mother? Or did she believe what Aiden had told her—that Richard would get custody of Emma if Jolie tried to escape with the child? She shook her head then raised it into the warmth streaming down upon her and tried to stretch out the knot in her back. Maybe she was no better than Richard.

More laughter from the den. Something welled inside her stomach and started into her throat. She spun away from the water and concentrated on the back wall of the shower as the urge to throw up subsided.

Richard's voice boomed from somewhere down the hallway, and Timothy answered from the den.

Jolie leaned back and took a deep breath to calm her racing concerns. She reached for the soap. Her hand froze when churning noises erupted from the pipes encased inside the shower wall. The stream of water now only trickled down the drain.

Something rustled outside the bathroom door. She grabbed the shower curtain and concentrated on the sound. "Jolie, that's enough. Don't you think you're clean yet?" Timothy laughed. Had she remembered to lock the door? Of course she had. Hadn't she?

She flinched and almost slipped when fists pounded the door. Her spine rammed the shower wall. Pain blazed in her back and wrapped prickly arms around her middle. She lunged forward and grabbed the shower curtain again, intending to wrap it around herself if the door suddenly flew open and Timothy burst inside.

Concentrating on the doorknob, Jolie waited. Two voices again in the distance. Timothy seemed to be back in the den with Richard.

"Just let me rinse off."

No answer.

Then a sound like someone crawling through the wall dragging a sledgehammer.

The water burst through the sprayer, first tepid then scalding. Jolie screamed and leaped out of the shower, pulling the curtain with her. She stumbled onto the rug at the foot of the sink, twisting it between her slippery feet.

"I hope you're not doing anything in there that you shouldn't be!" Timothy shouted from the den.

Laughter again. Then Emma's voice came like an eerie whisper from another world. "Dad? Where's Mom?"

Footfalls thundered down the hall after the sound of Emma's shifting voice. Was she crying out with joy or with panic?

"Stop! Stop!" Jolie grabbed her blouse and skirt off the ceramic counter and forced them over her sopping skin.

Timothy called from the den, "Emma, your mother's in the shower. She's trying to get clean, but her heart is still dirty."

Jolie stormed out of the bathroom, her clothes clinging to her. The dripping ends of her hair left a trail of droplets she was sure would spot the wood floor. But she wouldn't stop to wipe them now no matter how loud Richard would yell later.

She ran down the hall and into the den. Emma was cradling one of her stuffed animals and swaying back and forth, her watery gaze fastened on Timothy.

"Timothy Caine! I'll not have you abusing my daughter. I don't care who you think you are. You're nowhere near the man Reverend Lamont was. He'd be ashamed of you. In fact, sir, you don't even strike me as a reverend."

Timothy covered his mouth with his hand, but she could still see him smiling. He faced Richard. "Are you going to let your wife talk to me like that? To make such disgusting accusations?"

Richard's face flushed. His neck and arms flushed. Probably his entire body flushed. He stammered the beginning of what sounded like an apology as he stood babbling next to Peter.

Jolie hadn't heard Peter. Hadn't even known he was in the house until now. Nothing on his face or in his stance conveyed any expression. She instantly thought of a CIA operative, but the image wasn't amusing. Probably because, for all she knew, Peter was employed by the CIA. Peter arched an eyebrow at Richard, and Richard whipped toward Jolie. His eyes wide. He grabbed the first heavy object near him and lunged toward her.

She raised her hands before she realized his target. He stopped behind Emma. Hand raised in the air over the child's head and hesitated as tears filled his eyes. "Look what you're making me do."

"No, Richard! Oh, my God! What are you doing?"

Emma screamed, covering her head and running into her mother's outstretched arms.

"I'm sorry!" Jolie threw up her hands and lowered herself to her knees to catch Emma. "I'm sorry, Reverend Caine. I just forgot myself is all."

Timothy's eyes twinkled. A Cheshire grin unfurled across his lips.

Richard dropped the tape dispenser onto his desk. It sounded like a gunshot in the cramped room. Bewilderment and fear enveloped his face. His stubby hands quivered by his sides. His chest ballooned and fell.

She lifted Emma and fled the room.

Emma buried her face into Jolie's damp blouse. "Why did Dad do that?" The child kept asking between vicious sobs.

"Dear God, help me," Jolie whispered, "Help me now."

Jolie's mind raced with ideas, untested plans of escape. She could take Emma and flee in the night. The alarm would go off if she didn't disable it. Maybe a mallet would collapse its mechanical lungs. Or she could wait until Richard's next business trip to leave town. Maybe if Gena got free and came over while Richard was away, she could take her with her and Emma. They could take a taxi to the outskirts of town then hop a bus or two. But if Gena didn't get free at the right moment, she'd have to risk trying to come back for her as much as she abhorred the thought. But how far would they get anyway? Since Peter worked at the police station, if she passed a cop, she was certain Peter would get the word, and she'd be hauled back to Richard. Maybe Aiden knew the roads better. Maybe he would help her. That is if he'd even talk to her again. She could go straight for Chicago and report Richard to the authorities unless Timothy had that base covered too, so she would be just waltzing into a trap. If Timothy had the control Aiden implied the man had, then Jolie would be on the run for the kidnapping of her own child and possibly her mother.

Plastic rustled near the breakfast table, and Jolie twirled around, having forgotten she was standing in the kitchen. Emma sat at the table unwrapping a cheese sandwich. She held up her arm and offered her the sandwich with a stern look. "You have to eat, Mom. You don't want to end up like Mrs. Caine. You won't be able to stand up for us if there's nothing left of you."

"Emma." Jolie's eyes filled with tears. "How did you ever get so smart?" Jolie went to her daughter and took the sandwich. She laid it on the table and knelt to hug her little girl. Jolie felt Emma's heart racing when their bodies touched. Familiar pangs of self-pity filled Jolie. The child's face was flushed. Her freckled cheeks were on fire. But she was holding back her sobs now.

"My brave little girl."

Emma patted her mother's back and nestled her head against Jolie's shoulder. "My brave mom."

Jolie hugged Emma tighter before finally standing up. She put a hand to Emma's burning forehead. Emma's long red lashes fanned her palm. "Sit down, honey. I'll get you some juice to cool you down." She went to the cabinet to pull down a plastic cup. She filled it with juice and placed it in front of Emma. Then she went back to the counter and slapped her palms down, trying to get control of herself.

Jolie glanced at the bottle of Valium Richard insisted they keep behind the toaster for *emergencies*, as he called them. The faint urge for the taste of one of them licked at her insides, but she refused it. She hadn't taken one pill since their move to Redemption, and she had felt more alive in the pain than she had ever felt lulled in the arms of indifference.

"Honey, do you think I'm a hypocrite?"

Emma looked up from her chair. Furrowed forehead. How could Jolie be reduced to burdening her daughter? But she had to know what her daughter thought of her.

"A hypocrite is someone who pretends to be something they're not. Like when someone says they love you, but then doesn't protect you."

Emma raised her knuckles to her chin, propping her elbows on the table and stared forward. "You protect me as much as you can. But Jesus protects my heart. When it hurts, He makes it better like when you used to kiss my knee when I got a boo-boo."

"How does He do that, honey?"

Emma shrugged. "He just does. I don't know how. I just pray and know He'll be listening. He's always listening, even when I'm not praying with my head bowed like you showed me. He's going to get us out of this mess, Mom. And Grandma too. I just don't know how or when."

Laughter welled up in her throat along with fresh tears. Emma, an old sage speaking about the truths of the kingdom from the confines of an eight-year-old body. Jolie must be losing her mind.

Just like your mother, the gnawing voice whispered.

Jolie pulled up a seat beside her daughter.

"Don't cry, Mom." Emma wrapped her arms around Jolie's neck, and Jolie relaxed a little, enjoying the embrace a moment longer before withdrawing and wiping her eyes.

"Mommy's okay now, sweetheart. Don't worry. Things are going to be better. Mommy's going to make sure of it."

Jolie looked up, feeling someone's eyes on her from the doorway. Reverend Caine stared at her, the blue heat of his gaze like a blow torch.

He eased into a chair at the table. "Aren't you going to offer me something to drink? You wait on your little daughter like she's still a baby. You might as well wait on me too."

Emma jumped down from her chair and scurried out of the room.

"Smart little one. Shame she is just as emotional as her mother."

Jolie said nothing. Sounds of her daughter's feet thumping up the stairs calmed her. She scooted Emma's cup toward him. He narrowed his eyes at it.

"Brave little Jolie. One day all those emotions are going to get you into trouble too big for you to climb out of, even with those long legs of yours." He lifted the cup, sniffed, then plunked it down. Orange juice splashed the top of the table. Two long streams ran toward the sleeve and converged along the crack. Liquid dribbled onto the tiles below like raindrops.

Jolie took a seat next to him, biting her upper lip to control its trembling. "May I ask you a question, Reverend Caine?"

He leaned back in his chair. "You sure can. I always have time for my flock. Being a man of God is a nonstop occupation. Like breathing or raising children. Shame most people take the latter two for granted."

Jolie folded her hands on top of the table and tried to cool the anger she knew flamed in her face.

Someone thumped the doorjamb. Jolie looked up. Richard stood in the doorway. Desperation shadowed his face.

Timothy lifted his hand without turning away from Jolie. "Richard, I'm having a rather pleasant conversation with your wife. I think we talked about everything we needed to tonight. I'll see you tomorrow in Church. And don't worry, I'm not disappointed in you."

Richard wavered in the doorway before leaving. Jolie thought of Emma, and tried not to worry. She had to focus on keeping things from getting worse.

Timothy grazed Jolie's elbow with the back of his fingers. His overgrown nails snagged her skin. She winced, snatching her arm off the table. "How did Reverend Lamont die?"

He bent toward her face. She leaned back to avoid the warmth of his breath. Lines sprawled all across his face and spilled into deep wrinkles that deepened further when he grinned. His eyes sparkled like jewels. For a moment, Jolie thought his skin might tear loose at the seems along those deep wrinkles, that the fleshy mask he wore might peel free to reveal the monstrous face beneath it. "How did Reverend Lamont die?" she repeated.

He leaned back and folded his arms. "A tragedy really. The same thing that happened to your father. A heart attack."

Jolie watched his eyes. His dark blue gaze so steady. Too steady.

"I know how you admired Reverend Lamont. But when you leave home and don't call for years, things change. People die. And parents go insane with worry. Have you ever considered the possibility that your father died of a broken heart?"

Jolie stood up, pushing out her chair and felt her forehead. Her skin was so hot it seemed scalding. Worse than Emma's.

"Sit down, Jolie." Timothy's voice floated over her like in a dream. Then riding at her heels, it boomed. "Jolie, sit down! We're not done here. I will be heard. I am your reverend."

Jolie fell backward, not intending to resume her seat, but doing it anyway. Her spine smacked the back of the chair, and she veered sideways wanting to cry out from the blinding pain it sparked in the bruises on her lower back.

She squirmed away from the bars pressing against her.

Timothy grabbed one leg of her chair and dragged her closer to him. The floor screamed in protest as the chair legs slid across it. Fresh waves of pain washed over her, and her vision grayed, but Timothy's blurry face materialized again. His breath was hot against her cheek. The sour stench of it was like a moldy draft. But she couldn't scoot away because of the giant bee stings shooting through her back when she tried to even breathe. He whispered into her ear. "The way you're feeling, dear, I'm surprised *you* haven't had a heart attack."

Something definite flashed in his eyes. He had dangled something long enough for her to see it, but not long enough for her to understand it. *Dear God, is there something wrong with me? How can I pity this man the way Aiden seems to pity him? Surely, he has no pity for my mother.* But as Aiden had reminded her, if people can't love their enemies, what makes love so special? Anyone can love his friends.

Still, she couldn't bring herself to love this man.

Chapter Sixteen

Aiden stood dressed in a dark blue suit by the dining table, looking more handsome and more irritated than Jolie had ever seen him look. He tugged on his tie to loosen it and pulled it free from his neck. He tossed it on the table and folded his arms. "Jolie, what a pleasant surprise," he finally said, sarcasm sharpening his words.

Jolie fought the urge to cry. She had never heard him sound so much like Richard.

"She's worried, Aiden. Have a little sympathy." Barbara crossed her legs and arched her brows as though to make a point. "There was a note on the kitchen table this time. Richard's left again."

Emma giggled from one of the spare bedrooms down the hall, and one side of Aiden's mouth lifted in a smile. Jolie's heart leaped at the sight of it. Maybe he was just hurt. Maybe he didn't hate her. Maybe he would still help her.

He kicked off his dress shoes by the fireplace and looked up at Jonathan's portrait. He rubbed his hands together in front of the dying fire then added another log before plopping into the recliner opposite them. "Seems Barbara can't say enough complimentary things about this new partnership between your husband and the reverend. Seems to me she forgets a few things about what it was like for us when I worked with him." He lifted the newspaper on the table beside his chair and shook the pages out before disappearing behind it.

Barbara rolled her eyes. "Don't listen to him. He forgets how much we lost when he stopped working for Timothy. And not just financially, but spiritually too. Any luck at the courthouse today?"

"For the last time, I'm not trying to get my old job back. I just want to lend a hand where it's needed."

"Yeah, sure. I know what you're digging around there for with your old buddies. You think I'm blind?"

"I think you see everything," he snapped. "So, when will Richard call you?"

Jolie looked at him. He had lowered the paper and was staring numbly at her.

"He probably won't. I mean he didn't last time." She blinked hard and focused on the hands she clasped in her lap. "But he's different now. He's...Well..." Jolie let the tears fall. The sound of rustling newspaper made her lift her head. Aiden's face tensed. Then he snapped the paper back up over his face.

"He did something, well, almost did something to Emma." Jolie sniffed and cleared her throat. When she looked again, Aiden's face had softened.

"What could he have possibly done?" Barbara leaned to put a hand on Jolie's shoulder.

Jolie tried to calm herself. "He..." She massaged her throat with her jittery hand.

"Listen here, girl. The reverend will make a better man

of your husband. You should be happy. Every time Richard returns from a trip, he's going to be a better man."

Jolie stared into Barbara's muddy eyes. "He tried to hit Emma last night. Not a slap across the face, but much worse. I was in the shower. I heard him and the reverend in the den. When I went in something wasn't right. Emma was just standing there when I yelled at Reverend Caine. Richard grabbed a tape dispenser and lunged at her. There was something in his eyes I've only seen when he looks at me on the very worst occasions. It was pure evil. And that night, he told me if I ever tried to leave him, he'd make sure I never saw Emma or my mother again."

Aiden stomped his foot. Jolie looked at him. His face was a hot sheet of rage. He ran his quivering fingers through his hair and averted his gaze. "Why won't you let someone do something?"

Was he talking to her or to Barbara? Jolie wondered.

Barbara's voice was soft, but not a whisper. "Is something else wrong? Is Timothy not paying Richard enough money?"

"Barbara." Aiden slapped the arm of the recliner and stood up. Jolie flinched. "You'll have to excuse her. She can be more coarse than she's worth sometimes."

Jolie folded her hands together in her lap and looked down.

"Jolie won't you please let me help you?" Aiden begged.

Barbara narrowed her eyes at him, but said nothing. He matched her stare.

"I watch Mom from the window sometimes because the nurse won't let me in. I know what's wrong with her, and I know the reverend is keeping me from seeing her because he knows I could change things between them. He wants to keep her on those drugs, but it'll only destroy her mind. Then what good will she be to him."

"Your poor mother has a chemical imbalance," Barbara said. "It's not always safe for people to be around her. You're letting your emotions get the better of you. We as God-fearing women can't let our emotions dictate what we think. The devil will use that to confuse us."

"You shouldn't torture yourself." Aiden stepped closer. "Legally, there's nothing you can do if the reverend decides he doesn't want you seeing her."

"Stop coddling her. She's got to grow up. She can't keep thinking with her heart. She has to use her mind." Jolie didn't have to look to know Barbara's eyes were bulging.

"Mostly," Jolie continued, ignoring Barbara, "she just sits on the sofa staring at what I think are photo albums. I can't see too well from the window and it must be soundproof because when I bang on it, she doesn't even look up. Sometimes, she starts laughing or crying and won't stop until the nurse runs in with a syringe."

"You're right," Aiden said. "Your mother doesn't need medication."

"That's enough." Barbara stood up.

"Well, you know I'm right. She's only crazy when she's high. And she never tried to kill herself. She fell off that balcony by accident. She slipped in the rain. Tim was the one who convinced her she jumped on purpose so he could get custody of her, so she'd sign herself over to him to get out of being committed to that facility."

Barbara leaned over him, gritting her teeth. "I can make things difficult for you, Aiden, if you're not careful. I know where certain precious documents you keep hidden are located. I could put them into certain hands very easily if I wanted to do so."

Aiden folded his arms. "You'd be bringing yourself down with me," he hissed.

She turned away before Jolie could see the expression on her face.

"Bringing you down?" Jolie asked.

Aiden shifted his gaze.

Barbara finally sat down. She squeezed Jolie's hand. "Don't listen to him. He means well, but avoiding the truth about your mother's illness or trying to simplify her condition will only set you up for disappointment in the long run. There are so many things that I can help you with, dear. So many things we can talk through together. I want you to know that it's more than all right for you to come over here anytime."

"Just tell me, Barbara, how can it be good to leave your wife without telling her where you're going and when you'll be back?"

"It's all right." Barbara patted Jolie's hand. "It takes some getting used to, but I for one used to take advantage of Aiden's time away. Go shopping. Go out to lunch with your little girl. Sleep in. Enjoy the time to be alone. Don't worry. I'm not worried, and I should know about worry."

Jolie glanced at the table in front of the sofa. Little cakes sat on a plate under a glass lid. The thought that they might be poisoned or drugged crossed her mind.

"Go ahead if you like, dear. They're rum cakes."

Jolie shook her head. "Tell me about the reverend's business. What is it exactly that my husband is involved in."

Barbara leaned back. She blew a puff of starched blond hair off her forehead. "God has anointed Reverend Caine's business, but to an outsider who doesn't understand the call on Timothy's life, some of the aspects of his business might be difficult to accept. Basically, he travels the world, offering broken people the opportunity to get back under God's grace. You and me, Jolie, we don't need to know where our husbands are because God doesn't need us to know. It's all about faith.

Have faith in God that your husband will only become a better man through all this. Support him by waiting patiently for his return, and don't run him through a barrage of questions when he gets home."

Barbara reached over and selected a cake from underneath the glass. She bit into it slowly, eyeing Aiden, then crammed the whole thing into her mouth and swallowed, her throat bulging like she were a snake consuming a rat. "You do want one, Jolie." Barbara bore her gums as she smiled. She lifted the glass, and Jolie's stomach clenched.

"I'm not very hungry."

"Guess that's how you stay so slender like your mother."

Jolie's stomach tightened.

"Goodness, Jolie, you look pale all of a sudden." Barbara's breath smelled sour like alcohol and mouthwash, or maybe the odor was only from the rum cake.

Cupping the armrest, Jolie leaned back. "Why'd you cover for Amanda so she could visit me that day at my house while Richard was at work?"

Barbara stared at her as though she were studying the identity of a distant object. She brushed her frizzy pale hair back over her shoulder and narrowed her beady brown eyes. "She said she wanted to set you straight about a few things." Barbara grinned wide. Her little animal teeth gleamed white. "Did she set you straight, dear?"

Jolie suddenly realized why she had come to see Barbara. Deep down, Barbara wanted Jolie to know the truth about Timothy. That was why Barbara had allowed Amanda to visit Jolie. That was why she wasn't demanding that Aiden leave. Barbara just didn't want to be the one to reveal the truth and betray Timothy or be seen as the one betraying him. She didn't want Timothy with Gena anymore than Jolie did.

Jolie started to laugh and clapped a hand over her mouth.

Barbara frowned. The skin between her eyes didn't wrinkle under the strain of her expression. Jolie grabbed her chest, doubling over with laughter. Tears poured from her eyes. Barbara gasped. But that only made Jolie laugh harder, catching her breath in large gulps.

"What's wrong with her?" Aiden eased onto the sofa and put a gentle hand on Jolie's lower back. "What's so funny?"

Then the jaws clamped tight. The pain sunk deep. Jolie screamed and thrashed. Aiden tightened his grip. Then, as though realizing the pain he was causing, jerked back his hand. "Barbara, do something."

"I am doing something," she said, her voice flat.

Jolie looked up and saw Barbara had taken another cake from the plate. Her eyes were glazed as she licked the yellow frosting from the dessert.

Heat flushed Jolie's body. Jolie leaned into Aiden, and he slid a hand down her side. She flinched, but didn't scream. Aiden scooted back from her and placed one finger on her lower back. She shrieked. "Jolie? Why does that hurt?"

She moaned and tried to stand up. But he was too quick for her. He lifted the back of her blouse.

"No, don't," she pleaded, hardly able to catch her breath from the pain throbbing around her lungs.

"Barbara. Look what that monster did." He grunted, rose from the sofa, and stormed across the room. He slapped the mantel and spun toward her. His eyes flashed green like the eyes in the portrait above him. For a moment, the two faces held the same intensity, and the same secrets.

Barbara lifted another cake and stared at the fireplace, saying nothing.

Aiden sat back down next to Jolie. "Let me ask you something. Don't you think it's a little strange that there would be a suspicious death in Redemption for the first time in seven years?"

"You're talking about Mr. Rakes, and you mean since my father's death, don't you?"

"And there was Reverend Lamont's the year before that. But those are the only three I know about in all the years I've lived here."

Barbara clapped her hands together. "Now I can't even begin to imagine what you must be getting at, Aiden. This poor girl comes here for solace, and you go out of your way to frighten her, to reduce her to tears and tantrums."

"Something strange is going on in Redemption, has been going on since Timothy took Reverend Lamont's place," Aiden continued.

"What is with you too?" Barbara laughed, putting her hand on Jolie's knee. When the embrace tightened, the clammy jeweled fingers felt like tadpoles slithering across her skin. Jolie gagged once. Then the urge to throw up left her.

"We've never had a murder in Redemption. That poor man probably wandered out there drunk to kill himself. Evidently, he hadn't a loved one left in the world."

Jolie glared at Barbara. "Who said anything about murder?"

"Who knows what exactly happened to him? Wild animals could've dug that shallow hole the reporters called a grave."

"Barbara, that's ridiculous," Aiden snapped.

"Look, I didn't want to tell you this because it feels so much like gossip, and you know the evils of gossip, right Jolie? Well, I met that man at Church, and he wasn't exactly a steady Churchgoer. He complained of having problems at home, of going through a painful divorce. I even smelled alcohol on his breath. I have a trained eye for human suffering. Probably from the years I've worked with Amanda counseling people. Trust me. The man was riddled with guilt and desperation. He probably just decided there was no hope and killed himself. Who cares how a little dirt got dumped on him?"

Jolie tried to stare at Barbara with the same intensity Aiden had used earlier. "And during Timothy's next sermon, I'm sure we'll here all about the danger that strangers are bringing to his town. That'll probably make the women at Church even more suspicious of me."

Barbara's lips flattened. Her eyes gleamed, and Jolie read something in them. Barbara was glad the truth was coming out. She was even satisfied with the way she had pretended to disagree with them. It had been the way Barbara had asked the ridiculous question, *Who cares how a little dirt got dumped on him?* That had made her motives transparent.

Barbara clutched Jolie's hand. "Now, listen to me, girl, Reverend Caine is the finest man I've ever met. I have a feeling if you told him how you've been feeling, he'd settle all this for you very quickly and you'd feel a lot better. Sometimes, as women, we can be overly emotional about things that are hard for us to understand. Go talk to him. He'll be at Church this evening until very late. I'll tell him you're coming. He'll talk to you, and you'll see I'm right."

Standing up, Jolie shook her head. "Emma's life could be in danger, yet I'm afraid to leave the source of that danger because I fear what will happen if I do." Jolie gazed into Aiden's eyes, hoping he could help. "Sometimes, I don't see Richard get in or out of bed. He's more like a ghost than a husband. I don't know what to think about the late night conferences at the church. Sometimes they last into the early morning, and I'm not allowed to attend. I'm trapped, and I'm probably going to meet my untimely end too, unless someone who knows something finally opens up to me and gives me a fighting chance."

Barbara glanced at Aiden. Jolie read something in the woman's expression. Aiden was biting his lip and looking down at his fists.

"Have you been listening closely to the reverend's sermons, Jolie? Don't you realize he's working with Richard mainly to help him be a better husband and father? Richard isn't exactly the gifted business man he thinks he is. The reverend cares deeply about all of us. Even your sick mother hasn't depleted his patience."

Jolie tried to steady her voice. "He doesn't deserve to be called Reverend. He doesn't teach about Christ. There's no New Testament in the pew Bibles at his so-called church. And the way the people always seem hypnotized by him. It's like they can't think for themselves. Like they're possessed. It's more like a cult than a church."

"I get that same feeling," Aiden whispered back, "ever since he replaced the steeple."

Barbara snapped her fingers at him as though she were trying to silence a child. "You're not helping, and the reverend just might find out." But the gleam of satisfaction in Barbara's eyes belied her threat.

Chapter Seventeen

The house seemed wrapped in a mist of shadows. Jolie blinked hard to clear the tendrils of sleep from her mind, but they only crept deeper inside, coiling their spindly limbs around her heart. She slunk from bed and ambled toward the window. Richard's car was in the driveway. The floor mats were lying on the concrete. The trunk was up. And the yard hose lay nearby dribbling water down the driveway.

So, he had returned home. And he had needed to clean out the car. Why was that?

The smell of sausage and ketchup wafted into the room. A pan clattered onto the stove downstairs.

Jolie shook her head. She glanced back at the bed. Emma still slept on Richard's side, snoring softly, whistling lightly through her nose.

Outside, the landscaper Reverend Caine had recommended to Richard looked up at her as though he had sensed her appearance at the window. She raised her hand to wave, but he only nodded back before darting away.

Another one of Timothy's spies?

Church bells rang in the distance on her way to the shower. The Church of His Redemption. The name didn't quite make sense, she suddenly realized. Who was the he denoted by his? Christ? The Church of Christ's Redemption? That certainly didn't make sense. Christ is our redeemer, but he never needed redemption. She faced the bathroom mirror and pulled her pajama shirt up to the top of her ribcage. The bruises on her lower back had faded to a deep green, and her muscles ached less, but now whenever she would come to bed, she would sleep facing Richard.

Oh, well, the name is just another mystery to add to the collection of things that don't make sense around here.

Deciding against a shower, she left the bathroom, and followed a blooming sense of dread downstairs. At the living room window, she spotted Richard outside raking his hands through his hair beside the landscaper who kept tapping a baseball cap against his jean-clad leg while he spoke, his mouth moving fast and wide. The landscaper motioned in the direction of the car, but he could've been indicating the pile of leaves beside it. The lawn and leaf bags fluttered past them, but neither man looked up. Jolie raised a hand to the pane to knock, then decided against interrupting them.

She gazed down at the little Psalms book resting on the windowsill and lifted the book. Reverend Lamont had given it to her eight years ago before she had left town for Chicago with Richard. It had been the last time she had seen the dear man. He had looked so sad. Had he known she was leaving town? Had he known about Emma?

Her palms grew sweaty around the tiny book. This one little thing was the only material possession that meant anything to her, despite the many expensive gifts Richard had bought her over the years.

Why hadn't she seen through Richard's façade?

Oh, how her father had cried before she had left, shoulders rocking back and forth, his face buried in his hands just like he was praying, crying out to God to save her. Her mother had stood motionless at first. Tearless. All she had said was, "Jolie, if you should ever want to come home, you come on home, just don't bring him." Then she had flung her hand out at Richard, the father of the child inside her daughter's womb. The child Jolie thought her mother had known nothing about.

But there had been love in her parents' eyes too that day. Love Jolie could only understand now that she had a daughter. If only she hadn't been paralyzed with the fear of the unknown, the fear of what they might have thought about her if she had only told them what her mother had already known.

"Dear Jesus, take all these feelings away so I can think clearly."

Obey me, Jolie, and do what I've told you. Eventually those feelings will fade if you trust me instead of your emotions.

Emma ran past the archway with her puppet tucked underneath her arm. Jolie barely noticed the manic look on her daughter's face.

"Mom. Mom quick. Get the door. She's in trouble."

Jolie's mind snapped to attention. She wiped her eyes and skidded into the foyer.

Someone was trying to kick in the front door, she thought. Richard's voice boomed from outside, but he wasn't yelling yet. "Jolie, you dumb mule, let me in."

More kicking. Emma's feet scampered up the stairs. A door slammed in the distance. Jolie tensed at the sound then realized it had only been Emma.

Jolie grappled for the front door and flung it open. She

stepped back. The landscaper came inside first. The lolling head of a woman followed him. And Richard stormed in supporting the other side of the woman's limp body.

Jolie's heart raged, looking into the bruised face. "Mom, what have they done to you?

Jolie grabbed the wall to steady herself. Gena's wet and leaf-ridden clothes and hair reeked as though Gena had been lying in the gutter all week.

She lifted her head. Her red-rimmed eyes and swollen nose laced with a crust of blood made Jolie take a reflexive step back. Gena's voice sounded filled with gravel. "Don't be mad at your father. Deep down, he still loves me." Jolie gasped and reached for her mother, but Richard shoved his hip into her, making her stumble backward into his office.

"Mr. Needham. I'm very sorry, but I think we need to call the reverend," the landscaper said, supporting Gena as Richard approached Jolie.

"Of course I'm going to call him. I don't want her staying here."

He clamped his hands to Jolie's shoulders. Then everything made sense all at once.

"What did Timothy do to her?" Jolie begged.

He shoved her back when she tried to dart past. "Not for you to worry, sweetheart."

She skittered on her heels as he shoved her further into his office. "No, Richard. You can't lock me in here." She flung herself at him.

"Don't be a child, Jol. Do as I say." He shoved her harder, but she charged him again.

He stumbled into the mail table.

His fingers whispered past her waist as she charged into the living room. "Grab her! Don't let her near that woman!"

The landscaper stepped back from the sofa where he had

laid Gena and reached for Jolie, but she rammed him with her shoulder, and he fell over an endtable, toppling a lamp and yanking its cord out of the wall.

Jolie's heart thumped so madly in her chest she thought it might shoot out of her. She slumped to her knees beside her mother.

"Mom." Tears stung her eyes, blurring her vision. *Don't be dead. Please God, don't let her be dead.* Gena lay limp, sprawled out over the cushions.

Richard's hands encircled Jolie's waist and lifted. "Now Jolie, don't look."

She flailed and toppled to the floor in Richard's arms.

The landscaper bent over them, holding his knees, huffing and trying to suck in great gulps of breath. "Richard...the reverend...won't like this."

Jolie felt her eyes bulge. "What do you mean, he won't like this? He did this to her."

She struggled against Richard's suffocating arms. He lifted her like a doll, gripping her around the waist.

"No." She wrestled against him, drumming his arms with her fists.

He laughed. Spittle flecked her ear. "Why aren't you this spunky when we're alone?"

"Let me see. Lee me see her. She's my mother."

He cursed and let go of her before standing up. She lay there panting for a moment, trying to catch her breath then raised up and crawled toward the sofa, surprised Richard was letting her go. She gripped the legs of the coffee table in case he changed his mind and reached down for her ankles to pull her back. But he only laughed at her.

Her eyes felt frozen by her mother's blank expression.

Gena lay contorted while she moaned. Fresh bruises were welling up on the cheek facing the ceiling. One eye stared as though sightless, but Jolie knew that eye could see. It must see. Underneath one cheek, a pool of blood had dried in her mother's knotted hair.

"Momma."

Richard grabbed Jolie again and threw her into a chair.

The landscaper put his hands on his hips. "Reverend Caine's gonna be spit-fire mad if she's dead when he gets here."

Ignoring the man, Jolie stared at her mother.

"She's not dead. Just drugged out of her mind." Richard poked Gena's chest.

Gena's eyes snapped toward Richard, and Richard's jaw dropped.

Gena locked stares with the landscaper as he reached for her legs. She went wild, sitting up and pummeling his face and shoulders. He cursed and jumped back.

"Mom. Don't move. You could be hurt. Your head was bleeding."

Gena faced Jolie. Coherency lit her eyes, and her expression softened. Jolie held her hands over her mouth, not knowing what to say. Then the drugs took over again, and the light in Gena's eyes dimmed.

"Mom, don't go. Don't leave me."

"Dove? Where am I? Is your father home yet? I've had dinner waiting for an hour. I hope he's not hurt." Gena collapsed.

Jolie's heart locked up. She brought a fist to her chest and squeezed shut her eyes. "Dear God, give me strength."

"Get her a towel for her head." Richard swatted at the landscaper.

The man disappeared down the hall and returned with a white hand towel.

Richard shoved Jolie into the man's arms and snatched

the towel. He wedged it under Gena's head. "She's staining my imported Italian leather. Why'd you have to lay her here? Wasn't the floor good enough for the crazy witch."

Jolie stared dumbstruck at Richard's blanched face. He was more worried about the furniture than a human life. When had he become that callous? Then she remembered the gun and the car he had been cleaning out just a short time ago. If she were to go outside and look in that open trunk, would she find traces of something else she wasn't supposed to see?

"I need to call Tim now. He stuttered, "Ke...keep her head as st...still as possible." He unclipped his cell phone from his belt loop and hit a smart key before pressing the phone to his ear.

The landscaper finally released Gena and scurried about the living room shutting blinds and curtains. Richard kept his gaze trained on Jolie while he spoke into the phone.

"You know, Barbara," Gena whispered.

Jolie turned her head.

"Sometimes I get the feeling Johnny isn't dead after all...just missing."

"I hope the neighbors didn't see any of that," Richard said, drawing Jolie's eyes back to him.

"He'll be here in two minutes flat," the landscaper said, holding back the curtain and peering through two slats in the living room blinds that he wedged open with one long finger. "You mark my words."

Richard tapped the man on the shoulder and handed him a wad of bills. Jolie thought she saw a couple hundreds leave Richard's hand. "Why don't you just take this and go on home. I can handle the reverend when he gets here."

The man nodded. He lingered there for a moment, locked in Jolie's gaze, then left.

Jolie shook her head at her husband as he took the landscaper's place at the window.

"Jonathan? Where are you, Jonathan?"

"Shut up, you crazy old kook," Richard hissed between gritted teeth.

Jolie opened her mouth to say something then saw her mother motioning for her. Jolie crossed the room and knelt beside her mother. "There's no way out for me, but you and Emma still have a chance."

"Crazy old kook," Richard grumbled. "What's she saying to you?"

Jolie jerked her head toward Richard. He was still facing the window. Waves of relief rippled through her chest.

He spun away from the window and darted into the foyer. The front door creaked open. "Please hurry," he said. "I think she's hurt."

Shoes scuffled fast across the foyer.

An unshaven drooping face appeared in the living room. A man dressed in jeans and a polo shirt ran toward her. At first, she didn't recognize Reverend Caine. "Gena, darling," he moaned.

Richard smiled behind him.

"No." Jolie gathered Gena into her arms.

Richard wrestled her to her feet and pinned her arms to her sides.

Timothy gathered Gena into his arms.

"Oh, Jonathan." Gena kissed his lips, and Jolie gasped, clapping one hand over her mouth. "You've finally returned. I knew you weren't dead."

Timothy's eyes got wide. He slid one tremulous arm behind her head and pulled his fingers away wet with blood. "Oh, my poor dove." His voice was choked. "You're still bleeding."

Jolie gasped.

He cocked his head at her.

"You did do this."

He looked back down at Gena. "I'm never going to let you out of my sight again."

Jolie stared at him in disbelief then looked at her husband. He was smiling over her shoulder at the reverend. What was happening? Was she losing her mind?

When she looked back at Timothy, he was staring at her, hiding nothing about his feelings for her mother. She turned away, burned by the truth she saw in his eyes. Nothing but a miracle could save her mother now.

Chapter Eighteen

Holding the cool compress against her forehead, Jolie rose from the cot and ambled down the blurry corridor outside the dark room where she had been sleeping. No, she had fainted, she remembered as she flexed her fingers across the cool cloth. Light rose from the end of the hall. "Richard," she called out, hearing a slight echo in her voice. She turned a corner and entered a softly lit area. A man slept in a chair beside two open doors. She glanced up at the clock above the doors and froze. Already six o'clock?

Why had she fainted?

Norman Rakes funeral at the church. Yes, now she remembered. She had passed out when Richard had led her to the casket. She had taken one look at the man's powdery face. Then her world had swum in black and white. And Barbara had been right, or so it had seemed. Not a single stranger attended the funeral. Either Rakes hadn't had a loved one left in the world, or none of his loved ones had been informed of his death.

She crept closer to the open doors and peeked inside the room. It was the lecture hall. A separate entrance though. The other entrance doubled as an exit from the church. If she was right, the Sunday School room would be back down the hall on her left. And the room that had been used for the wake should be a little further down past the room where she had woken. All the rooms along that corridor had been part of an addition to Reverend Lamont's church. How many other additions had Reverend Caine made? Were there secrets here she could uncover with a little snooping?

The man snored from the chair behind her. "Richard?" she whispered, realizing the man was her husband. He shifted in the chair, but remained asleep. His elbow stayed propped against the armrest, his palm facing up to cradle his chin. A thin line of drool ran down the side of his cheek.

"Oh, God," someone moaned from inside the lecture hall. Jolie flinched. *Timothy?*

She studied Richard. The cry hadn't woken him.

She edged toward the open doorway and chose a seat on a pew in a darkened corner of the candlelit room.

Reverend Caine stood with his back to her in front of the large window behind the pulpit. One thick candle resting in a dish on the pulpit illuminated the area of the stage where his feet just touched the edge of the light. Past the pane, the dark horizon of the world swallowed the fading red light of the setting sun. Timothy paused with his arms spread out as though the face of God were disappearing with the sun. His shoulders tensed, stretching the fabric of his dark jacket. His arms shook. "Who am I?"

Jolie flinched, dropping the compress into her lap, and glanced behind her. Past the open doorway, Richard still slept.

Timothy tore off his jacket and flung it across the stage. He fell to his knees and ripped the white clerical collar from his neck. He cast it on the altar. "I am not worthy to be your servant, Lord. I have sinned and brought shame upon Your house. Dear God, have mercy on me. Forgive me. Help me give her up. I'm so tired of trying to force her to love me."

Timothy fell forward and slammed his palms on the stage. "Why can't I have her, Lord? And if I can't have her, why can't I stop wanting her?" He raised up and threw his hands in the air. "I give up." His body quaked. It seemed to ripple with an invisible current.

Jolie shook her head and blinked hard. But surely Timothy had no intention of giving up.

A fidgeting sound behind her drew her attention. Richard's eyelids flickered. He flinched. His eyes were rolling behind closed lids. She sighed. He was just dreaming. Maybe even having a nightmare. She gulped and turned back around and gazed up the aisle.

Timothy was staring at her, his blue eyes blazing.

Her heart jumpstarted.

"Tell me something, Jolie, if you're so smart, if you don't need my sermons like your mother claims she doesn't need them."

Jolie tried to rise, but found her legs untrustworthy. Timothy sauntered down the aisle, his shoes clicking against the floorboards. Oily strands of hair dangled over his face. His forehead was a gleaming sheet of sweat. The deep groves in his cheeks deepened as his face twisted in what could only be an expression of revulsion.

"What do you want me to tell you?" she whispered.

She glanced over her shoulder at Richard.

"You know he won't protect you from me."

Timothy stopped at the end of the pew were she sat. "I meant God, of course, not your husband. But Richard won't help you either." He slid in and genuflected before facing her. He slid an arm over the back of the pew, and scooted toward her. The surface of his eyes were wet glass. His weathered drooping neck was melting candle wax. "Don't worry, I'm not Catholic. I won't make you confess your sins to me. I just want to know why you and your mother honored Reverend Lamont so much and why you both seem to do your very best to merely tolerate me."

"Only if you tell me why my mother called you Jonathan before she kissed you."

Timothy glanced away and shaved his chin with the backside of his hand. The loose skin seemed to tighten when he drew his lips back in a snarl. "I can't tell you why she hallucinates. I'm not God. I can't see into her mind."

Jolie sniffed. "Reverend Lamont loved Jesus more than anyone I ever met. The only thing you seem to love is getting your own way, especially when it comes to my mother. And I'm no fool. I saw the look in your eyes after she kissed you. You didn't try to push her away. You'll take her love any way you can get it. And we both know I saw you the other time too."

Timothy thumped the heel of his palm on the pew. Spittle flew from his mouth while he laughed. The sound started small like a distant thunderclap, but grew into a rolling explosion that seemed to shake the pew. "What can you teach me about loving Jesus, Jolie Needham? Please tell me. I really want to know what the great and morally superior Jolie Krenshaw knows about obeying God's commandments."

She stared at him, winding her hands together in her lap. "So it's no accident, and I'm not misunderstanding you? You are talking about Aiden." She searched his eyes. A deep sadness loomed just past his false bravado. She shook her head and turned away, refusing to pity him or buckle under his accusations. "Why don't you tell me why the pew Bibles don't have a New Testament. Where is the life of Jesus? Do you even believe in Him? Have you ever taught one sermon about Him, or would that convict you too much?"

"Tell me, Jolie," his voice was deeper than usual. "Is Aiden telling you things about me he shouldn't be?"

He slid closer and dragged his ragged fingernails across his cheeks, drawing blood. Jolie winced, but wouldn't shift her gaze.

"You see," he said, "I am flesh and blood. I bleed too, Jolie. I need love too." He bowed his head. She could just see the blue of his eyes as he looked up at her. "Just as you and Aiden need love. I know how your spouses treat you. Deep down, I don't blame you for your feelings for each other. I just wish you could see not to blame me for my feelings for your precious mother. Am I not as worthy of love as you are?"

"Why do you keep her medicated? Are you afraid that if you let her mourn my father's passing, she'll realize something about you that you're trying to keep hidden?"

He raised his head. His smile widened until it seemed to consume his face, but the glint in his eyes told her she had almost uncovered a secret. He leaned back, lolling his head over the back of the pew and moaned, a deep low guttural rumbling in his chest that barely squeezed past his lips. "You seem to want all the answers, but do you know which questions to ask? I don't think you do. And that is good. That is very very good that you don't...for your sake as well as Aiden's...and..." He raised his eyebrows. "Of course for Emma's."

"Reverend?" Richard's voice startled Jolie. She turned her head. A tuft of his red hair craned over his sloping forehead. His puffy red-rimmed eyes stared out under copper-colored brows raised like question marks. "How's she feeling now, Tim?"

Timothy was staring at the altar. Probably at the collar that still rested there. "She's feeling fine now. We've had ourselves a little talk, and I think we both know where we each stand."

Richard scratched his head and yawned, arching his arms over his head. "That's good. I was starting to worry."

Timothy winked at her and put a hot sweaty hand on her knee.

Her heart clamped like a fist in her chest.

She looked down when he squeezed for emphasis. "She won't be anymore trouble for you now."

Looking once more into those blazing eyes, she thought of Richard's study and how she had found the plane ticket to Sacramento in there with the attached note about the gun. One weakly guarded secret no one had wanted her to uncover, yet it had been left there anyway. Would Reverend Caine have a similar hideout for his carelessly guarded secrets? She tried not to smile into Timothy's face and bit down hard on her tongue. Tears sprang to her eyes, and he leaned back, looking satisfied with his threats. Good, Jolie thought. He didn't suspect a thing. *You go on and keep pretending you'll never make a mistake.*

Chapter Nineteen

Aiden had told Jolie exactly where to find the key to the reverend's study. In a metal box behind the lilies that Amanda had planted last year. Jolie could enter by the back door of his house and slip directly into the room. She wouldn't even have to turn the lights on because there were enough windows for sunlight to illuminate every file cabinet and every shelf.

It hadn't taken her long to find the metal box. The task had almost seemed too easy.

Steadying her hand on the doorknob, a burden lifted from her that she hadn't even known was there.

She prayed the house would be empty like Aiden had said. It didn't matter that he promised she would find nothing incriminating there.

The heels of her flats touched down on marble, making a startling sound she nearly mistook for another's person's footsteps. A breeze riffled a few papers on the reverend's long mahogany desk. She panicked, slammed the door and dove to catch them, then stopped in mid-swoop to squeeze shut her eyes.

"Stupid. Stupid. Stupid," she hissed at herself, then slowly opened her eyes and carefully lifted the papers with her fingertips.

No one stormed into the room. The house, or at least the first floor, seemed empty.

She turned the papers over, searching for soot, animal hair, and anything that might indicate someone had opened the door and allowed the papers to spill onto the floor. Running a finger across the marble, she found it immaculate. Maybe she should have removed her shoes. Even in the bright sunlight, there was no trace of dust floating in the air.

And probably no fingerprints now but yours?

She placed the papers back on the desk and leaned over the spot she'd touched on the floor. She slipped off one shoe and buffed the floor with her trouser sock before putting the shoe back on. She stood and eyed the papers now resting, hopefully in their proper order, on the desk. She couldn't easily remove her fingerprints from them. And she wasn't about to wipe up the faint tracks her shoes might have made.

You're being ridiculous, she told herself, then walked around the hulking desk.

The desk calendar lying flat in the center of it read *family picnic—everyone must go* in the square marking today's date.

Thank you God, she mouthed. Aiden had been right about the house being empty. But how had he known? No matter, she decided, and started rummaging through the drawers. Nothing unusual caught her eye until she reached the bottom right drawer. The single item inside was a .38 Rossi handgun. She stared at it for a long time before shutting the drawer. Her father had once owned such a weapon for protection, not that he had ever needed it.

"No matter," she whispered. *Find what you came for, girl.*

Her gaze circled the room. There was too much to take in. All the textbooks and papers. She had never guessed the reverend was so intellectual. His collection would even impress Richard—although, the reverend had probably read at least half of his collection, by the looks of the ragged edges. Only the red leather Bible resting on one of the middle shelves looked untouched.

She lowered her gaze to a gray file cabinet marked, *Amanda, do not clean.*

Jolie glanced at the doorway, certain she would find the reverend's heavy gaze upon her. But no ominous figure stood there. Her steps felt unsteady as she went to the cabinet and opened the top drawer. The wheeled tracks squealed. Her gaze drifted past a blank folder.

This is a waste of time.

Jolie's hands shook while she lifted the contents of the folder, telling herself it couldn't be anything important. She searched for a chair. The cot behind her would do. She sat down and laid the pages in her lap. Most were scribbled inventory lists that had something to do with the church. Not too interesting, but not too legible either. Some were medical documents listing medications prescribed for her mother over the years including Halodol and of course, Thorazine. Jolie was not surprised. The doctor's signature on each document was identical, but illegible.

Jolie reached the last page and was about to shuffle the papers back into a neat pile and return them to the cabinet when phantom fingers constricted her lungs. She stood up, spilling all the papers except the last one, and not caring if she ever picked them up.

On the paper shaking in her hands, she read what was supposedly her father's admittance report from Covington Hospital.

Covington? Hadn't her mother been admitted there?

She looked closely at the name of the admittance doctor, Edmond Caine, and the corresponding signature, identical to the others on the prescriptions.

Edmond. Timothy's chauffeur?

Caine. Timothy's brother?

Was Timothy's chauffeur, her mother's doctor? Was this a real admittance report?

At the bottom, under the heading, Reason for Admittance, was written *head trauma*. She repeatedly turned the paper over until she was sure there was nothing more written about her father's death on either side. Hadn't Barbara said her father died instantly from a heart attack? Why would there be a head trauma and no acknowledgement of death when her father arrived at the hospital? Unless he wasn't dead or hadn't died instantly.

There's a reason Amanda acted so funny about your father's funeral being closed casket, the soft voice prodded.

If my mother wasn't medicated, Jolie wondered, uncertain where she was going with the thought, would she have the mental clarity to question my father's death?

So many people had remarked in one way or another about it. So many had expressed their sorrow when they found out she was Gena's daughter. Could the whole town be just as deceived as she was?

Hadn't she overheard Timothy apologizing to her mother that day in the foyer for something he had done. Could the reverend have plotted to kill her father like Aiden seemed to think he had? Beaten Jonathan over the head and waited at the hospital for him to die from blood loss or brain damage?

Why wasn't there a record of the exact cause of death from the admitting hospital? It was simple, wasn't it, the coroner's report would be in the cabinet too. She riffled through the contents in the top drawer then tore open the bottom drawer and rummaged through its contents. Nothing allayed her fears.

She looked back at the reverend's desk and let her eyes fill with tears. "Oh, God. Dear God, what is going on? I don't understand."

She gathered the papers that had scattered across the floor, shuffled them back into a reasonable pile, and returned them to the file cabinet as neatly as she could.

So Aiden had been right. She would find nothing incriminating here. Just more unanswered questions.

Intending to search the bookcases and every other square inch of the room for the coroner's report, she spotted another paper lying under the desk. She knelt and stretched out her hand. Her fingers grazed the corner. Excited voices rumbled from somewhere near the front of the house.

They're home, she thought, snatching the paper and accidentally crumpling it. There wasn't time to return it to the file cabinet. The voices were drawing closer. She stuffed the paper underneath her jacket and hurried out the door.

"My heart," Jolie gasped, looking down at the hands in her lap as though they held the aching muscle that thumped madly in her chest. As though they could just start squeezing until the annoying thing burst. But all she held was the handset of her master bedroom phone while she sat in Richard's armchair. She tensed her fingers over the power she now held and wiped the sweat from her eyes. Her breath felt foreign escaping her lips as though someone else was breathing through her.

She started dialing.

"Dear God," she whispered, "give me Your perfect

strength." She clutched the handwritten letter postmarked Sacramento that she had taken from the reverend's study and waited. The phone rang in her ear. One. Two. She counted the rings, staring at the familiar handwriting and the phone number scrawled across the top. Three. Then a voice picked up on the other end, and she choked trying to get the words out.

"Hello? I said hello. Who is this? Timothy, is that you again? I'm getting sick of these games. And I didn't enjoy you sending my son-in-law to threaten me. The big oaf doesn't scare me one bit, gun or no gun. I told you, you can't blackmail me any longer because I've been cleared of all those charges you tried to pin on me. If you want something from me, you'll have to tell me where my girl is. That's the only way I'll play your games again."

"Dad," Jolie blurted.

"Excuse me?"

"Dad." Tears clouded her eyes. She blinked them away and clutched the phone with both hands, dropping the letter. "Dad, it's me, your daughter, Jolie. I came home. They said you were dead. Reverend Caine said you were dead, but you're alive. Dear God, you're alive. I found the medical document in the reverend's study. Dad...the reverend tried to kill you, didn't he? But he only knocked you unconscious."

"Jolie, my little girl?" The change in his voice was a healing balm for a broken heart. I've missed you so much. Please come out to see me. It's not safe for you there. I'll give you my address. I've been trying to find you for so long. Are you still with Richard?" Jonathan sniffed. "Please say you'll come see me." His voice quivered. "There's nothing for us in Redemption anymore now that your mother's gone."

"Dad. Listen."

"I know, honey. I know about the child. Bring her too."

"Oh, Dad, how did this all happen?" She wiped her

sweaty palm on her skirt then tightened her grip on the phone. "I can barely understand this madness. I don't understand how Timothy—"

"It wasn't Timothy who attacked me. It was his brother, Edmond. Somehow, they got into my room. Your mother was downstairs in the kitchen making breakfast. The sound of her radio woke me. I don't know why she had it turned up so loud. I saw Timothy and Edmond standing over me wearing surgical gloves. Timothy held a needle. They were whispering. Arguing, I think. I made a run for my gun. Edmond wrestled it away from me, but not before it misfired into his face."

Jolie remembered the gun she had seen in Timothy's study and clapped a hand over her mouth.

"I was surprised your mother didn't hear the commotion. But she wasn't well. I could see that the night before when I returned home from my last business trip with Timothy. Then when she killed herself because she thought I was dead…We both weren't well after you left. Oh, Jolie, it's not safe for you there and…" He started to cry. "I'm so sorry. I never would've left Redemption if I had known there was any chance of you returning." By the sound of his breathing, he was leaning as close to the phone as she was. "Honey. Please come see me. Let me give you my address. Give me a chance to make things right between us. Timothy is an evil man. Promise me you'll stay far away from him."

"Oh, Dad, I don't know how the reverend deceived you, but Mom is very much alive."

Chapter Twenty

Jolie clutched the cushion of the sofa beside the Krenshaws' fireplace and stared down at Aiden as he knelt before her.

"I lied to you," he whispered, unable to meet her gaze. "I lied to you by refusing to tell you the truth when you practically begged me for it, but I didn't want you to get hurt. I didn't want Timothy to threaten you like he had threatened so many others. And Barbara? She's not your friend. She never wanted to help you."

He grasped her hands. "Please say you'll forgive me, Jolie. I couldn't bare it if you hated me." He raised his watery gaze to hers, and she stroked the top of his head. He closed his eyes while her hand lingered in his soft curls. "Oh, Jolie, you're so kind to me. I'm sorry for being angry with you. I had no right."

She shook her head, unable to answer.

He kissed the hand she had lowered to her knee and her face warmed. He raised up onto the sofa. The intensity in his gaze told her she still had to be careful with him.

"Aiden, now that he knows, he's coming back. How much danger will he be in?"

Aiden shrugged. "Timothy won't just let him waltz back into town and steal away his only solid reason for remaining in Redemption all this time."

"How'd Timothy get into the house that morning? Dad didn't know."

Aiden shook his head. "I honestly don't know unless somehow in Jonathan's rush to get home to Gena, they had forgotten to lock the door. Did he tell you it was supposed to be his last business trip with us. On the plane ride home, Jonathan told me Timothy had agreed to let him out of the business. I was surprised because I thought by then there was no way Timothy was going to risk losing his grip on Gena. But then we both know what happened after that. I should have known something was wrong. I should have warned him."

Jolie raised her fingers to his lips to silence him. His gaze warmed as he kissed them. She pulled her hand free and held it in her lap again. Then she stood and crossed the room. She paused in front of the mantle and gazed up at her father's portrait. She glanced over her shoulder. Aiden stared at her, his hands pressed on his knees to rise.

"I gave him Mom's new address and told him where I am. I told him about you too. You'll have to forgive the things he said about you."

Aiden stood up and shoved his hands into his pockets. "I'm sure nothing he said was inaccurate."

"He wouldn't listen to me. He said he's going to confront Timothy at Church—not tomorrow but next Sunday—during the evening service if his plane arrives on time. He refused to meet up with us first. I know he's afraid I'd try to talk him out of it again. He says he'll call me if his plane doesn't arrive on time. I hope he's late. I don't think he has any clue what Timothy must be capable of now after eight years of this obsession with my mother. Dad thinks Timothy still won't kill him. That, worse case, he'd get someone else to do it and that certainly, no one will do it in front of the church congregation."

Aiden reached into his pocket and withdrew his cell phone. "Call him back and let me talk some sense into him."

Jolie shook her head. "You can try, but he won't answer. He wants to confront Timothy, *where all the town will see*, was how he put it. He said it's the only way he'll get Gena back because too many people are on Timothy's side. And Aiden, I think he might be right. This may be my mother's only chance."

Chapter Twenty-one

Today too many eyes watched Timothy. Normally, he'd love having the church packed with parishioners. People he could sway so easily one way and then another. But today his palms effused with sweat as slick as his well-polished words. Maybe it had something to do with the way one set of eyes watched him in particular. Jolie Needham. She was getting dangerously close to the truth about her father.

She glared at him while he spoke, and something in her eyes made his voice tremulous. Just slightly. Just enough for him to notice and maybe her too. But no one else. Not even Amanda or Aiden. And for that he was infinitely grateful.

Oh, Gena. How my heart breaks. How my mind aches for you, my beloved.

Neither Peter, Barbara, or Richard had been able to stop Jolie's quest for the truth. Maybe God was using Jolie to bring him back to Christ. He had been thinking this for so long he wasn't sure when he had first started thinking it. He should never have allowed her to see him crying out to God. She should still have been sleeping off her nervous breakdown, the one he was hoping would allow him to convince Richard that she needed the same medications that Edmond was prescribing for Gena. Richard should have remained alert, but the oaf had screwed up and fallen asleep, just like he had screwed up the elmination of Norman Rake's body. Thankfully, Peter had smoothed things over at the police department and stopped the case from being investigated as a murder. It was deemed a suicide, and an autopsy was not performed. The body would be cremated and the ashes scattered, preventing any future inspections of the body.

If only he could be strong enough to do what needed to be done. But Timothy couldn't risk what effect it would have on Gena now. Especially considering the ground he had gained when she had called him Jonathan and kissed him.

Yes, eliminating Jolie now was not wise.

His hand slipped on the side of the pulpit. Sweat may have allowed the loss of friction, but he thought the trembling that had snaked from his voice to his limbs was the more likely culprit. Several gasps erupted around the room, but Timothy regained his composure and waved off any embarrassment. *Dear God, what do you want from me? What point are you trying to prove?*

You must not put Gena above Me. I am God. You will have no other gods before me.

Timothy shut his eyes. He wanted to shake his head at the voice, but he knew his audience would not understand the gesture. His hands slipped again. Before his head smacked the side rail, he caught himself and strained upward. Cries of distress filled the room. The veins in his neck burned so hot his skin almost seemed to boil, but he managed to raise his head and smile.

Barbara lurched from her seat and darted onto the stage.

Only the flight of Amanda's hand to her open mouth alerted him of her concern, or maybe he had only sensed her astonishment. Jolie didn't even flinch. All the others were a blur of tensed bodies and widened eyes. He saw them all in the blink of an eye. The ones for him and the ones against him.

He narrowed his eyes on Barbara, and she halted in front of him, her back to the congregation, concealing from them all he meant to convey to her with his glare. She backed down the stairs and resumed her seat next to Aiden. Amanda must be the one to comfort him in public. How many times would he have to remind Barbara of her place?

He waved his hands over his head. "I'm fine, just working a little too hard lately, everyone. Don't worry. I'm going to have a good rest tonight. Amanda will see to that."

The congregation applauded as though they were marionettes whose arms had been lifted merely by his words. Controlling them had been too easy over the years.

Barbara leaned forward in her seat and slowly turned her head toward Amanda, but Amanda didn't take the hint. Timothy lifted his arm to her and she rose. *Why God did you ever give me such a dense woman?*

She raced up the steps onto the stage and ducked so he could drape his arm over her shoulder. He whispered a sarcastic "thank you" in her ear and reached behind the pulpit for a microphone. "You know what to do?"

She nodded and took his place. He fled the stage and headed down the center aisle.

Amanda tapped the microphone, hopefully drawing attention away from him with the amplified sound.

The speech they had rehearsed tapered off behind the heavy doors that shut behind him. A blinding stream of yellow sunlight enveloped him. He sat on the church steps and breathed deep. Peace seemed to fill his lungs.

A breeze cooled the sweat dripping down the sides of his face. With his arms wrapped around himself, he shivered. In the light that seemed to dance between the shadows cast by the swaying trees, Gena stood before him, an oblivious little nymph. Long black hair streaming down the sides of her breasts to the pinch of her waist.

He opened his arms, but her image winked out. Shadows took her place, leaving him feeling like her foolish puppet.

He fell forward, hacking. God was pressing down on him with a stronger hand than ever, and he hated knowing that soon he would be forced to make the biggest decision of his life. With his mouth nearly pressed against a concrete riser, his mind cried out to God. *Father forgive me for what I'm thinking of doing. Bind my hands, Lord. Bind my thoughts.*

Barbara pivoted away from the windowed wall of the Sunday School room that provided a view of the parking lot and grabbed Jolie's elbow. "What's worse, Mrs. Needham, having once considered aborting Emma or knowing the one person you love most came from the one person you come the closest to hating?"

Jolie clutched her purse against her and snatched her coat from the bench where she had sat watching Emma participate in Barbara's lesson plan. "Where did you hear that? I never considered that."

Other people's purses and coats toppled to the floor. Bending to gather them, Jolie kicked a woman's baby carrier. The infant inside squealed. The mother locked gazes with Jolie from across the room where the woman had been entrenched in a deep discussion with a group of other women. Heat blazed in Jolie's cheeks and she mouthed an apology, but the woman stormed past the children's desks toward Jolie. "You have about as much respect for a helpless infant as you do our dear reverend." She poked Jolie in the chest. "You're pathetic." She wrested her child into her arms and let her eyes get wide before spinning away and heading back across the room. The other women glared at Jolie then folded their arms, turning their backs to her.

Avoiding Barbara's smug expression, she headed for the door. Richard would be outside with Emma about now, grilling her about what she had learned in her new Sunday School class. Jolie could only pray Emma hadn't learned anything.

Barbara's pumps clunked close behind. Then Barbara was in front of Jolie, wedging herself in the doorway. "Ah, if only things weren't always so confusing. If only the sword weren't always double-edged." She grabbed Jolie's forearm and dug in her fingernails.

People were staring at them.

"Let go. You're hurting me."

Barbara ground her teeth. "I look at you sometimes, Jol, and I see myself."

Behind them, Aiden appeared with Barbara's coat draped over his arm. "What's wrong with you?" He pulled her arm free and flung the coat at her. "Put it on. We're leaving."

She clutched it tight against her chest and glared at him before turning back to Jolie. "Men don't stay with you long. We always cling to them for dear life, but they leave us. Sure they may stay physically, but soon enough they leave mentally, emotionally and spiritually, in all the ways that count. It's only when you play hard to get like your mother does that they seem to stick around and then it's only for the competition of it all."

"Leave her be." Aiden put his hand on the small of Jolie's back, raising eyebrows all across the room.

"They'll make you think you're the most important thing in their lives and then, when they get bored, they'll leave like they never knew you. And believe me, there will be no arguing with them. Arguing with them will only strengthen their resolve to leave as fast as possible. Believe me, dear, with all the admiration I have for the reverend, he's a man and not capable of loving anyone for long."

Gasps filled the room. Women grabbed their children and held them close.

Barbara stepped closer, eyeing Jolie up and down. "How long do you think you'll stay young and beautiful, so that men will love you in the only way they are capable of loving any woman?" Barbara glanced at Aiden before turning back to Jolie. "Men know exactly what they want from you and for how long, and if you ask the right questions, you might just see past the end of your pretty nose."

Aiden raised a hand to Barbara's shoulder, but she twisted away from him. She faced the room full of stares.

Whispers ignited like firecrackers across the room.

Barbara faced Jolie again. This time, fear had crept into her voice. "Listen to me girl. There was a time not long ago when I denied reality, but you can no longer live in darkness when you've been forced to see the light."

"What exactly are you saying?" Aiden asked.

Facing the windowed wall, Barbara stared into the parking lot. "I wish I could convince you he's only playing with you, that he'll be done with you soon. But no one could have convinced me I wasn't in love with him when I thought I was, so you can have him Gena, until he breaks your heart." Barbara shook her fist.

Aiden stepped between the women, wavering in some resolve for action.

Facing Jolie again, Barbara licked her lips. "But

remember this, there will come a time when you'll be with him for the last time, and when you've realized that it's the last time, he'll already have long abandoned you in his heart."

"Are you still talking to me?" Jolie whispered.

"Barbara? Are you all right?" A tiny voice asked.

Jolie turned.

Amanda stood behind them. Worry wrinkled her face. A huddle of women had gathered behind her like troops prepared for battle.

"Oh, sure I'm just fine. If only someone here could convince me I'm wrong, then I'd be even better. Then maybe living might not seem so much like dying—getting one step closer to the grave with each unremarkable day."

"Gena, who am I?"

Clad only in a slip, Gena turned in front of her cheval glass and smiled with one side of her mouth. She took a step forward and stumbled into Timothy's arms. The Rohypnol the nurse had given her in a glass of lemonade was finally starting to wear off.

He eased her toward her bed then stood over her. "Gena, who am I?" he repeated.

"Where's Jolie?"

He gritted his teeth "Oh? Not asking about Jonathan today?"

Gena shook her head. "Jonathan's dead."

Timothy backed up and clapped his right hand over his heart. "Do you mean that?"

She raised one hand to her forehead and rolled over.

"What do you think about me?"

She shrugged, and for a moment his heart sank.

"I think you've done so well with your congregation. Reverend Lamont would be so proud."

He closed his eyes, savoring her sweet words. "Does that mean you'll come to Church to see me preach?"

"I've been thinking about that."

When he finally opened his eyes, she had gotten out of bed and had slipped into a light sweater and an ankle-length skirt. She had never looked more stunning to him.

"Do you think anything else about me?"

She paused. "Sometimes, I wonder why you spend so much time with me." She twirled toward her mirror and began brushing her long black hair. It shimmered even in the meek light of early evening.

His lips quivered. "You need me most of all."

"Yes, I do need you. I don't know what I'd do without you." She gathered her hair in one hand and reached for the Scrunchie on her nightstand.

He rubbed his sweaty palms against his slacks and watched her hair dangle over the nape of her neck as she secured it in a ponytail.

"I told Jolie how much you've helped me since Jonathan died."

He grabbed her ponytail and let it slip out of his hand when she walked past for her shoes. "You're very beautiful. Did you know that?"

He followed her down the hallway.

"I'm pretty," she said with a shrug of her shoulders.

"And you're very sweet and very gentle."

"I'm nice."

"And I love you."

"I love you too," she said. She turned around to hug him and bounced just as quickly out of his arms as she had bounced into them. Like a child. Why always so much like a child?

His voice felt strained. "No, I mean I *love* you, Gena."

She stopped and stared at him with unblinking eyes. "I *love* you," she said again. She took his hand in hers, and his heart thumped madly.

Could this be true progress?

She patted his hand once before dropping it. "Don't worry. You're going to be as great a reverend as Reverend Lamont one day. I just know it."

He cringed as though she had slapped him across the face. "Do you still miss Jonathan? Do you wish Jolie wanted to see you?"

She focused on him. Today he had let her medication slide again. To see if she would react the way he had hoped she would since kissing him. Her face was changing, second by second. A clear-minded woman, the woman he knew she'd be without the medication would soon stand before him if he didn't give her another injection. "I miss Johnny, but as long as I have his memory in my heart, he'll always be with me. I miss Jolie all the time because I know she's still alive, and I have a chance to be with her, but I think Milly is stopping her from seeing me. I just can't prove it. I've been trying to go see her, but Richard won't let me in. Seems I'm flanked on all sides."

Timothy stepped toward her, hiding none of his feelings for her in his gaze. It was another test, he supposed. "If I talked to Mildred and convinced her to allow another visit with your daughter, would you come to Church this Sunday and watch me preach?"

Her eyes got wide. She nodded empathetically.

You ridiculous excuse for a man, the vicious self-hating voice screamed in his mind. Whether it was his father's voice come back from the grave or Satan's voice, he didn't know. *And even if you do win Gena's affections, she will never love you for the right reasons.*

"He comforts me when I'm scared, when the thunderstorms threaten to come like they did the day I lost Johnny, and not just the storms you can see and hear, but those inside my head." She batted her eyes as though clearing a film from them.

His heart ached. "Who is this he, Gena? You're not talking about that man you met after the women's group at Church?"

"No, not Norman. Jesus."

Timothy recoiled as though stung.

"He comforts me. I don't think I need my medicine anymore. I don't think I ever really needed it." Her eyes glazed over. "I hate this part," she whispered.

He lowered his head. "I know, dove."

She went back down the hallway to her bedroom.

He followed with the syringe he had pulled out of his back pocket. "Gena, I'm sorry," he whispered. It was doubtful she heard him. "I only want you to love me like you loved Jonathan. Your love would redeem me, dove. It would justify all the sacrifices I've made. Without it, everything I've done to earn your love has been in vain."

Chapter Twenty-two

Having heard a knock on the doorframe of his church office, Timothy looked up from the sermon he was crafting for this Sunday, the Sunday Gena would be watching him preach. A brunette version of Barbara stood hugging her elbows to her chest in the doorway.

Gena, his mind whispered. And he felt a chill.

But it was Barbara standing there. Her features lacked their usual severity, and he suspected it was the lack of dark foundation that was doing her justice. Her hair lay loose over her shoulders and arched inward to her collar bone. It wasn't teased into an over-processed heap of curly fuzz. He smiled, knowing the expression would please her. Or maybe it was her meltdown in the Sunday School room nearly a week prior that made him smile. Fortunately, Amanda had smoothed over that awkward incident, had even somehow justified Barbara's ramblings to make it appear the woman just needed his unique spiritual counseling to win the battle for her mind. But Amanda hadn't turned the crowd on Aiden and Jolie like he would have preferred.

Barbara smiled back, and he thought he glimpsed Gena in her face again.

He swiveled out of his chair and cast his reading glasses across his desk. The sermon could wait. It would be perfect soon anyway. He waved her in and joined her at the bow window. They sat on the ledge, facing each other, saying nothing for a long time. He considered telling her how beautiful she looked when she wasn't trying to look beautiful, then thought better of it.

Finally, she ended the silence. "I've been thinking."

"Hmm?"

"I've decided it's not good for me to stay with Aiden anymore. He..." She reached up and with her fingertips, traced his jaw. He closed his eyes, holding them closed until she removed her hand. If only she were Gena. If only Gena could love him the way Barbara did. "He doesn't love me anymore."

"Aiden hasn't loved you for a long time, dear."

She winced. He hadn't meant to hurt her, but hurting her was a habit not easily broken.

"Does Amanda still love you?"

He stared into her eyes, trying to search out her motive for asking such a question. He tried not to let his anger show. He saw nothing but resignation in her eyes. He sighed and lifted her hand, wishing he could stop teasing her with his affections. "What am I going to do with you?"

She blew a puff of dark hair off her forehead and leaned against him. "You could love me and stop thinking of me as a substitute for Gena."

"Have you tried prayer?"

Barbara averted her eyes. "God, doesn't talk to people like me."

"I know." He gripped her shoulders. "I know you think that, but you should try to understand sometimes our prayers are wrong because our motives are wrong."

Was he listening to himself?

Her eyes narrowed to slits. "What do you pray for?"

"You know what I pray for. My congregation. My family. The world."

"And what do you ask God to give you?"

"Patience, love, hope, confidence."

"And? And what...who do you pray for most?"

He pushed aside thoughts of Gena, and tried to focus on Barbara. He had missed being with a woman. He squeezed her hand. "Come live with me for awhile...until we can figure out something permanent."

She raised her free hand to her mouth. "What will Amanda say? What will the congregation say?"

"I have a bunch of spare rooms just waiting to be filled. You could fill one of them."

Someone knocked on the doorframe.

Timothy looked up. "Amanda, dear. I was just telling our dear child, Barbara, that she could move into one of our spare rooms while she's having some trouble with Aiden. Isn't that right, Barbara?"

Barbara nodded, teeth clenched.

Amanda stepped into the room and began fingering the sermon on Timothy's desk. "So, the honeymoon's finally over?"

Barbara frowned.

Timothy rose and started toward his wife. The fist he usually concealed behind his back when he was rough with her appeared in front of him now, and he only partly hated it. He had never hit her, but she still took a step back.

"Yes," Barbara replied, "the honeymoon was over before it even started."

He took a deep breathe then unraveled his fingers.

Amanda reached for the bookshelf beside the door and

retrieved one of her Bibles. "Well, by all means come stay with us. Don't let me get in the way." Returning his hard stare, she held the Bible against her chest. "God will be your judge, Timothy Caine. I won't cover your sins with my own anymore."

She spun away from them and left the room. He stared at the empty doorway and listened to the uneven tempo of her pumps clicking down the hall. The sound made him think of Jolie. She had walked with the same tempered rage. Had Jolie inspired these recent changes in his wife?

He tried to imagine what secret meetings they might have had while he was away with Richard and Peter. Barbara hadn't mentioned anything in that regard, and she was supposed to be the one keeping the closest watch over Jolie.

He glanced at the sermon on his desk. *No matter. Gena will be mine soon enough, and Jolie Krenshaw will get exactly what is coming to her.*

"While you're at it, why don't you get Gena to move in with us?"

Timothy rubbed his head. He hadn't been home more than a minute before she had started in on him. He guessed the empty suitcase she had placed on her side of the bed was supposed to be some kind of threat.

"Don't start, Amanda," he moaned. "I've had a long week. I don't need any of your female craziness right now."

"Oh, no, you sure don't need anymore of that. You get enough of it from Barbara."

Timothy stepped toward her. She clung to the bedpost. Her frail body had withered to a skeleton not much bigger than the post. Why was she still alive?

Oh, God, that's exactly what I've been trying to do, isn't it? Kill her. My fat jokes were never just jokes. They were tiny nails in her coffin.

He could never divorce her and remain in good standing with his congregation or with Gena. But if Amanda died, or if she left him, he would be a very misfortune man. Someone they would encourage and support.

Self-hate filled him. *God forgive me. I'm no longer the man you wanted me to be.*

No soft voice responded. No conscience uttered a word. Had God finally abandoned him? Of course he would deserve it. He didn't even deserve to live.

"I'm sure Barbara would be thrilled if I were gone," Amanda said just short of collapsing onto the bed.

"What are you so angry about?" He stomped his foot.

Her eyes bulged. If she had ever looked like a deer caught in headlights it was now.

God forgive me, he thought as he laughed. He couldn't stop laughing. Leaning over and putting his hand on her vanity, he tried to slow his breathing.

"You just don't stop. You promised me there would be no more affairs." The words barely finished on her lips. Her fingers loosened, and she flopped onto the bed. Except the bed didn't seem to know something had fallen on it. It hadn't shifted. Could she weigh so little?

She moaned and curled into a fetal position.

"Amanda." Timothy rushed to her side. "What's wrong?" He lifted her in his arms and held her close, shocked that he could still care for her.

"Not so tight. Everything hurts. It hurts all over."

He pulled the bedcovers down, tucked her legs under the sheet, and crawled in beside her, cradling her as she tried to free herself from his arms.

"It hurts when you hold me. I can't breathe. Why don't you just leave me alone." She glared at him like she wanted to throw him across the room. But she had barely enough strength to turn her head.

"All right. You lie here and feel sorry for yourself." He climbed out of bed. "That seems to be all you're good at anyway. I'm going to go be with a real woman."

"Run, you fool. Run into the arms of Hell." She seemed to strain to shout, but the words barely came out in a whisper.

He watched her from the doorway. She probably thought he had left.

He could suddenly feel how her bones ached for flesh to cushion them. He could feel her relentless shivering under the sheet just by seeing it.

She managed to prop herself up on her elbow and grab the cordless from the nightstand before her arm collapsed. Her shoulders quivered while she dialed. "Jolie?" She finally mumbled into the handset.

A pause. "I'm in trouble, Jolie, and I need your help. I wouldn't ask, but I can't help myself. You were right." Amanda gasped and panted for breath.

"Yes, I'm here," she said through sobbing bursts, "but I feel like a fool. It even hurts when I cry. Please come get me."

He wanted to reach for her, to take her in his arms and tell her he loved her, but he didn't love her. He had needed her, yes. He had even pitied her. But love was more than an emotion. It was an action. He had never loved her.

Then what about Gena? Did he love her? He had never treated her with the respect she deserved.

Maybe he wasn't capable of loving anyone but himself.

"Timothy. Could you help me with something?" Barbara's throaty voice rang from down the hall. How he wanted to smack the wench. She was always butting in at the worst moments. Just like his own mother did to his father before she left.

Amanda struggled upward then fell back against the bed. A thought from earlier returned. If Amanda left him, he wouldn't be to blame. He could still preach at the church, and people would still come to hear him. He could even marry Gena.

Go on then if you want to go, he thought. *Let little Jolie come and get you. We'll just see how the two of you make it on your own.*

Amanda opened the front door and careened into Aiden's outstretched arms. "He's with Barbara."

Aiden easily lifted her and cradled her in his arms. Barefoot in her pajamas with bright red trails of tears running down her face, Amanda reminded Jolie of Emma.

"Mandy," Aiden choked out, "you barely weigh an ounce."

"I let him convince me I was fat and ugly." Amanda sobbed. "I let him convince me God wouldn't love me without his approval. I couldn't convince my girls to come with me. They're staying with him. Can you believe that? Even knowing that woman's in the house." She cringed. "Sorry, Aiden."

He shook his head. "She hasn't been a wife to me in years. Forget it."

He glanced at Jolie and whispered. "She feels like sand slipping through my fingers."

Amanda's eyes clouded, and Jolie thought of her mother.

"He's in one of the guest bedrooms with her," Amanda

muttered as though the words hadn't deserved the mouth that had spoken them, "and I don't care. They deserve each other." Amanda curled toward Aiden's chest.

Jolie stroked Amanda's thinning hair, wondering how the woman had lost so many glorious blond curls. She rested her hand on Amanda's shoulder. The bony prominence seemed as hot as a poker drawn from a fire and nearly as sharp. "It's going to be okay now. Don't you worry about a thing."

Amanda placed her hand overtop of Jolie's, and Jolie felt the tremors wracking Amanda's body.

Jolie looked up into the brooding sky and narrowed her eyes on a thatch of gray clouds. A storm was coming. And not just any storm.

Faint moans rose from inside the house. She shut the front door. "Let's go, Aiden, if there was ever any doubt in my mind that I had misjudged them, it's gone now.

Chapter Twenty-three

The phone rang in the Needham household around one o'clock in the afternoon, and Richard picked it up. Emma was sleeping on the couch when Jolie entered the foyer and spotted Richard running out the door with his car keys.

Jolie stood in the doorway watching his Mercedes zoom down the street in the direction of the church.

Emma stirred on the couch.

"Honey, Mommy's got to go see her friend. Will you be a good girl and come with me?"

Emma's feet thumped down, and she padded into the foyer. Rubbing her eyes, she nodded.

Jolie bent and kissed the crease between Emma's puckered brows. "That's my good girl. There's nothing to fear."

Aiden swung open his front door and eyed the bulging Hefty bags by Jolie's sides. "Uh..." He glanced at the taxi in his driveway then at Emma who hid behind Jolie.

Jolie stroked Emma's hair. "It's okay."

"I know, Mom, but he looks scared to see us."

"No, dear." Aiden reached for the bags. "I was just coming to see your mother. Please…please come in. What's all this?"

He closed the door behind them.

"Some personal items I need you to hold for me." She laughed with effort. "Whenever I pack a suitcase, it gets tossed across the room."

She eyed the keys jangling in his hand before he formed a fist around them.

"Where's Amanda?"

"She insisted I drive her to a hotel last night where Timothy wouldn't find her. A dump on the outskirts of town. Not that Timothy seems interested in finding her. What did Richard say to you?"

Jolie shook her head. "I don't even think Timothy told him we came to get her." Jolie cleared her throat. "I have to talk to you too, Aiden. I need to ask you to do me the biggest favor I've ever asked of anyone. I don't know how much time I have before Richard gets home."

"Please. Me first, Jol. What I have to say is very simple, I've been wanting to say it for a long time. Could Emma wait in the kitchen?"

She smiled down at her daughter. The child's face wrinkled into an expression of disapproval.

"Come on." Jolie led Emma into the dining room. "Just sit at the table. I won't be long."

Emma plopped into a chair. She stared at her mother while Jolie closed the doors.

Aiden dropped the keys on the coffee table and strode across the living room. Jolie backed away from him, uncertain what the look in his eyes meant. He grabbed her by the shoulders, and she realized what he wanted to ask her.

His heart was racing. His body felt like a high idling engine, but there was nothing mechanical about the way he stared at her. But something held back the question he most wanted to ask. "How well do you know me, Jolie?"

Realizing she was shaking her head, she froze and concentrated on his hands. They seemed safe enough descending to his sides.

"I love you more than anything." His voice sounded strange to her, pleading and small. "And I'm willing to do anything for you. Barbara wants a divorce." He hesitated once more before blurting, "Marry me."

Her heart said yes, but her mind said no.

"I never told you who I caught in bed with Barbara, but I think you should know. It was Timothy. That's what I meant when I told you she had been dead to me for a long time."

Jolie opened her mouth to speak. She was determined to be rational. But cotton filled her mouth.

"I love you. At least admit you have feelings for me."

She reached for the arm of the recliner next to her. "I have to sit down."

He knelt in front of her and took her hands. Traces of his cologne lingered in the leather upholstery. She wanted to curl up in the recliner and never let go.

"Do you love me, Jolie? Honestly, do you love me?"

She wiped her eyes. "I do, but I won't marry you. If I divorce Richard, it will be because he's bad for Emma and bad for me, not because you'd be good for us."

His smile was bittersweet, and she wanted to kiss him more than she had ever wanted to kiss a man. But she turned away.

"Timothy's liable to snap when your father confronts him at Church tomorrow. You do realize that with Amanda having left him, he'll be wanting your mother now more than ever. I have no idea what he might be planning to do with Barbara."

Remembering what Amanda had said about her girls refusing to leave their father, Jolie wondered what would happen if Emma refused to leave Richard. Blood pumped so hard in Jolie's ears it was hard to hear Aiden whisper. "What?" Jolie asked, seeing his lips moving and his eyes filling with tears.

"I'm dead without you."

She threw her arms around him, drawing him onto the couch. "You're not dead. You're very much alive."

He clung to her, burying his face in the crook of her neck. She ran her fingers through his soft dark locks, rousing curls she hadn't even known he had as his lips brushed her skin. She nudged him back. "You have to be strong for me. I need you to help me do something very important. I wouldn't ask if it wasn't absolutely necessary."

He laid his hands on top of hers and stared into her eyes. "If I'm so alive, how come I feel so dead inside? Why is it so wrong for us to be together?"

"You don't have to understand everything God asks of you to know His way is always best. You just need more faith in His wisdom than in your own."

Aiden massaged the backs of her hands with his thumbs. She reveled in the sensation it sent through her body, hating that she couldn't quell her desire for this beautiful man.

"I need your help. Will you drive me to Church tomorrow after Richard leaves? I'm going to pretend I'm sick so that he'll go without me. He'll leave Emma home so he won't have to deal with her. That'll be the last time I ever return to that house. If Richard fights me for custody of Emma, he better be willing to put up the fight of his life."

"You're not afraid?"

"God is on my side. Besides, I can't stop Dad from

confronting Timothy if I stay with Richard. And I can't help Mom or Emma either if I stay chained to fear."

"Stay with me tonight. Tomorrow, we can stop your father together."

"I can't risk raising Richard's suspicions. I have to stay with him as long as possible. Dad's life might depend on it."

"But you're leaving Richard?"

She nodded, biting her lower lip.

He put a finger under her chin and raised her head. "Oh, Jolie, you're leaving Redemption with me after all? You know I won't be able to sleep tonight."

She squeezed his hand, trying to tell him to be serious, that she wasn't finished.

"I need to make sure Emma is prepared. There's no one I can leave her with tomorrow. She'll have to come along with us, but I don't know how dangerous it's going to be. I couldn't even risk leaving her with Amanda."

He scooted closer to her and leaned his head against her shoulder. "I'd do anything for you. I'd even be your friend for the rest of my life when I desperately want to be so much more."

"Oh, Aiden. My father. My father is alive, and tomorrow my mother will be too for the first time in years. Maybe there is hope for us down the road if we do things right."

Aiden pressed his face against hers, but didn't try to kiss her. "Please tell me you're saying what I think you're saying." He exhaled against her ear and slid his face to her shoulder.

Her gaze shifted to the keys on the coffee table. "I'll have to get home soon. Richard will only be gone so long, and there's still something I need to ask you."

Aiden nodded. "Thank God Timothy doesn't know about your father's return."

Jolie faced the dining room doors and flinched. "Emma, how long have you been standing there?"

Emma was cradling herself, rocking back and forth. Her face contorted.

"Come here." Jolie held out her arms.

Emma ran to her mother and crawled into her lap. She looked at Aiden, and he stood.

"Mom, I still love Dad. Don't take me away from him."

Jolie stroked Emma's back. "Honey, listen to me. This is very important. I want you to do something very important for Mommy. It's the most important thing I've ever asked you to do. Will you try for me?"

Emma shook her head and buried her face against her mother's chest. "I don't want to."

"Try your very best to be brave tomorrow and do everything me and Mr. Krenshaw say without asking any questions?"

"Are you leaving Dad?"

Jolie sighed. Aiden touched Emma's shoulder, and the child spun toward him as though she had been burned.

"I won't listen to you! I just won't!" She spun back toward her mother. "Please don't make me."

Jolie squeezed Emma's shoulders and looked her in the eyes. "Remember when you had those bad nightmares about Mrs. Caine and Reverend Caine?"

Emma whined and tried to wrestle out of her mother's grip. "I guess."

Jolie started to cry, and Emma froze. "Mom?"

Jolie let her shoulders quake through silent sobs. "Lord, give me strength."

"Mom?" Emma put her hands on her mother's face. Jolie let the little hands raise her head. "Mom, please don't cry. No, Mom. I'm sorry. Please don't cry."

Aiden reached for Emma, and the child glared at him. He stepped back, and Jolie gazed into his face, hiding none of her love for him.

"Mom?" Emma gasped and pushed away from her mother. "You don't love Dad anymore? You love Mr. Krenshaw?"

Jolie nodded. Emma said nothing. Her chest rose with a deep audible breath.

"Daddy doesn't love me," Jolie whispered.

Emma squirmed. Her face tensed. "He doesn't love me, either. Does he?"

Jolie lowered her head, hating the adult tone in her daughter's voice, hating that it had slipped in while Jolie was busy trying to protect Emma from the adult world. "I'm just afraid he's going to hurt us real bad if we stay with him much longer."

Emma wrapped her arms around her mother. "I'll listen real good for you and Mr. Krenshaw tomorrow. You love me, don't you, Mom?"

"Of course she does," Aiden said. He put a hand on Emma's shoulder, and the child didn't pull away. Jolie hugged her daughter, holding back the tears of relief that wanted to come. Aiden's hand rested on her back, and she ached to be hugging him too.

"Emma, sweetheart, I love you more than you could ever imagine."

"I love you too, Mom."

"Jolie?" Aiden whispered.

Jolie eased out of her daughter's tight embrace and stood up.

"If Timothy tries something crazy, will you promise me—"

Jolie raised her hand. "I won't make you any promises, but you'll make me one." His Adam's apple bobbed. "You must make me this promise." She leaned toward him, hoping Emma wouldn't hear. "If Emma is ever in danger tomorrow, you'll leave with her."

"No, Mom." Emma tugged on Jolie's arm and wailed.

"You'll take her and get out of here as fast as you can. Take her to Amanda. Amanda will help you if she's still around." Jolie looked down at Emma. The child stopped tugging on Jolie's arm and threw her damp face against Jolie's abdomen. Jolie smoothed back Emma's hair.

"And just leave you?" he asked.

Jolie nodded, biting down on her lower lip to still its trembling.

He gasped as though he had been holding his breath under water. "I'll protect her with my life. You have my word, but I will never leave you."

She turned away before tears fell from her eyes. She led Emma to the foyer and stopped with her back to him. "I would die if something bad happened to her. You know that, don't you?"

"I know it."

She faced him. Emma had raised her shirt and was wiping her face against the fabric.

He nodded, indicating the child with his eyes, and Jolie knew he would honor her wish. Emma would never know what he had promised, and Jolie loved him even more for it.

Chapter Twenty-four

Pictures flew off the walls behind Jolie as she ran through the upstairs hallway with the car keys clenched in her fist. She should've just stayed with Aiden.

"Come back here! We're not finished yet!"

She tightened her grip on the keys. Butterflies swam madly in her stomach. "Stop chasing me. I'm not a prisoner in this house." She took the corner a little too sharply and nearly collided with the wall at the top of the stairs.

"You tell me why Timothy spotted you leaving Aiden's in a taxi last night. I'll break your pretty face with one of these frames if you don't give me a good answer!" Something whizzed past her head and bounced down the stairs.

Emma stared up at her from the foyer, shifting back and forth like she had to use the bathroom, but Jolie knew she didn't.

Richard took the stairs two at a time to catch up to her, still smacking things off the walls. "You knew Barbara was gone, so what could you possibly want to talk to him about? Or did you two even do any talking?"

Her torn blouse flapped at her side, and she was glad she had thought to wear a slip underneath. Richard growled close behind her, and she tried to run faster.

"Get in the car." Jolie lunged off the staircase toward Emma, spreading her arms toward the door.

"Stop right there, or I'll shoot her."

Jolie twirled around, pulling Emma behind her.

Richard had an automatic aimed at her. "Move aside, Jol, or I'll shoot through you."

"Richard, don't."

"You think that Aiden Krenshaw will put up with half the crap I've put up with for you?" He worked his way down the remaining stairs, taking them one exaggerated step at a time. A Cheshire grin unfurled across his lips.

"You've no right to keep us here against our will."

He cocked an eyebrow at her and sneered. "Tim warned me about your infatuation with Aiden, but I didn't believe him."

Jolie backed into the living room with Emma wedged behind her. He followed them, keeping his eyes trained on Jolie's face.

"What do you want from me? Why won't you let us leave?"

Watching Emma, he ground his teeth and popped his jaw. "Oh, you can leave, but she stays here where she belongs, with her daddy."

Jolie's heart froze. "Where did you get that gun? Did the reverend give it to you on one of those so-called business trips?"

"Now, Jol, you should know it's not smart to antagonize the guy with the gun." He darted past her, shoving her to her backside, and grabbed Emma's arm. The child squealed while he forced her across the living room.

Jolie scrambled to her feet. "Stop! This is between you and me. Leave her out of it."

He ignored her, pulling their wide-eyed daughter around the couch.

"You said you'd never hurt her. You promised me. That's the only reason I stayed with you."

"Awe, Jol, now you know that's not true."

"Let her go or I'll…"

He rested the muzzle of the gun against Emma's forehead. "Or you'll what?" The child twisted, but Richard easily held her.

Jolie's mind raced with implausible plans of attack. *God help me. God help me.* She gasped for breath. She had to stop the panic seizing her. Had to think. And she couldn't let her face soften to comfort her daughter. Richard would see it as weakness. Tremors overtook her bottom lip.

"It's a shame we had her. She took the romance out of you. Maybe with her gone, we can try again."

She bit her lip until she thought she tasted blood, letting anger steady her nerves. "I will never feel for you what you want me to. Never. But if you hurt Emma, we can't even be friends."

Richard looked down at Emma. "Honey? You don't like when Mommy yells, do you? Tell her you don't like it." He shook her. "Tell her!"

Emma's face wrinkled, but she didn't cry.

"Do what I say."

Emma raised her head to look at him, but he wouldn't meet her gaze. She looked at her mother, and her face became stone. "I don't like when you yell, Mom."

Richard laughed, lowering the gun from Emma's forehead.

Jolie shifted her eyes. She spotted a large statue on the end table beside the couch, one of Richard's many prized artifacts, and edged toward it, absently thinking the mad thought that she were that warrior statue with its spear raised high in the air.

"Stop right there," Richard snapped. "That's far enough."

Chills spread through Jolie's body. But nothing in his expression indicated he knew what had captured her attention.

She bent and laid the keys on the oriental rug beside her. "Richard, we'll stay. I don't want to leave anymore. Just let me hold Emma for awhile. Please. Come here, honey. Let Mommy hold you. Everything's going to be all right now. I promise."

"Don't make promises you can't keep." Richard shook Emma for emphasis.

Emma tensed her cheeks like she had done on the mountaintop overlooking Redemption. The same inexplicable peace Jolie had experienced that day overtook her.

Richard's forehead creased. "Remember when the minister at our wedding said, 'Until death do us part'?" He stopped, obviously waiting for her answer.

She nodded.

"It was the proudest day of our lives, wasn't it? I remember how my mother said what a beautiful bride you were and how you'd make me so happy. She made me promise to make you happy too. I..." The gun shook, and his hand seemed to lose its grip.

What was this? An opportunity?

He ducked his head and lifted his shirt to wipe his face, exposing trails of sweat beading down the red hairs on his round freckled belly.

She beckoned Emma with her eyes, but the child seemed frozen with fright.

He stepped back, dragging Emma with him. "You can't have her."

"You don't want her. You never wanted her."

Emma's stoic facade started to crumble. Her eyes glimmered with tears.

His eyes glazed over. "I suppose you think Aiden would make a better father to her than me?"

Jolie glanced down at the keys and suddenly wondered if she had made a mistake laying them there. *Dear God, save my little girl.* Tremors raked her shoulders. Her heart ballooned in her chest. This was it. He was going to kill them, maybe even kill himself too.

Richard started laughing. Not his usual sarcastic, clipped laughter. Nor his heavy, room-flooding laughter. But mad, hyena-like laughter that made him sound insane.

She bent and snatched the keys from the rug, clearing any emotion from her face. Richard stopped laughing and focused on her hand.

Drawing on the vestiges of peace inside her, she steadied her voice. "All right, you can have her. I wouldn't be any good to her anyway if I stayed with you." Jolie turned sideways, holding her fingers crossed low behind her, hoping only Emma saw them. "If you must keep her, then so be it. I've already seen how I'm becoming with her now because of you. I'd rather give her up than ruin her life."

"Is this some kind of joke?" He gripped Emma with both hands, smashing the gun against her shoulder.

Jolie fought to keep her expression blank. Richard was studying her face now, searching for any indication of a lie. "You don't care if I kill her then?"

Jolie kept her eyes on Richard. She refused to look at her daughter.

"But we were so in love." His hands trembled. He wiped his forehead with the arm that held the gun then stumbled and lost his grip on Emma.

"Now!" Jolie grabbed the statue with her free hand and

thrust it at Richard's head. He ducked, and it only grazed him. But he slipped on his own clumsy feet and sailed to the floor, loosing the gun. Emma jumped onto the couch and leaped over the back of it ahead of her mother.

"I'll *kill* you." He growled and stretched for the automatic. "I won't lose you."

A tiny scream escaped Emma's throat. The sound hit Jolie like a punch in the face as she trailed her daughter to the door. She wanted to weep for all the evil she had done to Emma by staying with Richard, but regret would have to stand in line and wait.

"That door won't get you out of this house." His voice came from behind them in the foyer. Already too close.

Jolie threw open the front door.

Timothy blocked the exit. In his right hand, he held some kind of printout with lines of numbers all over it. Phone records, her mind offered.

"I thought you were leaving?" Richard's stubby nails ground into her shoulder.

"Let me go!" She twisted free and slashed at Timothy with the keys. He tried to grab her hands. "Get out of my way!" She swung hard with her free fist and connected with soft flesh. She was rewarded with a grunt.

The paper sailed to the floor. Timothy slumped over, grabbing his middle, but quickly recovered and reached for Emma.

Jolie kneed him in the face. He stumbled backward, grabbing his nose and cursing at her.

She raised her arm and jabbed the automatic power unlock on the sensor attached to the key chain. The Mercedes beeped in the driveway.

Richard came at her with an oddly comical look of exasperation and disbelief. Holding Emma by the shoulders, she backed away from him.

Fingers whispered past her head and snagged her hair. Timothy yanked hard, but she brought an elbow up into his ribcage. He moaned and clutched his side. She shoved Emma past him out the door. "Run!"

"Making calls to Daddy won't help your mother now that she loves me." Blood pooled in the grooves of his cheeks and in the gully of his chin.

Jolie made a run for the door.

Fire blazed in her elbow, and she tightened her grip on the keys, afraid she would drop them. The ground seemed to slip out from under her as she was spun around and dragged back over the threshold. She looked down at the hand still clutching her and saw the long nails burrowing into her skin. "Oh, clever little Jolie, clever little, too smart for her own good, Jolie." Timothy slapped the paper against her face and jolted her arm like he intended to dislocate her shoulder. "An eye for an eye, Mrs. Krenshaw. A tooth for a tooth." He flung her into Richard's arms. "Tell me, how you uncovered my little secret, and maybe I'll spare your little girl the experience of watching you beg for your life."

One of the doors slammed shut on the Mercedes. Jolie's heart leaped in her chest, knowing Emma had made it to the car.

Timothy faced the open doorway and planted one hand against the doorframe. With the other hand, he cupped his nose, whistling through it as he panted for breath.

"No! You sick monster! You leave her alone!"

"Give me those." Richard reached for the keys in her hand, loosening his grip. She stomped backward, crushing his foot, then twisted, slamming her good elbow into his ribcage. He gagged, and she slipped free just like she had in self-defense class.

She shoved Timothy off balance and sprinted from the

house. Her legs throbbed with adrenaline as she raced down the driveway, barely aware of the neighbors now watching from their lawns and driveways.

"You're letting her get away."

Something breezed past her. She spied Richard's sweaty face out of the corner of her eye. He held his hands out like a linebacker, but doubt clouded his expression.

"Stop her, you fool. She's stealing your daughter."

Richard looked down, reaching for something in his pocket that might've been his gun. Jolie swung her arm, clipping his chin. He stumbled away from her and tried to orient himself.

She clambered into the car and slammed the door.

"Jolie, don't you dare." Timothy ran down the driveway, arms splayed. His gaze swept up and down the block while people kept pouring outside. "You're a sick woman. You need help. Don't do this to your husband. For God's sake, think about what you're doing!"

Jolie jammed the lock button as he flung himself onto the hood. She met his hate-filled stare through the windshield as she fumbled the key into the ignition. For a moment, she thought, *he's lost his mind, he's actually lost his mind. And he's still trying to keep up appearances with the neighbors? No, maybe you're not mad after all, Reverend Caine.*

He slammed his fists on the windshield, and she revved the engine.

Emma balled into a fetal position in the front passenger seat and whined. "Mom, I'm scared."

Jolie narrowed her eyes at Timothy. "Hold on tight."

Something smacked the driver side, and she jerked her head. The muzzle of the automatic was touching the pane. But Richard's hand was too badly trembling. He dropped the gun. His eyes filled with tears.

"You fool." Timothy thumped the windshield. He was talking to her. Then his voice changed, and he was talking for the benefit of his audience again. "Where'd you get that? Don't hurt her, Richard. We just want her to get out of the car."

I'm sorry, she mouthed at her sobbing husband. *I'm sorry for you.*

She faced Timothy and ground her teeth, letting her face fill with rage. Then she threw the car into reverse.

"Stop!" Timothy clawed at the wiper blades. Blood from his busted nose smeared the windshield. "This is only going to get worse if you keep going."

A neighbor shouted. "Mrs. Needham, what on God's green earth are you doing?" A few of the other neighbors ran for the car.

Emma whimpered, curling into a tighter ball.

Jolie jerked the wheel at the end of the driveway to back into the street and glanced in her rear-view mirror to check for oncoming traffic. She didn't recognize the mad grin in the reflection as her own until she realized Timothy was screaming from the ditch where he had rebounded. The thought that she might've run him over if he had landed in the street crossed her mind, and the corners of her smile stretched wider.

"Where'd he go?" Emma raised up to look out her window, and Jolie slapped a hand to Emma's chest.

"Stay down. Put your seatbelt on."

Emma sobbed hard. "Why are those people blocking the street?"

Jolie flexed her hands over the steering wheel, wondering if she should jerk the wheel and drive straight through her mother's house. No, she decided, even if she didn't hurt anyone in the process, the growing mob would prevent her from rescuing her mother.

Emma wouldn't stop crying. Jolie tried to block out the sound, but the awful noise only filled her head, making it harder to think. She bit back the urge to scream, knowing she was dangerously close to losing it.

Dear God, keep Mom safe until I can return with Aiden. Don't let Timothy take her away from me now.

She floored the accelerator and zipped around a couple in the street like they were obstacles on a driving course.

Aiden reached across the center console of his truck to hand Jolie two aspirin. "Don't loose it now, honey. Hang in there. We've got to get your mother out of that house. There'll be plenty of time to cry later."

Jolie's arms quivered. "If she's still there." She tried to swallow the pills with a mouthful of water from one of the bottles she had lifted from a console cup-holder. "No more tears," she whispered.

She glanced into the back seat and watched the two Hefty bags she had used as makeshift suitcases bounce around behind Emma's head.

"I hope Amanda's safe," Aiden said through clenched teeth. "She wouldn't answer the phone earlier."

Jolie glanced at the baseball bat propped against the back of Aiden's seat. "I'd feel better if we had a better weapon. If only I would've thought to grab that gun when Richard dropped it in the living room."

Course the reverend might be dead now, her mind offered, and she shoved aside the thought.

Aiden's forearms bulged when he adjusted his grip on the steering wheel. "To think I almost lost you to those..." He was going faster on the bumpy road than he should have been, but they needed to get to her mother's unnoticed and by the fastest route possible if they had any hope of rescuing Gena now.

"Oh, God, let her be safe, wherever she is," Jolie whispered. "And keep Dad safe too. You think Tim will actually have the audacity to hold services today?"

"For your father's sake, I hope not. Timothy's goons will be looking for him now, not just us."

"I wish I could get in contact with him, but he's still not picking up his cell. I hope that doesn't mean Timothy's gotten a hold of him."

Emma scooted forward from the backseat and patted her mother's shoulders. "Don't worry, Mom. I've been praying for all of us, and God is good."

"God is also cruel," Aiden whispered.

Jolie didn't like the strange expression on his face. He was hiding something again. He readjusted his grip on the wheel and glanced at her. She leaned over and kissed his shoulder. His expression didn't change.

What kind of secrets were still locked in the man's heart? "For what it's worth, Aiden, I'm glad you're with us right now."

He gave her a hint of a smile as they turned onto her street, but nothing more.

Emma squealed.

Jolie pressed her feet against the floor as Aiden slammed on the brakes. The truck skidded to a stop. Mildred stood on the curb of Gena's house with her shoulders hunched over the barrel of an antique rifle, looking like some surreal gunfighter from the Old West. There was no sign of Richard or the reverend.

Jolie leaned over her seat and shoved Emma's head down. "Stay put."

Aiden nudged Jolie's arm. "Keep calm. Stay still. She would've pulled the trigger by now if she wanted to shoot us. This is just a warning to keep out. Your mother must still be inside."

"But where's Timothy?" Jolie glanced at the front of the house. "Where's Richard?" Someone moved the curtain aside. Long dark hair appeared behind the pane. "Mom." Jolie gasped. "Thank God she's still here."

"You see her?" Aiden asked.

"At the window." Jolie pointed.

Mildred shot the front bumper.

Aiden zipped the truck around. "What was I thinking? We need help."

Emma screamed and pitched against Jolie's seat.

Jolie twisted around to watch Mildred's shrinking face through the rear window. "Mom, I'll be back for you. I promise."

Mildred lowered the rifle. Worry knitted her brow.

Losing your nerve, Jolie wondered.

"That's one thing I never did, Jol. I was never willing to kill for him like his siblings. Like Richard almost was. I was never as close to him as they are, as Peter is."

"His siblings?" Jolie kept her eyes on Mildred.

"Yes. You might as well know everything now. Mildred's his sister."

Jolie gasped. Suddenly, the Caine resemblance became apparent in Mildred's jaw and forehead. Even in the shape of her eyes. "Of course. How could I miss those eyes?" She lowered her window and leaned outside.

Aiden grabbed for her arm, but his fingers slipped before he could reel her back. "No, Jol."

"Mom, no! She'll shoot you."

"I'll be back, Mildred Caine!" Jolie raised her fist outside the window, but Mildred didn't shoot again. "I'll drag her out of that house if I have to, my body full of bullets and walking dead on my feet."

Chapter Twenty-five

Barbara unlatched the screen door and stepped into Gena's kitchen.

Gena rose from the table and dropped her drawing pencil. It clattered across the floor and stopped at Barbara's feet. "What…what are you doing here?"

Mildred stormed into the room and propped a rifle against the wall. "Gena Young. I'll not tell you again. The reverend will have my head if you get away from me today. Where are they?" The nurse extended her hand. "Come on now. Don't play dumb. Give me the keys to that door. I heard you trying to open it."

"I didn't. Barbara did. Tell her, Barbara." Gena turned and stared at the corner of the kitchen where Barbara stood almost like a mirage.

"Oh, Gena." Mildred patted Gena down. "Humph! Now you know I'm not leaving until you tell me where you hid them."

Barbara took a step forward and slipped the keys into Mildred's pocket.

Gena pointed. "Isn't that them?"

"What?" The nurse ran a hand over her pocket. Her fingers tensed over the lump in her white slacks. "Gena, you put them back when I wasn't looking. You sneaky little...I'll have to be extra careful with you today." She took a step toward Gena and raised her hand to smack her. Something rolled across the floor. The nurse looked down and glared at the drawing pencil now resting at her feet. "Maybe I should talk to the reverend about revoking your drawing privileges again." She raised one eyebrow. "That would teach you some respect."

"But I didn't..."

"No. I suppose Barbara did, and I suppose she kicked that pencil at me too." Mildred hoisted her hands to her hips. "The dead can't unlock doors and put keys in other people's pockets, Gena, nor can they kick things at people they might not like."

Gena pointed at Barbara. "But she's not dead. She's right there beside you."

The nurse threw up her arms. "Never mind, you loon. Just don't think those kids are coming back to get you. They've probably forgotten all about your sorry self and are driving out of Redemption right now, kissing and thinking how fortunate they are to be rid of you."

Gena's eyes watered. Mildred smiled and went to the doorway. She collected her rifle and left the room.

"Do you know where your husband has been for the past seven years?" Barbara whispered while Gena continued to watch the doorway.

"What are you talking about?" Gena pivoted her head.

Barbara was sitting at the table with her hands folded, staring at her. "Well, I know for a fact he isn't in Heaven."

Gena chose a seat across from Barbara underneath the

emergency wall buzzer for Mildred. "What are you talking about?"

Barbara nodded at the unfinished drawing on the table. "Does Tim know you're sketching Jonathan again?" Pushing aside the drawing, Barbara locked gazes with Gena.

Gena leaned back against the fanned wooden rails of the chair. They reminded her of prison bars pressed against her back. She gazed up at the buzzer and thought about pushing it. "I don't care. I need a way to remember him. Sometimes I feel like I'm forgetting he ever even existed."

"I used to think you deserved what happened."

Gena stared into two brown eyes, brown like the color of soil without Barbara's usual amber highlights. "What exactly did you come here to tell me?"

No response.

"Barbara, he was saved. I know he went home to Jesus."

"Listen to me, Gena. Whatever you do, don't take any pills today. You're going to need to be clear-headed. Today Jonathan is coming back to Redemption."

Gena froze.

"Didn't you even notice the blood from the head wound? You poor fool. I used to hate you, but now I can only pity you."

Gena shook her head. "Stop speaking in riddles, Barbara."

Barbara sighed. "All right. I'll spell it out for you. Timothy and dear Doctor Edmond sneaked up to your bedroom while you were making breakfast and attacked your blessed Jonathan. But Tim messed up. He hadn't counted on your father having that gun. You remember turning the radio on to block the sounds that were making you so nervous? You left the front door unlocked after you went downstairs to answer it. Tim did knock that morning. He wasn't even sure if he was going to go through with his plan. But you left the door unlocked, and you made up his mind for him. He took it as a sign from God. Remember that morning? Remember thinking you were losing your mind? Remember the presence you felt behind you when you entered the kitchen after leaving that door unlocked? Remember thinking it was just that stupid cat of yours?"

"How could you know all that?"

"The dead see all." Barbara paused. "A lethal injection when given at the right dosage can render a person unconscious for many hours, if not kill him. Sodium thiopental. Courtesy of the reverend's brother. Quick acting too. But Tim didn't get that far. The misfiring handgun stopped him. Timothy and Edmond fled down the balcony, thinking you'd come rushing upstairs, but you didn't, did you? You thought you were hearing things, and you had that blasted radio cranked too loud without even realizing it. Good thing though, or Jonathan would've never woken up in time to defend himself. The insanity started early, didn't it, Gena, it crept in like a spider on soundless legs."

"I was never crazy. I was just under a lot of stress."

Barbara shook her head. "And everything would've been okay if you hadn't tried to kill yourself. Jonathan would've eventually regained consciousness. But when Tim saw your swan dive from the balcony, he seized another opportunity. He convinced Jonathan you died instead, and he blackmailed your precious husband into leaving Redemption.

"It's really sad if you think about it. Add a medicine cabinet full of prescriptions and voila, you never had the clarity of mind to question anything. No more perfect love to throw in everyone's faces. No more staunch Christian example parading around Redemption, hand in hand, big smiles and lots of sickening little kisses."

"How could you know all this unless you were in on it?"

"I already told you how." Barbara stood up. She reached over and crumpled the drawing. Gena screamed and tried to snatch back the paper. "Don't take any more pills today, Gena." Barbara slammed her fists on the table. But the pine top didn't move. "Don't let your thinking be clouded today. Whatever happens, don't let that woman give you your Sunday sedative. You'll be too vulnerable when Timothy comes by after Church."

"What are you talking about?" Gena leaned too far and almost slid off her chair. "You're just not making any sense. Jonathan is dead. His body went into the ground. I saw it myself."

Barbara's eyebrows flexed. "Did you now? And I suppose you saw him lying under the lid of that closed coffin?"

Gena glanced at the wall buzzer and swallowed hard. "You're lying. You've always been mad at me. First because Aiden loved my Jolie before he settled for you. And second because Timothy thinks he loves me instead of you. If it were up to you, I would have to suffer even more than I have."

Barbara smiled, but it was a sad smile. "Your smart little girl discovered Tim's secret, and now Jonathan's coming back, but guess who he's looking for before he tries to come for you?"

"Where is he?" Gena pounded her fist on the table. Barbara didn't even flinch. She seemed as relaxed as a corpse in its grave.

"It's a shame you're never going to see him again, but if you can stay coherent today, you might have a chance of seeing your daughter again."

Gena held her fists against her chest and stared at her kitchen door.

"Now, don't go thinking you can find him again at my house. I can tell you for a fact that he no longer likes to be seen peeing on my lawn or digging through my flower bushes."

"I never thought Johnny was your dog."

"Never? Do you remember much about these last seven years of your life? You really tortured me, Gena." Barbara's face wrinkled. "You really tortured me, and you were so doped up you didn't even realize it."

"Why are you telling me all this? Why are you playing with my mind?"

"I want you to know the truth so that when Timothy finally does kill your precious Jonathan, you'll know who is truly to blame."

"I never meant to torture anyone. I just wanted my mind back."

A tear slid down Barbara's cheek. "Don't we all, honey." Her eyes glazed over as though she were entranced. "I didn't realize I was going so fast. The car pitched before I knew I was doing nearly sixty around that turn. I sailed right over the cliff. I was furious, so furious Tim ended everything with me after all I suffered for him, after giving me that final grain of hope that we might be together without Amanda's interference. He wants you bad, Gena. Bad enough to do his own dirty work this time. I never saw him look at me like that before. Something flipped in his mind when Peter came in with the phone records. A routine search of theirs, mostly done to monitor Jolie's calls to you. But when Tim saw that Sacramento call to good ole' Johnny, he became livid. It was like he wanted to kill someone, anyone who got in his way first. He's going to go over the edge if anyone tries to stop him from killing Jonathan this time. He'd even kill your precious Jolie. He might even kill you."

"Over the edge?"

"I just came to warn you while you've still got a chance.

While you're still on the safe side of that cliff. What you do with that warning is up to you."

Tears welled in Gena's eyes. She turned away from Barbara and depressed the buzzer. She went to the kitchen archway and yelled for Mildred. Turning back around, she saw a table and two abandoned chairs pulled out on opposing ends. Barbara had vanished. Gena glanced at the kitchen door. It was still locked.

Gena awoke in a cold sweat and sat up in bed staring at Mildred's back. Mildred was leaning over a tray, dolling out Gena's weekly medicine. The nurse turned with an open bottle of water in one hand and her fist closed around something else. "Goodness, sleepy head. I thought sure that nightmare was never going to end. I wanted to wake you, but I wasn't sure I should. Was it as pleasant for you as it was for me?"

Gena clamped her tongue between her teeth and looked down at the pills resting in Mildred's upraised palm.

"Strangest news on the television earlier. Barbara Krenshaw's car was found wrecked in a ravine. Paramedics rushed to the scene, but it was too late by the time they hoisted the body up. I'm sure you'll be happy to know, they don't think she suffered…much."

Gena guarded her expression while she put the pills in her mouth and brought the bottle of water to her lips. She wedged the pills under her tongue and swallowed the liquid before sinking back down into bed, feigning exhaustion.

Mildred grabbed the bottle. "You sure are a piece of work. What? No comment about your dear friend Barb?"

Gena let her eyelids droop and rolled over. Mildred laughed. A cold hard laugh like her brother's laugh. And instead of checking underneath Gena's tongue like she usually did, the reverend's sister left the room.

* * *

Timothy gazed out at the room full of his parishioners and knew he was being foolish expecting Jonathan to confront him here during evening services. Peter had contacted the local airports and used his badge to get information on Jonathan's arrival flight. Edmond would be meeting old Johnny boy there soon, and this time, the job would be finished. Jolie would never be reunited with her father—or her mother, for that matter.

Timothy's only worries now were Jolie and Aiden. Mildred had stopped them from getting to Gena, but Jolie could still show up at Church and make a big fuss. But Richard would be handling that little worry for him if she did. Richard was just mad enough to shoot her this time. Right in the church aisle. And that would be a relief. Timothy would finally be rid of her— and her tiresome husband when Peter shot back to feign protection of the church body.

All Timothy had to do now was wait for Edmond's call to confirm things had gone according to plan at the airport. Timothy glanced at Peter. The man put his hand to his cellular ear piece and shook his head. Still no call.

"My children. God's voice is clear!" Timothy raised his hands above his head for emphasis. This was supposed to have been his second sermon that Gena would attend, the one that would have proven to her he was a better man than Reverend Lamont. But Jolie had ruined that. He still didn't know how she had discovered her father's phone number. Not even Aiden had known Jonathan was still alive. But it was of little concern to him now that the damage had been done.

Underneath the bandage that covered his nose, his bones seemed to throb. The pain made him flinch. Concern swam in the watery gazes before him. As far as his parishioners knew, Jolie Needham had done this to him because he had finally confronted her about her wayward beliefs in hopes of leading her back to God. He couldn't help but smile at that thought. He concentrated and made his face fill with an almost peaceful sadness. "He commands that we listen and heed His word. I understand most of you have already heard the news about Barbara Krenshaw, but may I assure you that I knew her better than most of you, and I'm certain her soul rests with God now."

Gasps filled the room. Women folded their hands in their lap or whispered wide-eyed to their neighbors. Men grabbed their wives' shoulders to comfort them. Women grabbed their children. It was evident on every face. They believed God was testing their dear Reverend Caine. First with the disappearance of his wife and the reckless suicide of Barbara Krenshaw, his most loyal deacon, because of the poor woman's realization that her husband was cheating on her with that terrible Jolie Needham. Then with Jolie's assault of him and abduction of little Emma from a heartsick husband who didn't even suspect his wife's relationship with one of his closest new friends, Aiden Krenshaw. What a mess. Poor Reverend Caine, their faces said. Poor dear man. Dearer even than Reverend Lamont. We must pray for him. He has been burdened with so much, and yet he continues to guide us.

Everything was working according to plan. Better in fact. When he left Redemption with Gena after Edmond finally killed Jonathan, any authorities who might come searching for Timothy would be turned away because no one would be able to say anything against their dear reverend or give any clues to his whereabouts.

"Now, I know you're all very upset. It's a hard thing to suffer the loss of a loved one, but please, have joy for Barbara.

She was one of God's children, and she has gone home to her Heavenly Father." Timothy lowered his face into his right hand, and raised the left one for emphasis. "Behold, I say to you, we should all be so fortunate to be so close to God right now—to be able to sit in His presence." The words soured on his tongue even before he raised his head. *How long have I been such a good liar?*

The congregation grew silent while a man in a dark suit slowly approached the stage.

Timothy glanced at Peter. The man's eyes were already trained on the man, his hand under his jacket.

"Excuse me, reverend."

The familiar voice gave Timothy a chill like a draft on the back of his neck. His skin prickled with goose bumps. Jonathan Young, he thought, trying to slow his breathing. Timothy grasped both sides of the pulpit and slowly turned his face to exaggerate the rudeness of the man's interruption. "Surely you can hold your questions until I am finished, sir."

Two plain-clothes security guards were already headed for the man when he removed his hat. It was the queue Timothy had anticipated if Jonathan somehow made it past Edmond. "He's got a gun!" Timothy ducked behind the pulpit.

Jonathan raised his hand. "No, don't. I'm unarmed."

Peter pulled the gun from his jacket, but a male parishioner grabbed his arm, forcing it upward. The bullet shattered one of the skylights over Jonathan's head. Timothy locked gazes with the man. That one man had changed everything now. Who was he? No one special. Not even a member of the church. And from the look on the man's face, he didn't even know why he had reacted so quickly.

Shards of glass showered the crowd huddled underneath the exploding skylight. They raised their arms to shield their faces as they ran. A woman crumpled onto a pew, grabbing awkwardly at her back as she tried to sit upright. She shrieked in pain as she clawed futilely at the shards of glass that had sprayed her back and now poked out like teeth along her twitching spine.

"Someone call an ambulance!" a man shouted.

People rushed toward the woman, crunching glass underneath their shoes. Some skidded and fell on the glass, crying out in pain.

Timothy's heart dropped. It was over now. He couldn't fix this. Jonathan was still alive. He had to get out of here and get to Gena before someone stopped him.

The security guards tackled the man who had interferred with Peter's shot and took him to the ground with a couple punches to the face and ribs. Then they descended on Jonathan.

Gasps and screams erupted around the room.

"Jonathan!" a voice rang from one of the back pews.

Then another. "Jonathan Young!"

And another. "Gena's husband! Come back from the grave?"

The room filled with whispers that soon united to a dull roar. The rolling undercurrent of panic seized Timothy's lungs in spasms, and he could barely breathe, gazing out at the looks of disbelief and revulsion. How could Peter have missed and injured that woman? Now no one could shoot Jonathan and end this. And what had happened to Edmond? Had Jonathan gotten the upper hand on the man?

"What did you do to my brother?" Rage suddenly pumped through Timothy's veins.

"I treated him with more respect than you ever treated me. That's for sure. He's safe in police custody, just like you will be soon. Are you afraid yet, Tim?"

"You're the one who should be afraid. I'm an innocent man." Timothy slammed his fist on the pulpit before heading down the center aisle and shoving people out of his way, knocking some to the floor.

"Reverend?" someone cried out. "Don't you care about that woman?"

Timothy stared his accuser in the eyes. He turned and looked down at Jonathan. *No Lord, I can't give Gena up now. Not when I've come so close to having her.*

"Let him up," someone said. "He wasn't armed. I didn't see a weapon."

Timothy averted his eyes from the accusatory glares and spotted Peter. The man's face blanched as two male parishioners latched onto his arms, restraining him. Timothy's guards backed up, releasing Jonathan. No, Timothy's mind whispered. He had to get out of here.

Timothy couldn't still the trembling in his body. He tried to speak, but found himself mute. He shook his head. He couldn't escape their stares. They knew. How could they know? He broke into a run down the aisle, knocking more people aside, and tore through the front doors, racing into the parking lot.

Tires squealed as he reached his Jaguar at the curb. When he looked up, Aiden's Ford Ranger revved in front of him, blocking the closest exit from the parking lot. It would take some manuevering to get around them. Jolie sat in the front passenger seat, her head cocked toward something or someone in the back.

Emma, his mind whispered. He reached for the .38 Rossi handgun he had hidden in the waistband underneath his black jacket and blocked out his festering concerns for his brother.

* * *

"I said do you have anything to say to me, reverend!"

He glared at Jonathan. Those green eyes that had once seemed so blissfully naïve now brimmed with self-righteous disdain, and he almost pulled the trigger with his hand still underneath his jacket, shooting the fool right there with his own gun.

Timothy spun toward the crowd and wondered if his reputation could be salvaged. No, he decided, feeling a strange smile creep onto his lips. "Big surprise, huh? Looks like you've all been worshipping at the wrong altar." Gasps filled the parking lot. "You've been following the wrong God." If only his father were here to see this mockery of a life's work. Yes. The old man would've loved that. Now that would be worth a little wasted time before he whisked Gena away from Redemption, never to be found again.

Rage boiled inside Timothy. His tongue burned with hatred as he spoke. "So, you think she'll be happy to see you now that she's had so many good years with me?"

Voices buzzed around him like bothersome flies.

"Who cares what all of you think? You were never my goal. I always had my eyes on Gena."

More gasps.

Someone said, "I thought so."

Another said, "I knew it. I bet there was even truth to the rumor about him and Barbara." Then another. "But she's dead. You don't think he had anything to do with that?"

"You wanted to come here and have it out with me in front of everyone, huh? Well, fine! Have it all out!" He spun and pulled out the gun, brandishing it in the air for all to see.

Heads ducked. Then everyone froze.

"Yes, I used good ole' Barb, and now that she's dead—

not that I had anything to do with that fine fortune, but now I don't have to worry with that loose end anymore, emphasis on the loose end part."

"Reverend." It was Jolie. "Please don't. Think about what you're doing."

Timothy faced the Ranger. She was jogging toward him with Aiden at her heels. Already her obedient puppy. But an obedient puppy dragging a wooden bat.

Timothy stepped back and leveled the gun at Aiden's head.

"Look at you. Suppose you're thinking about starting fresh with her now that Barbara's dead? Suppose you think that bat's going to do you some good."

More gasps and whispers. The sea of faces blurred into one hypnotic current washing over his raw nerves.

Don't do it, Timothy. Stop now, and turn yourself in, the faint voice inside him whispered. He felt a tinge of shame as tears came to his eyes.

What kind of spell are they trying to cast over me?

My son, they aren't doing this to you. I am, the voice said, the voice he thought had abandoned him.

Timothy shook it off, hating how tender it still sounded, and blinked back the tears threatening to drive him to his knees. He wouldn't ask for their forgiveness now. He couldn't. Not that they would give it. He had to keep his mind focused on Gena. She was his redemption. He glared at the crowd.

"Why can't you all mind your own business?" He raised his fists to them. They stepped back, revealing two blank-faced girls. He focused on them and realized they were his two daughters. How could he have grown so distant toward them that he would hesitate to recognize their faces? How could they look at him so void of emotion just like Amanda had done the last time he saw her?

Oh, God, what did I do to my family?

"What's the matter with you!" he shouted.

Finally, emotion registered on their faces. Fear, he thought, feeling the fingers of self-hatred tightening around his heart.

They stepped back and hid in the crowd. Why hadn't Amanda taken them with her? They should never have been allowed to see this. But then, he knew that answer. He never would've let them leave with her, and for some inexplicable reason, their allegiance had remained with him. At least until now.

"What's wrong with you, reverend?" a deacon of his church asked, jarring him from his thoughts. "Why'd Peter try to shoot Jonathan?"

"Yeah, what's going on?" a woman asked. "I thought Jonathan Young died a long time ago. We all saw his burial."

"Yeah, we saw it," the same man said. He held his wife tight against him now. "But it was closed casket. Remember?"

Whispers filled the parking lot. A woman stepped back, but another woman moved in front of her and glared at Timothy. "Why don't you care about that woman suffering inside? Why don't you check on her? What kind of man are you?"

Timothy shook his head. "None of you are in any place to judge me. God will be my judge and God alone."

"When's that ambulance getting here?" a voice rang from inside the church.

Timothy cringed. How could he care so little about people he had spent so many years shaping into a...Into a what? he wondered. Into a family, he realized. That's why he had stayed here so long and not taken Gena away sooner. He had wanted these people to respect him...to love him and respect him like his father, his own family, never had. It hadn't only been about not upsetting Gena any further.

"Timothy, you're not going to get away with this. Everyone knows now." It was Aiden's voice. "The authorities are researching the evidence I gave them right now. No matter how this ends, this will end badly for you if you keep going."

Timothy eyed Aiden, searching his face for an explanation.

"I'm calling your trump card, Tim." Aiden licked his lips. His Adam's apple bobbed. His next words held a tremor of what could only be fear. "I've decided I'm going down with you after all."

Jolie gasped. "Aiden? What are you talking about?"

Aiden seemed unable to face her. "I'm sorry, Jolie. I never wanted it to end this way, but there's no other choice if you want your mother back. Tim will never let her go unless he's in a place where he can't reach her. Like prison. So, go ahead and shoot me Tim. I'm as good as dead anyway."

Unbelievable, Timothy thought. So Aiden had grown a backbone after all. But it was too little too late as usual.

Timothy turned his head at the sound of gravel crunching underfoot. Jonathan was sprinting toward him. He locked eyes with the man and realized he had let the gun drop. He slowly raised his arm, savoring the look on Jonathan's face.

"Stop!" Jolie's shoulder slammed into his side before he realized she had dived between them. His hand bucked, and he nearly dropped the pistol. Jonanthan ducked out of sight behind a car. He cursed and shoved her onto the pavement then clambered into his Jaguar as the parishioners rushed the vehicle, some throwing stones at his windshield.

He backed out of the parking space and zipped around, looking nose to nose with the Ranger. He floored the accelerator, letting the engine scream. The smoky smell of rubber wafted up as he slammed into the quarter panel, crumpling it, in an effort to shove past the behemoth. Two of his tires bounced up onto the curb then dropped down again before the car finally burst free. He fired one good shot in the direction of the truck's tires and sped off.

Chapter Twenty-six

As he reached the turnoff for Gena's street, Timothy savored the memory of the look of desperation and disbelief in Jonathan's eyes. Even if he had missed Aiden's tire, with the main road out like he had planned, it would take Jolie and her crew an extra fifteen minutes to catch up to him unless they also knew about the shortcut, but by then, he'd be gone with Gena in his backseat sleeping off the pills Mildred had given her earlier that day.

"Oh, God, what's become of me?" His voice sounded foreign to him, from another world. But he would worry about that later.

He jerked the wheel and skidded into Gena's driveway.

"I can't live without you!" Timothy felt invincible standing in Gena's living room. He tossed his keys onto the mail table and started up the stairs to collect his sleeping beauty. "I have so much to tell you. God has told me to take you as my wife, the wife I should've had. He has released me from my marriage to Amanda and her children. I'm free to marry you."

"I don't want you. Go away!" Gena's voice came from what sounded like her bedroom.

He cocked his head then froze. He hadn't expected for her to respond. Where was his sister? "Milly?" No answer. "Milly!"

A faint sound, like muffled screaming. He snapped his head toward the closet at the top of the stairs and ran, taking the risers two by two.

Where Gena had once tried to hide a packed suitcase, he found his sister and the syringe that had been jabbed into her thigh. Timothy ran his hand over his forehead and shrank away from the door, already feeling less and less in control. "What happened to you? Did you give her the medicine?" But of course he already knew the answer.

Mildred clawed the wall for stability and wobbled out of the closet. Her eyes were glazed over, and her hair was a mess of static. The collar of her nurse's uniform was torn. Dried blood spotted one ripped pocket of her skirt and dribbled down her offended leg. He took her hand to steady her and tugged the dangling syringe free.

"Did Gena do this to you?"

Mildred whimpered and fell against him, then pushed herself off, looking around as though she were trying to look everywhere all at once. "I thought she took them, but I didn't check her mouth. I should have checked her mouth."

Rage rose inside him. His hands had begun to tremble. The first faint sounds of thunder rose outside. They drew him back to that fateful day he tried to get Edmond to kill Jonathan.

Am I afraid? No, surely not! But of course he knew he was.

He looked down at his wide-eyed sister and slapped her across the face, hoping to strike some coherency into her.

She stumbled and fell then started crawling for the stairs, that inane whimpering filling his mind.

"Oh, just go!" he screamed, balling his hands into fists. "You're too weak. Just like Mom. You can't tell me Gena did this to you." He rammed one fist into the wall beside him, punching through the drywall. He stared into the hole for a moment then at his throbbing fist. Somehow the pain barely registered. "Where's your rifle?"

She hobbled down the stairs, grabbing her useless leg.

"Well?"

She stopped, gripping the railing, and faced him. Lightning flashed in the dry sky outside the living room windows, illuminating one side of her face. He glimpsed the whisper of a smile. "I'm not going to kill for you anymore, and I'm not going to let you kill anyone with my gun. My sentence will go a lot lighter if I stop now." She started to look away then her gaze swung back toward him. This time a distinct smile was perched on her lips. "It won't help you stop them anyway. God is on their side."

He suddenly felt nauseated. His vision flickered like old movie film reel, and he thought for a moment, somewhere between the front door slamming and Mildred's car starting, that he was going to faint. He tried to grab something supportive on the wall, but found nothing, and plummeted to his knees, breathing hard. His lungs seemed to fill with burning acid. Mucus dribbled down his upper lip. He hacked and spat out the salty taste, spraying the floor with saliva. A migraine started at his right temple and quickly spread to his left, clutching his entire head in a vise. His eyes felt like two hot pokers pulled from a blazing fire. He leaned over and stared at the swimming floorboards, concentrating on the raspy panicky sounds coming out of him, knowing all at once that they couldn't be his own even though they were, and tried to focus on what remained of his plan. All he had to do was knock Gena out and get her in his car in the next…He looked at his blurry watch…the next five minutes.

He rose to his feet and moved the pistol around to the back of his waistband. He took off his jacket and wiped his face clean with it before tossing it down the hallway toward the bathroom. He spun to face the other direction that led to Gena's bedroom.

Gravel crunched outside as a vehicle skidded into the driveway.

"Jonathan," he hissed.

"Help!" Gena cried from her bedroom and started pounding on what sounded like the window that overlooked the driveway. "Jolie! Aiden! Oh, God, help me!"

Timothy flexed his hands, trying to will the tremors out of them. The image of the front door flying open flashed in his mind.

You left it unlocked? Just like Gena did on that fateful day. Is that a sign from God too?

"Gena!" He stormed toward her bedroom and yanked hard on the doorknob. It wouldn't budge.

She's locked herself inside, genius. He felt his pockets for his keys then suddenly remembered he had left them downstairs.

Go back and get them, you fool, or shoot out the lock and hope the bullet misses her fickle little heart.

The reflection of Gena's wrenched face in the shiny brass knob shook, and she recoiled from the door. *Oh, Jolie, Aiden, hurry up.* "Go away, Timothy, you're not thinking right. I never loved you in that way and you'll never be my husband. You're scaring me! Go away!"

"You're mine, dove. God commands it."

Keys jangled in the door. Thunder clapped in the sky.

Gena took a deep breath and closed her eyes, wrapping her arms around herself. Her body was quaking. She wondered if her dream about Barbara had only been a dream. A soft rumble of lightening shook the window behind her. She spun toward it, almost expecting to see Barbara standing there offering her a weapon.

"Go away! I called the police."

A succession of stairs squeaked underneath pounding feet. *Jolie. Aiden.*

He laughed, shoving open the door. "Oh, Gena. You know Peter is the police. And you know no one ever came for you before."

"No." She bowed her head, inching around the bed. "You were the only one who came."

"And I will always be the only one, dove."

"Don't call me that." Her eyes filled with tears. "That was Jonathan's name for me. I told you only he may call me that."

"Oh, Gena. Don't be like that. You know I'm your true husband."

"Mom!" Jolie's voice rang from the doorway.

"Gena!" Aiden's voice now.

Gena jerked her head, unable to see past Timothy, but straining to see anyway. She heard another set of feet pounding up the stairs.

Timothy's laughter chilled her. He reached behind himself then turned and wielded something at the open doorway. Her husband's old pistol, she realized. So, she hadn't lost it after all.

Just past his shoulder, Gena thought she glimpsed a ghost in the doorway. She shook her head, trying to deny it and accept it all at once. "Jonathan?" she whispered. He had slightly grayer hair than she remembered, but his intense stare was the same as it had always been. It seemed to want to swallow her whole. She tried to speak, but found her chest too full of joy to do much more than breathe. His still chiseled but rounder face broke out in a myriad of emotions. The muscles of his jaw seemed to be working to utter all the things he was unable to say, but he said everything she needed to hear with his eyes alone. Barbara had been wrong. Jonathan had returned to her, but Timothy was still going to kill him.

Her body bowed. Her knees buckled, threatening to take her to the floor. Aiden clapped a bat against his palm. Jolie heaved by his side, her large round eyes brimming with hysteria when she spotted the gun. Jonathan charged past Jolie and Aiden.

"I won't miss this time."

Jonathan locked eyes with Gena. "My love." The sweetness of his voice melted over her like chocolate. She ached to kiss his sweet lips just once more. She shrieked in agony and sprang forward, thrusting her fists into Timothy's lower back.

Timothy stumbled as he fired. The bullet sailed into the hall and slugged the wall.

He grunted and grabbed his side, dropping to one knee and losing the pistol. It skidded across the floor.

Gena darted for the gun, but he quickly recovered and sunk his fingernails into her calf like teeth. He stood and flung her backward. Her back cracked audibly against the dresser, and she slumped to the floor. Streaks of lightening streamed across her vision.

"How *dare* you." Jonathan growled.

She glimpsed a blurry object rising from the floor, knowing somewhere in her fading consciousness that it was the pistol. Then Timothy pulled another surprise from some kind of holster just above his ankle.

"No, get out of the way!" she tried to shout, recognizing the long slender body of the weapon. But her lips wouldn't budge.

A fist of darkness seized her mind.

Jolie grabbed the gun, vaguely registering Aiden's warning about another weapon.

"Leave her alone!" Jonathan latched onto Timothy's shoulders from behind and shoved the reverend at the door. Timothy slapped his free hand against it to keep his balance and turned like a crab into the swinging arch of Aiden's bat. Timothy ducked at the last second before impact. The weapon cracked at the handgrip when it slammed into the door.

Timothy thumbed off the protective cap of the syringe and locked gazes with Jolie. The gun shook in her trembling hand. She grabbed it with both hands to steady it and squeezed the trigger. It clicked off an empty chamber.

"Again!" Aiden shouted.

She kept squeezing until she had exhausted the chambers. All empty.

Thunder much closer than before crackled outside. The floorboards seemed to reverberate in response.

Aiden dropped the broken bat and lunged for Timothy, but the reverend bent, using Aiden's momentum, and tossed him over his back.

Jonathan grabbed Timothy's hair, raising the reverend's head, and tried to punch him in the face, but Timothy was too quick. He sunk to one knee and plunged the syringe upward at an unexpected angle into Jonathan's neck before grabbing the man's ankle and knocking him off his feet.

Jonathan sprawled on his back, pawing at the protruding object like someone might swat at a spider. He shoved with his feet to wriggle away.

"I should've done it right the first time." Timothy yanked the syringe free and shoved off Aiden when he came at him again.

Jonathan's eyes drifted closed.

A shriek died in Jolie's throat. She threw the pistol at Timothy. He swatted it away, laughing.

Aiden took a step and swung at Timothy's midsection with the bottom of the broken bat. Timothy leaped back. The bat hit the window, shattering it. Shards of glass sprayed the floor. Timothy wrenched the weapon away from Aiden and brought it down on the man's shoulder. An audible crack erupted, and Aiden dropped to the floor.

"No!" Jolie rushed Timothy, but he shoved her away. She skittered to remain on her feet.

He thrust the bat through the shattered window. It clattered onto the sidewalk below.

Gena moaned. Jolie jerked her head toward her mother. Her heart leaped in her chest. *Thank You, God. She's still alive.*

Timothy kicked Jonathan's motionless form. "I never should've let you live."

Words froze on Jolie's quivering lips. How had the reverend seized control so fast?

She surveyed the room for the syringe and any other makeshift weapon.

"I hate you!" Gena hissed at Timothy. Jolie pivoted her head.

His jaw dropped. Sadness dulled his expression. His eyes watered. "You don't mean that. You couldn't hate anyone if you tried."

Gena glanced at Jolie then at something else near the foot of the bed.

Timothy knelt on one knee and touched Gena's cheek. "It should have been me in bed with you that morning celebrating my return home."

Jolie knelt and lifted the bedskirt. The tip of the syringe glinted strangely from underneath the bed.

"I would never have hurt you like he did by being gone so long. That's why you got confused. A woman's delicate heart can only take so much pain. He killed you, Gena, whether you know it or not, but now I'm going to help you live again."

"I could never love you. How could anyone love someone like you?"

He let out a guttural cry, and Jolie spun to face him, thinking he had seen what she was doing. But he hadn't. He was responding to her mother's words. He slapped Gena hard across the face.

Oh, God. Jolie grabbed the syringe. Feeling its cold body in her hand, she knew what had to be done.

Timothy cradled Gena, his head buried in the crook of her neck. Her eyes were closed, and she lolled in his arms like a doll. "Wake up. I can't take losing you." Timothy kissed her forehead, but she didn't move.

Jolie arched the syringe in the air as she approached him. She aimed for the back of his neck and sliced downward. The needle sank into tensed muscle.

Timothy twisted and screamed, grabbing at the syringe and choked on what Jolie hoped was blood. He dry heaved and clutched at the needle again. Finally, he got one hand around it and yanked it free.

He flung it across the room and spun toward her. The veins in his forehead pulsed. He blinked furiously and stumbled. "You never learn," he hissed.

Rain splattered the floor, and Jolie felt like she were on a sinking ship. Freezing droplets smacked her face. The jagged edges of the broken windowpane reflected a strange light like the syringe had done from its hiding place under the bed.

A shroud of darkness settled over the sky and swallowed most of the room's light. Timothy's dark shape flew to her like a demon in a nightmare, but she darted away from him around the bed.

Wind swirled throughout the room, rattling furniture and moving the perfume bottles and jewelry on Gena's dresser. The sky rumbled. Timothy's mad laughter paralyzed Jolie. She wished she could reach a light switch, a table lamp, anything that could illuminate him.

Behind his dark form, the sky was now one swirling mass of deep blue and steel gray brushstrokes on a black canvas. She locked her gaze on him as he knelt and retrieved something from the floor. Light flashed, briefly illuminating him, and she saw the pistol in his hand. Light flashed again, and she saw him reach into his pocket and fumble for something.

Ammunition?

Thunder rolled. A silver streak of light fell across the constricted pupils of his feral-looking eyes. Then a flash of blinding light filled the room. Something exploded past the edges of broken windowpane, and Timothy squealed in pain. Jolie's ears popped, and Timothy's screams went mute in her head. A meaty smell like fried pork filled the room.

She fell onto the bed, realizing as she saw her mother's blank-faced clock radio that lightening had taken out the electricity. It would be useless to try the light switch now. A deep ache filled her body, and she wished things hadn't gone so wrong so quickly.

She spotted movement from around the side of the bed and clawed the sheets with her free hand as she tried to scramble away. Her legs were almost too sore to move. Her knees almost felt locked in place. She slid a hand down one leg and found tiny splinters of what must be wood and glass embedded in her skin from the lightening strike that had taken out the rest of the window. Then her fingers tightened around something hard and cylindrical. A bullet. She raised the marvel to her eyes. But it was no good without the gun.

Timothy's moaning sounded distant, but she knew by the changing perception of his voice that her hearing was returning. She rolled off the bed and fought to stand while rocks seemed to roll around in her head. She crumpled to the floor on liquid-filled legs.

Timothy rose, slapping one charred hand to the foot of the bed, cradling his hip with the other. For a moment, she could see nothing in his eyes but pain. Smoke billowed behind him. He twisted, and she saw the gash in his hip where the lightening must've struck him.

"Jolie, where are you?"

She turned her head. Aiden was crawling toward her.

Oh God, thank you, she thought before realizing her parents had been trapped closest to the shattered window. Her mother still lay hunched on the floor, but her father was inching toward Gena over fragments of wood and drywall. And Timothy was hobbling toward the window.

A memory seized her mind, and she saw her husband approaching their bedroom window with his back to her. For a moment, she thought Richard had taken Timothy's place. Then Timothy turned, and she saw the tears streaming down one side of the reverend's wrenched face. Her face, she remembered, thinking of a time when she had been struggling with God against leaving Richard for Emma's sake. *Deep down, I'm no better than he is.*

She gulped back something rising in her throat. Who was she to hate someone God still wanted to save? But she did hate him.

He slapped his hand down on the window frame and bowed toward the blue-gray abyss. "Oh, God, what have I done?" The curtains flapped like excited arms behind him.

Push, Jolie's mind raged. *Now.*

He bent, and Jolie thought he was reaching for her mother. "You leave her alone! Haven't you hurt her enough?"

Fighting against the pain blazing up her legs and slicing into her knees, Jolie ran toward him and thrust out her arms to shove him through the busted window.

He bent again, to get leverage, she realized. He ripped something from the frame and faced her. She stopped dead.

In his upraised hand, he gripped a jagged shard of glass. Blood poured down his arm like water. His blue eyes seemed unusually dark. "No one's going to help you now." He limped toward her, favoring his injured hip.

He managed to swat her knee away when she kicked at his groin. She fell and landed painfully on her backside.

His bloodshot eyes were bulging. His pupils were dilated. Gashes scissored across his face. He grabbed her foot when she kicked again, and he yanked her leg. Her knee made a popping sound, and fresh starbursts clouded her vision. She bit down on her lower lip to stifle the pain. She kicked hard with her other leg, aiming for his face. But missed again. He grabbed that foot, dropping the other one, and slid her toward him. She screamed, and he pulled harder. Fragments of glass dug in like splinters along her spine. She tried to roll onto her stomach and cried out as the fragments ground deeper.

She reached across the floor and latched onto a shard of glass half the size of the one he held, forcing herself to blot out the searing pain in her hand like he did. She arched her arm and rolled into a sitting position.

Lightning flashed again. Her vision flooded with alternating strobes of light and darkness.

"Come to Jesus!" a Southern Baptist voice blarred through the clock radio as the electricity came back on. Timothy jerked his head in the direction of the sound. The clock radio blinked green, frozen at twelve o'clock.

Jolie met the reverend's widened eyes.

"Dear God, I'm sorry," he whispered before she slammed the shard into his foot. He screeched then recoiled from her as she pulled the shard free. His eyes locked on the busted window as though he were looking through it into the face of God.

She held the weapon tighter, feeling the edges embedding in her flesh, but not caring just like he hadn't cared. If he came at her again, she wouldn't hesitate to slice an artery, but she knew he wouldn't come.

Horror contorted his features. He turned, hesitated at the door as though lifting something or touching his punctured foot, then tore from the room.

Jolie rolled onto her side, clenched her teeth, and pried the shard free from her hand. Something tugged her waist. She screamed and spun toward her captor. But it wasn't Timothy who held her. It was Aiden. His jaw was clenched. His muscles shook.

"Your legs?" He brushed her skin with his fingertips then sobbed against her neck. "I thought I lost you."

"I'm fine." She ran her hand over his back. She wanted to stay locked in his embrace forever.

"Where's Tim?" He frowned.

"He ran out." Hearing sobbing, she turned her head.

Her mother was hugging her father's motionless body. *Oh, God, please don't take him now.*

Aiden put a hand on Jonathan's chest. "He's still breathing."

Jolie reached out to her mother. "Mom, we shouldn't move him if he's hurt."

Gena shoved her away.

"Mom, please. Please…" Jolie tried to pry Gena's arms free from Jonathan's neck.

Jonathan gagged and opened his eyes.

Gena gasped. "Oh, thank God."

His head lolled, and he smiled up at her. Tears ran down his face as Gena stroked his hair.

"Dad. You're alive."

"Yes, honey."

Aiden ran a hand up Jolie's back. "Of course he's alive. He's not going anywhere."

Jonathan stared at Aiden, unable to speak, but as if to ask, "You really have changed, haven't you? Like Jolie said?"

Gena smiled, throwing her arms around Aiden and Jolie. "I couldn't have gotten him back without your help. God bless you."

Jonathan wrestled upward, coughing.

"Don't move, Mr. Young." Aiden put a hand to Jonathan's shoulder.

"That's right, honey." Gena curled against him. "Don't try to sit up. Just rest."

Jonathan's eyes rolled in their sockets then seemed to focus on the busted window.

"Shh." Gena cupped Jonathan's cheek. "Shh. You're here now. God has given you back to me, Johnny, even though I didn't deserve it. All in His time. All in His perfect time."

He struggled upward anyway, and she kissed his cheek, trying to ease him back down. "Emma," he whispered.

Outside, a distant scream rose past the sound of a slamming door. A slamming truck door.

Jolie gasped, remembering Timothy's awkward bending at the door, and slapped a hand over her mouth hard enough to leave a bruise. "The gun."

Chapter Twenty-seven

Timothy flung open the passenger door of Aiden's Ford Ranger and yanked Emma out by her hair. She scrambled down the steps and landed in a puddle of water, splashing Timothy's trousers with mud. He slammed the door and felt reflexively for his clerical collar, uncertain why he'd want to protect it now. The white band suddenly seemed more constricting than a metal brace. He found the clasp, ripped the collar free, and tossed it in the mud. Emma stopped wrestling against him. Her hands fell limp at her sides when he pulled the gun from his waistband, the gun he had retrieved from Gena's bedroom doorway. She turned away from him and stared at the sinking symbol of his life's work.

"What's this?" He placed the gun under her chin and raised her face toward him. "Are those tears for me?"

"Mom!" She lurched toward the house, and he almost slipped and fell backward trying to restrain her. He growled when thunder boomed, turning the swirling gray sky bright silver.

Jolie's faint voice rose above the storm, and he realized Jolie was calling for Emma from Gena's smashed bedroom window. He wound Emma's hair tighter between his fingers and pressed the now loaded gun to her head. When she screamed, he was glad Jolie heard it. *That's just the beginning.*

But Jolie spared your life because I wanted her to spare it, the soft voice he had been ignoring for years insisted. *I love you Timothy, and I want to heal your broken heart. Why won't you let me? I will never allow Gena to love you the way you want her to love you.*

Timothy shook his head. "No!" He shook the gun at the torrent above him. "I tried it your way, and it doesn't work! You won't let me be happy! I don't want to do it Your way anymore! It's too hard!"

He stared down at Emma. Her tiny face streamed with more tears than raindrops. "What do you think of God now? You think he'll protect you from me?"

"He can save me if He wants to." Her body was trembling, and her voice was faint under the fury of the storm, but her words cut through him as though she had shouted.

"What makes you believe He'll do anything for you? What makes you so sure He can stop me?"

"I didn't say He would. I just said He could. Everything is better His way. Don't you know that Reverend Caine?"

She started to sob. He tried to believe the sound meant nothing to him. He stared down at her. "Why would he care about someone so insignificant as you?"

She stopped crying and again met his eyes.

Brave just like your mother.

"I'm not supposed to feel sorry for you any longer. God wants me to tell you He's going to work it all out if you'll let Him. He'll fix everything if you just believe in Him."

Timothy couldn't help but chuckle at that. "What are you talking about, child? I believe in God."

"No. He wants you to follow Him."

"Emma! Don't you hurt my little girl, you sick monster!" Jolie was racing down Gena's porch steps, slipping and flailing her arms to keep her balance. Her shoes slid off, and she landed barefoot on the flooded walkway. Veins bulged in her face. Her damp clothes clung to her. Aiden wasn't much farther behind.

Gena appeared in the doorway. She met his gaze.

Where was Jonathan? *Hopefully dead once and for all.*

Gena's gorgeous black hair swirled around her angelic face. Even now, after it was clear she would never love him, he still ached for her. He pointed the gun at Emma's head. Then a soft voice stopped him. Not the voice of God unless God was speaking through Emma. "I forgive you, reverend. Whatever you're going to do, I forgive you."

He looked down dumbly at the child.

"He wants you to follow Him. He wants you to want Him more than anything else."

Timothy raised the gun, uncertain what to do with it. "I can't do that. I can't follow Him. He wants too much. He wants all of me. He won't take just a little." He shoved her away and dropped the gun. It sunk into the mud beside his discarded collar. "So he'll have none of me!"

She slipped and fell onto her backside into the same puddle. Mud slashed her face. She looked ridiculous to him then, and he felt the mad desire to laugh.

"Emma!" Her mother wailed like a siren, finally reaching her and clutching her shoulders. She thrust Emma behind her.

He turned away from all of them. It must've been God, he thought, who made Emma feel tenderness toward him. There was no other way anyone could love his enemy. Not even a child. Had that been how he had made Gena feel about him, like he was her enemy? The tears of defeat he had been damming back for so long prickled the corners of his swollen eyes. "You love Him for me, child." He hated the weakness in his voice, but he couldn't hide it. "You just go ahead and love Him with all your heart because it's too hard for an old stubborn fool like me."

He headed around the rear of the Ranger, staring into the rain-slicked street. He couldn't hate them anymore. It hurt more than trying to get his own way with God. Yellow lights like lasers lit up one side of his peripheral vision just like the lightening had. He just kept walking, walking into the light and at the same time ignoring it. He didn't know where he was going, but he couldn't bear to stay here and hate them anymore. Not Jonathan. Not Jolie. Not Aiden. Not Amanda. Not his earthly father or his Heavenly Father. Not even himself.

Tires squealed. Air rushed past him. Screams rose in an unpleasant chorus he only vaguely heard as his body whirled upward then downward. Then the lights went out, and blackness seemed to swallow him whole.

Chapter Twenty-eight

People filtered in and out of the Chicago courthouse. Some wore casual attire and looked down at the concrete risers while they walked, obviously trapped in their own thoughts. Others wore business suits and carried briefcases, looking hurried with their cell phones pressed against their ears or their hands-free pieces locked in place. They spoke in commanding or slightly inconvenienced tones, and their faces wrinkled in emphasis. Beside the door Aiden held open at the top of the courthouse steps, Jolie smiled at them. They were so blissfully unaware of her life, of her story. But the world would soon hear about it if the news crews pulling up at the curb were any indication.

She turned sharply and felt Aiden's hand on her arm. "Let's hurry. They haven't seen you yet."

She hesitated, watching Gena take Emma's hand and lead her into the building. Jolie looked back at the reporters climbing out of their vans and peered past them into the clear sky. Jolie chuckled. *Dear God, you've been so patient with me.* She bit her lip when she saw the furrowed brows of confusion beside her.

"You don't have to do this if you don't want to. It's not necessary in order to convict him. The police have all the evidence they need," Aiden said for the third time that morning.

Jolie looked at the door he still held. She kissed him on the cheek and caressed his arm before entering the courthouse. He raised a hand to the spot where her lips had touched him and smiled.

At the end of the second hall, Gena led Emma to a bench outside the room Jolie would soon enter with her attorney, Mr. Caldwell. She forced the image of Richard's red sweaty manic-looking face out of her mind. But the images of the automatic he had pointed at her and Emma wouldn't budge. Jolie closed her eyes and forced herself to concentrate on her breathing.

Emma's tiny fingers wound around her wrist, and she looked down at her daughter and forced a smile. The child still had the same worried pout with which she had left the hotel that morning before their two-hour drive to the courthouse.

"Jolie, please don't do this." Aiden still didn't trust God like he said he did even after he had been pardoned in exchange for divulging critical information that had helped convict Timothy, but life was a continuous test of one's trust in God, so he was in good company. And they would have their lifetimes to learn that lesson over and over again, hopefully together.

She faced him, but spoke mostly to Emma. "You don't have to worry. Mr. Caldwell is one of the best lawyers in this whole state and he'll protect me in there. Nothing bad is going to happen. I need to do this in person, or I'll always look back and wish I had been more brave."

Gena rose from the bench. "Don't let him bully you. Remember, he can't hurt you anymore."

"I know, Mom."

Two hours before his trial, Richard wasn't going to enjoy getting more bad news from his wife, but Jolie was determined to make her intentions clear.

Emma leaped from the bench and clamped her arms around her mother's legs. She glared at Jolie's attorney as the man approached with a Styrofoam cup that smelled of burned coffee. "Don't go in there."

Jolie bent down and hugged her daughter. "It's okay, sweetheart. Nothing bad is going to happen to me. I won't be long, and Mr. Krenshaw and Grandma will take care of you while I'm inside." Emma twisted toward the bench where Aiden and Gena now sat exchanging glances.

Emma rubbed her eyes and scooted onto Gena's lap. "I wish I could go with you."

Jolie leaned down and kissed Emma's forehead. "What a brave girl you are, honey, but I won't be long."

Gena smoothed back Emma's hair and kissed the child's cheek. "Honey, your mommy can take care of herself, but I need you out here with me."

Emma gave her mother a pleading look then scowled at the attorney sipping his coffee like their display was inconsequential to him. Finally, she buried her head into her grandmother's chest with one last whimper of protest.

"You be careful in there." Aiden's smile seemed forced. "Don't let the..." He glanced at Emma. Her face was nestled against Gena's shoulder, but she was peeking at him with one exposed green eye. "Don't let him rattle you. He's not worth it."

"Be quick, dove." Gena winked. "Say what you have to, but don't let him change your mind. Then we can go back to the hospital and be with Dad."

Jolie felt herself smile. "Thanks, Mom."

"You ready, Mrs. Needham?" Caldwell asked.

Jolie turned. The man held the door open.

She nodded and entered the room, wondering if she were making a mistake.

The door whined on its hinges. Richard looked up from a large square table and focused his bloodshot gaze on Jolie. After Richard had confiscated $2.5 billion of the money he had helped Timothy extort from churches and charities all over the country, he had been chased down by police cruisers and one helicopter just outside Tampa Bay, Florida. What kind of reaction was she hoping to get from him after that ordeal?

God, help me stay calm and do this.

He brought one hand up to scratch his blackened eye where a bruise was just beginning to fade. Had he gotten that shiner from resisting arrest?

"Come in, Mrs. Needham," Richard's attorney said from his place at the table. "We're all friends here." The man's beard still held a bit of the sandwich he had shoved aside when she had entered the room.

The rumbling of Richard's steady laughter chilled her, but she was determined to tell him what she had to say. She followed Caldwell to the table and took a seat across from her husband. "I have something to tell you, then I won't be speaking to you anymore."

"Oh yeah?" Richard pivoted in his seat and cocked an eyebrow at her. "And what more could you say or do to ruin my life?"

"I didn't ruin your life…" She stopped herself. She was playing his game, and she was sick of it.

"You know, Jol, you're just as guilty in your heart as I am by my actions. You know you liked all that money I was making, but here I am the one sitting on this side of the table."

"Now, Mr. Needham, I don't think we have to get into specifics here," his attorney interrupted, wiping at his chin with a napkin. "This isn't the trial."

Richard's stare didn't lift from Jolie's face. "Oh, I'm already on trial. Just let me talk to my wife."

"About that..." Jolie began.

Richard's eyes narrowed to slits.

"I want a divorce."

"A divorce?" The slow smile spread across Richard's face, twisting his otherwise normal-looking features into monstrous deformity. "What would you do without me? Where would you go? What would you do for money? You think that miserable Aiden Krenshaw will be able to support you?"

"Money isn't everything. Don't you realize that by now? I don't know what God has planned for the rest of my life, but I know it will be better for me and Emma without you in it."

"So, it's back to God again, huh, Jol? He's the one you think will lead you on your narrow little road to happiness? You know you're more pathetic than me."

She stood up, pushing out her chair. The wooden legs scraped the floor. Richard flinched. Or maybe he didn't move at all. "I'll pray for you, Richard. I'll pray your heart will open to Jesus and that you will come to see the line that separates us because of Him."

"Some big talk for such a small-minded woman. It was probably a good thing you lost that second child. Maybe God decided you couldn't handle the responsibility of caring for another life since you never could take proper care of Emma. I may have hurt her, but you let me do it. Seems you're the real monster."

She knew what he was thinking as another grin stretched across his face, that he had hit a nerve, and she would soon cry.

He rapped the desk before reclining against the back of his chair. He puffed up his chest.

She studied him, feeling a deep ache in her heart. Richard was still pretending to be important. "I refuse to hate you. And I won't dwell on you or the choices I could have made differently when we were married. I won't let your memory consume my life. I'll move on and so will Emma. And if I do marry Aiden, that will be mine and Emma's business."

Richard averted his gaze and stared past her, his face unmoving. He balled his hands into fists. They said everything for him just as they had done so many times before. But finally, what they said, couldn't hurt her or Emma.

Epilogue

Seven Months Later

Timothy stuffed a few of the most recent letters from his former congregation back into his Bible, leaned against the wall of his prison cell, and closed his eyes. So many people were still angry with him, but there were others God had allowed to forgive him. "Beautiful Savior. How could you forgive a man like me? You know the souls I've tried to corrupt in Your name."

Convicted of one count of murder for the death of Norman Rakes, a retired trial lawyer from Minnesota, one count of attempted murder against Jonathan Young, seven counts of extortion, two counts of tax evasion, fifteen counts of grand theft, and various other charges including bankruptcy fraud, mail fraud, and money laundering, Timothy considered himself fortunate. God had forgiven him and wiped his record clean. The only sentence he would serve to pay for his crimes would be on Earth.

Tell them the truth, Timothy, so I can repair what you have broken.

Timothy recalled the words he had felt in his heart so long ago and found himself smiling while he raised the Bible to his lips to kiss the still gleaming golden inscription, Holy Bible, on the worn red leather cover. Even Jolie had started to forgive him. Little by little her letters had gotten softer, almost tender. He lifted her last letter. Tears trickled from his eyes as he read the last few lines: "I think I'd like to see you. I think I need to. I want to see if I can have the same mercy on you as God has had on me for what I did to Emma and my parents by staying with Richard all those years."

Timothy sighed. "How God? How could she of all people forgive me?"

Not even Amanda or his two girls had forgiven him. And Gena and Jonathan? He hadn't had the nerve to inquire about them to Jolie. He was certain his feelings for Gena had changed, but he knew it was probably better if he never saw her again except in his mind, a part of himself that God was still repairing. They had every reason to hate him.

Oh, God, will you ever bring healing to my marriage and my relationship with my sweet girls?

God didn't answer him. But that was okay. He no longer wanted to control everything. If he was meant to know that answer, he would know it when the time was right.

"You have a visitor, Rev."

Timothy blinked away his tears and looked up to find one of the prison guards waiting past the bars of the cell. The one with deep set eyes and a deep set heart who had spent twenty years serving his own type of prison sentence in this place. The man was flashing his crooked toothy grin again.

"Someone to see me?"

"Yeah, I'm as surprised as you are, old man. It's a Ms.

Jolie Krenshaw." The guard smacked his lips. "She's very pretty if you ask me. She your daughter—not that I think for one second she could've gotten her looks from you."

Timothy stood up and stretched. "Nah. She's not my daughter." The spot where the lightning had struck him still hurt all these months later. He'd probably always walk with a limp, but after wrestling with God for so long, he was glad to have a reminder of the eternal love that had saved him. "How did she seem?"

The guard called up the prison row, and the cell door whined open. "Pleasant enough for someone coming to see you." The man chuckled.

Timothy stepped out of the cell.

"Hey." The guard put a hand to Timothy's chest. "Bout what we were discussing the other day..."

Timothy followed the man's eyes to the dog-eared Bible spilling with letters and lying open on Timothy's cot. But even months of actual use hadn't dulled the gleam of that golden inscription.

"Most people would admit they believe in God, Rev, so why do you reckon He doesn't just save us all?"

Timothy couldn't help but smile. How many times had he wondered the same thing in one way or another even though he knew the standard answer by heart? The confused look on the man's face made Timothy laugh despite all the inmates staring at him from across the cellblock.

"Come on now, Rev. Be a pal and answer a dumb old heathen like me. Clear this thing up for me and all the prisoners here."

"Yeah, reverend. Tell us," a prisoner shouted, the man Timothy had surprised yesterday in the cafeteria by handing him back his tray instead of beating him with it.

Timothy shook his head. Tears trickled from his eyes.

How had he changed so much so quickly? How could he feel so free in a place like this? Or had he been on the verge of change for longer than he had thought? Timothy stared at the guard's crooked grin. It was an expression he could only now understand. There was so much pain there. There was so much pain all around him—so much of the bitterness and desperation men were often compelled to hide behind sarcasm and violence. But there was one good man here too, just like Jolie had mentioned in one of her letters, one good man who could take all the suffering away if He chose to take it away, if we chose to choose Him, one good man who could save us all and keep us all from perishing.

And why won't He save us all? What had Emma said that had made him realize he had never listened to a single one of his own sermons?

Timothy stepped forward, watching the guard back away from the bars. The man's smirk faded a little—not much, but a little.

"Not everyone who believes in God's Son will follow Him. Most people try to compromise with God. They rely on themselves for answers when His Word is as true today as It was when It was first written. God never changes just because the world does. And His expectations for us to follow His will never change." Timothy's voice sounded deep in his ears, and he started to tremble at the foreign sound. It seemed at least two worlds away. It was the tone he had used from the pulpit before his heart had turned away from God. "You must," Timothy continued, speaking more to himself than to the men around him, "surrender your will to His, and trust Him completely, or it isn't worth trusting Him at all. Everything is better His way." He smiled to himself, remembering what Emma had said to him. "In order to follow Christ, you must want Him more than you want anything else. Nothing must separate you from Him. You have to know you're nothing without Him yet know you're everything with Him."

For the most part, none of their faces changed, but the twinkle of sarcasm in the guard's eye had dimmed. Not much, but a little. Thank You, Lord, Timothy thought. Thank You for Your Son. Thank You for saving me.

~End~

About the Author

Melissa Hart is a freelance novelist and poet. Her education in mathematics and computer programming has given her a unique blend of artistic and structured creativity that helps her intertwine plot and characterization to create thought-provoking, emotionally charged thriller novels with unusual plot twists. Her ten-year writing background and her experience as an editor has taught her that most things in publishing are slow and unpredictable, but by dedicating your work to God's glory, publication becomes less important than the call to write. The Redemption of Reverend Caine is her debut novel. Melissa resides in Severn, Maryland with her husband, Paul, and her wonderfully bad dog, Angel. You can visit her website at www.hometown.aol.com/LaughHeart for further information about her and her other novels as well as some helpful writing tips.